THE RAID

What Reviewers Say About Lee Lynch's Work

"Lee Lynch has not only created some of the most memorable and treasured characters in all of lesbian literature, she's given us the added pleasure of having them turn up in each other's stories. *Beggar of Love* ranks with Lee Lynch's richest and most candid portrayals of lesbian life."—Katherine V. Forrest, Lambda Literary Award-winning author of *Curious Wine* and the Kate Delafield series

"Lee Lynch reads as an old friend, and in a way she is."—Joan Nestle, Lambda Literary Award-winning author and co-founder of the Lesbian Herstory Archives

"I've been a fan of Lee Lynch since I read her novel *Rafferty Street* many years ago. Her books—especially her deeply human characters—never disappoint. *Beggar of Love* is a story not to be missed!"—Ellen Hart, Lambda Literary Award-winning author of the Jane Lawless Mystery series

"*Sweet Creek* is Lynch's first book in eight years, and one that shows the maturing of her craft. In a time when much of lesbian writing is more about formula than finding the truths of our lives, she has written a breakthrough book that is evidence of her unique gifts as a storyteller and her undeniable talent in creating characters that move us and remain with us long after the final page is turned."—*Sacred Ground: News and Views on Lesbian Writing*

Sweet Creek "…is a textured read, almost epic in scope but still wonderfully intimate. Lynch, with a dozen novels to her credit dating back to the early days of Naiad Press, has earned her stripes as a writerly elder—she was contributing stories…four decades ago. But this latest is sublimely in tune with the times."—Richard LaBonte, *Q Syndicate*

"…the sweeping scope of Lynch's abilities…The sheer quality of this work is proof-positive…that writing honestly from a place of authenticity and real experience is what separates literature from 'books.'"—*Lambda Book Report*

"[Lynch's stories] go right to my heart, then stay and teach me... I think these are some of the most important stories in the dykedom."
—*Feminist Bookstore News*

"Lee Lynch fills her stories with adventure, vision and great courage, but the abiding and overriding concept is love. Her characters *love each other* and we love them for caring."—*This Week in Texas*

"Lee Lynch explores the elements of survival, the complexities of defining community and the power of claiming our place..."—*Gay & Lesbian Times*

"[Lee Lynch's work] is a salute to the literary and bonding traditions of our lesbian past, as well as the acceptance we continue to demand and achieve within a larger society."—*The Lavender Network*

"Lee Lynch is a mature novelist who retains the freshness of outlook of a young writer. Her independent, self reliant women...are ever ready to face the challenges that all lesbians meet."—Sarah Aldridge

"[Lee Lynch's] writing is a delight, full of heart, wisdom and humor."
—Ann Bannon

"The highest recommendation I can give Lee Lynch's writing is that you will not mistake it for anyone else's. Her voice and imagination are uniquely her own. Lynch has been out and proudly writing about it for longer than many of us have been alive...A good book can make the reader laugh, feel desire, and think, sometimes all in the same scene."
—*Queer Magazine Online*

Visit us at www.boldstrokesbooks.com

By the Author

From BOLD STROKES BOOKS
Sweet Creek
Beggar of Love
The Raid

From NAIAD PRESS
Toothpick House
Old Dyke Tales
The Swashbuckler
Home In Your Hands
Dusty's Queen of Hearts Diner
The Amazon Trail
Sue Slate, Private Eye
That Old Studebaker
Morton River Valley
Cactus Love

From NEW VICTORIA PUBLISHERS
Rafferty Street
Off the Rag, Edited with Akia Woods

From TRP COOKBOOKS
The Butch Cook Book, Edited with Sue Hardesty
and Nel Ward

THE RAID

by

Lee Lynch

2012

THE RAID

ISBN 13: 978-1-60282-753-0

This Trade Paperback Original Is Published By
Bold Strokes Books, Inc.
P.O. Box 249
Valley Falls, NY 12185

Credits
Editor: Shelley Thrasher
Production Design: Susan Ramundo
Cover Design By Sheri (graphicartist2020@hotmail.com)

Acknowledgments

Thank you:

Nel Ward, Sue Hardesty, and Elaine Mulligan Lynch, for your time and your excellent counsel.

The Golden Crown Literary Society for the hours and hard work you give to us all and for honoring my work in so many ways. Among others: Lori Lake, Patty Schramm, Mercedes Lewis, Mary Phillips, Judy Kerr, Karin Kallmaker, M.J. Lowe, Renee Bess, Nat Burns, Claudette Dillard, Lizz Gibson, Mary Griggs, MaryLou Heintz.

Shelley Thrasher, for your poet's eye and literacy.

Radclyffe, my butch cap is off to you always.

Connie Ward, for sharing stories of your life and for your unconditional support.

James Duggins, a much-appreciated supporter of our community.

Paul Willis, Jean Redmann, Greg Herren, for the Saints and Sinners Literary Festival.

Lisa Girolami, DJ Garden, Ruth Sternglantz, Sterling, Mark Leach, KG MacGregor, and Stonewall Library.

Bobbi Weinstock, who has informed my characters for many years.

Lynette May, Rachel Spangler, Nell Stark, and Anne Laughlin for writer friendships. Cate Culpepper for terrorizing me with love and affection by proxy.

Hank Lynch, my writing companion for 16 years—I miss you, little guy.

I also want to pay homage to my Great-Aunt Jo Murphy, who I never met and only learned about recently. She was a laundry worker and a "big strong woman" whose best friend Vera would visit her and stay overnight.

Dedication

This book is dedicated to Elaine Mulligan Lynch.
The heroine of my heart.
My storybook princess.
The woman I never dared dream.

PROLOGUE

1957

A teenage girl darted into the doorway of the Old Town Tavern. She wore a shiny, green top hat decorated with a shamrock and the Hansfield High School initials.

"Excuse me!" she yelled over a drum major's whistle and jingling ice-cream cart.

Two young men looked over her shoulders, leering. Their arms snaked around the waists of girlfriends, hanging on tight.

The girl's voice sounded high with excitement. She had the local Massachusetts accent, but her features and complexion were distinctly those of someone with ancestors from India. Her large dark eyes were filled with mischief above a wide smile and a nose slightly large for her thin face. She looked like a little scarecrow in her Peter Pan collar, no makeup, no nail polish, blue-green blouse half-hanging outside her flared skirt, and long, dark hair parted in the middle.

She shouted, "I'm looking for a bar, not the city zoo!" Her friends laughed in hilarious triumph and dashed away with her, only to return: brazen, naughty children on the cusp of growing up, their faces flushed, verboten beer bottles in hand.

It was both St. Patrick's Day and senior week, Class of 1957. The football team was the Hansfield Fighting Irish so it was traditional for the students to play hooky and, along with co-eds from Hansfield College, line the street and cheer the parade, drinking green beer in full view of the police, who looked the other way every March 17.

"How many times do I have to tell you kids?" JoJo, one of the two bartenders at The Old Town Tavern, shouted over the cacophony of the marching band. "Get out of here!"

"Hey, guys," the scarecrow girl cried out. "They won't let us in! You have to be *queer* to go in there."

"What a wisenheimer," I mumbled, trying to hide my face behind my glass.

JoJo sounded disgusted. "I'm calling the cops right now." She started back toward the pay phone across from the toilets in the hallway. Two older men left then and there, their drinks unfinished. "Cops" was a dirty word in a gay bar.

"Did you hear that?" the kid shrilled over her shoulder. "She's calling the cops. On us. They're lucky they're allowed on the streets with us normal people."

A young cop behind the kid sniggered, egging her on.

From her barstool, which she straddled like a horse, Murph said, "You might want to hold off on that call, JoJo. The last thing we need is more cops. Kid—hey, kid, I'm talking to you."

The young woman stared at Murph with something like fascinated horror.

"Don't they teach manners anymore, skinnymalink?" Murph asked.

Norman, the other bartender, looked skyward and said with bitter good humor, "Oh, Murph, don't you know this is exactly what they teach these kids? The parents are rude to queers and the criminals, the crippled, and us dark-skinned folks. Their broods become bigots-in-training." He called out the door, "Try it! You might like it!"

"Hell, no! It could be catching." The girl's friends guffawed behind her.

Something struck me about her little gang. The boys and their girlfriends were light whereas the kid was darker, were on the beefy side while she was all elbows, knees, and nose. Why was she their mouthpiece? Had they goaded her into this? Was she out to prove herself to them?

Then, arms flailing, she came through the door like she'd been shot from a cannon. One of the boys stepped back as she careened smack into JoJo. The boy had shoved her into the tavern.

"Eewww!" his girlfriend cried. "Dirty Deej is touching one of *them*!"

It was true. JoJo reflexively put her arms out to keep them both upright and they stood, arms as good as around each other, for a long, drawn-out, teetering moment.

The other boy was ready. A big round flashbulb went off and his friends watched while his Polaroid whirred and ejected a picture of the embrace.

By then, the girl called Deej was backing away from JoJo. She turned and ran to the boy with the camera. He was pinching the edge of the picture, air-drying it. Deej made a grab for it, but the boy was tall and yanked the photograph out of reach.

"You liked it!" The shover's girlfriend, fleshy and blond, in a light-green sweater set with matching knee socks, goaded her.

"No!"

"You like wearing men's hats too," the boy who shoved her said. "You even want to do a man's job. Come on, admit it!"

"Why did you ram me in there, you jerk?" Deej asked in a voice that sounded like she was fighting tears.

"Why did you glom onto that she-man like that?" asked the girl who'd cried "eewww." She stabbed a finger toward the bar. "Is it because you *belong* here, like *them*?"

"I didn't! He—"

The tall boy with the photo did a twitchy dance around Deej. "We're going to mimeograph this baby and plaster the school with it!"

"Why?" Deej asked, looking bewildered. "I thought we were friends. I'm the one who stole the beer for us."

"*Sure* we're friends," the girl in light green said with an acidic drawl. "I always wanted a lesbo friend."

"But I'm not a lesbo," Deej squawked.

JoJo leaned on the bar beside me, watching the kids jostle Deej in the doorway. "The straights can always tell, can't they? Then they cut us out of the herd."

The shover held up his beer bottle, tipped back his head, and poured the last drops down his throat. His Adam's apple went up and down with each swallow, like a peacock displaying or a bull lowing. "We're out of beer!" he said. "Come on, you guys. I know where the key to the mimeo machine is."

I remembered those cruel days when the other girls all turned to boys at once, hacking off childhood ties with those of us who didn't follow their lead.

Deej stood marooned, her bravado wilted, a desperate panic on her face. She wiped her eyes with closed fists, glared in the door of the bar, then bolted, sprinting after her tormentors, calling, "Hey, wait for me!"

CHAPTER ONE

Four years later, in 1961, the St. Patrick's Day Parade fell on a Friday. Sunlight fought its way inside the Old Town Tavern through a big rectangle of glass bricks that replaced the plate-glass window vandals had cracked. JoJo was still bartender, a pint-sized woman in perpetual motion who wore her black hair like Elvis Presley's and had the same bruised look around her eyes. The black frames of her glasses matched her hair.

Norman waddled out of the kitchen. Always in a pullover sweater, white shirt, and cuffed slacks, he never missed an opportunity to bat his long dark eyelashes, roll his eyes, make suggestive remarks to the male customers, and otherwise present himself as a typical bar queen, complete with his perfume du jour, usually Shalimar. A little too round in the middle to successfully pull off a feminine walk, he always gave it his best shot. With JoJo, Norman kept the bar as immaculate as a bar could be kept. The outside of the glass bricks he left dirty to further obscure what went on inside, hopeful the frat boys and football bulls wouldn't pester the customers.

A group of Cub Scouts trudged past, completely out of formation, giving occasional gap-toothed smiles and waves of their tiny American flags. Behind them, also mostly gap-toothed, a contingent of Spanish-American War, and maybe even Civil War, veterans rode on a float—red, white, and blue garlands around their necks, slightly larger flags in their hands.

Firemen rang the large bells on their trucks as they brought up the rear of the parade. This was Northwestern Massachusetts in its patriotic glory. I loved it. Most of it.

JoJo made for the pay phone in the hallway. Originally from California, and estranged enough from her family that she wanted a whole continent between them, JoJo was quiet and a great listener even on the go. She picked up the phone, then paused.

"Gone," Murph called back to her from where she slumped at the bar in her well-tailored vest, a glass of ginger ale in front of her, sleeves rolled up, right arm swathed in gauze to the elbow.

Almost every year the Old Town and its customers were harassed by youngsters or drunks along the parade route. Murph was giving the all clear that today's set of hecklers had left.

Murph, Murph, Murph. How could anyone ever forget Murph? Slacks creased to an eye-catching edge, cuffed shirts that wouldn't dare wrinkle; hair dense, dark, swept back, she was city-pale and handsome, an unpolished yet dapper forty-something, hoarse from shouting over machines at work and telling stories in the bar.

The Old Town Tavern was Girolami Avenue's neighborhood—and gay—hangout. The locals pronounced Girolami wrong, and the hordes of students that helped the neighborhood thrive didn't bother to try; they knew it as The Avenue. The bar itself was located in an undistinguished brick building, never packed, often lively. Treed older homes, small shops, Hansfield College, the railroad station, and a private hospital completed the neighborhood. The bar's entrance sat smack-dab at the corner of The Avenue and College Street.

Earlier, at the start of the parade, JoJo had stood in the open doorway, to let fresh air sweep out the smells of smoke and alcohol and Mr. Clean. Norman adored the image of Mr. Clean. JoJo had marched in place as a band, all booming drums and shrill horns, passed the row of shabby storefronts across the street.

Now, as JoJo returned to the bar, Murph said, "Such a fine parade they run in Hansfield. Did I ever tell you about the time—"

"Probably." JoJo threw a grin my way as she popped back behind the bar at top speed. A tremor shook the building and went on and on as a train hauled freight right through Hansfield Station. The bottles lined up against the mirror always clinked a bit.

Murph seemed to be at half-mast already. She slurred her words, not from drink, but from working a double shift at the hospital laundry. She moved her Scotch-plaid blazer and, with work-reddened hands, carefully hung it on the back of the bar stool. Her clothes carried the faint scent of Bay Rum, the men's cologne. We all wondered where she got such neat duds, as they fit so well they had to be custom-made. Some people spent their money on the ponies, some on booze; I thought this was where Murph's money went, to a sympathetic tailor. The Avenue remained relatively quiet between bands; Girl Scouts and Boy Scouts trudged by, nearing the end of their route.

Murph took a swallow of ginger ale. She was born right in The Old Town Tavern section of the city, yet came across as Irish as if just off the boat. She moved into her characteristic story-telling stance, head up, leaning over the back of a molded plywood bar stool, glass in hand. Many drinks she'd upended when The Old Town Tavern got crowded, waving her arms so emphatically she'd learned to turn her back to nearby glasses. The rest of us kept our reflexes toned by catching flying drinks. A tuba blasted outside. Through the door, I could see a young man holding a beer mug with one hand, getting sick into a green bowler hat. I turned away, my stomach queasy.

"Listen," Murph said, "I marched in the St. Paddy's Day parade in Boston. Nineteen fifty."

I could picture her. Murph looked taller than most people her height because her bearing could have been military, if she'd been a man. Her eyes were nothing like a soldier's, though. They had a sad slant belied by a crouching humor always ready to pounce into action. Murph loved to laugh and to make everyone around her do the same.

"I lived outside Boston, working a god-awful job. I looked forward to my once-a-week Girl Scout troop meeting. And never mind rolling your eyes at me behind my back, JoJo. To this day I can be trusted with a troop of girls. And hell, I was only twenty-four and in love with the other leader. She was my boss's wife, little and pretty and wonderful with kids. I taught them how to build fires, chop wood because I grew up camping out."

She told the story in her rough voice with a sigh and a smile.

"Give me another ale, will you?"

"Don't tell me she let you march in the parade," Norman said.

"She made a mistake all right. Here I am, wearing the old Girl Scout leader uniform, a drab and shapeless green dress, marching up 5th Avenue as proud as I could be. From the sidelines I hear whistling and cheering to beat the band. It was my gang from the gay bar, in green. They didn't exactly look like Scouts. Green derbies and ties it was, and these were women. 'Don't she look cute in drag!' they're yelling. I can't describe the terror. I didn't know if I'd be better off running or ignoring them. Didn't they understand this could ruin me? I wished I could wrap myself in the flag and not take it off till I got home. I bore their bedeviling till my co-leader asked, 'Who are they?' I about-faced then and melted into the crowd. Aw, I knew all along I didn't belong with those nice people. I never went back to my job, much less the troop." She gave a dry laugh. "I'd never touched a woman, but knew what they'd think."

For all her bluff and bluster, Murph could be extraordinarily shy. Part of that, I suspected, came from self-consciousness about her odd-colored teeth, some of which were missing. Irish teeth, she called them, and blamed them on the generations who had to get by on soft potatoes and poor dentistry at best. The way she back-pedaled when anyone tried to get near her made me wonder if she'd ever been with a woman in anything but her dreams.

"We love you, Murph!" said a rosy-skinned regular at the bar. He held a martini with some delicacy, but he wasn't gay. He'd come from the Philippines as a kid and stopped in every day on his way home to his wife and daughter. We'd all seen wallet photos of the three of them skiing. Murph gave him a big smack on the cheek befitting The Old Town. He hugged her.

The Old Town Tavern drew a delightful mix of customers, many of them graduates of the college. Some wore heavy, dark-rimmed glasses, and their hair, under striped railroad caps or black berets, tended to be a bit too long and mussed up for squares. They brought girlfriends with earrings that dangled under long straight hair, and they all played whatever jazz they could find on the jukebox. The men dressed in denim and army-navy surplus jackets. In the warmer months the women's pants, in odd geometric patterns, ended below their knees. Another customer was a doped-up painter who wore droopy chinos smeared like a palette. Sometimes store owners from the little neighborhood businesses would lock up and quickly visit the cigarette machine in the bar, then return later for a drink.

The long cry of a train arriving at the station came through the door with Lisa Jelane. Head high, she stood silhouetted in the doorway and glared at the hecklers, who had returned. Over her long black wool coat her hair was the shade of sparkling apple cider, center-parted so it curled inward, under her jaw. She wore a black skirt and a patterned green top that flattered her soft, resigned-looking blue eyes. An ever-present brown leather purse hung on a long strap from her shoulder. I'd have given a million dollars to trade places with that purse.

Lisa didn't have to say a word. Her stance was enough to shame the hecklers and they melted into the crowd. She turned and made her regal entrance. Whenever I saw Lisa Jelane in a bar it was like spotting President Eisenhower at a Cub Scout meeting. Maybe John Kennedy too, though I hadn't seen enough of him yet to know. Broad-boned and a spare five foot eleven, she had the face of an Irish goddess. Lisa told us that the ring she wore represented the Celtic goddess Danu, mother of magic and the fae. The fae are supposed to remain in Ireland, an invisible race of magical, ever-youthful beings. To tell the truth, they sounded like gay people to me.

She eased her bag onto the table, then greeted us with a tired smile. "I tried waiting out the nasty delinquents. They got me anyway."

Murph deepened her voice and imitated them. "'You don't belong with those people. Come with me, baby. I'll show you what you're missing.' Miserable cusses."

Norman headed back to the kitchen. "What a shame they're so cute at that age," he said, his Jamaican roots unmistakable in his voice. With a two-handed grip on the dishtowel around his neck he laughed and vamped as always, all plumpness and budding belly. His small brown eyes shone with a bright, steady liveliness muted by—what—his years behind a bar? The bullying that would follow such a man all his life, especially a dark-skinned man?

"My apologies," said JoJo. She set a cloudy-colored daiquiri and slice of lime in front of Lisa. "I really didn't want to risk a major confrontation with the parade going past."

I got up and shut the door. It trapped the cigarette smoke inside, but maybe the kids would go away. We could hear the parade. The drunken high-schoolers horsed around in front of the glass bricks. Their ghostly silhouettes pointed at us and they made pistols of their fingers into a sinister show.

"Thanks for the antidote, JoJo." Lisa slowly lit a cigarette, her long, freckled hand elegant in movement. One of those women who wouldn't be caught dead without makeup and accessories, Lisa wore smoky-gray eye shadow and liner that made her blue eyes darker. Her collection of sleek scarves seemed endless. Today she wore one with a light-green border, white background, and blue bicycles running across it.

Murph had the wiry look of someone who earned her leanness through hard work. Not as tall as Lisa, both of them carried themselves with postures so erect they could be models, though for very different products.

Lisa took a ladylike sip of her drink and a long pull on her cigarette. The movement of her arms was both fluid and restrained, very much like herself. Even the smoke she exhaled had a controlled grace and drifted in two streams that fused as they rose toward the lazy ceiling fan.

"Damn Adam and Eve," Lisa said. "I can think of much better ways to fill my days than working for a living." She looked at her drink. "Should I be sober when the woman of my dreams walks through that door?"

"Mind your p's and q's, colleen," said Murph. "Be grateful you've got that work, whatever it is you do."

Lisa never spoke about her job, her home life, or her past. She was a mystery who kept me hoping for a glimpse behind the curtain. It was all I could do not to fall for her. I had no business pining for someone more sophisticated than anyone I'd ever known; I was a scruffy old dyke in her presence, outclassed by leaps and bounds. Her New York accent, though not grating, leveled out her magic just enough. New Englanders looked down on New Yorkers. Don't ask me why. Red Sox, Yankees, I didn't care, but without that tiny flaw in her speech Lisa would intimidate me.

Murph stifled a burp with a powerful-looking hand. The veins on the back of it were ropy. The detergents and water and heat at her job both reddened and bleached her fingers. The cracks and splits in her fingertips must, I thought, be painful all the time. She finished her advice. "You could be in the hospital laundry room like me, wearing a hairnet, a gray dress with your name embroidered on it, white stockings, and sensible shoes. Not a pretty thing to see, I can assure you." The idea of Murph looking like that was absurd.

Lisa nodded and raised her drink. We'd celebrated her twenty-seventh birthday here a month ago. A complete flirt, Lisa Jelane also had periods of isolating depression. When things went her way she could be warm and loving; when they didn't, she could be cold. I suspected that chill covered up some chink she feared in her pretty armor. She answered Murph. "Not that there's any disgrace to laundry work. I helped my mother when she cleaned other people's dirty clothes for food to put in our mouths. Work is all dirty laundry. As soon as it's clean, it turns into dirty laundry again."

The guys at the bar thought that was hysterical.

The shoemaker stroked his scant beard and said, "I'm making that into a sign over my counter."

"And some of us have more dirty laundry than others," Murph confided to her glass.

She spoke as if she had some history the rest of us didn't know about. I would have thought she'd laid bare all her secrets based on the countless stories she told. "Where did you find this kook?" Lisa asked JoJo, with a smile and the flick of a wrist toward Murph.

JoJo laughed. "I tried taking her back for a refund. No luck."

The front door swung open and one of the hecklers reappeared. "Oops," he called out. "Sorry. I'm looking for some real men."

He backed out, but not before one of the longhairs from the neighborhood, a former college guy turned shoemaker, called to the hecklers, "Give up! There's worse things than queers."

Like a squall, Carla Jean, as always holding a lit cigarette in one hand, rushed through the door. Her short, curled hair was hennaed to an orangey red, which did nothing for her olive-hued skin. She wore overlarge blue plastic hoop earrings, and two shopping bags hung over her arms. She waved a large business envelope in her free hand. Carla Jean was a Girolami, a descendant of the guy the street was named after, and proud of her family, proud of her town. She'd been JoJo's lover since high school. They owned a little shop that made awards, plaques, and trophies: Girolami Awards. They inscribed glass and made wood signs and everything in between. JoJo's bartender job and Carla Jean's office-manager work at her parents' car dealership kept them afloat while they worked to make a success of their business.

Carla Jean acted as The Old Town Tavern's biggest cheerleader. "Where will it end?" she asked. "Tormentors at our door, Communists aiming missiles at us, and now look what comes in the mail! Give me a hair of the dog, JoJo. This hangover's been with me all day long."

She handed the mail to JoJo, who scanned it, then calmly read it aloud. "Can you believe this? 'According to regulation la-di-da, the city has received a report of unpermitted structural renovations upon your commercial property at the above address.' What are they? Nuts?"

Norman took the letter. A powerful spike of naptha from urinal cakes clung to him from cleaning the bathrooms. "Well, excuse me. We only want to use our old stove safely. It's not like we're opening a restaurant. Who in the world told them what we're doing?"

"You have to get a permit to fix up your own property?" asked Lisa. "That's outrageous."

"They should give you a medal. This area isn't exactly upscale and never has been," Murph said.

I'd dealt with the city many times; the letter sounded par for the course to me.

"Wait a minute, darling," said Norman. "Heavens to Mergatroyd. 'A representative of the department will inspect said premises within thirty days.' I can't stop for thirty days and leave a hole in the wall! Getting a permit to vent a stove in this old building will take months."

Lisa asked, "Can they shut you down for this world-threatening infraction?"

"Shut us down." Carla Jean set her wineglass on the table for a refill and lit another cigarette. "Board us up. We might as well surrender before we start. No way Norman and Hugh can afford a licensed contractor to make these repairs on what this bar brings in."

"I suspect the fixit guy," Norman said with certainty. "The one who tried to sell us an electric stove instead of repairing our old one? He must have really wanted that commission."

Hugh arrived as if Carla Jean had summoned him. Norman's pallid, bookish boyfriend since high school, Hugh taught at the college. He blinked his owlish eyes behind old-fashioned wire-rim glasses as he quietly said, "You know they're doing their level best to harass us, people." Hugh liked to tell us he taught dead languages to make living languages more alive. Considerably taller than Norman, he had bushy eyebrows that contrasted with a neatly groomed beard lining the edges of his jaw and chin. Although he had a certain dignity, he sometimes got downright cuddly with Norman, and he loved to dress in a dark, sober style of drag. Otherwise, he kept a very low profile while he waited for tenure. "They want to drive us out, like the Romans did the Jews."

Norman sighed loudly. The parade ended. There was no sign of our tormentors. "I can see the business page now," he said. 'Unemployment swells. Norman turns to hustling. Oh, well. Just call me Marilyn-Between-Movies!" His whole name was Norman Eugene Monroe, and he called himself Norma Jean every chance he got. He even did Marilyn behind the mike now and then, giving us a whispery rendition of "Knick-Knack Paddywhack," "Old MacDonald Had A Farm," and other ridiculous offerings until we laughed ourselves silly.

Murph, who, as usual by the time day drifted toward evening, reached a level of fatigue that made her depressed, said, "I suppose Hugh's right, as always. This is an excuse to raid you with building inspectors instead of cops."

"You win the prize," exclaimed Carla Jean. She thrust her heavily freckled arms around Murph from behind. "I wonder why, all of a sudden, they're bothering with a complaint like this. They never enforce these ancient regs."

None of us knew Carla Jean's stake in the bar. She might be trying to keep JoJo employed. Maybe she loaned Hugh and Norman money.

Exuberant as she was about most things, she chose to keep her mouth shut about this. Or that might have been the simple answer: Carla Jean Girolami was exuberant about The Old Town Tavern.

"Maybe they never enforce them except for struggling gay bars?" Lisa normally saved her anger for acts of cruelty and violence. Did she think the city's letter qualified? "This is a decent place. Even the straight customers are pleasant."

Murph slowly swiveled her stool toward Lisa. I don't know where the boys got the idea that stools shaped like modern art, with smooth blond wood molded into a curve that perched on four tall, shiny shafts, fit in at The Old Town. If these were a sample of their taste, I hoped they'd never have the money to redo the place.

"Did I ever tell you about the time I was superintendent and the building inspectors came?" Murph asked.

I heard affection in Lisa's laugh. "Did I ever tell you about the time JoJo tossed Murph out of the bar for telling stories until the sky fell?"

Carla Jean fussed with the letter. "We can do it, my little Carla Jeanie," said JoJo. She tried to enclose her short, stout lover with an arm not quite long enough for the job. Laughing, she said, "Norman, why don't you take over the bar while we give Murph the old heave-ho."

Carla Jean had left the door wide open when she arrived with her packages. One of the high school boys stuck his head in and made a smart-ass comment with a forced laugh. "Look! There's a man in there now! Oh, excuse me. My mistake. It's nothing but one of the sissies."

Carla Jean rushed at the boy, wineglass in one hand, cigarette in the other. She stumbled and righted herself. "Enough already! Shoo! You troublemakers are all I need right now."

The boy backed off, revealing a familiar figure. Slight, long-haired with shaggy bangs, she hesitated, then came through the door. She was alone this time and held a plastic cup of green beer.

"Wait," Carla Jean said. "I'm trying to place you, but I don't think this is where you want to be. How old are you?"

"Old enough."

"You know the law about minors in this state."

"I'll be twenty-one in three months," the young woman said, her tone sulking and defiant.

"Like hell you will be!" Murph rose ominously from her stool, at her most imposing. She lowered her head as if she had horns and bore down on the kid. Her rough hand jabbed at air. "Then come back in three months, jail bait!" she roared. "I remember you. Out with you now!" The kid turned away, her big, dark eyes as pitiful and accusing as a scolded puppy's.

Carla Jean shook her head, eyes shiny with tears. She got weepy when she had a glass of wine. "I shouldn't take it out on that poor confused kid. How can I protest what the city's trying to do to us, what the world wants to do to us? There's no face to blame, no name to plead with, no way to fix what's behind this kid's attitude and whatever the city plans."

"If that girl isn't the butchiest thing I've seen in a while..." Lisa said.

Murph declared, "It's the ones who fight the hardest today who lie down with us tomorrow."

"The child may die fighting her nature," Lisa said. "Why is she back? You'd think she liked it here." She laughed in the full-throated way she found after a couple of daiquiris. "Don't let her—or anyone—block the door, Norma Jean. The love of my life may try to get in."

CHAPTER TWO

After the parade, I went into work for a few hours. Then I walked my dog, Colonel Mustard, ate some dinner, and, once *The Red Skelton Show* was over, planned to read until I couldn't keep my eyes open. I'd taken the best seller *Anatomy of a Murder* out of the library that day. An English tea cozy it wasn't. The everyday evil of the book drove me out of the house to find some companionship.

I live across the street from The Old Town Tavern, at The Avenue Arms, about twenty minutes from where I own a bookbindery. My shop does quite a bit for the college press, and for a few little publishers and magazines around the region. I make enough to live simply and pay my crew well. Why should I be richer than they are? Our skills are only different, not better or poorer. I donate as many bindery services as I can to the public library.

By ten o'clock that night I was back at The Old Town. As I went in I got a little teary-eyed over the way Norman and Hugh used small lamps along the bar and on the tables instead of overhead lights and beer signs. They'd assembled the lamps one by one from straw-wrapped Italian wine bottles. This gave the impression of a congeniality and warmth that drew me the way someone's living room might. Besides us homosexuals, The Old Town appealed to locals from the apartments and businesses. These customers were hesitant about rock'n'roll more recent than Elvis's. I thought of it as one of thousands of low-lighted bars strung out across America offering to drown loneliness and provide escape from lives that at times seemed unbearably hard. I welcomed my chilled vodka-tonic glass with its spiky sweetness.

"So Rockie is back too," Murph said to me by way of a greeting.

"Surprise!" I practically lived there and took a number of their gay waifs under my wing to give them whatever work they could handle at the bindery. I was older than many of them, had found my place in life and enjoyed the chance to catch a gay person who's falling. Like the rest of the folks at the bar, Norman pours his big hurting queen's heart out to me, and I never tell a soul what he's said. "Every queer," Norman claims, "needs a gay auntie." He elected me because I wear my hair braided and pinned at the top of my head, as I have since I was a kid. My mother thought it balanced the heavy jaw I got from my father. Norman said his aunts did the same and their hair was as silver as mine. Of course, the resemblance ends there—trust me on that. Before it went gray in my thirties, my hair was a dark blond. Add my blue eyes, fat rosy cheeks, and I looked like a *goy*. Now, although I'm only fifty-three, this head of hair is almost pure white. Lucky for me I still have my mother's charcoal arch of eyebrows, which keeps me from looking even older than I am. Whatever it is about me—my face, my braids, how happy I am to give my gay kids the attention they want, even when they're older than me (they often act like young fools)—they confide in me; that's a true honor and I love them for it.

Someone hammered behind the kitchen's swinging wooden doors. Two of the regular boys huddled at the bar with Tipsy, our resident straight eccentric. She had to be in her late seventies, with blued and marcelled hair, highly rouged cheeks, and the makeup of a forty-year old. She couldn't hide the wrinkled pallor of her neck. She lived on alcohol and bar nuts, but didn't seem frail and dressed like someone in her thirties, right down to the low-cut tops. She was a bottomless well for nicotine and martoonies, as she called them, and treated the boys like a cross between boyfriends, stellar sons, and movie stars.

Quick little JoJo was behind the bar, wiping, clanking bottles, in motion as usual. Norman swept around the stools, something he was given to do obsessively.

"Goodness gracious," Lisa said as she slowly exhaled a curl of cigarette smoke. "Some night Norman will sweep me under the bar with the rest of the trash." A barely touched daiquiri before her, she murmured to JoJo, "Say hello to all my exes under there, will you, hon?" She indicated the bar with her shapely hand. "I've heard good butches don't go to heaven. They're buried under their favorite barstools."

It was strange to hear our lingo coming through those refined lips. From the way Lisa spoke you could tell she'd been to college, though she'd mentioned dropping out to marry halfway to graduation. College had probably taken the edge off her accent.

"Speaking of good butches," Lisa said, "here's to you, Murph."

"What brought on the compliment?" Murph asked. At a certain point, she always seemed to find a second wind.

"I've wondered all evening, Murph, about your bandage."

"You don't want to hear about that."

JoJo winked. "Don't tell me Murph's passing up a chance to tell a story."

Lisa could be very seductive in her dignified way. "Come on, honey," she said, to encourage Murph.

Were they finally lonely enough to go home with each other, I thought? Looking at them, the striking, urbane Lisa and the handsome, sinewy Murph, I thought how ironic it was to look so good yet be as mopey as they sometimes were.

Murph sighed. "You know I work at the hospital laundry."

"You got your hand caught in the mangle?" Lisa asked, eyebrows raised.

"Mangles? They're long gone. We clean millions of pounds of laundry a year at the hospital and it's all got to be done yesterday. I get the mistakes and fix them with chemicals, or I might hand-iron an item. We use a lot of high-pressure steam. If there's a little leak anywhere, in a hose or a line, this can happen." She unraveled the bandage and exposed the inside of her right elbow. A deep burn ran across it. Red patches on her well-muscled arm were in several stages of healing.

Lisa said, "You need to get out of there."

"Don't I know it. What else can I do? It isn't a high-wage job, but it's steady and pays for vacations and major medical. Listen, I grew up in the Depression. I know the price of a pound of beans and a stick of celery to make soup. During the war I earned grand money. When the men came home and took their jobs back, I used my savings to live on until I got the hospital-laundry job."

Murph replaced the dirty bandage and Lisa stroked her hand. "This isn't right. Isn't there somebody you can complain to?"

"Listen, doll, life's not safe for any gay girl, whatever she does. What've I got for all my work? What do any of us have? It's not that I ever wanted to be president of the United States, but even Carla Jean and JoJo, what do you have, with both of you working your jobs night and day? An apartment? A couple of forbidden cats, a small business you have to support with outside jobs?"

JoJo dimpled one cheek every time she made a crack. "Where else in this town can we be with our own?"

Lisa lifted her glass in agreement.

"Then it wasn't you I heard a while ago going on about your weariness, JoJo?" Murph asked. "You're right, though. You're the lucky ones. The rest of us pay for the privilege of one another's company. Do you hear that? It's Norman out in the kitchen late at night, butching it up to make improvements in secret—damned if he does, damned if he doesn't, because the city dislikes our kind. And look at you, Lisa, you lost your kid because of it. What can we do except keep our whole lives secret?"

Poor Lisa, I thought. I didn't know she was a mother. That was the thing about her. She could be a princess or a prostitute and you'd never know it from her say-so.

Carla Jean's words were no longer very distinct. One cigarette was in her hand and another in an ashtray. Her penchant for red wine often took her past the mellow phase. "You two are about as cheerful tonight as—"

"Two people about to go home alone. Again," Murph said, with a look at Lisa. "Still, I remember when life was better."

"Before you were born?" I could tell Lisa was teasing Murph by her sidelong glance and the way she watched for a reaction.

Murph scowled. "I'm trying to cheer you up."

"Okay, cheer me, Murph."

"Uh-oh," JoJo said, making that deep dimple again. "I have a hunch another Murph tale's coming on."

"Oh, I love that dimple!" Carla Jean said. She held JoJo's face in her hands and tried to kiss the dimple. JoJo squirmed away from her and said, "Carla Jeanie," her long-lashed brown eyes cast down, as if she could hide herself. She grabbed a bin of empties and fled with it to the kitchen. We could hear her fill the bottle crates for the delivery guys to take away. She wouldn't show her face again for a few minutes.

We all laughed.

"Got yourself a little charmer, didn't you?" Murph said.

Lisa added, "JoJo's sweet."

"Don't I know it." Carla Jean's smile was sloppy.

When JoJo returned, Lisa asked, "How'd you get the name JoJo?"

For once, JoJo stood still. She looked very serious as she explained. "My father is Joseph. My brother is Joe, Jr. He's in the army. My big sister is JoAnne. Mom took to calling me JoJo as a gag because we all answered to the same name."

We laughed and JoJo got back to work. Norman sang "JoJoJoJoJoJoJo" in falsetto to the melody of "The Star Spangled Banner" until JoJo gave him a smack on the butt and told him to quit, which only made us laugh more, and Norman picked up the pace of his song until he, too, gave in to laughter.

The fact that only Norman served the longhairs made sense to me. JoJo probably assumed they were anti-nuclear-weapon-pacifist types and refused out of loyalty to her brother.

I overheard Spence ask JoJo where her brother was stationed. "I got back from Korea last year," he said. Spence, who looked like a big white motorcycle-gang member, but wasn't, and Seneca, who wore her short black hair straightened, worked at the city jail. The Old Town was their home away from home. They were comfortable with the rest of us oddballs. As always, they had a penny-ante card game going, either between themselves or with other regulars, and they really did play for pennies.

Murph turned back to Lisa. "What about you, doll? I'll bet you've got some stories to tell."

Lisa replied in her unruffled way. "Nothing exciting."

"How do you know what gets me excited?"

"Oh, Murph," Lisa said.

She closed her eyes and I could see her relive coming out as she'd confided it to Murph. As exhilarating as the experience had been for her, the story was only about two office mates alone all day, day after day, never bored, always laughing, so enthralled with each other they grew to hate going home to their husbands.

"We kissed a few times in the office," Lisa said, "then spent a couple of evenings in the bleachers at the Jones Beach Theater. We'd take the train and a bus to get there—at least a two-hour trip." She lit a cigarette and laughed smoke out of her mouth. "We literally sat on our hands so we wouldn't touch. The outdoor performances made us dreamier. The Guy Lombardo Orchestra floated past at intermission on a yacht, playing romantic songs. Every visit we stayed overnight at a motel in Freeport. She had exquisite hands."

"Where is she now?" Murph asked.

They talked at the bar. I was two stools away. The noise dampened their voices like a curtain insulating them inside their story world.

"Back with him. She was too scared to stay with me." She smiled and slowly shook her head. "I thought you planned to tell me a story, Murph."

"You must be tired of them."

Lisa laid a hand on Murph's arm. She leaned toward her. "We're in a tent, Murph. It's pouring outside. We're chilly and inside our sleeping bags. It's too soon to go to sleep."

Murph grinned wolfishly. "I can think of better things to do in a dark tent than tell tales."

"Oh, Murph." Lisa swatted her arm. "Indulge me."

Murph smiled, her look both exasperated and benign. She led Lisa to the scarred wooden banquette against the wall and I soon wandered over, not quite next to them. I laughed at myself for being such a *yenta*. "We'd walk for miles through Chestnut Forest Park, me and my friend Rose. I'm named Rose too, if you can believe it, so we were always two peas in a pod."

"Were you—"

Murph patted Lisa's hand and smiled. "She was such a nag, my little Rose. She came to me as soon as I dropped out of business school, fit to be tied. I told her, 'Rosie, I got on at the plant. I'll make $2.25 an hour and put half of it away for an apartment.'

"We'd touched and frolicked alongside the river all through high school, and sometimes in the water. 'Trouble!' she'd call me, then we'd sit against a rock and she'd lay her head in my lap. Those were the best days of my whirligig life."

Lisa didn't move. We watched Murph form pictures with her hands as she talked. Rose was shorter than Murph, I could see, and the park was filled with trees. The river, as her hands described it, flowed swiftly. "One day we were at our rock, only my head was in her lap." Murph would speak in the voices of other people and now, in a pitch softer and sweeter than her own, she said, 'Do you know the reason I spend so much time with Vi, Murph? Do you know I'm attracted to a woman? Do you know I'm funny that way?'"

I saw that the bar had disappeared from her consciousness: Murph was at the river, Rose stroking her head. "'Funny?' I said to Rosie. The poor woman went through the whole thing, explaining what made her and Vi funny. 'So that explains why my heart does cartwheels at the sight of you,' I told Rose. 'Of course you are, of course I am. I knew we were special.' I was so excited. I asked how she found out, and if there were others like us, if I could meet them and, finally, if maybe I could kiss her." Murph put her hand to her mouth and kissed her half fist where the thumb met the soft, fleshy juncture.

"Did you?"

"Rose told me to hold my horses. That was the first time she called me little Romeo, even though, standing, I towered over her. She said she was taken.

"'Taken?' I said. My heart broke right in half. 'You mean you're with Vi? Rose, no, you know we were born for each other.' A tear dropped to my cheek. She kept smoothing back my hair. 'I didn't know that a year ago, Murph, when I fell for Vi.'"

Murph's dreamy eyes returned to focus on Lisa. "Vi Derizzi was thirty-eight then, twenty years older than Rose. As for myself, I've looked for a Rose of my own."

"Is that why you're still in Hansfield? To look for one more, where you started?"

"I don't know, Lisa. I'm tuckered out. It's dangerous to be out in the world when you look like the crown prince of lesbians. I hoped life would get a little easier when I moved back to Hansfield."

"And?"

"It's been years since I returned. My father died, then my mother. I don't see much of my relatives. What do we have in common except memories? Maybe that's all family is anyway. People you happen to have memories with."

JoJo came over to their table. The two blinked as if someone turned on a light. "This is the slowest parade day ever." JoJo shook her head as she looked toward the front door.

"The hecklers scare people away," Lisa said. "You had a good crowd of men for a while. And that cute retired het couple. The ones who confess to living in sin every time they get a little bit stewed."

"So fill 'er up, JoJo. I got a little story I want you to hear." Murph sang words close to the familiar lyrics.

"Figures."

Lisa gave a bubbly laugh I'd never heard from her before and leaned toward Murph as if for warmth.

Without a word, Murph slid an arm around her and patted her back as if to make her intent ambiguous.

"I've had it," Carla Jean said as she emerged from the kitchen and joined us at the banquette. She was disheveled, with cobwebs in her hair. "I like Norman's idea of finishing before an inspector arrives so we can claim nothing's changed." She stretched her arms. "But if someone warns us the inspection is tomorrow, I couldn't do a thing about it."

"Don't come near me until you take a bath." JoJo looked disgusted.

"Have a nightcap with us, you two," Murph said. "Don't stand on ceremony, Rockie. Bring your drink over."

I've never been shy, but I appreciated the invitation. I looked at my watch—an Omega my parents gave me for my college graduation. Colonel Mustard would be fine for another couple of hours.

"Get me another splash of wine, JoJo?" Carla Jean said, and explained to me for the hundredth time, "It helps put me to sleep."

Murph guffawed. "Is that all you two do at home? Sleep?" She was always predictable, our Murph, making the wisecrack that came to everyone's mind and was as obvious and old as civilization.

"When JoJo opens at ten a.m. at our shop, works till two a.m. at the bar, and starts all over the next day—you bet it is."

JoJo said, "Meanwhile, before she comes to The Old Town, Carla Jean does her nine-to-five bit over at the Girolami GM dealership, fighting with customers about their bills."

"They think car repairs should be warranted forever."

Murph said, "They have a point."

Lisa, ever the mediator, said, before Murph and Carla Jean got into it yet again, "How much do you have to do before the inspector comes?"

"Everything." Carla Jean flung her arms up over her head.

"Seriously," Murph said. "May I tell you, Carla Jean, about the time I put in as a building superintendent?"

"You've told stories all night. That's really what drove the customers away." JoJo grinned. There was actually quite a crowd.

"Don't look a gift horse in the mouth."

Carla Jean asked, "Meaning?"

"I mean I was a super. You know—repaired kitchens, plumbing, walls—like in what you're trying to do quickly?"

"Is that an offer to help us?"

"You might think I'm a dumb cluck, but I'm very good with my hands."

Lisa's eyes fastened on Murph.

"I can fix about anything with these." She held them up and spread the fingers. Lisa watched them move. "I once brought my twelve-story building with a hundred and twenty apartments to code in three weeks. Of course—" Murph was all modesty—"I kept it up pretty well to start with."

JoJo headed back to the bar for last call. She looked over her shoulder to ask, "So why didn't you say so?"

Murph hit her head with the heel of her hand. "You never asked!"

"We couldn't pay you much," Carla Jean said.

"Listen, you babes in the woods. I need The Old Town to be here as much as you need me to spend my dollars here. You're my family now. I'll take payment at your free Thanksgiving Feed."

"Are you kidding?" Carla Jean asked. "Cook for the hordes on Thanksgiving? The stove doesn't work yet."

Lisa asked, with some excitement in her normally modulated voice, "Can you fix a gas stove?"

Norman strolled over and said, "If you can do that, you're on for Thanksgiving." Norman was pretty much in the bag by that time of night too, but hid his liquor better than Carla Jean.

"Stoves were one of my specialties," said Murph. "Tappan ranges included."

"I need to talk to my husband about it," Norman said. "I can't imagine he'd object. He can dress as a pilgrim lady."

"How big is the oven, Norma Jean?" Lisa asked.

Norman answered. "Ovens. Two restaurant ovens. We'd have to get a license to use them commercially, and that isn't about to be granted to this lowly queen."

JoJo drifted back. "I worked my way through college cooking with the institutional ovens at the school."

"I have a lovely stuffing recipe," Lisa said.

"Seneca makes scrumptious pumpkin pies," said Spence.

"Norman and a couple of his friends would be stunning waitresses." Carla Jean draped an arm over Norman's shoulder and tried to give him a smooch on the cheek.

"Six dollars' donation for a turkey dinner and all the trimmings? Maybe a glass of champagne?" JoJo suggested, kind of shyly. "Except for you, Murph. You'd be helping in the kitchen." We all pretended that we didn't know Murph didn't have a penny to her name.

Murph said, "Seven, and cover some of the repair parts." She stood and made to hug them all in her excitement. "Invite everyone. All the regulars. The gay ones and Seneca and Spence. The others can take care of themselves."

Lisa was the only one who stayed in Murph's embrace. "The whole darn family!" she said as we moved to leave.

Months later, Murph told me the story of the rest of the night.

"I let myself be persuaded," she said. "I went home with Lisa. I remember our conversation."

"You're awful pretty," she told Lisa. "And so young."

"Young?" Lisa sighed and reminded Murph she was twenty-seven.

"God, tell me that isn't young when you're over forty."

Lisa said, "If I ever reach forty. I might as well be about a hundred now. Young women are so unstable. They think something better is around the corner no matter how happy they could be with what they have."

"Sounds like you've been through a lot." Murph pulled Lisa close, then held her tentatively, respectfully.

Lisa rubbed a cheek on one of Murph's scarred hands. She avoided the implicit question, instead commenting, "Not as much as you've been through."

"Hey, you have to take the licks in life."

Lisa smiled. "And lesbians take more than anybody?"

"I didn't mean that," Murph reported saying, and explained to me that she got awfully shy when she was alone with a femme.

"Make yourself comfy, Miss Innocent, while I freshen up." From the closed bathroom door, Murph said she heard Lisa chattering. "I know it's only March, but I can't wait till Thanksgiving. Can you?"

Murph said she'd sat on the edge of the bed and bent stiffly, like an old person, she said, to remove her shoes. Then she lay back, hands behind her head. "It's a long way from now," she'd called through the door. "And everything depends on getting that bar past its predicament."

"You will."

"See how young you are? With all you've been through you still believe in happy endings."

"Some of us have to end happily. Why not me?"

Murph said when she'd tried to sit up, her head whirled from exhaustion. She'd worked a double shift and hadn't slept since.

Lisa opened the bathroom door and stepped out in what Murph saw through mostly closed eyes was a provocative nightgown. "You know, we ought to have Thanksgiving dinners every year, in every gay bar. No more being scared and lonesome," Lisa was saying. She slipped the nightgown off one shoulder and went to Murph. Murph knew she'd regret it if she moved a muscle, said a word, opened her eyes again.

It was a bad idea, her and Lisa, Murph told me. The lost daughter, Lisa's secrecy, but mostly how classy she was, with some college education and growing up in New York City. She'd been too damn tired, she said, to start something she hadn't a hope of finishing. Someday Lisa would know it was for the best. Drained as she was, coward that she called herself, she knew she was dropping toward sleep and didn't respond when Lisa said, "Till then we at least have this, don't we, hon? Murph?" She touched Murph's hand, then grasped it with tight fingers.

It almost broke my heart to hear that Lisa said, "Oh, Murph. Not even this? Damn you!"

CHAPTER THREE

It was a rainy night in May, and I was tempted to stay home with my dog rather than go to The Old Town, but we'd had our long walk and spent the day together.

Of course Colonel Mustard goes to work with me. I've got a special arrangement with a friend who owns the cab company because I can't be bothered to own a car for personal use. Why pay insurance and repairs? Why waste time battling employees at the college and hospital for a parking space? I'd rather take a bus unless the Colonel is traveling with me. We're very close, my golden dog and I. She makes me laugh and laugh with her antics. She's a beauty, a Border collie-golden retriever mix with a long feathered tail, a smile on her face, and the eager eyes of a puppy, though she's seven now.

At The Old Town, work in the kitchen continued, two months after the notice came in. No inspectors had shown up yet—further evidence the city was picking on the bar. Murph would open the door and sing, "There'll Be a Hot Time in the Old Town Tonight!" from the old song, then disappear again. Problems stalled the original kitchen work. We heard her bang and curse at whatever got in her way.

Carla Jean carried a tray of clean glasses to the bar and held up a cigarette for JoJo to light. She hadn't started to drink her wine yet. She sometimes reasoned aloud that she wasn't a drunk because she never lifted a glass until after work at her family's dealership, was never late, and never took sick time.

"What I can't figure out," she said, "is why the inspector never came."

"I'm sure we're still on his little list," said Norman, wiggling his shoulders. He made a check in the air with his pinkie finger.

JoJo stopped moving long enough to say, "I'm not so sure." She stared toward the street again. "What's worse than an inspector?"

"Arson." Norman swept the floor behind the bar with choppy double-time strokes.

JoJo chuckled and smacked him lightly on the bottom as she sped past him.

"Oh, do that again, darling. The girl knows what I like!" Norman cooed.

Carla Jean paused behind the counter. "Yes! You're right. It's worse when he doesn't show up and the inspection hangs over our heads."

"Yup," JoJo said, eyes on the door every time it opened. "When you think of all the other little things that keep happening…"

"Like?" Carla Jean asked.

"Like those two straight guys who come in every day. I told you about them. Sometimes they bring their buddies. They come in once or twice a week during the day, order the cheapest draft, and take up a table for a couple of hours. No conversation. They watch. They give me the heebie-jeebies."

"They come in when I'm on too," Norman said, stopping to lean on his broomstick. "At first I thought they were super-butch closet cases. The way they look at me says something else."

JoJo said, "Agreed," with some enthusiasm. She dried each glass to a shine. "They glower. Like they want me to know they disapprove of me and can get rid of me if they want to."

The door opened and Lisa backed in with uncharacteristic awkwardness. She closed her umbrella and left it to lean against the wall.

"Look who's here!" said JoJo.

Lisa also set down a large wet bag. "It's not fit for a duck out there," she told them.

Murph laughed. "Not even a queer duck?"

Lisa's smile looked patient.

"Quack!" Murph said.

JoJo and Carla Jean quacked along with her. I thought they must be the cutest gal duo in history, really like a couple of silly ducks waddling around the wet floor. Just about everyone had the boozy giggles as we watched this show.

A tiny, gorgeous pixie of a man, an androgynous regular named Paul, who taught English at a parochial school in town, arrived a little after Lisa. Also dripping wet, he quacked over to Carla Jean and JoJo, boots sloshing. They circled around Lisa, who tolerated their clowning with her usual reserved good humor. It took a lot to rattle our resident princess. Not that anyone called her Princess. Maybe it was only me who couldn't help but think of her that way.

Lisa, who had her impetuous moments, set her bag on the floor, held her arms high, and pretended to do the breaststroke past the ducks. They stopped quacking and applauded themselves. Norman picked up the shopping bag.

"Webbed feet?" JoJo suggested as she tried to peer inside the bag.

I wondered if someone of Lisa's height had a hard time of it growing up and if her sometimes-aloof manner resulted from defending herself from the cruelty of other children and the unintentional barbs of a family probably like herself, and different from others. In my family we all have loud laughs. Mine never fails to draw curious stares, and as a kid, other children mocked me for it.

A table of beatnik types looked over at me when I couldn't stop laughing at my duck-walking pals. Down to a man, the beats wore light-blue chambray work shirts. They were in the bar preparing to read poetry at the bookstore across the street. Norman's boyfriend Hugh sat with them. It didn't surprise me, professor that he was, when he arrived with a net shopping bag filled with book purchases. On their third pitcher of beer, the poets argued with one another in strident tones.

"No, not webbed feet," Norman said. "Thanksgiving tablecloths!" He opened one and held it up. "Absolutely stunning! The table covering every woman yearns for." He wrapped it around himself like a cape and pranced on tiptoe until he was behind the bar. He folded the tablecloth and returned it to Lisa.

"What a woman's touch you have, Lisa," Murph whispered.

"Is this an attempt to make up for our night of wild sex?" I heard Lisa whisper back.

Murph studied her highly polished shoes and mumbled, "Regretting missed chances."

Seneca came over and hugged Lisa. "I'm so glad you're back, woman! You add class to our watering hole."

Carla Jean barged in on them. "You haven't been around for a long time, Lisa. We've missed you." It was true. Lisa hadn't come back for a while after her night with Murph. Lisa had been so mad that Murph, when she woke at four a.m., said she'd found Lisa asleep on the couch.

Lisa nodded that regal head of hers. "No place in town is as much like home as The Old Town Tavern."

The door crashed open and bounced off the wall. The kid who had taunted them on the day of the parade stood there, disheveled, swaying and glowering. Every head in the bar was turned toward her.

"Look what the cat dragged in," Murph said.

"I see nothing's changed around here," Lisa commented.

In a stern voice JoJo announced, "You know the rules, kid."

"Call me Deej," the kid said, her voice slurred.

Lisa looked skeptical. "Deej?"

"Nobody wants to say my name. I don't want to say my name, so D.J. is okay, or Deej. Deej Garde, pronounced the Indian way: *gur-day*. And yes, my dad and mom run a motel. Three of them, as a matter of fact."

This was unheard of, giving out a last name and family business details to anyone listening.

"Okay, Deej," JoJo reminded her, "but rules are rules."

"Yeah. You have to be twenty-one. That's why I'm here—I'm twenty-one today. To show you I'm as legit as you." She offered her ID.

JoJo took a look at it. "What else do you have in the way of an ID? You look twelve."

"What do I need, a passport? Here, my work badge."

"You work at the helicopter plant?"

"My cousin is an engineer there and my uncle is purchaser. I'm part-time."

JoJo flipped the badge back to Deej. "You're an intern. What are you interning in, the effect of alcohol on pilots?"

Lisa's voice was soft, concerned. "Or have you come in out of the rain, Deej?"

I could see that the kid was spellbound by Lisa's striking looks and kindness. She stared as if she wanted to run into Lisa's arms. All too quickly she said, "I wanted to show you."

"Let me buy you a drink," Lisa offered. "To celebrate."

"I've got to get back to my birthday party."

Norman said, "You left your birthday party to come here? Sounds to me like you're about to fall off a certain fence, kid."

Lisa urged her. "Come on in, Deej. You're safe here. What are you drinking?"

The kid stopped about two inches inside the door.

"Everything. Anything," she said.

Carla Jean laughed. "Are you ever going to be sick tomorrow!" She looked at the clock. "Cuckoo-cuckoo! It's after six, JoJo. Have you forgotten me?"

JoJo filled a wineglass from a jug of red.

Deej still glared at Carla Jean. "You're not my mom. I can hold it."

Lisa went to the door. "Come in, Deej. No one will attack you, I promise. This open door is making me chilly."

The kid was like a stray cat in that entry, ready to escape, longing to come in.

Lisa took Deej's hand and led her to the stool next to Murph.

"What is it with this place? I dream about it."

Norman said, "Oh, gawd, kid. You're a goner then. If you're a dreamer, dream of the heights! Partying at Liz Taylor's house! Or," he said, hand over his heart, "with Miss Troy Donahue!"

"Glitz isn't for everyone, Norman," said Lisa.

"Then call me the whoopee girl!"

"Can't someone shut that fag up?" Deej complained.

Norman whirled on her and sniped back. "Would you notice who's calling the pot black."

"I'm not like him." It was clear that Deej wasn't as drunk as she'd first seemed to be. Who hadn't at some time used that illusion as a threadbare ruse?

Lisa spoke quietly. "I can tell you why I love The Old Town Tavern, Deej. I can be my real self here. I have lots of love to give, and I know some day there will be a strong butchy woman by the fire for me. But I'll always need my friends as much."

Deej closed her eager dark eyes and said, "I had a friend by the fire a long time ago. I'm not seventeen any more. I'm trying to get into life now, you know?" She opened her eyes and glared with defiance at each of us. "There are other reasons you might not fit in, aren't there? Besides being queer?"

"A thousand," Lisa said.

Norman laughed and said, "This is the best one." He draped a yellow dishtowel over his head, like a blond wig. "Just call me Marilyn!"

The table of poets filed out the door, laughing at Norman's pose. Two of them applauded. Norman called out, "Good luck!"

When the group was gone, Deej asked, "Do you really want to be called Marilyn?"

"They used to call me Norma Jean, honeybuns, until I grew out of that."

"You think I'm like him, don't you!" She swept Murph's empty glass to the floor where it shattered. "AM I? Go ahead, say it. You think I'm queer like you because of what happened at camp. It could have happened to anyone. I grew out of it for real. Not like him." She pointed to Norman.

"You poor confused kid." Lisa reached toward Deej. "What a shame you have to come to a bar to find yourself."

The kid pulled away with an abrupt movement. Then, in a plaintive voice, she remembered aloud. "She was so soft to touch. We were buddies, counselors on the waterfront, and we'd sing love songs in the night air while the rest of the camp slept. Back at the tent her mouth was like the campfire. Her hands were like the songs. The rest was swimming. Does that make me queer?"

"Do you want it to happen again?"

Deej chewed on her nails. "I—I liked the sensations."

Lisa told her, "I married a man, briefly, and fought being a lesbian for a little while."

I didn't hide that I was listening again. I'd collected clues to Lisa for a very long time.

The kid cringed—was it at the word lesbian? "Why'd you give in?"

"I didn't give in. I got brave enough to be who I really am."

"Brave enough?"

Norman butted in as he often did after he sampled too much of his wares. He gave his characteristic sniff and upward thrust of the chin. "You think we're not brave, sister? To come here every night and get an earful of the names you call us?"

"You ask for it, swishing around."

"I don't do it for you. I don't invite comments. It's who I am."

Deej turned back to Lisa. "How come you're queer, Lisa Jelane? You're beautiful."

Lisa frowned. "How do you know my name?"

"It's on your mailbox."

"You followed me home?"

Deej didn't answer.

"Come dance with me," Lisa said. "I'll tell you my story."

"I can't dance with a girl."

"How do you know till you try?"

The kid looked like a daughter of Murph as she stared at her feet. "If you really want me to—"

It took a while for Lisa to instruct Deej, but eventually Deej's hands stole around Lisa and she quickly grasped the knack of leading a taller woman. She did better when the fast rock songs started playing. I don't know how Lisa kept up with the irritating silliness of the song "Tossing and Turning." The younger people are welcome to their rock and roll.

I left to walk Colonel Mustard again and to reapply my lipstick. Although I wasn't big on makeup, I wasn't completely dressed unless I had some color on my lips. It was time to air myself out anyway. Dr. Everett, a caring man near retirement who practiced across from the hospital, came in. We all claimed him as our doctor and begged him to keep working. Finding another physician who admitted he was one of us wouldn't be easy.

"What are those police cars doing along the side of the building?" he asked.

CHAPTER FOUR

When I returned from walking my dog in the lovely spring rain, I ordered my second and last vodka tonic of the evening. I'd noticed, on my way, that the bookstore was jammed. I liked the liveliness the store gave the area, with the poetry-reading and folk-singing nights. Tonight, after the store closed, its customers would come back to The Old Town, quote lines from Dylan Thomas poems or sing the sea shanties they'd heard. Right now, the light wind carried cheers from the high-school stadium. I imagined there was a night baseball game underway and silently wished the home team luck. I liked to go to a game now and then, eat popcorn, drink a beer; I hadn't been to one since Geri left. It was something we did together for many years and she probably still did, with her new improved lover. I still imagined myself the margarine Geri left for real butter. Tonight I looked forward to my John O'Hara book, *From the Terrace*.

Everyone at the bar spoke about the police cars. Apparently, this was not the first sighting.

Carla Jean studied a ledger. JoJo paced behind her and hurried to peer over her shoulder each time Carla Jean tapped out figures on the adding machine and announced a total.

"You can see what nights they must have parked outside," Carla Jean said, pointing at the adding machine's printout with her cigarette. "We should have noticed it months ago. The comparison to last year is so clear."

"People are afraid to come in," Murph said.

"I wonder how long the cops stay?" JoJo asked.

"Too sadistically long," Norman said and he stamped a foot behind the bar. His slightly high heels made a clomping sound. "They're probably encouraged to hang out here, the savages."

"Have neighbors complained about us?" Carla Jean asked. "I thought we all got along."

"Somebody's got it in for us," JoJo muttered.

"And who it is, is the mystery," Murph said.

Norman, on his toes now, one small hand cupped at the side of his mouth, trilled to Lisa and Deej. "Did you two ever think about entering a dance marathon? I clocked you. An hour and seven minutes, including trips to the jukebox for that Dusty Springfield song."

"No wonder I'm thirsty," said Lisa as she lifted her shiny hair off the back of her neck. "How about a Coke?"

Deej ordered a Scotch on the rocks.

Carla Jean, over at the bar, said, "Oh, kid—"

"Shut up, *Ma*."

Norman raised his arms in exasperation and went toward the bar.

"Everybody always nags at me." Deej whined often. "I wouldn't even be here if I could find a decent guy."

Lisa's laugh was a silky rumble suitable to royalty. "Meanwhile, you might as well spend time with me?"

"You're different," I could hear Deej mumble.

"I enjoyed dancing with you, Deej. If you ever decide you are gay—"

"You want to go to bed with me, right? Like all the guys?"

You bet, I thought. I couldn't stop a short laugh.

The two of them were so enmeshed in their attraction and the denial of it that they never noticed anybody could hear them. Lisa fingered the tiny vase of plastic flowers that graced their table. I found the movement of her fine hands sensual and didn't like the tiny jab of jealousy in my solar plexus. Deej didn't deserve Lisa. "I didn't say my motives are more pure than theirs, but I never want only sex."

"What do you want with me, anyway? I'm only a kid."

"I wasted some good years married when I could have been with a girl like you. I'm not much older than you, Deej. I've got some of my best kid years left."

Murph stopped playing pool with a couple of gay guys. She approached Lisa and Deej's table and flashed the twenties she'd won. "Is this a private party?" she asked. "Can I buy you girls a round with my winnings?"

"Not looking real sleepy tonight, Murph, are we?"

I'd seen Lisa sarcastic before. This time it was muted, as if she wanted only to wound, not kill. I wondered at her air of hurt pride. Who could stay angry at a madcap character like Murph?

"How come," Deej asked Murph, "you can't get a girl? You must be the oldest queer in town."

"It's none of my doing that the girl I loved was married all my life."

"Was?" Lisa asked.

"I got Rose's letter today." I couldn't tell if Murph's expression was glad or sad. Maybe it was a mix of both. "She's finally on her way home. Her lover Vi died."

Deej seemed to talk half to herself when she said, "I never thought of queers dying, like anybody else."

"Where'd you find Miz Tact here?" Murph asked Lisa.

"Same place you did, hon. Chalk it up to being suckers for younger women in bars."

This time Lisa hit home: Murph flinched.

"Just because you two are old—"

"Old! Rose's lover was too young to die. Vi was only sixty-three."

That hit me pretty hard; I was fifty-three. I planned to live a lot longer. Probably Vi Derizzi had too.

Deej asked, in her caustic voice, "What does a sixty-three-year-old queer look like?"

"Listen, I never met Vi. Couldn't bear to, but, kid, I'm certain she looked like you," Murph answered, "with a few more miles on you. If somebody doesn't murder you first for your lovely manners."

"Murph." Lisa pleaded. "Don't bait her."

I laughed at the exchange; I could have predicted every word. Trust me on this. Murph was jealous of Lisa's interest in the kid. And the kid? She was spitting mad she wasn't a grownup, though Lisa seemed to think Deej was grown up enough for her.

Deej stood, the ancient wood chair she sat on wobbling behind her until I caught it. "I'm no queer, you—"

"We're all people, kid. Would you stop trying to make out that we're some kind of monsters! Vi looked no different from us because she was as human as you get."

"Because she played the man is more like it." Deej mocked Murph.

"It's true." Lisa cautioned her. "Some lesbians are very masculine."

Deej looked at me and said, "Yuk."

I laughed long and loud, and so did Murph and Lisa. I remembered reacting the same to women who didn't particularly want to look like women. Of course, I'm no one to talk. I'm not as tall as Lisa but, I admit, I have more meat on my bones, especially around the chest, though only my lovers know that. In my kind of work, I couldn't be bothered with dress-up clothes. You get dirty when you bind books; you crawl around the guts of machines, haul heavy cartons, load the delivery van, and you need to wear loose clothing that lasts. It might be rough to the touch, but I can take it. Tell me where I can find women's duds that take that kind of punishment. I look like a mother in her son's work clothes.

Murph confessed. "I've been afraid of a few of the butchier gals myself. Then I found out they're tender lambs inside. They dress like they do to protect themselves from threats like the cops outside—and you." She pointed an unsteady finger at Deej. "I want you to remember whenever you meet anyone in drag—"

"I don't plan to—"

"Girls!" Lisa laid a hand flat on Deej's jacket until Deej sat again.

I was kind of surprised Murph and Lisa would give this smart-ass the time of day. The kid was obnoxious, to say the least. Then I remembered Lisa's comment that Deej was the butchiest thing she'd seen in a while, and I caught on. Infuriating as she might be, Deej was one of us and would not be turned away.

"If you ever should meet someone in drag," Murph said, "by mistake, I need you to remember that Vi must have been the sweetest lady you'd find in any clothes anywhere or Rose wouldn't have loved her. And Rose—there was another parade. Right along The Avenue here. An Easter parade. We were probably all of nine years old, in our Easter coats and white shoes. We strolled along like the cream of the crop. Our mothers made us Easter bonnets. We were still neighbors, our two families. My hat was round and flat, a wide brim all around that my little pointy head popped out of on top, looped around with pink yarn and a pink-ribbon strap. They must have gone to a millinery shop, our mothers, to get the flowers and the forms. Rose's hat was an upside-down pail shape, white, flowers of yellow and lavender, with a wide lace ribbon tied in an enormous bow under her chin. I wish I had a picture of those two little girls hand in hand."

Deej seemed entranced while Murph spoke, and Lisa relaxed, her hand on the kid's shoulder. Then Deej ruined it all by asking, "What will the girlfriend do now? Check someone out of a nursing home?"

"Damn you! She's a spring chicken at forty-three. She has decades ahead of her."

"Her girlfriend was almost twenty years older?"

Murph breathed deeply. Her face was patchy pink. She counted aloud to ten and said, "It worked. They were together a lot of years—

since Rose graduated from high school. That may be more than I'll ever get to be with someone."

Lisa rejoined the conversation. "Maybe. Maybe not."

I read encouragement in Lisa's words, but doubted the look of longing on Murph's face was what she'd meant to evoke.

Deej leaned into Lisa's hand. Lisa stroked across the back of her spine. I thought Deej would purr. Instead she said to Murph, "Maybe you should marry Vi's girlfriend. You want to, don't you?"

Deej leaned forward, breaking contact. Lisa put her hand in her lap. She watched it as she would a broken creature that needed its mate to cradle it.

"It's a hard thing. I've waited for this day a long time," Murph said, "but I didn't want Vi to die. In spite of the fact that she knew I loved Rose, she was always there, maybe like an immigrant father who supports the family from afar. Through Rose, Vi helped me understand it was okay to be gay."

Deej's laughter sounded mean. I saw by her posture that she'd shut Lisa out. "So what was she? Your dad? Your granddad?"

"Wouldn't you have liked a gay adult on your side when you got caught with your campfire girl?"

"How'd you know we got caught? And how did I know back then to be careful? What did we have to be afraid of—love? When I got back to school, someone had blabbed. Everyone knew. Put that together with a darker skin and I was the perfect target." She shot up and moved away from the table to act out the boys at school and herself at Campfire Girl age.

"'We'll show you what a real woman likes,' they told me. 'We'll cure you, you dirty queer.' They backed me against a wall, out by the school dumpsters and away from any windows. What could I do?" She stood and struck a provocative pose and batted her eyes.

Lisa entwined her hands in front of her lips. Her eyes, usually unfathomable, held a look of shocked compassion.

"'Hey,' I told them, 'where have you been all my life?' They fell for it. The ringleader, a boy from another neighborhood, said, 'So you know what's good for you, do you?'" The change in Deej was complete—she looked like a sultry young tramp. "I said, 'Yeah, but I didn't think I had a chance with you.'" She strutted away, arm crooked as if linked with her attacker.

With her hands flattened against her eyes now, Lisa looked up. "You poor kid. Only a little girl."

Deej whirled, herself again, and strode to Murph. "I learned to act smart and saucy, like all the other girls. Why couldn't I stand up to them like you do, and let them know I—" Deej squeezed her eyes shut and swallowed. "I could be happy about who I am?"

"Me!" Murph said. "I may look bold," she said with a scoffing laugh. "Inside I'm as timid as a mouse."

Deej hung on to Murph's words now, the storm between them passed for the moment.

Murph gave a long sigh. "I wish every kid could have a family like the one I grew up in: a family that knows who I really am and loves me anyway. A family where a kid like you can go when things get rough, without changing your colors."

"Fat chance." Deej was seated again and stretched her arm along the back of Lisa's chair. "When Dad found out about camp he stopped talking to me. It's never been the same."

"Rose's whole family turned against her and she wasn't welcomed by Vi's. I plan to be her family, including the day-after-Thanksgiving dinner right here at The Old Town."

Norman collected empties from the tables. "And Christmas. Maybe we'll have Christmas dinner here too."

"You can be the sugar-plum fairy," said Deej with a snort of laughter.

"I'll bust you in the chops next comment, missy," Murph said.

"No, Murph." Lisa took her arm. "Let her get used to us. Why don't you come to Thanksgiving, Deej?"

"Well…"

Lisa teased Deej. "There's our song. Want to dance?"

Deej examined her glass and peeked through it at Murph. "Maybe one more time."

Watching them, Murph said, "I'm amazed that kid can still dance, with all the spirits she's imbibed."

"I notice she's listing a little from the weight of that chip on her shoulder," Norman said. "I don't know which will fall down first, the chip or the child."

"I think Lisa would like to rub it off."

"As long as that's all she rubs. This is a classy joint."

"She's too smart to take on a ragamuffin like that, Norman."

"Oh, honey, don't kid yourself. I can see the shooting stars from here."

As we watched, Deej jerked away from Lisa and returned to the table.

"What did I say?" Lisa asked.

"You know damn well."

Lisa reached to her. Deej pulled away. "I only want to give you a place to stay so you don't have to face your parents drunk."

The kid picked up and downed another drink. She didn't seem to care whose it was.

"Sit down, you." Murph's voice was gruff. "Lisa's not like that."

Deej threw out a childish challenge. "How would you know? Has she been through you already?"

Lisa slapped her. I was as shocked as Deej.

Deej scraped back her chair. "What the hell?"

"Oh, God!" Lisa cried. "I've never done that before. I'm so sorry, Deej!"

Murph said, "You asked for it, kid."

Deej rubbed her cheek. "I thought only guys hit girls."

"It's—" Lisa frowned. "It's all this wanting. Wanting life to be a little more than work and the bar, wanting a lover, wanting a lover who stays, wanting a decent place to go where I won't be put down. I thought I was safe here until you showed up, Deej. I only offered you shelter."

"Sure, lady. That wasn't what it seemed like, the way you danced."

"Maybe that's how I shelter, the only way I know. It's what I do best for a woman: take her in, comfort her, share myself. If love was what you wanted, you'd have it. I'd never push it on you."

"I've heard that one before. As you very well know."

Murph intervened, her arms held wide open. "You've got it all wrong, kid. We opened our hearts to you. We told you our secrets and you told us yours. Where else can you get that?"

With a sharpness that scythed through us all, Deej snapped, "Don't you nag me again."

Murph pushed back her chair and stood, hands at her sides in fists, "Don't you talk to me—to any of us—like that again."

CHAPTER FIVE

My first visit to Murph's rented room, a few days later, was both depressing and uplifting. It was comfortable as furnished rooms go, but oh, how sad it made me that she lived in one room and, at the same time, that she had to live so much of her life away from it. Big piles of record albums teetered on her dresser and around her easy chair. She probably spent as much time listening to music in this little home of hers as I spent reading in mine. That's how I got into binding; I was a big reader as a kid. One of the badges I did as a Girl Scout taught some bookbinding, and I loved the mix of skills. My troop visited a bindery where we watched people stitch and glue, design, restore old books, operate machines to press and trim.

I was there to take Murph's old friend Rose to my apartment. My convertible sofa would be hers until she found a place. Rose wasn't due for another hour so, as we spoke, I checked out Murph's room, which smelled of shoe polish and crushed pine needles. The polish I understood—her shoes always looked at least burnished, if not downright shiny. The pine scent took a little longer. Eventually I saw that she'd placed little sachets of pine needles here and there.

"My mother gave them to me almost every Christmas," she explained. "I have about thirty of them. The scent transports me to Chestnut Forest Park."

What appeared to be the only piece of furniture she owned was a beautiful blond-wood tabletop hi-fi console with both a turntable and a radio. She must have saved for years to buy it. Not that this surprised me, as Murph had a nice voice and sang in a choir at her church as a kid.

The rest of Murph's room was comprised of bed, wardrobe, and a hope chest by the window, which she explained had belonged to her mother. Under an embroidered cover on her dresser was a tray that held an electric burner, a teakettle, and a small saucepan with cover, a mug, bowl, plate and one set of silverware. A metal breadbox shone next to those items. The room smelled faintly of toast and maybe canned stews.

"All the comforts of home," she told me with a proud smile, with a gesture at what passed for a kitchen.

An American flag was tacked over her bed, and around it she had used masking tape to exhibit several dozen photographs. When she shut the door behind us a piece of poster board slapped against it. Dozens more pictures hung from that—photos, postcards from across the U.S., magazine clippings of James Cagney and Virginia Mayo, Janet Leigh and Robert Mitchum, and other popular movie couples.

What really held my gaze, though, were the tiny, framed embroideries that sat on her dresser. I picked one up. It was all in shades of purple, from stitches dark as eggplant to an almost-pink lavender. The design was of jewelry, long chains, and pendants with a few elaborate bracelets. I moved on to one in blues and greens. This looked like the coat of arms for a family of fishermen. There was a boat surrounded by interlocking shellfish, all cushioned on what looked like the hint of a jellyfish. An embroidered doily covered her night table. I lightly ran my fingertips over the fine stitches.

"Some are my mother's and some her sister and mother's. It's a family tradition."

Then I noticed she'd stitched her initials into a towel that hung over the radiator. I looked at Murph and raised an eyebrow.

"I get a little creative. That fishing piece is mine. Patterns are so predictable I don't use them anymore." She looked unhappy. "Every year I plan to embroider something for The Old Town, but I'm darned if I ever get around to it. I better before I get too creaky."

Imagine, I thought, framed embroidery in a bar. To cover my laugh at the absolute queerness of it, I pointed to what looked like a skyscraper, with vertical lines that cut white spaces of fabric. Stars poked through the lines. It was magical and I told her so. I never would have taken Murph for a person who did needlework, especially work this imaginative. All I did in my spare time, other than read, was occasionally try to keep up with my skeet shooting. I was county champ in my twenties. Instead of needlework on my walls, I have dusty old plaques and trophies galore.

I had an unexpected thought. "Do you make your own clothes?"

Murph's face flushed. "Some of them, yes."

"Your vests and jackets?"

She bent and pulled a portable sewing machine, in its black case, from the low shelf of her night table. "Saves me a pretty penny," she said.

Murph made a quick change of subject. "You've been out of town all week for your job, haven't you?" When I reminded her that I'd gone up North for my father's surgery she said, "Then you don't know what's going on outside The Old Town." She sat on the edge of her bed and patted a spot for me. "Remember the patrol cars that idled on the street?"

Unfortunately, yes, I told her and explained. "They scare me. I own my own business, and some customers are funny about spending their money with people like us."

"Now they stop drivers and ticket them for anything they can think of—like a bulb that's out, drifting through a yellow light, or following too close."

I shook my head. Would even The Old Town be denied to us?

"We don't know if they're doing this in other parts of the city and to the other gay bar or not. Norman's taken to unlocking the back door so customers can park down the hill and come in through the kitchen—those that dare come in at all. This all happens after dark. The goons who come inside at odd daylight hours haven't helped business either."

The sound of footsteps on the stairs led Murph to heft the tray of items that served as her kitchen and slip it into her hope chest. She closed the combination padlock in a hurry and scanned the room for, I assumed, additional forbidden objects. What a way to live, I thought. It was second nature to Murph to hide like a fugitive. Subterfuge pervades our lives. Yet she dares to go to The Old Town. Dares to love women. I'd never thought much about this contradiction. Were we tearing ourselves apart inside to live our secret lives within the rules?

"Could be the landlady," Murph said. "She always drops in at the wrong time. Probably wants to make sure I haven't brought a man up here."

We laughed over that one, me with my hand over my mouth to mute myself, and then there was a knock at the door.

"No rest for the weary," Murph said with a sigh. She opened the door. "Why, Mrs. Lange, I was about to step out for dinner with—"

She went silent and stood so still for so long I was about to ask what was wrong when I heard, "Hi, there, Rose Murphy," from the landing. Rose Murphy? I remembered then that they shared the same name. An unlikely one for the stalwart Murph, but it suited the delicate-featured Rose. No one could look more Irish.

"Rose!" Murph exclaimed. "Rosie! I didn't expect you till four."

The other Rose saw me. A look of confusion crossed her face.

"No, Rose, no," Murph said. "This is my friend Rockie from the tavern I told you about."

"Of course. I'd forgotten. I don't know where my mind is these days." Rose seemed relieved. Had she thought I was a lover and gotten jealous? No, I thought. She'd come home to a person of relative safety and I could have been a threat. "I made it to the station sooner than I expected and caught an earlier train. Aren't you going to let me in?"

Murph, boisterous roustabout that she can be, grabbed Rose in a hug and lifted her over the doorsill.

"Ask you in? A royal twenty-one-gun salute is more like it. Come on. Are those your only bags?"

"No, the rest are downstairs. The cabbie brought them in."

Murph gawked and grinned, happier than I'd ever seen her. "Hello," she said. "Hello, hello, hello!" She stopped herself and became serious. "I'm as sorry, Rose, as a person can be, about your Vi. She was good to you, wasn't she?"

Rose gave a big sigh. Murph ushered her to the easy chair.

"We had a lovely life together, Murph. She was such a sensitive soul, not really strong enough for the life she was given. I helped her as best I could. All the lying and fear that went along with our love took its toll on her poor heart."

"So that was it?" Murph asked. "A heart attack?"

"It killed her immediately, outside our home, while she dug a hole for a chestnut tree. She knew how I loved them. And now, I don't know that I'll ever stop missing her. I thought to follow her, then I thought of you—and of Hansfield, how Settlers River rolls through Chestnut Forest Park, and of the snooty old mansions falling to boarding houses and doctors' offices. And the birds." Rose's smile was sweet, with an edge to it I couldn't identify. "Wherever I am, the sounds of the birds take me back to childhood in Hansfield. It's good to be home."

Murph held her arms open and they hugged. Then Murph took a quick, nervous step back, as if afraid her touch would be misconstrued. Murph rattled on. "I can't get over living in the old Goodlette house. Remember? Hot dogs and sausages made them so rich Papa Goodlette named his first son Frank." She smiled. "I still find that ridiculous enough to be funny. Frank's become a city councillor, he's one of the biggest employers in town, and I live in the room he grew up in! Too bad he's such a nasty man. He must have bought the councillor election.

He's running for mayor on a morals platform now. Morals?" she said, with contempt in her voice. "They don't care about morals. They feed them to the voters to get themselves elected." Murph shook her head. "Remember when Frank Goodlette tried to court you in school?"

They laughed together. I could see the tenderness between them flare up like flames in a fireplace swept clean of ash.

"And he'll be mayor of Hansfield. Who would have thought it." Rose looked around the room. "So this is your humble abode."

"Every night I see my life flash before me." Murph indicated the photos with a movement of her hand. I saw some I'd missed between the two windows bayed over the front-porch roof where her hope chest served as a window seat.

From her purse Rose took a pair of glasses with modest wings and peered at the pictures. "Your Aunt Una and your Grandmother Murphy and all your cousins. Who's that one of, Murph?"

"That's Lisa."

"Oh?"

"No. Nothing like that. I thought so once, for an evening. Now we're—well, I think we're friends. She flirts with Deej, a youngster who comes to the bar. You will join us at The Old Town Tavern tonight? It's my living room."

"Oh, Murph, are you drinking night and day?"

"Of course not. I gave you my word when we were kiddies that I wouldn't end up like your father. It was an open secret among the adults that he was bothering you. When I found out about it, you were long gone and he was long dead."

"If that kept you on the straight and narrow, then there was a reason for it to happen."

"Credit where credit's due, Rosie," Murph said. "The bar is a place to go beyond these four walls. Let me help carry your bags and I'll tell you all about it—on one condition, doll. That you'll come to The Old Town for Thanksgiving dinner next month."

"A bar that celebrates Thanksgiving?" She got up from the chair and held her hands out to Murph. "Sure. Sure I will. I've been here how long?" Rose looked my way and I read the time on my watch out loud. "Not ten minutes and you've invited me on an outing."

CHAPTER SIX

November that same year, 1961, was dreary. My apartment was stuffy with the smell of closed windows and steam heat. I struggled through *Ice Palace* for a week. It was sad, but the movie was better. Fortunately, Fanny Hurst's new book, *Family!* was on my coffee table ready to enthrall me.

Rose Callaghan took an open room in Murph's boarding house when she learned how dear apartments were in this college town. Since then, the two of them parted only to sleep. They were at The Old Town when I arrived.

"What do you think?" Murph asked me. "You like the floor lamps? The couch Norman found? I think it makes the bar more relaxing."

"Any excuse to buy new furniture," Norman said. "The bookstore put in armchairs and that new track lighting they make down in Fall River. They practically gave these to us. What a steal."

Paul said, "I'm the one who found out about it." He pointed at Norman. "Catch her going into a bookstore."

"Are you kidding? I adore bookstores," Norman said.

"That wasn't a reference to X-rated bookstores, Marilyn."

Rose was laughing. "I could spend my life in this place." She wore a faint flowery perfume. I wondered if it mingled well with the pine scent of Murph's room.

Norman laughed too. He'd breached his polite drinking limit; anything could come out of his mouth now. "I hate to break it to you, honey. You already do."

"You, zippy little JoJo, and that sweet smokestack Carla Jean make it pleasant. And my dear Murph."

"Why don't you two pool your incomes and get a place together?"

I barely stopped myself from jumping up, clapping my hands over my head while doing a split, and chanting, "Norma Jean! Norma Jean! Make them do it!"

I didn't want them to leave the neighborhood. The little movie theater all prettied up in neon lights. The tattoo parlor with its strange pipes and risqué greeting cards. The messy upholstery shop, the Italian-ice place, and Old Town Bowl back to back with a transmission-repair shop. Wooden houses from early in the century. A storefront library branch, a tiny music shop called LP Land. The ghostly Uneeda Biscuits sign high up on a brick wall. Avenue Cantonese—deep, narrow, cheap, and a favorite of the college crowd and us barflies, with its purple-neon rice bowl in the window. Sometimes the bar itself smelled more of Chinese food than beer.

"Now, now, Norman. Murph may still have an eye for the gals," Rose said. "I've had my springtime and I look forward to a nice, restful fall."

"As roommates, Rose. Besides, you'll get younger the farther away you get from," he hesitated, "your loss."

Murph added, "And I'd give you plenty of room to breathe. I'm seldom home, and when I am, I'm likely to be on my way here."

"Have you seen the rents though?" Rose asked. "They're through the roof."

"Tell me about it," said Paul. "I pay seventy-five dollars for my third-floor loft over Goodlette's railroad warehouse. Truck fumes, workers yelling, doors clanging." He lowered his voice as if in humility and said, "Illegal for a dwelling, but fabulous, if I do say so myself. I have a view of the river. I've made that monstrous old space cozy."

"We could do the same, you know, Rose. And shop on nights before trash collection for furniture left on the street. Paul could help us decorate."

"You wouldn't have to ask me twice!" Paul said, his pretty eyes glittering and his Nordic skin flushed with excitement.

Rose looked over her glasses and shook her head. "You are impossible, Murph. I already gave in and rented the room next door to you, despite the fact that you spirited away the landlady's keys to connect the rooms!"

"I admit it. I like connecting to you, Rosie. I know how strong a lock is as well as how thin a door can be. Did I ever tell you, Norman, about Aideen and me and the adjoining rooms?"

"Yes, Murph," he answered, with a grimace of patient suffering. He put a hand over his forehead.

"What's wrong?" asked Murph.

"I have an awful headache from last night's fun and frolicking."

"You have those headaches every day."

"John Barleycorn gets less kind to me with every year."

It was then that I noticed Deej. She skulked to one of the small dark-wood tables that matched the banquette. Her clothing was completely different: dungaree pants, flannel shirt open to display a white undershirt, a fur-collared nylon flight jacket I'd seen in army-navy stores, and a hat, one of those stiff, stingy-brim souvenir hats you bought at the beach and could wear with the brim rolled up or peaked. Like Rose Callaghan, Deej looked as if she'd come into her own. I imagined Deej as the young Murph with Rose when she was that age. It didn't work; Rose needed someone older then.

Murph ignored Norman and told her tale. "There were two benches down at the river that sat back to back. One faced the water, the other faced the street," Murph said. "They'd been washed together like that from rising waters a few years earlier. Aideen faced the water. I sat behind her and leaned over the benches. I talked to her in the most enticing voice I could manage."

A guffaw came from Deej over at the corner table. She hadn't changed quite enough.

"'Go away with me this one weekend, Aideen,' I begged her.

"She kept the back of her head, with its long, curly hair to me, but said something like, 'Oh, you. Here I am spanking brand-new to America and you're wanting to act like this. Is that what the new world does to young Irishwomen? I've told you and told you, Murph. I plan to marry a rich American gentleman and live a life of ease. What can you offer me?'"

"I told her, 'Can I show you how you get under my skin? You're so lovely, Aideen, like an Irish song. I want you, not to marry you myself. I want to touch you, to wake you up before you settle for some man and have his kiddies. I want to take you to the top, to see what you can be, quivering and full of yourself under my hands, full of the best life can give you.'"

JoJo gave a low whistle. "You said that to a straight girl?"

"Sure. What did I know at seventeen?"

"What did she say?"

"I recall her exact words. 'How vain you are, Murph, to think you can do that for another woman.'

"'No,' I told her, 'it's not me. It takes a woman to show you. Outside you look like all the rest, Aideen. Inside you're like my Rose, hot as the sun. If I can't have my soul mate in this life, I at least want to give as many girls as I can this gift of themselves. One weekend is all I ask, Aideen.'"

"'Oh, Murph. You're a charmer, you are.'

"She came round to my bench and let down her long, thick hair. 'I love you like springtime, Aideen. I couldn't wish for anything more than you here at the riverside with me and a whole night ahead of us. Are you sure you want to lock yourself away from me tonight?'

"Aideen laughed and fluffed out her hair.

"'Ai,' I said, 'if your spirits got any higher, you'd float right up the river.'

"She got up and walked away, saying, 'I'll see you tomorrow, Murph.'

"I reached to her. 'I'll walk you home.'

"'It won't get you a thing.'

"'It'll get me beside you, the way I want to be beside you all night, your magnificent hair streaming over our pillows. How will I sleep tonight with you far from me? Won't you let me lay beside you, still as a mouse?'

"'You Yankee Casanova, you,' she said.

"That night, she flew under my hands like an angel. She was a night bloomer, more than a dream and had skin so velvety I was afraid to caress it. Next day we walked Main Street, not touching. Maybe I'd dreamed what we'd done. We were chaste as two sisters, and I never saw her again after she married the middle-aged refrigerator repairman."

Had they or hadn't they, I wondered. Murph's stories always left room for assumptions she never confirmed.

Norman quietly applauded. "And she never stopped thinking of you while they made babies."

Murph nodded. "I'm certain she had a flock of kids and now has grandkids. Surely no man could keep his hands off her."

"Like you could?" came Deej's voice. "Like you're more pure than any man?"

All heads turned Deej's way.

"It's that walking, talking chip-on-the-shoulder," said Norman.

"At least the ninny looks more like who she is," Murph commented.

The kid pivoted. "Do I?" She took off her hat to show us her short hair.

"She sure sounds the same." JoJo darted around behind the bar.

"Methinks the child is trying to tell us something," Norman said. He set a Shirley Temple on Deej's table.

"What the hell's that?" Deej demanded.

"It's called 'On-the-house-now-say-thank-you!'"

Deej shook her head. "Come on. Bring me what I asked for."

"Something's happened to you." Murph beamed like a proud dad. "You have a girl of your own now, don't you?"

The kid went from angry moth slamming against the very light she was drawn to, to a butterfly, soaring with a beautiful pride. "Crista's gorgeous! Long blond hair, big blue eyes. I took her away from the captain of the football team."

"A football queen?" Norman said. "I've had a few of those myself."

I'd taken a sip of my drink and gulped it down before my laugh escaped.

"Aw, never mind. I thought you guys would be glad."

Murph complained. "You don't make it easy. Where have you been?"

"I've been around, learning the ropes, paying my dues. I wasn't sure you'd want me back."

"Me neither," Murph said.

"You raced out of here," said Norman, "like your future was about to catch up to you. Ah, to be young and scared instead of old and jaded."

"I went down to the river and thought about your riverbank story. About you and Rose."

Murph looked pleased. "This is Rose," she told Deej.

"Wow. You're pretty."

"And you're a handsome youngster."

Deej, whose coloring I wouldn't have expected to redden, managed to blush and look embarrassed. "Anyway," she said, "I wasn't allowed out of the house except for classes after Dad caught me and Janey."

"The blonde?"

"No, Janey came first, before Beth and Denise and Sandy—" She was grinning like a kid let loose in a toy store.

"All in five months? You made up for lost time," Norman said.

"I've been with Crista six weeks now."

"Practically married!" Norman said.

Murph took a seat next to Deej and asked, "What kept you away so long, kid?"

"How could I come back after I made such an ass of myself?" She ducked her head, as if Murph could hide her. "In front of Lisa."

"That," Norman said with a sniff, "is what bars are for. Fools like us."

Someone fumbled with the front doorknob. Carla Jean came in, all smiles, exhaling cigarette smoke. She announced, "We got the commission for the school district!"

"You're joshing me!" JoJo said. "Do they want us to do their awards? Plaques? Trophies?"

"The whole deal. Honest to God. They said Rockie's recommendation counted a lot."

"Trust me," I said, "I was pleased to endorse you. You two do a fine job." My pride couldn't have been greater if they'd been my own kids. I bound the school yearbooks and embossed them. "Let's have some champagne, JoJo. We need a celebration!"

Quiet JoJo practically hugged the life out of me, then circled Carla Jean in a tiny flamenco-like victory dance and held a wineglass out of Carla Jean's reach.

At the bar, Norman screamed.

CHAPTER SEVEN

Certain gay guys scream at the least provocation, like silly six-year-old girls. Nevertheless, everyone in the bar turned to see what Norman was staring at. A man staggered in, shirtfront bloody, his hand over his nose.

"Somebody do something." Norman clutched the bar, pale, his skin abruptly shiny with moisture.

Although I have a pretty strong stomach, I was a little faint at the sight too. The guy had been an Old Town Tavern ornament for as long as I'd gone there. Shiny black hair worn long enough to show off curly waves, an ivory complexion, and light-green eyes so pretty you'd swear he wore makeup to enhance them. Not tonight.

Two men rushed up to him, called him by name, and helped him to sit at a table. The poor fellow was crying.

Spence charged outside, Seneca right after him.

"They broke a forty-ounce beer bottle on my head," he said. "I reek of beer." The sharp neck of the bottle had slashed his chest.

JoJo gave Norman a glass of water. She led him to a chair and helped him to sit, his face away from the injured customer.

"The sight of blood," she told us, then ran to the pay phone to call a cab. The injured man's friends soon took him away.

"They're afraid the attackers would see which cars belong to them," JoJo explained.

Norman held his head in his hands. "What are those brutes doing to us?"

Hugh strode in, so we knew JoJo had called him too. Hugh and Norman lived upstairs over the bar.

JoJo told Hugh the victim had approached the back door and was grabbed from behind. "There were three guys. He didn't recognize them, but they sound like our daytime goons. They held him while a third gorilla-type punched him. The last thing the gorilla did was kick our guy in the belly and head. His friends thought it would be safer to get him checked out at the hospital downtown."

Hugh folded his arms. As large as his bearded head was, his ears were too big for it, yet his nose was small and delicately formed over his pouty red mouth. His eyes, which normally seemed focused on the heavens or whatever professors thought about, glowered. "They want to shut us down."

"But why?" Deej asked. She sat by herself and watched. JoJo made a come-here gesture with her arm and, when Deej didn't obey, thrust her pointing finger at the bar top. Deej tightened her lips until they almost disappeared, squinted with a look of distrust, then stood and sauntered toward JoJo, hands in pockets.

Seneca and Spence returned, out of breath. "There's no sign of the attackers," Seneca said, panting and leaning over, hands on her knees.

"They must have taken off in a car," added Spence. He pulled a handkerchief from his back pocket and wiped sweat from his face.

We regulars were in shock about the attack. I could hear snatches of conversation about our fates should we lose The Old Town. I tried to think of ways to help: pay off the whole police force? Were the police all of the story, or even behind the violence? I doubted that. The bar downtown wasn't under siege, nor was the one out by the turnpike. Both were a lot bigger and strictly gay. The Old Town was much more mixed. Yet it was the target.

Murph put an arm across Deej's shoulder. "It hasn't been that long since you thought we were the scourge of the earth."

"That was me and some high-school kids. Lots of people don't like queers, but they don't tyrannize businesses."

If we'd been in a lighter mood, we might have laughed. I tried not to cry with the horror of it. All I could think of was the stories my relatives brought from their *shtetels* when they escaped to America, those who did escape. I wanted to take the whole bunch into my arms for a never-ending hug. Instead, we looked to Hugh, our very own professor.

He said, "Someone is intimidating our customers. No customers: we're out of business."

Norman echoed my puzzlement. "Why in the world our customers and not one of the other bars'? Or all of us?"

Hugh brought his bushy eyebrows together and fiddled with his cufflinks. "The Old Town is as straight as a gay bar can be, sugar-britches. We don't serve minors or let people smoke weed or have sex in the johns like the other bars, so they need to get at us another way. The fact that we haven't been raided before only means we've been good boys and girls."

"A while ago I probably would have thought it served you right to get pinched by the fuzz." Deej frowned. "No, that's not right. I would have thought I had to think that. I didn't want to be like you."

"After what just happened, no one will believe they're safe here, no matter who they like to spend their time with," Rose said. "I'm afraid to leave."

Murph said, "They wouldn't hurt women."

"Stop your blustering," Rose told her. "Of course they would."

"Well, they can't scare me away," Deej said. "They have the whole world. We have The Old Town Tavern."

Murph chimed in. "Out of the mouths of babes…"

Carla Jean studied Deej. Cigarette in her mouth, she ran her hand along the ragged bottom of Deej's haircut.

"What!" Deej said, and brushed her off like she would a pesty bug.

"Who gave you this cut?" asked Carla Jean. "Come in the bathroom with me. It needs some help."

"Murph," Rose said after Carla Jean shanghaied a protesting Deej, "don't you think we could talk to Frank Goodlette? He's a big man about town now: city council, top dog at the hot-dog factory. See if he could help?"

"You know a Goodlette?" Norman asked. "I adore their maple franks."

"Sure," Rose said. "We went to school with Frank." She smiled at Norman. "Did you know he was named after their hot dogs?"

"That's a laugh," Hugh said.

Norman's mouth was open. "You're not joking, are you?"

"The Goodlettes always called him their best frank. I prefer Teo's Hot Dogs down in Pittsfield."

Murph said, "Rose got to know the family when she went out with Frank." She looked at Rose and held out her hand. "He was sweet on her. Can you blame him?"

"Murph." Rose's tone was pleased and chiding.

"Seriously, ladies, we could use any influence you might have to find out what's going on," Hugh said. "Everyone is our natural friend. Everyone is our enemy."

Hugh often talked in riddles like this.

"It might be worth a try, Rosie. Better you go with someone else though. I might not be a good ambassador," Murph said, gesturing to her appearance. She was handsome to us, but told us she scared the daylights out of women in public bathrooms. Trust me, it happens to me too, braids and all. Could be the way we walk. I think, really, being gay marks us in some way. I can sometimes tell from a woman's voice. I can certainly tell most of the time when I look at a gay person. There's some indefinable, indescribable air about us. Whatever it is, my heart beats a little faster when I sense it. Straights run a little faster when they sense it. I suppose they'd be happy to herd us into zoos. Maybe human zoos are called prisons, or concentration camps.

"I lived with a lawyer. There are ways to make him see us. Or," Rose said, her eyes on Murph in her work clothes, "maybe you're right and I should go alone."

Murph stepped back. "You've changed a lot from your shy young days, haven't you, Rose?"

Rose slid her glasses down her nose to study Murph's face. "Enough to have the gumption to try and get this harassment stopped," she replied.

Norman rapped the flat of his hand on the bar and said, "Go get 'em, Miss Rosie!"

The door opened again and this time Lisa stepped inside. She paused like a dancer might, one hand up, feet poised and pointed in low blue heels.

"Has something happened?" she asked. Then she spotted Deej. Trust me, I saw their eyes meet with such warmth my heart went all soft like it did at the sight of newborn puppies and kittens. If those two hadn't spent time together, close together, my name wasn't Rockie Solomon.

Deej moved to Lisa, took her hand, and led her to the bar.

"So my little crazy is back," Lisa said, her tone tender. "Did you bring your running shoes, Deej?"

Murph said, "She doesn't need them anymore. She converted, didn't you, Deej?"

"Converted?" Lisa asked. She rested her purse on the bar after JoJo wiped down a space for her.

"Why don't you bring Crista to Thanksgiving?" Rose suggested. Murph scowled at Rose and shook her head behind Lisa's back. I winced. Deej was about to be in hot water.

Lisa asked Deej, "Who's Crista?"

Deej looked down at the floor. "A friend."

"Out with it, girl," Norman said. "She must be the pinnacle of a series of conquests, Miss Lisa. Little Deej walked in here and announced that she was living the good life now."

Deej emptied her glass and said, "I better get going."

"Hot date?" Norman asked.

Deej narrowed her eyes at him, then edged away. "Hey, Lisa. Why don't you give me your phone number again. I lost it."

Lisa looked like she would smack the kid. "You'll find it if you want to," she said, and took a seat next to me.

Laughing, Murph said, "And give Crista's to me."

"You dirty old lady," said Deej, shaking her head. She shook a fist at Murph, then grinned and marched to the door. Before she stepped into the street, she leaned out, looked all around, then turned back, thumb raised.

Lisa asked, "What was that all about?"

Norman said, "That's the all-clear." He explained the problem.

"You're kidding me. Who got hurt? Will he be okay?"

Norman answered, "Oh, Prettyboy. You know the one, with all the hair. He came to meet friends here, apparently. I know him, not the friends."

"Maybe he brought the trouble with him and it had nothing to do with the bar," Lisa suggested.

"Could be," Hugh said. "We can't ignore a pattern of harassment."

Before Hugh could don his lecturer's hat, Deej was in the doorway again.

"They're out there! Around the corner. One car, two cops. Bye!" With that warning, she took off on her bike in the opposite direction from the police car.

Hugh and Norman shared a look.

"Why," Rose asked, "can't they leave you in peace? What harm are you doing?"

"None," said Hugh, "except frightening their moral high horses, saddlebags stuffed with religion, superstition, and ignorance."

"It's 1961!" Norman proclaimed. "You'd think it was the Middle Ages, not the middle of the twentieth century."

"What can you do?" Murph said with a shrug. "Go straight?"

Norman grabbed Hugh's arm. "Bite your tongue, girl."

On the barstool that might as well be labeled with her name, Tipsy, the old, straight, bar mascot patted her nose after a cough and tucked her hanky into the V of her neckline. "I happen to like my men."

A queen who went by the name Honey Delight leaned over and put her arms around Tipsy. "We love you, Miss Tipsy-Lou! You can't help being a square."

Tipsy was obviously drunk as a skunk, but, as usual, a happy drunk. She gave Honey a big wet kiss on the cheek. "There!" she said, her laugh as raucous as a tropical bird's cry. "Now you have as much makeup on as me."

With a laugh, Rose lifted her wineglass. "Let me think about visiting Frank Goodlette when I don't have a drink in me." She wore a navy-blue button-front dress patterned in cerise-colored petals and low, thick-heeled black pumps. She and Murph had come in earlier after the movie *Gidget*, the silliest show, they reported, they'd seen in their lifetimes. I doubt The Old Town had ever hosted a more matronly customer than Rose. She drank port, one glass each evening. "I've learned to channel Vi's clear way of thinking. I may want some advice before I knock on Frankie's door."

"The woman calls him Frankie! Have one on the house," Norman said as he tipped the port bottle to fill Rose's glass.

"I'll drive home," Murph joked.

"You may have to carry this old dame tonight," Rose said. I think it had been a while since she'd enjoyed herself this much, regardless of the evening's events.

Rose leaned toward Murph. "I remember Chestnut Forest Park."

"We strolled and strolled," Murph said. "Beside the river. The leaves under our feet in fall. The birdsong in spring."

"Do you still love the birds, then, Murph?"

"You know I do."

This was a surprise as I never saw Murph outside a bar, except for her room.

Rose said, "You once knew every breed and gender and what the young looked like."

Murph's smile seemed to cast a glow around her. Rose had a little trouble pronouncing her words. "I remember the thrill of the first owl you pointed out to me."

Murph put a hand over Rose's and I was filled with hope for them. As slowly as she'd spoken, Rose withdrew her hand and I saw that, though Rose and Murph loved each other, Rose's was a different kind of love and Murph was destined to disappointment. I turned away.

The joint was as full as it ever got, while the noise level was higher than normal, probably because of the earlier incident. The music from the jukebox vibrated through my feet. These were my people: they didn't let a little blood and terror ruin our time together. The straight world seemed to think homosexuality was all about sex. I had news for them. It was also about companionship, about spending time with the people we wanted to be with, intimately or socially.

My family would be horrified to know where I socialized. They thought I dressed like Rose Callaghan and spent my time being wined and dined by square businessmen. They were correct about one thing: I hadn't found the right man! What they didn't know, the poor things, was that I wasn't looking, and neither were most of the other fine women at The Old Town.

Rose left Murph's side and linked an arm with Lisa. She said, with an affectionate gaze toward Murph, "These younger butches are quite something, aren't they?"

"Yes, yes they are. I can't hold on to one. I expect Deej was a silly idea."

Murph heard them. "You haven't lost me, woman. You're a classy act, too classy for me. We simply aren't right for each other." Murph sounded as if she wanted Rose to hear the end of that story.

"You'd led me to expect—"

"A little love and affection? And I went and worked myself into a stupor instead. I've had all these months to think about it, Lisa, and you know what I've come up with? Something in me knew I needed you more as a friend than as a lover. Can you forgive me?"

"I've swallowed my pride for less. If love plans to pass me by, I'll need my friends more than ever."

Rose hugged her. Carla Jean approached with a bottle of wine and two glasses, then took Rose away for some girl talk they'd promised each other.

Murph, not one to fear a question, asked, "Whatever did happen between you two after the night you danced with Deej?"

Lisa's face froze into a mask. I thought she was deciding how much to tell and I expected that to be nothing, but I forgot that Murph could charm a Secret Service agent into spilling state beans. Even in front of someone else. I wanted to give Lisa privacy by moving away and, at the same time, wanted to be as still as I could, not to interrupt her exchange with Murph.

Lisa's tongue must have been loosened by the horror of the attack on Prettyboy. She said, "Deej was—amazing. She followed until she led."

Murph laughed softly. "Think what a champ you'll have with some tutoring."

Lisa went all shy then. If Murph pushed her she would clam up. Instead, into the silence she told her story.

"Deej danced me into my apartment and hummed an old romantic song. I wish I knew the name of it. I hear it in my head."

She hummed it and Murph, an old romantic herself, immediately sang a few bars of "That Old Black Magic."

"That's it!" Lisa said. "I was surprised Deej knew it. As it happens, she's a big fan of crooner music: Jo Stafford, Nat King Cole, all those singers."

"That's something in her favor," Murph said. "She sang to you all night?"

"Of course not. She even gave me a foot massage. She's got hands that could melt a glacier."

Murph waggled her eyebrows. "Don't stop there."

"Oh, Murph, that's enough. Use your imagination."

"If I use my imagination, I won't be able to control myself, now will I?"

Lisa looked down with a smile and shook her head. "No more ginger ale for you or I'll think you really are a dirty old lady."

"Old, no. Dirty—what's wrong with dirty?"

"You're impossible. I will say we somehow got past the nervous stage very quickly. She's a natural."

"Did she let you touch her?"

I couldn't believe Murph asked that.

Lisa looked taken aback. She started to say something, then turned away.

Nice reaction, I thought. Despite her marriage to a man, Lisa respected the subtle and wordless butch honor system more than Murph did.

"Well," Murph pronounced after a silence, "someone needed to bring that kid out."

"Oh, Murph!" Lisa got up and threw her balled-up napkin in Murph's face. "That's not all it was! Why do I ever tell you anything?" She snatched up her purse and jacket and stalked out of the bar. She lucked out. The number 46 bus slowed for the traffic light and she was able to hail it. Lisa lived somewhere on the other side of downtown. Usually she left so late Norman called her a cab.

Murph looked at me and said, "I guess stepping on Lisa's sensitive toesies saved her cab fare tonight." She breathed out a sigh.

Who knew what Murph was really thinking or could guess the emotions inside that handsome head?

"Foot massage," she said with a devilish grin. "Why didn't that ever occur to me?"

CHAPTER EIGHT

I left Colonel Mustard with my neighbors, who adored her almost as much as I did, and took the train ninety minutes north to be with my family for Thanksgiving. I tugged at my bra straps the whole visit and straightened my nylons obsessively, like I was about to go onstage. While I love and enjoy my family, they don't know who I really am. Even at my age, with a good business to my credit, I'm as scared as a little kid that they'll find out I'm gay. Geri and I had separate bedrooms in case anyone from either family came to visit. I get the runs every time I go back home.

When I got to the tiny station, Dad waited in the old family Buick. Wipers kept snow off the windshield. The flakes gathered on my head and braids. I prayed they wouldn't pile up to leave me trapped with my folks. Once at the house, I stamped my boots and went in through the big kitchen where practically everyone was gathered. It was steamy hot and smelled of mashed sweet potatoes and turkey. Immediately, my mouth started watering. I dipped a spoon into the gravy and nodded my approval to my mother, who always used me as a taster. She raised her arms and welcomed me home with an embrace. Then came her sisters and their families, then my father's side, and my brothers' wives and kids. It was a houseful this year, noisy with laughter and scolding, kids crying and singing along to a recording of songs of gratitude.

In the kitchen, the women asked me the usual questions and I gave them the usual answers, variations on the word *no*. No, I hadn't met a man good enough for me; no, I wasn't about to lower my standards; no, I hadn't heard from that girl Geri I used to room with; and no, I wasn't moving home, I had a company to run. In the living room I spoke with the men about business and world affairs. They're good people, my family. They're also old-fashioned, very traditional. They buy kosher products for the holy days. There was a temple in town, but we didn't see the inside of it often because we're not as pious as most of the congregation. The Solomons' Jewishness is more a home thing, a time to get together with family, to teach the kids our history, to cook traditional dishes.

I didn't say that I might never have left if they had given me a role in the family business, which is the manufacture of children's shoes. They groomed me for it, as they did my brothers, one older, one younger. Despite my loud protests they gave the boys the reins and told me I'd be the face of the company. I was to deal with direct customer and retail-sales problems. In other words, the receptionist, their little rock, holding down the fort while the boys did the real work. My name, Rochele, means little rock, which is one reason they called me Rockie for short. That, and I'm built like a small boulder. In pictures from my childhood I'm usually running, my legs sturdy, my hands in fists, a serious look on my face. I was the kind of toddler who would run full-out at adults, slam into their legs, and hold on until they pried my fingers away.

After college I didn't go back up North to my family, but stayed here in Hansfield. I studied business and made my own way through the Great Depression. I saved every penny and turned my anger at my family into ambition, learning everything about the first job I found where the employer would hire a girl to do hands-on work. It was in a bindery. Fourteen years later, when the owners decided to retire and move to Florida, I used my savings and borrowed more from the big-cheese family in town, the Goodlettes, whose company's lending arm helped foster small Hansfield businesses. All I owned was my clothes and The Durable Binding Company, but I repaid the Goodlettes in ten years. One of my nieces got into a scrape back home and came to work for me. She married my foreman and now their two daughters work with us summers.

I grabbed an early southbound train the morning after Thanksgiving and watched northwestern New England pass by, the banks of its rivers and brooks made even prettier by new snow. At the same time, I couldn't wait to get back to my apartment and take off my dress-up clothes. I collected the dog from my neighbors, changed to wool trousers and boots, and had an exciting reunion and a good walk to the park with her. I'd given my loyal crew the Friday off with pay. All the time Colonel Mustard tugged me along at the end of her leash I thought about how much I missed my friends at The Old Town—much more than I ever missed my family. I was eager to get to the day-after-Thanksgiving dinner.

For this private party I knocked on the side door. The sight of the old gang made me all wet-eyed. Despite our recent harassment, I was happy in their company. We were used to being beleaguered. I might miss it if we should suddenly blend in with the square world. Our special place in society had its good points. I looked around at all these fine people. Every table was filled, and spirits looked and sounded high and noisy. Rose and Murph grabbed an unoccupied chair, pulled me between them, and hugged me from both sides. My hands found the embroidered tablecloth Murph must have brought. Someone told me Rose had made the crocheted lace table runner. Rose and Murph were like two peas in a pod. Although the scents of turkey and stuffing were similar, the contrast to Thanksgiving with my relatives was drastic: I'd left the snow behind; rivers and brooks of love flowed through me here.

Carla Jean rose from her seat, a fancy silver goblet in one hand, a cigarette in the other, her speech only slightly sloppy. They'd unplugged the jukebox during dinner. "I want to tell you how this warms my heart, to see all our friends together. Thanks to Norman and Murph for sprucing up The Old Town."

There was a smattering of applause while Norman stood up and twirled, arms clasped above his head. Murph settled for a wink and a nod.

Carla Jean continued her speech. "Lisa and our Miss Norma Jean and Rose prepared this gourmet spread!" The applause was stronger now. "I hope we celebrate many more day-after-Thanksgiving dinners with you!" She bent over JoJo and kissed her a dozen times around her head and face.

Rose said, "Please, God, protect all these lovely men and women."

Murph said, "You've heard of the blessing of the fleet and the blessing of the animals. This is the blessing of the homosexuals!" I shook with laughter, spraying my vodka tonic as I did. Murph swatted me on the shoulder. Her smile was proud.

"And bring back your souvenirs next year!"Carla Jean and JoJo's little trophy business had inscribed goblets, gratis.

"Never mind waiting till next year," Paul said. "I'm moving in!"

"They'll never root us out," said a hefty woman in a plaid blouse and green dungarees, "with all of us homesteading here."

"Root you out?" Deej asked. "Could they do that?"

JoJo, who'd begun to clear dishes, stopped short in front of Deej, like she'd hit her brakes. "It sounds like that's somebody's plan."

"But that's not legal! The city can't make the police do it if it's not legal, can they?"

Carla Jean asked the crowd, "Do you folks want a Christmas dinner too?"

After the cheers, Norman leapt to his feet again, his hands folded for prayer. "Blessed Mary the Fairy will appear in person!"

Norman is too much. I was in stitches at that remark. I checked out Rose to see if she was offended, but her laugh was one of the loudest.

Even before the laughter died down, Carla Jean and JoJo scuttled to push the tables aside for dancing. Hugh helped as much as he could in his severe dark women's suit. The straight black skirt had a very short slit at the bottom. Between its hip-hugging form and Hugh's high heels, his tight white blouse with black-bordered ruffles, and the tailored jacket, he had little freedom of movement. As incongruous as his neat beard looked with a long, banged pageboy wig, his professorial black-framed glasses tied his outfit all together and, somehow, it worked. I never noticed Hugh laugh or flirt with Norman as much as when he was dressed in severe schoolmarm garb.

You had to see Lisa, though. She wore a simple, elegant sexy black cocktail sheath that clung to her body. I didn't recognize her tantalizing scent, but I bet it wasn't cheap.

Murph and Rose, both in their best dress-up clothes, guided me to the bar with them. Murph wore brown slacks that complemented her tan, spread-collared shirt. Rose was in a pale-orange crepe dress, short-sleeved, with a loose shawl collar. An intricate silver brooch closed the collar and I got a whiff of her flowery perfume.

"What a wonderful idea this was," Rose said. And to Murph she added, "Thank you for inviting me, Rosie."

"Rosie?" Deej asked, angling in to order drinks.

Rose explained. "The Murphys and the Callaghans both chose the name Rose. As we grew up, we never knew which one of us was being called home to dinner or to speak in class."

Deej pinched Murph's cheeks. "What a lovely rose you make!"

"Back off, kid. What did you do with that pretty little Crista of yours?"

"She's no little girl."

"You made sure of that, didn't you," Murph said.

"Don't start anything, Murph." Rose frowned. "The day has been so peaceful."

"That's what families are for, isn't it? To squabble on holidays?" Norman quipped.

Dr. Everett laughed. He'd been coming in every evening after his last patient to help plan this shebang. He sat at the bar, in a dated gray suit, a Windsor knot in his tie, a bit sloshed. With his near-perpetual smile, he looked like a proud granddad.

At the back of the jukebox JoJo kneeled and snaked her arm behind to plug it back in while Carla cried over the din, "The music's on us! Dance your hearts out!" She and JoJo fed a mound of quarters into the box and left the partiers to punch in songs.

"Not yet!" Deej said. "Crista's out in the kitchen washing dishes."

"There are other women who'll dance with you," Murph said.

Deej grinned at Murph. "Oh. Yeah," she said, her voice higher than usual. She seemed unable to stand still. "Uh. Lisa? Would you like to, you know, dance?"

I laughed in pleasure to see them move into each other's arms as if they were testing the temperature of a pond before they swam. They started out at arm's length and gradually danced more and more slowly. My heart was as big as the sun, huge and shining with gladness for Lisa, as if she in some way belonged to me.

"I think those two ought to stay together," Murph said.

Norman nodded. "Someone better tell them."

"They're such a young, good-looking couple, why aren't they together?" Rose asked.

Carla Jean tried, unsuccessfully, to walk a straight line as she delivered clean glasses to the bar. She commented, "Deej's pretty young. She disappeared on Lisa."

"Don't tell me about age differences," Rose said. "I wish people would stop thinking up reasons not to love one another. There's not enough love in the world as it is."

I noticed Rose and Murph look at each other. Rose turned her head away. Murph wiped her hands on her pants, and I knew what those sweaty palms wanted.

"How about a Thanksgiving dance for your old friend Murph, doll?" she asked.

Rose's face froze briefly, her eyes staring at nothing, as if she could find an answer outside herself.

Murph backed away from Rose. "Too soon? I'm sorry. I shouldn't have asked. Forgive me."

Rose spoke so quietly I almost missed what she said. Not that I needed to know, but I suppose I'm a nosy parker when it comes right down to it. "Oh, Murph, it will always be too soon."

She was looking down and couldn't see the dejection on Murph's face. At that moment Murph looked a hundred years old. Most of the time her eyes sparkled like she was about to turn a very hip sixteen, and when they did, everyone around her acted sixteen. I know I did. To liven Murph up, I grabbed Dr. Everett and dragged him onto the dance floor. He groaned when he realized Frankie Avalon was singing "Venus," which is practically unnavigable. Of course that's why I chose the doctor—neither of us can dance worth a bean.

"Where's Tipsy?" I asked. The doctor and Tipsy were long-time drinking buddies.

"In Florida with her ancient school chums," he said. "She goes there every year. One of them has a big house and a big boat. Haven't you noticed she stays tan in winter?"

"So it's all gay tonight?"

"Except for Seneca and Spence. And they're family."

Lisa and Deej came back to the bar after "Venus" and talked right beyond my stool. Deej leaned with her elbow against the bar, her other hand in a pants' pocket. She pulled out a bill and let it drop on the bar to buy Lisa and herself drinks.

"That's it, though. I'm now too broke to buy you anything."

"This is my limit anyway." Lisa sipped her drink. "So, how have you been?"

"I have my ups and downs."

"What's your up's name again? Kristen?"

"Crista. How about you?"

"I think I have lover's block. I want to love, and I don't."

"Nothing?"

Trust me, if I were fifteen, even ten years younger I'd rise to the challenge and unblock her.

After a pause Lisa answered. "Nothing I know how to fix."

Another pause and Deej, who apparently learned fast, said, "I think you're beautiful, Lisa."

Oh, how I agreed. I would have to visit a museum before I found a face as appealing. Lisa's hair was longer and must, I thought with warmth, tickle her shoulders when they're bare. The familiar resignation in her eyes looked more like surrender.

"And I don't want to be another notch on your bedpost, Deej."

"No. I think you're beautiful. I sit in class and daydream about you."

"When you're not dreaming about Kristen."

"Crista. All the Cristas in the world," Deej told Lisa, "don't match up to you."

Deej was so young she probably didn't even know what an old line that was.

"I daydreamed at work too. My boss caught me."

"Work? You work too?"

The kid got defensive so easily, but this really was a shocker. "Why? You thought I was some deadbeat? My internship at the 'copter plant is part of my curriculum. I work in the engineering department."

"Receptionist?"

"Way off, Lisa. I do drafting on a project to design new running lights. I hope they'll make me an engineering assistant when I graduate."

"That's unusual, isn't it, for a girl to be an engineer?"

"Only if you think you can be nothing more than a receptionist."

Lisa winced, although by now I'd learned she had a decent bookkeeping job.

"What about your parents," I asked. "Aren't Indians strict about what daughters can do?"

"My parents are very forward thinking. When I was tested in school and found to have a good brain, they saved for university. I'm lucky to be the only daughter or I would have been given a motel like my brothers. They didn't think that was a fit occupation for a woman." Deej laughed. "I'm expected to marry another engineer, but they don't approve of dating. They want to pick him."

Murph elbowed her way to the bar. "Jesus, kid, how'd you luck out? I would have gone to college in a flash if I could have. It was the Depression, though, and I wasn't much of a student. I still live paycheck to paycheck."

"I am lucky. My family does okay and they approve of my interests. My father's youngest brother teaches industrial design in India. When I was thirteen we went over for a visit and I asked a lot of questions. I fell in love with everything about his job: drafting tools, blueprints, slide rules. Drafting and engineering are subjects I understand, like I was born to be an inventor."

Lisa looked puzzled. "Industrial design? It sounds like you make machinery."

"You can." Deej looked more passionate about this than about either Lisa or Crista. "The part I like is kind of machinery for life. Industrial design is—" The kid looked up, as if she could find the words she wanted in the cigarette smoke. "It can be a way to make beautiful objects that help people. You could design," she picked up an empty beer pitcher on the bar, "a better way to serve beer. Or a more efficient broom. Or, take my grandfather. He suffered a lot in India before he came here. He fought for Indian independence and his own people. The Indians who lived well under English rule jailed and tortured him. He's in a wheelchair except when he's in bed. He's a really lively, curious old guy. If we can make jets that can fly him to India, can't we make some kind of special scooter so he could go to the library on his own right here in the US? Or design a bus so you could stash your wheelchair on it and get across town to a museum?"

"Bless you," Murph said. "Don't let being like us get in your way. Be careful who you sleep with and keep your nose clean."

Despite what she'd said about not wanting to be another notch on Deej's belt, Lisa seemed unable to look away from her. When Deej looked back, there would be a pause in the conversation as if one, or both, of them had to catch her breath. I remembered that sensation. Part of me never wanted to experience it again; it led to blizzards of hurt. And I caught my breath too because I remembered it led to a paradise of passion.

As the day-after-Thanksgiving party wound down, I realized my heart was tired from so much pleasure. Crista came out of the kitchen, looking as fresh as when she went in. She had the strangest eyes, unsmiling, that always darted sideways, as if too busy to engage with mine. With a quick, discreet peck on the cheek and a glance at her wristwatch, she said good night to Deej. She had her own car, a sporty '58 Plymouth Fury, parked right out front. Deej watched her head back to campus.

Before anyone else could leave and before Norman got around to locking the front door after Crista, I heard a squeal of tires and a flash of whirling lights. Dread froze me where I stood. Was someone else hurt? Why were the police here?

CHAPTER NINE

Norman, with a little yelp, gave his lover a shove. Hugh grabbed something from under the bar and ran to the supply closet at the end of the bathroom hall. He must have picked up the key, I thought a long time afterward, because he never came out, and when the police used a crow bar to open that door, Hugh wasn't inside. Norman and Hugh owned the whole building and lived in one of the two apartments upstairs from the bar. I envisioned a trap door in the ceiling and a hidden rope ladder. Hugh's job was too valuable to them to risk.

Soft-spoken JoJo stood still for once and roared, "Fuzz!"

An enormous uniformed cop with captain's bars opened the front door.

Couples jumped apart, the crowd surged toward the kitchen exit, but blue uniforms and shotguns blocked the swinging door from inside. This wasn't a large bar. They trapped us in seconds. I tried to make myself small, invisible, but I shook so much I couldn't think. I needed to get to the bathroom before my quavering bowels embarrassed me. No such luck. I could hear the police kick open bathroom-stall doors so hard they slammed off the stall dividers. A man was pitched into the main bar; the windows in the bathrooms were too small for escape. Murph gathered Rose to her as if to shield her from view. My heart beat between beats, and I closed my hand around the keys in my pocket and pressed the pointed ends into my palms. Other than that, I couldn't move.

I'd noticed Carla Jean dive behind the bar. She was no lightweight, but when a cop found her he dragged her out by one ankle. Carla Jean neither resisted nor cooperated; she lay on the floor where he left her, skirt hiked up to her thighs, her cigarettes spilled beside her. Half my brain was like a trapped mouse looking for a way out; the other half cheered Carla Jean.

Danny Bernato and his Avenue Revue were dressing in the kitchen for their Thanksgiving show. A local boy, Danny was the former owner of the bar and was now a well-known drag performer all along the East Coast. Their screams and pleas made it clear they were taking the worst of it, as queens always did. Dr. Everett, one of the first to attempt flight through the kitchen, now looked confused. These were not only his friends, these were his patients. I supposed the police could report him to the medical board if he brought attention to himself by announcing that he was a doctor. I could see the struggle in his face: he wanted to help.

JoJo caught his eye and, eyebrows drawn together, gave a quick shake of the head. Dr. Everett nodded, looking angry. He knew we needed him too much to let him lose his license. The expression of surrender I'd seen in Lisa's eyes was all around me; we'd long ago accepted that we would be punished for our queerness. The doctor drew his fedora low over his eyes and dropped into a seat.

Murph motioned for Deej to take off her hat and mash it into a jacket pocket. Deej, young enough to think herself invincible, gave her a defiant look, then complied. Hats made men nondescript, while the women who wore them might as well ask for punishment. These sex rules reminded me of growing up Jewish. Kids need to learn so many things: to use a toilet, tie shoes, left from right, red from yellow—that boys could grow up to be rabbis and girls could not, that a Jewish last name could make people hate me, that young was better than old. That night, I was a triple target: gray-haired, a Solomon, and queer.

Two small women edged behind the police at the front. I recognized them. Korean War veterans, one was a retired army nurse, the other a driver. The first pulled her girlfriend by the hand and darted past the cop in the doorway. He caught the girlfriend by the breasts and pushed his shotgun between her legs. A tall young cop who stood outside the door reached out and eased the shotgun away from the girlfriend. He glowered at the cop in the doorway. The first cop then lunged toward the other woman, aiming at her head, but, again, the tall young officer blocked him. After a split second struggle of wills the cop in the doorway laughed and let the women go. "Faggot lover," he said to their defender.

Eventually, everyone went still. There was silence except for a woman crying and a guy who whimpered over and over, "My heart, my heart."

This was an outrage. I had friends in the police force. They'd helped when the bindery was broken into—more than once. One of my neighbors was a cop. This group was nothing like them. It was like a Gestapo inside the Hansfield Police Department. They didn't give an inch and acted as if they were enjoying themselves. Outside the open front door I could see more of them taking down license-plate numbers. Inside, the sweat of fear smelled stronger than the smoke of cigarettes abandoned in their ashtrays.

"What did we do?" shouted a husky man with a brush mustache when a cop asked for ID.

"What's in your purse?" another cop asked a woman, grabbing it. The woman tugged back and lost; he upended it and dumped the contents on the floor. The last I saw, he was checking inside a tampon holder while another cop patted down her burly companion.

"Having fun in the kitchen, boys?" the captain called. The queens stopped screaming.

An out-of-uniform cop opened one of the swinging doors. "You want a turn, Sarge?" The captain was too busy.

He lined us up like school kids. Murph was still trying to hide Rose. In the kitchen someone wailed, "I'm sorry. I'm so fucking sorry." It sounded like our Miss Scarletta of The Avenue Revue.

The tall cop at the front door let a couple of older men leave when none of the other officers were looking. Seneca and Spence were told to leave or be arrested for gambling. Spence gathered their cards and went for the roll of pennies. Seneca stayed his hand. "For you," she said to the cop, gesturing to the pennies, disdain in her eyes.

"I ought to arrest you for whoring around with a white man. Is this real or is it a wig?" He yanked at her hair, then wiped his hand on his pants. Seneca, eyes looking down, cringed away from him.

Spence put an arm around Seneca's slim shoulders and drew her close. "This is my wife," he told the threatening cop and hurried Seneca out the door. I heard the pride in Spence's voice. The officers were white.

"What have we here?" the captain asked. He pulled Rose forward by her skirt. "A girly bulldyke?" He laughed at her and examined Murph. "And you're the top-captain?" He palmed Murph's crotch. "You're old enough to know nothing's there."

Murph stepped back from his touch, fingers outspread and stiff at her sides, as if forcing herself not to make fists. When I say the man was enormous, I mean girth as well as height. He had to have close to

300 pounds on a six-foot frame. His presence was as threatening as all those guns.

"Why are you dressed like a man?" he asked her. I would not have said she was. Her trousers zipped at the side, her blouse buttoned on the left. Her jacket, unlike the kid's, was a woman's. Sure, it was a bat-wing jacket like the guys wore in the war, cinched at the waist and blousy under the arms, but it was woman's clothing. She was so proud of that thing; she must have splurged on it and kept it pristine for years.

The captain grabbed Murph's collar and jerked her to him, then thrust her away. She fell over a barstool and tumbled down on top of it, splintering its wooden back. The captain kicked at her. She rolled to avoid his polished black shoe, and the kick landed on her rib cage. She flung out her right arm to deflect another blow. He tromped on her hand several times, snarling, "No woman will want that hand on her once I get through with you!" Laughing, he opened his uniform pants and urinated on her jacket.

Rose gagged beside me. I looked away; I couldn't imagine the degradation Murph must be experiencing. Lisa started to go to her, but a cop who moved down the line cuffing people clutched first Rose's, then JoJo's arms. Rose cried; JoJo stared ahead, her hands tight fists. I guess he ran out of handcuffs because some of us were still free.

Deej started toward the captain as he finished defiling the mound that was Murph. Lisa and I held her back. "You'll make it worse for Murph," Lisa told her, the calm in her voice and her uncompromising posture an antidote to all our panic. "You need to choose your battles or you won't win any."

Meanwhile, Paul gasped and told the cop to stop. Paul was like a porcelain doll: long eyelashes, rosebud lips, no sign that he needed to shave. The captain turned, spat at him, then drove a fist down onto his cheekbone once, twice, a third time. It sounded as if he'd crushed it. Paul shrieked. Blood immediately covered that side of his face, some of it from his eye socket. Norman whimpered, then retched. Dr. Everett gave in to his instincts and clutched Paul. He held him, then called that he needed ice. JoJo managed to crawl behind the bar to tie ice into a bar rag for Paul's face. The doctor moved to Murph and asked for more ice.

Deej looked from person to person, group to group. Her eyes reflected the horror of the scene. For so many of us, this was business as usual. Most had been through busts in one bar or another. I'd never seen police this brutal and had at times been told by merciful officers to leave the area.

The cop who'd been called a faggot lover stood at the back door of a vehicle. Our eyes met. His seemed apologetic.

"Get them in the wagons," the captain ordered now. "Be as gentle as I was." He slipped something shiny from his crushing fist into his pocket.

A young lesbian at the end of the lineup rolled herself under a car. A cop made a grab for her. Wriggling at top speed, she managed to scramble out the other side. Another officer let her run. He saw me watching and shrugged. "What the hell," he said.

"This old biddy too?" a baby-faced cop in uniform asked. His hand clutched quiet Rose's upper arm like she was subhuman and not bound by handcuffs.

"Leave her alone." Murph's voice was a scratchy whisper.

"Oh, Murph, no." I tried to warn her.

The captain gave the order. "Bring her along."

Murph looked half-dead, but managed to kick him. He raised his billy stick high over her head. She let herself fall to the ground and he missed. We managed to get in front of her.

"I never forget a face," he said, and looked at each of us with deeply mean eyes. His thick, straight eyebrows crawled almost to his hairline.

Three by three they marched us out, except for Murph, who shuffled, ice against her injured hand, and Carla Jean, who continued to make herself dead weight. The paddy wagons looked like armored ambulances bound for a madhouse. Two real ambulances stood along the side of The Old Town. Men carried a queen on a stretcher; her finery drooped from the side. This had to be a newsreel from Germany, the police forcing us toward the cattle cars, like some of my father's family or like my mother's great-great-grandfather, stolen as a child from who knew where and made to work for the railroad as a brakeman. This was my nightmare—that they'd gather us up and do what they wanted. It could happen in 1961 America.

Norman was still sick. He coughed, choked, and asked, "What about the bar?"

"With any luck," said his escort in blue, "it'll be looted and burned to the ground."

"What do you hateful hoods have against us?" Carla Jean asked as two cops carried her outside.

The captain spit at Carla Jean and called her a string of lewd names after the others swung and dropped her by Norman's feet. Norman hung his head. He listed like a tree in high winds, keened like a storm wind himself.

By this time I was in shock, terrified of what would happen once they got us to the police station. My underwear was wet. Whose wasn't? I thought. I knew my niece would keep the business in good shape when I didn't show up. It was better that I didn't: I'd have to keep a low profile or risk losing clients. All this because I spent the evening with people I was closer to than family. This was not the country I loved.

"Is it the election?" Carla Jean demanded as she wiped her face with vigor. "You've never bothered us before. Is this part of some ruthless conspiracy to drive us away?"

Through his tears, Norman found the courage to say, "Never. There will always be homosexuals and gay bars."

The sight of police vehicles and flashing lights and armed men brought people out of the apartment buildings, the bookstore and bowling alley, all the businesses still open along the row.

My next-door neighbor at The Avenue Arms stood on the corner. He yelled, "Who can I call for you, honey?" I pointed at another man's dog. He nodded. He and his wife would move Colonel Mustard back in with them if I couldn't get home. Everyone else I could think to call for help was being arrested too. I would never get my niece involved in this sordid scene. Gay people took the knocks. It wasn't as if prejudice would disappear. Maybe I'd better quit The Old Town, I thought with some sadness.

Deej muttered, "Whatever you do, don't call my dad. He'll kill me as it is. I should probably kill myself and get it over with."

I thought, that won't change either. Families will find out their kids are gay, teach them that they're immoral, wrong, mentally ill, so that when the kids are out on their own, they have zilch to sustain them when the rest of the world colludes to destroy them.

Lisa hadn't let go of Deej's arm, as if to restrain her from attracting attention.

Murph bent over as she walked and gasped from the rib pain each time she drew breath. "Make a run for it kid," she told Deej. "They'll ruin your life."

"Don't be silly," Lisa said as Deej looked around for an escape route. "They could shoot her down."

"Give her a chance, Lisa," Murph said. "The police can hurt me all they want—don't let them touch the kid."

"What about you, Lisa?" Deej asked with a desolate look.

"You can't help Lisa," Murph said. "Go."

At that moment, the tall, sad cop yelled at my neighbor, I guessed because he'd talked to me, and hustled him across the street. Deej took advantage of the distraction, pulled away from Lisa's hand, then spun free and took off behind us. She was small, fast, and not handcuffed. We all kept our eyes front, like a submissive queer chain gang, except for Carla Jean, who was throwing up in the other direction. I slowly shuffled forward to fill the empty space Deej left. I don't know how, but Murph managed to wink at me. Lisa's neck looked taut. She stood as if poised to turn and see that Deej had safely fled and, at the same time, stayed frozen so she wouldn't alert the police. What a time to be looking for love.

The tall cop came back across the street, his eyes toward Deej's escape route. Again, we exchanged glances. One corner of his mouth was up and his eyes looked triumphant for a split second. Van Eps, his name tag read. His face was kind of goofy: jug-eared, wide-mouthed, with a long nose that flared more to the left than to the right. Had Officer Van Eps created the distraction on purpose?

The captain was back and asked where the jailbait went. No one answered. He asked me then, no one else, while he stared into my eyes. Though I was with all my friends, this homosexual Jew shook so hard I might as well have been alone. Even so, I wasn't about to go along to get along and looked away, silent.

He took hold of my shoulders, shoved me to the side of the wagon, then, one huge hand at my brow, bashed the back of my head on the hard metal. The others told me later that, with each of four hits, the captain demanded I tell him where Deej was. Trust me—the blows hurt like nothing I'd ever experienced before. I saw, if not exactly stars, bursts of light. He jerked me back after each hit and I heard my neck crack each time. I tried to twist away from his giant, clamp-like hands. My knees gave out. He held me up and shook me. My brain moved inside my skull. Why was he so angry at us? May his *shiksa* wife leave him for another woman, I prayed.

The man's rage took him over completely. I was astonished at Rose's courage when they told me later that she'd leapt on the cop's back and clawed him away from me.

"Get off me, you dirty old bitch!" he'd yelled.

Ultimately it took two other cops to get the captain to release me. They shoved me inside the wagon. I was too disoriented by the battering to maneuver the step up. My toes caught and I pitched forward between the benches that lined the vehicle, onto the long slatted skid that covered its floor. I was so grateful the blows had stopped I never wanted to leave the sanctuary of that floor, despite the bloody scrapes on the heels of my hands. To anchor me to a seat, JoJo and Carla Jean sat me up and held hands across me. I recall the smell most clearly: Murph's sopping jacket, Carla Jean's sick breath, years of sourness soaked into the wood benches, my own sweat.

I remember as if I dreamed it that Carla Jean, much more sober by then, said, "I hope to God Deej got away. Could she get expelled from college for this?"

"God?" Rose asked, her voice hoarse from crying. "This wouldn't happen if there were a God."

I could see a fuzzy Murph. She wiped her shirtsleeve under her nose and started to talk, then cleared her throat. "I've got a frog in my throat," she said to cover her emotion. "Don't let them take your faith from you, Rosie."

Lisa cradled Paul's head on her lap and held her scarf against his bloody face.

The ride was short. My head hurt so much I threw up between the wagon and the station.

"The perverts are here!" hollered a cop who stood outside with a cigarette.

"Up yours," Murph rasped. Her arms hugged her ribs. She'd left her handsome, ruined jacket in the wagon, yet streams of sweat seeped from her hairline.

Now, as she reached to steady herself with the stair rails that led into the station, the plain-clothes guy, who seemed to be the captain's right-hand man, said, "Get inside, you damned battle-ax," and brought the butt of his gun down on her already-crushed right hand. There was a horrible sound—Murph in agony. I don't know how she stayed upright.

I was in such pain and so dizzy, Carla Jean and JoJo supported me into the station. Dr. Everett told me to lie on a bench and stay still.

A reporter shot pictures. His flashbulbs blinded me. The cops stopped him before he could get shots of Paul's bloodied face.

Dr. Everett, who a few hours ago convivially had donated a case of champagne to the dinner, was beside me. He'd staunched Paul's bleeding and broken ranks to demand more ice for Murph's hand. He got ice for the back of my head. The reporter zeroed in on Paul again. Paul, barely able to form words with his broken face, begged the reporter not to take his picture. The reporter's response was to get a shot of Paul, bloody hand outstretched in supplication as Dr. Everett held him.

Fewer women gathered at The Old Town, so they fingerprinted us first. Dr. Everett objected when the finger printer told me to get up. Officer Van Eps, the sad cop, in a rough voice, told me to get lost. I could see my horror from the last hour reflected in his eyes.

"And take this wreck with you," he added. He hauled Paul up by the armpits and pushed him toward me. I tried to thank the cop with my eyes, but he looked toward the reporter and made a slashing motion across his neck. Once more, the reporter put his camera down.

"Thank God they don't want anyone to see us. They might get stuck paying our medical bills," Paul sort of hissed. He held half-red paper towels to his face. Still, blood slid along his jaw. He had difficulty staying upright too. His eye was already closed. I wondered if his sight would be affected long-term. "They've got us over a barrel because they know we can't report this."

I told him about Officer Van Eps.

He managed to mumble, "If some of the bad cops find out, they'll make him their plaything. He'll have to leave his job." I asked what he meant, truly puzzled, and leaned close to hear his answer. "Oh, girlfriend," Paul said. "Policemen have come to my door after a raid. They had my address and knew I was gay. You figure it out."

The back of my head, my neck, and now my heart hurt so horribly I wanted to give up. My faith in human nature was, at that moment, as shattered as Paul's face.

JoJo, a circle of flesh around one eye already going purple, got on her high horse and ordered me to go to the emergency room. Carla Jean and Lisa pleaded with me to get checked with Paul. I didn't dare say it aloud—I had to think of the bindery. I wasn't the only one who'd be hurt if we lost business. Dr. Everett told me not to spend the night alone. Since I'd already decided I wouldn't ask for help from my niece, and the neighbors had my dog, I tried to come up with one person in the whole stinking world who I could comfortably ask for help. Maybe Geri—but, no, anyone other than Geri or the others I'd brought out or gone out with and who had moved on, usually with my blessings.

There wasn't anyone. I had work to do the next day anyway, work I could do with my office door shut, so I called a cab from a phone booth outside the station. The driver would take Paul to the hospital downtown and deliver me to the plant. I had a cot stored there for sick employees. If I got worse, they'd find me in the morning. I'd be fine,

I decided, it was only a headache. I'd be able to get money out of the bank for Murph and Rose's bail.

"Let her be," Murph told JoJo and Carla Jean. She sat on a bench with them, all handcuffed like felons.

"Get out of here," Murph told Paul and me, "while the getting's good." Her breathing was shallow, but her job gave her a mass of muscles and she was used to pain. Her hand, already swollen, must hurt like hell. Would she ever be nimble enough to embroider again?

Norman said, "I'd give you a key for the bar if they hadn't taken it from me."

I promised to get help if my symptoms worsened and to make sure Hugh called a locksmith for the bar. Hugh would already have contacted a straight lawyer friend. None of the local gay lawyers would help us; they were too scared they'd get tarred by the same brush.

"And tell that neighbor of yours to keep an eye on you," Dr. Everett instructed me as I helped Paul out the door.

By Sunday morning I still saw things blurry and couldn't keep food down. Me, not keep food down? That was a switch. If I sought help, would they believe I fell down the stairs while walking my dog?

I was bad enough off all these hours later that I walked the block to the emergency room where I got x-rays, stitches, and diagnoses for whiplash and a bad concussion. I was forbidden to drink even the little alcohol I was used to and didn't go back to the bar for a month. The doctor told me I'd be depressed and, trust me, he wasn't kidding.

CHAPTER TEN

I t was like this," Murph said about a month after the raid when most of us were back at the bar.

Her hand and ribs still healing, she tried to smile and was quick to tell me she was being held together by spit and Aspergum. Her hand was still swollen, discolored, and disfigured. Her left hand held her ginger ale. When I asked about the damage, she said the doctor was worried about the nerves, and she showed me how she'd never be able to straighten her ring finger all the way. Now that her cast was off she could exercise so the hand wouldn't stiffen.

"It's just plain wrong to break a gay gal's hand," she said with a wink and a good try at a smile.

She looked like she'd lost a quarter of her weight. The skin on her neck hung slack, like an old person's. I knew that laundry workers at the hospital were not unionized and Murph's health insurance ended with her vacation days. On the one hand, she couldn't afford to pay for the initial procedures, much less more repairs. On the other hand, if she didn't go back to the specialist, she couldn't do her job, or anything else she'd ever done, without pain.

Without funds, Rose and Murph spent extra time inside. Fortunately, the judge set bail low; he acted like the whole raid was a nuisance and seemed to know we weren't the ones who hurt anybody. Paul showed up for court in a wheelchair after days in the hospital where doctors tried to save his eye. Half of his face was still behind white bandages. The bones of his eye socket and right temple had been broken and displaced. He couldn't chew and still couldn't talk in more than a mutter. I dipped deep into my savings account to free Rose. It took longer to find the cash for Murph because I'd always poured any money I didn't need to live on into the bindery. What I made on a job we'd finished plus what Norman kept in his kitty for unanticipated expenses got her out.

I was nervous about returning to The Old Town. I missed the old gang, so I asked my neighbor to take care of Colonel Mustard should the bar get raided again and screwed up my courage, what was left of it, to cross The Avenue. I'd also feared Murph would be ashamed to return after the humiliation she'd experienced. Nevertheless, she was at her post, with her ginger ale, and told anyone who would listen of her adventures in jail.

"That first night," Murph said, stopping now and then only to gnaw her lip, a practice I'd never seen her indulge before, "they piled us into a holding cell. Two beds hung from the walls. The bathroom was an open toilet and spigot on the other side of the room, a drain in the floor. The police took the guys downstairs to the jail right away. They won't talk about it, so you know it was bad. I wish Spence had been on duty at the jail that night. Seneca works there too, in the office. By the grace of God, one of the cops is a friend of Spence's so he was able to intervene a bit."

Poor Murph, I thought. Paul and I were lucky: because of our injuries we didn't get records and didn't have to spend a minute behind bars. I know Paul says he looks like he had a stroke, but his smile is adorable, lopsided like that. It's the droopy eye that I suspect will turn the boys off. As for me, I'm depending on what Dr. Everett told me about recovery being slow, because I'm not as sharp as I once was and I found I lost patience with everyone and everything, including life.

Murph sighed and took a swig of her soda, then went on with her story.

"One by one, Lisa, Carla Jean, JoJo, and the other women bailed out, leaving Rose and me. Oh, the stench of that cell. Every human excess had left its stain on the floors, the wall, in the air. It smelled like the inside of an unkempt toilet bowl. I said to Rose, trying to keep her spirits up, 'So, I finally get to live with you.' She burst into tears. 'Did I say something wrong?' I asked. Rose shook her head. She told me, 'You were always trouble, Murph. From the day they caught us skipping CYO till tonight, trouble finds you.'"

Murph's face looked like a model's posing for a portrait called "Grief."

"I admitted she was right. Then she told me, 'Why do you think I went off with Vi? She was a good Catholic woman except for loving me. We went to church every Sunday and confessed our love to the priests every Friday before I made our fish dinner. Oh, Vi, look what you've gone and done by dying so young.' I held her while she cried for her dead lover and, believe me, I should go to confession myself for the pleasure I took in holding her."

Murph waved her glass in the air with her good hand and sighed over the empty until JoJo brought another.

"Tell her, JoJo. Tell her how you haven't seen hide nor hair of Rosie at The Old Town since the night of the raid."

JoJo nodded in agreement and backed away, quickstepping, wordless. She'd never been a big talker, but now—now she worried me. She'd taken some knocks to the head too and one eye was still angry with burst blood vessels. I hadn't seen her dimple since my return to The Old Town.

Murph spoke again. "I finally got my Rosie back in town and now she's gone." She looked at me and put her swollen hand up. "Oh, not for good. She still lives in her room and we visit." She sighed. "Rose is mad as a wet hen. She paces and paces her room, plotting vengeance. Damning the city to hell. Reciting letters she wants to write. She's even mad at Vi for dying, mad at herself for being an odd one, as she says."

Someone played the jukebox. We waited to see what the song would be. With Murph's depression like a sonic boom through the place, I was glad when the song was cheerful. Murph raised her voice and called, "Play it louder! Louder still! Let's dance at this wake!"

Tittering came from the bar. *Murph is in her cups again*, I could hear them thinking. It was only her intimates who knew that, aside from an occasional celebratory root beer, she drank ginger ale exclusively, preferably Buffalo Rock Ginger Ale. She'd found it on a trip through the South, liked its zippy taste, so Norman ordered it by the case for her.

"She says she won't be seen in public with me and she won't set foot in a bar ever again. That was a humdinger, to learn she'd never been in a bar, much less a gay bar. She loved it here, loves you all. Now she sits in that little room looking at pictures of places she visited with Vi and pictures of her dead family everywhere, and grieves even harder than she did when I brought her here to help her get done with the mourning."

She sipped, looked at the big window of glass bricks at the front of the bar, where lights and shadows passed. "I even offered to go to church with my Rosie. She told me she'd rather watch mass on the TV in her room. She's lost weight although she feeds us both since I lost my job. Vi had a good life insurance policy through the veterans. Rose wants to find a job so she can put the money in a bank for her retirement. There's no telling if she'll ever be able to get a job in this town now. And if I don't go back to work soon, I'll lose Frank Goodlette's room."

Two clean-cut men, one leaving, the other arriving, greeted each other in the doorway with a hug.

"Bring it inside, boys," JoJo called.

Murph went on. "Rose picks at her food. I wish there was someplace else for her to go, other people for her to return to." She grimaced as she had when her ribs hurt. "I never meant her harm and that long night in jail really did her in. She can't think of anything else. I don't know if I'm more afraid she'll hurt another person or herself."

The stately Lisa came through the door and settled on a stool, but no one greeted her effusively. No one greeted her at all. Murph wasn't the only one down in the dumps. The Old Town Tavern atmosphere I loved was no longer there. Was it gone forever?

"It's not that I thought Rose would fall into my arms the minute she came back to Hansfield. She was a widow—is a widow, for crying out loud. Whatever the outside world calls her. She was lucky no one claimed Vi—the Derizzis only wanted Vi's money and property—so Rose could tend to her at the hospital and bury her as she wished." Murph let out a bitter guffaw. "Now it's me she's charged with the death detail. You know that Vi went to a veterans' cemetery? She was in communications in the war. Rosie said she had them play taps and all. She has Vi's folded flag in its own case. Of course Rose can't lie beside her as she never served, so she wants to be put near her own family in the cemetery outside Hansfield.

"All this she told me that long, sleepless night in the holding cell. My hand and ribs kept me awake. I got no medical attention after the ice back at the bar. Rosie's heartsickness wouldn't let her sleep in such a place. What must we have looked like, talking all night, sometimes her head in my lap for a pillow, sometimes sitting side by side—two depraved criminals?"

Of course I laughed at the thought, as Murph meant me to.

"At least we had the cell to ourselves. They brought men past us, drunken, sometimes bloody men cursing in foreign languages, some of them. Many were dark-skinned, the white ones doughy and belligerent or scrawny as weasels. All of them spitting bullets they were so mad to get caught doing whatever they'd done. I was ashamed: we looked no better than those thieves and brawlers in the eyes of the world."

Murph wiped tears from her eyes with her drink napkin.

"My Rosie," she went on. "You can't get more innocent or more honest than Rosie Callaghan. They might as well have snatched her heart from her body and let every one of those criminals tread on it. You could see how broken she was. It only started with Vi's sickness and death. I brought on the humiliation and the insults, the fingerprinting and the mug shots, the handcuffs and the hoosegow."

Lisa toasted us from the bar and shook her head, in sympathy, I assumed. Murph didn't notice.

"Life can't all be singing and dancing, can it? I should be thanking my lucky stars there's a Rosie still on this earth. She could have been the deceased." Murph's grin looked forced. "Maybe I should stay home with her and away from the bar too. What else is there? What else could there ever be for the likes of us?"

Murph, her own napkin soaked from crying, took mine. She was as schmaltzy as someone who'd been drinking. "God bless you all," she said, "for being my family."

Norman came out from the kitchen and flung himself into a chair, wiping sweat from his brow. He'd suffered cuts to his head and a gash across his chin, which had hardened to a red scar.

"Gawd!" he said. "The renters who moved out left the apartment a pigsty. I cleaned for hours!"

"You little mollycoddle," Murph said, and gave him a push. "You reek of Mr. Clean. Is women's work too hard for our boy?"

Norman pretended to lose his balance.

"It is hard work, my dear woman. And I no longer have you to help."

"Help?" Murph exclaimed. "I can't even help myself." Her eyes squeezed shut in pain when she tried to make a loose fist.

Norman stared at her, big-eyed. He said nothing for a long minute. Without a smile, he said, "This raid-iation is killing us, all of us."

Our very own miniature catastrophe, I thought in silence.

"No," Norman said. "I don't want you to clean up after my renters in the other apartment upstairs. I want you to be my renters."

"I can't afford your real estate," Murph replied with some emotion. "I wish I could!"

"Not just you," Norman said, with an excited waving of his hands. "You and someone else. It's a two-bedroom. We've got to stick together. With you upstairs, we'd have another set of eyes. I'd make it affordable. This building isn't much more than a write-off at the moment, with the neighborhood like it is. Thanks to Carla Jean's help with the down payment, Hugh's salary almost pays our mortgage. JoJo's wages come from the bar's earnings. But, who knows, maybe the beatniks will start new crafty businesses like the shoemaker's shop and make pottery and sell arts and crafts. The young people have already decided the army-navy store is stylish. The Old Town area could get trendy."

"Next you'll select my roommate for me, won't you?" Murph said, her teasing mirthless.

"What about Lisa?"

"She loves her place."

"Deej?"

"I'm too old for her shenanigans."

"I know! Your friend Rose!"

Murph slumped against the banquette. "My Rose live above the bar where she lost her pride? In the building that's a target for the cops?"

Norman said, "I want to make up for that."

"It wasn't your fault. You helped bail me out."

"It happened at my bar. We put our customers at risk somehow. I don't understand why the cops are going after us and no other bar."

"Your customers pick The Old Town, don't we?" Murph asked.

Norman let a fist fall on the table. "We'll figure something out. You need a place to live and I need good tenants."

"Maybe I like living in a rooming house, Miss Norma Jean. My ma took in roomers during the Depression while us kids shared beds all in one room. There was no shame to it. Maybe I like not preparing meals and cleaning one room instead of four. Maybe I like to see the waitresses at the diner. Maybe I don't want to live in the same space as someone else." She gave a scornful laugh. "Maybe my landlady won't decide to toss me out on my ear after all. Dear God, forgive me for being who I am." Murph turned to look at me. "Do you know what my landlady said when she saw my picture in the paper? She claimed I'd turned her house into a place of degradation. She won't have her grandkids visit her till I leave." She shook her head. A streak of gray had become prominent at her left temple.

Norman looked thoughtful. "I don't think your landlady will change her mind any time soon. Have you ever lived with someone else?" he asked.

Murph rubbed her eyes. "Sorry," she said when she stopped. "I don't sleep much nights. I even heard a freight train rumble by about four a.m. Aspirin doesn't do a thing for this hand misery. May that cop burn in hell."

"Oh, no, you don't. You're not getting away with changing the subject on me," Norman said, wagging a finger.

"You think you can read my mind, don't you?"

Norman's voice lost its usual girlish shrillness when he answered. "No, Murph. Just your heart."

Murph shrugged her wide shoulders. "Of course I've lived with other people."

"Besides your family?"

She glared at Norman.

"Like who then?" Norman asked.

Murph looked annoyed. "I don't kiss and tell."

Norman leaned forward, pretending unbearable suspense.

She looked again toward the window, dark like a worn window shade that lets pinpricks of light into an unlit room. "In the end, I always knew it wasn't the love I wanted, the love I had for Rose, the love I could never match again."

"How long did you live with them?"

"None over six years, and she worked outside Boston so she was gone most weeks."

"What did she do?"

"Put an end to my job!" She nodded. "She hired attendants for coin-operated laundries. Traveled all over New England. Hers was the first chain of Laundromats and also the first to put in attendants. I was trying to make a living cleaning clothes, as I am today. I was eating, sleeping, and breathing the solvents we use, lifting other people's dirty underwear in and out of a machine that swallows eighty pounds of the stuff at a time."

"Is that why you broke up?"

"Oh, that." Murph shrugged, then made a face filled with pain. "It was a relief to be free of her."

"Not your type?"

"Who could be my type after Rose? That one was small and dark, nuts about me. It was lovely, but my heart was otherwise occupied."

"And don't I know it," Norman said, drawing his lips into thin lines. He caught Murph's expectant look and explained. "You never know what you'll get till he moves in with you. If he was the guy who always kept his cool, he loses his temper at everything that doesn't go entirely his way. If he was a 'creative' type who always insisted on paying his way, he'll suddenly lose his secure job and promises a new one will come knocking at his door while he's 'researching' soap operas because he's going to write one, act in one, or produce one with your money."

Murph nodded like a woodpecker on a pole. "For a while I lived with an artist. The apartment smelled like oil paints and turpentine all the livelong day. She was a looker. Couldn't keep my eyes off her. One day I came home to a finished painting—her only one in all our time together. She announced that she hadn't been to work for three weeks so she could stay at home and finish the painting. She expected me to tell her it was worth losing the income. Did I? No, not on my nickel you don't make your masterpieces. Not long after that she found a new patron."

"Was she any good?" Norman asked.

"She was very talented—oh, you mean the art?" Murph tried to make a joke for the first time since I'd come in. "How would I know? I can tell you that she's got the same paintings up for sale at the street fair year after year."

"Which was your worst?"

"Oh, the older one. I was, let's see, twenty, I think. Rose had gone off with Vi and here was this married lady, must have been in her forties. She was a real knockout and so caring, like a mother. Got me a job where she worked. I needed that caretaking then, and I stayed with her a couple of years. Then, all of a sudden, I couldn't breathe. I discovered I'd become a complete infant, dependent on her for the least little thing. If we hadn't needed the money, she'd have locked me in the house—the house she lived in with her husband—and a gorgeous big house it was. Never let me out of her sight. The bathroom door had to be open in case I fell in."

Norman laughed vigorously at that and asked why Murph and Rose didn't work out.

Murph gave a whopper of a sigh. "Rose says we aren't suited. I don't know how that could be since God Himself made us for each other. Why put her in my life, only to have her go to Vi?" Norman topped off her ginger ale while Murph went silent. "And then I brought her back only to be scared off by a raid? Was that some kind of test?"

"If it was, it tested all of us."

"And how did you score on your test, fearless leader?"

I curled my hand and put it to my mouth to stifle a laugh at the thought of Norman as fearless and a leader.

He passed his fingers through his hair, as always uncovering his bald spot as he did. Norman was not a tall man, and the roly-poly belly he was growing made him look shorter, even seated. "We haven't been raided in years. We're always good to the police and never had any complaints, except a few from the apartment upstairs," he amended, giving the ceiling an exasperated look. "We make a point to be ready, though, with bail money in the freezer inside the Swanson TV Dinner box. We know these things can happen. Hugh made it up to our apartment, waited out the cops, then locked up the bar and came for me. Apparently straight neighbors looked after the bar until it was safe for Hugh to come out of hiding. See? That's your proof that we don't disturb anyone here. The straights protect us. None of the gays can afford to do that. "

"But inside, Norman," Murph said. "Didn't you think someone came and took a slug at your soul?"

"Oh, you mean that gnarled little thing that fell out of my pocket when the boys greeted me in that cell?" He appeared to shudder. "How frightened was I after the guard shoved me in there like I was a wild animal and announced for all to hear that I was a fairy? The cell door clanged shut behind me and my bowels let go. Embarrassing, yes, and I was so proud of them! No one came near me. Then I prayed Hugh would hit only green lights on his way with the bail."

"You must have been terrified. I know I was."

"No question. Terrified, humiliated, alone, helpless, defeated, stripped down. I was sweating and shitting and speechless. I could *not* form words in my head. I could *not* use my hands because, an exciting extra for the other men, I was left cuffed with my hands behind my back. I could do nothing except lie there, stinking like an animal."

"And you always so spotless, with your Mr. Clean. They couldn't find a worse way to torture you," Murph said.

Norman's face was anguished. "The only thing that made me a little bit human was my imagination. I imagined dying there on the cold floor. I imagined a kind soul lifting me up and protecting me; I imagined being onstage in drag and that my voice, my real voice, was exactly like Eydie Gorme's and Hugh's like Steve Lawrence's, and we were knocking audiences dead all over the world."

What resilient wonders we are. In his own bottomless pit, Norman saved his sanity with a drag fantasy.

"When they released me I couldn't meet Hugh's eyes, though he was all kindness and apology not to have gotten there before they locked me up. It took a while—it's still taking a while—to think he could love me after he saw me like that. I know he believes I've rejected him. I can't get into bed with him yet."

"Why?" Murph asked.

Norman shook his head. "While it's true nothing physical happened in that cell, I think I had a taste of what a raped woman goes through."

"Oh, Norman," Murph said, and put her good hand on his.

He leapt up. "The show must go on!"

After he left she whispered, "I hope he talks to someone more about the raid. This fake cheerfulness worries the living daylights out of me. Norman's the kind who decides to end the pain for all time." The same thought crossed my mind, but about Murph, not Norman.

"Rose, though, she was red-faced furious. Fit to be tied. I could see her try not to be mad at me in that little cell where the guards could hear. It was too much for her. She blew up."

"Now I understand why she doesn't want to share a place with you," I said.

"She gave me Hail Columbia. Went on about how I'd wasted my life and got nowhere and the only good thing I'd ever done was let her go. At this point I'm the Antichrist. How as a child I was always the finest, the bravest, the smartest, and she'd expected—she didn't say what she'd expected of me, only that I was a sore disappointment. One minute she yelled all this, to the great amusement of the guards, and the next moment she was asleep, her hot head in my lap where I sat on the hard bottom bed. I spent the rest of the night biting my bottom lip to stay awake, afraid Rose would take it the wrong way if I smoothed her baby-fine hair or if I so much as brushed my left hand against her or dared to worship her face with a fingertip. I am who I am, I whispered to Rose. With you, I told my sleeping beauty, I could have been anything. Then all my strength went to live from one day to the next. I had no stake in a future without you.

"I didn't blame her, I only blamed myself. I was convinced I had no value without Rosie by my side and here she was, letting me protect her sleep while I feared the unruly passion that would wake in me if Rose touched me with any tenderness at all."

You didn't hear a peep out of Norman or me. We also didn't take our eyes from Murph. This was a side of Murph we didn't know, the earnest unlocked version you sometimes saw when people got drunk. Our sober drinking buddy wasn't known for letting down her guard.

"As I'd expected, when Rose woke up she did so with a start and it was only my hand, finally curled to the shape of her head, that kept her from hitting the bed above us." Murph held up her right hand and I saw that the wrist was swollen too. "As the trusting sleep left her eyes and reality bled into them, I saw a misery I'd never wanted to see.

"That's when the morning jailer came to tell us Rockie was there to bail Rosie out."

CHAPTER ELEVEN

Rose had been pale almost to the point of translucence when I got her out. She looked as if she'd aged ten years overnight. I knew Murph would give me a hard time the rest of my life if I didn't get Rose her freedom first.

Though I trembled from emotional shock and the pain from my head, I took Rose home in a cab and walked her to her room. Someone at the hospital told me not to lie down after a head injury, so instead of going to my apartment to hit the sack, I went over to the bar to drum up the money for Murph's bail.

"After Rose left I was a bit peaked," Murph said, "and lay down to get what I could of the sleep I'd missed while she was close." Norman moved around behind the bar. I could see, by his sharp intakes of breath at the worst parts of Murph's story, that he was all ears. "They gave me small meals, aspirin for the breaks and bruises they denied causing, let me use the toilet in the hallway—the one in the cell was broken, thank goodness. By nightfall, ignoring how sore I was and the pain in my hand and wrist, I had the guards joking and laughing whenever one of them walked by. They insisted they knew nothing each time I asked what was going on and how soon I could see a doctor.

"It was after midnight when they brought me two things. One was the headlines. A guard read it to me, laughing. 'Mayor Purges City of Homos! In a tavern known to attract homosexuals, beatniks, and other lowlifes, city police rousted...' He read the list of all of the people arrested. Rose Murphy's name hit me like an explosion of dynamite. I knew my goose was not simply cooked, it was overdone, with her. I fully expected her to be gone from the rooming house, gone from her hometown, never to be heard from again.

"The other item they brought was a drunken straight woman who'd never see forty again. She had long hair dyed to look red-brown. Her lipstick was garish, to say the least, and she wore fake eyelashes along with other eye gunk, much of which had rearranged itself around her face instead of wherever she'd aimed. One of the guards called her a hellcat. I climbed to the upper bunk and lay there.

"It was the wrinkled cleavage that got to me," Murph said with a laugh. "The poor woman had not aged gracefully and deodorant had not been on her shopping list for a very long time. She was drunk as a skunk, almost ready to pass out. The guard took her to the bathroom when she threatened to get sick. She looked at me as she came back through the cell door.

"'You have to be shitting me!'" she said. "'Since when do you put girls in with guys?'

"'That's not a guy. It's one of those queers we picked up in a raid night before last,' the guard said.

"'You telling me that's a female?'"

I winced in humiliated sympathy with Murph.

"'Yes, it is,' the guard said, and gave the drunk a push into the cell. 'Have a good time, girls!'

"I was sweating bullets from the pain by then, so I said nothing when my cellmate broke into a rant. The alcohol fumes that came out of her mouth made her words like fire. Up on the top bunk I lay back. I didn't want to see her face ugly with hate. For crying out loud, this was a common criminal—she'd begged the guard not to take away her driver's license. The guard laughed at her too. 'This is your sixth DWI, and with your kids in the car. Your license is the last thing you should worry about losing.' 'You'll tell me if my baby is okay?' she yelled after him. Turning into the cell, she said, 'There was so much blood.'

"Not an hour later, this paltry excuse for a human being told me I was a filthy pervert who should be locked up for life. After the dressing down I got from Rose the night before, this criticism from the dregs of the earth and pain from the beating—by now swords plunged into my hand and ribs—

"I was convinced I'd died and gone to hell. The city couldn't have found a more demoralizing cellmate. Surely it was done as part of their whole get-rid-of-the-homos campaign. I turned my back on her and slept until you came and got me."

What a shambles Murph looked when we got into the November sunshine. I'd brought her a warm, clean jacket and draped it gingerly over her shoulders. She shivered out of control and cradled her hand in her other elbow. She even let me support her weight as she took her first steps into daylight.

"I took a long shower, scrubbed all seventeen yards of me with one hand, shared bathroom be damned," Murph said. "Rose didn't answer my knock, so through her door I asked her to go out for a meal with me. All I got back was a faint no. The double blow of her losses made me fret. I knew she had pills her doctor gave her to help her through losing Vi. Would she swallow them? I asked if she was okay. 'Let me be,' she answered. Her voice was so unlike her own I thought she might have company. Or be dying.

"I threatened to get the landlady. Rosie said the door was unlocked. I never expected to stumble into a room dark as night. She'd pulled the shades and hung a blanket across both windows. Rose lay on her bed, a musty closed smell like a cloud around her, hands folded across her chest. I might have walked into a wake.

"'Come on, girly,' I said. I took the folded hands into my own and pulled her up. She'd lain there like that since she got home. 'It's not good for you,' I told her. 'It doesn't matter,' she said.

"I don't know what made me say it, but out it came, the way her mother used to say it. 'Get up, Rose Bridget Callaghan!' She got up. I took her to the diner for a nice chicken dinner and made her laugh. God knows how I got my funny bone to work. It was the best thing I could have done for myself, too, except for my hurting ribs. It was a trial to feed myself left-handed. It stopped me thinking about how, if I couldn't pay my fine, they'd put me back in the clink and how, if I wanted to challenge the fine or the arrest, what judge would see things my way? Even the fruity judge who was so easy on us would protect himself, not me."

Norman and I both shook our heads at the uselessness of fighting back.

"I'll give you money for the fine, Murph," Norman said.

"No, I couldn't take it from you, Norman. You already helped with the bail. I know you don't scratch much of a living out of this place, and Hugh's already paid your own and the bar's fines."

"Dear woman," Norman said, "don't for a minute think I'd be doing it for you. I'm the proprietor here and I want to protect my interests."

"How?"

"I hoped you'd ask that," Norman answered with a wink. "It's bad enough we made the papers for the raid. Business has been down almost by half. If we get paraded around the TV and radio stations because you've gone to trial, no one will dare come into The Old Town. Not to mention that we cannot—cannot—take a chance on Hugh's name getting out or poofter! There goes his chance for tenure."

"Well," said Murph, "you've got a point." I could see her struggle with herself. "Consider this your good deed for the year. The decade even."

Norman unlocked the cash drawer and started back with a blank check. Tipsy caught his apron and stopped him to whisper something. Norman raised his eyebrows and turned to watch some activity behind us. In the mirror I saw a very young-looking man pause to look back toward a man at the bar. The young man had short, dark hair, heavy eyebrows that gave him a smoldering look, and he wore a tight striped jersey, a windbreaker, and cuffed chinos. He strode on. The man who stood at the bar had thinning gray hair. He held a hat and carried a coat over the arm of his double-breasted business suit. He downed the last of his drink and followed the young man toward the back.

"You let me know the amount," Norman said. His worried eyes still followed the two men. When Murph hesitated he leaned her way and said, "If you get locked up, or stay away from the bar to save your pennies for the fine, how will I ever use up all that ginger ale?"

Murph laughed. Norman patted her cheek as he got up from our table and headed toward the men's room with his quick, light steps.

CHAPTER TWELVE

Norman pushed open the bathroom door and called out, "Yoo-hoo! Boys!"

Murph looked at me. Norman was without doubt breaking up a quick assignation.

"Stay right there, fag! Police!"

"Oh, no," Murph said.

Norman stepped back so quickly it must have been reflexive. He always kept a fifty-dollar bill in his shirt pocket. Candy for the cops, he'd explained. I saw him reach for it when a jersey-clad arm dragged him inside.

"Wait!" we heard him yell. "I came in to stop anything illegal."

I grabbed Murph's bony arm as she pushed back her chair. She shook me off. "I've had enough of this," she said.

Murph, in a blinding-white Boston Red Sox sweatshirt, starched slacks, and black loafers, always freshly polished though worn down at the heels, stormed to the back and, with her left arm, flung wide the men's room door.

The young cop was on his way out. He stuffed something in his pocket with one hand and shoved the older guy ahead of him with the other. The older guy's wrists were cuffed, his belt hung from its loops, his hat was backward on his head, and his coat rested on one shoulder. A hiked-up pant leg exposed a black sock garter.

After the cop and his prisoner left, Norman emerged and fell against Murph.

"Lord a mercy. I'm shaking like the last leaf on a tree."

Murph led him back to the table. JoJo dashed over; Lisa followed, concern on her face, despite the calm in her step. All I could do was pat his hand, while Lisa leaned over in her grand fashion and held Norman's head to her chest.

"Did what I think happened just happen?" JoJo asked.

Norman nodded. Sweat shone on his face. "I don't want that kind of thing in here. How dare that old fairy think he can meet a trick in our lav. How dare that cop use The Old Town to set up a bust. We've never allowed such goings-on."

JoJo, mouth drawn to one side, cheek undimpled, said, "Getting trapped when you trick goes with the scene for you guys."

"Oh!" Norman replied. "Like girls have never disappeared into the ladies'."

JoJo laughed. "Don't get your feathers ruffled, Norman. I never saw a cop lure a gay girl into the can. They have better ways to get at us, like taking away the school-district contract."

"They didn't," Lisa said. "You actually lost the contract?"

"Mysteriously," JoJo answered, disappointment in her sigh. "After the raid."

Lisa shook her head, eyes closed, as if she couldn't believe what she was hearing.

JoJo's face registered disgust. "Maybe they thought we'd leave gay cooties on the football trophies."

"And maybe if laws didn't outlaw us, we wouldn't have to resort to bathrooms in bars," Norman said.

JoJo said, "Bars invite that kind of behavior. If this town is out to get us for some reason, they can bust guys in here right and left."

Lisa said, "It's a good thing I already lost my job or I'd have to stay away."

"That's exactly what we're afraid of," Norman said, chin on his hands, looking gloomy.

"You haven't found work yet?" Murph asked.

Lisa emitted a sound that fell somewhere between a laugh and a sigh. "Not for lack of trying."

"I wish I could hire you here," Norman said. "We'd send JoJo outside to be a scout and you could man the bar."

"Maybe I'd woman the bar," Lisa said.

Norman looked puzzled. "What?"

"When JoJo's behind the bar, she doesn't turn into a man."

That sounded like something I'd say. I clapped Lisa on the back. "Trust me. If I employed office staff, you'd be on my payroll in the blink of an eye."

Norman was still frowning. "Woman, man, whatever you girls want to say. The problem is, I can only see what happens out front, not around the side or back of the building. I'm going to have to send JoJo out to sweep the sidewalks a lot."

"I can picture it now," JoJo said, her dimple finally coming up like the sun. "Me as bouncer, prowling the alley, shooing tough young men who could tie me in knots and roll me down the hill onto the railroad tracks with one hand." She closed her eyes and shook her head as if to erase that image, then got up from our table and went back to the bar.

Norman raised his chin, sniffed, and said, "I know there's tricking, but I draw the line at following through in our lav. I need to go call Hugh. If I hadn't had the fifty ready, I'd probably be in jail again and you'd all be out on the street. What is going on around here? Is the jukebox too loud? Do the neighbors see monkey business outside? Do we dump trash? Do they think we are trash?" He flung his arms wide as he went to the pay phone.

"I think the kid jinxed us." Murph rubbed at her bandage. "We lured her into a life of sin and debauchery, and God's got it in for us." She smiled. "That's my Catholic guilt talking. My insides are coated with frankincense from all the childhood years I spent at mass."

"You don't believe any of it now though."

"No, not a bit of it. Listen, that doesn't mean it never seeped into my pores. Or that Rose, besides turning my head and heart, couldn't win back my spirit."

"Mad woman," Lisa said, with a warm laugh. "That's no way to get to God, through falling for a woman."

Murph looked surprised. "What are you saying, darlin'? All those squares who convert to some religion because they want to marry— aren't they being lured to the light by their hormones?"

"That's different."

"How? Because we're gay? Love is love. When I love a woman I want to share her life, care about what she does, go where she goes. An hour a week in church isn't too much to ask."

Lisa looked at her and was quiet.

"Oh, I know," Murph said. "It's about more than the hour and the church. I can only do what I can do. If a woman believes in the Easter bunny, then I'm going to do my darndest to provide pretty eggs for her basket."

"I'm not sure that's real honest, Murph."

"Religion is not real honest, Lisa."

They were starting to step on each other's toes. Lisa knew enough to steer the conversation away from Murph's biggest bugaboo, the

Catholic church. She'd spend hours sitting at the bar expounding on the church's condemnation of gays. Murph said she'd met more than one priest with a boyfriend.

"Personally, I think we did Deej a favor," Lisa said, looking kind of helpless. I noticed for the first time that she must be saving her good clothes; she wore a sweatshirt with the zipper attractively low and a skirt I hadn't seen on the streets in years. Instead of her usual nylons, she had bobby socks on under short boots with squat heels.

Murph smiled. "Or maybe it was you that we did the favor for."

Lisa tried to hide her blush by taking a sip of her drink. "My favor doesn't seem to favor me," she said.

"Oh, you'll land her all right, if you want to," Murph told her. "You need to give her a long line right now and reel her in slow. She's got a lot of living to do before she'll settle down."

"If I'm here that long. I may have to move back with my parents in New York unless I find a job soon. I'll be collecting scrap metal like I did as a child, only not for the war effort this time—to support myself. I can't even ask for a reference from my old employer. They fired me for my so-called criminal record."

"You never know," Murph said. "They may not want to work with you, but sometimes these people will give a good reference out of self-righteousness about doing the right thing both coming and going."

"Do you think so?" Lisa seemed to consider her advice. "I'm not getting anywhere this way. I have no other references. I started with this company right after my divorce and never worked before, except at my ex-husband's company, which his parents own. That's where I met him, during my second year of college. Sometimes I think I might have been better off staying married. I lost my kid, can't admit to my past jobs."

"I'll give you a reference," I said. "We'll say you worked part-time for me while you had the other job. If I could, I'd hire every last one of you at Durable."

"You'd do that?"

"Before you can say Jack Rabbit, Lisa," I said. "We've got to help ourselves out. No one else will. I'm now an invisible owner at the bindery so we don't lose business. That reporter didn't take my picture. He did print my name in the paper. My niece deals with our customers now, while I hide out in my office."

Murph said, "The best thing that happened to any of us, Rockie, was you coming out. You're a gay United Way." I was pleased as punch to hear that. Murph touched Lisa's hand. "What'll you do, Lisa? You can't go back to a closet even in the anonymity of the New York crowds. You wouldn't survive."

Lisa shrugged. "For right now, the rent's paid, and I have a lot of canned meatballs and spaghetti and the time to make meals from scratch."

"You could always rent a room. Not at our place, of course. We have to be out by the end of the month and I haven't found anything that's fit to live in. I think rooming houses may become a thing of the past." Murph pretended, badly, to laugh. "Merry Christmas."

"I don't think I could live in a house full of strangers. Isn't it uncomfortable when you all eat dinner together?"

"Rose and I eat in our rooms and cook on forbidden hot plates. The landlady told us we can keep our rooms till the end of the month, no longer. She said she won't have us at her table or eating her food. Fend for yourselves, she told us. You'd think we tried to murder her barehanded."

Lisa said, "Someday, I want to be the one in charge. I want to lay down the rules, not some landlady or some man who thinks he owns me." She looked at the door where a streetlamp was on. The traffic light gave a green, then red glow. When I'd stood in the doorway for a breath of fresh air earlier, it made me smile with affection to see the lights in my apartment building as people came home from work. I loved having windows that faced the bar. "Someday," Lisa went on, "I want a home of my own, any kind of little house, enough for two women who like to be cozy."

Murph watched Lisa. "That's a dream I gave up long ago," she said to Lisa's profile.

Lisa turned back quickly. "Oh, Murph, don't give it up. Someone like you—steady, sweet, good-looking—you're a prize!" Her smile was both amused and wistful. "You even do laundry."

"And sew. Don't forget I sew."

"You do?"

Murph hung her head, wincing. "I hope to again. Someday."

I remembered the fine embroidery on Murph's dresser and her flair for design. It was tragic that her fingers weren't fit for intricate work anymore. She carried a small black rubber ball with her everywhere, trying to exercise her fingers back to normal.

"Then that makes you the perfect catch," Lisa said.

"Hell," I told Murph, "if you and I didn't go for the same types, I'd marry you!"

We laughed and Murph said, "A lot of good perfection does me!"

Hugh came in the front door and Norman rushed to him. They shared a fast, brotherly hug, then whispered together. Hugh gave Norman some cash and left again.

"He stopped at the bank," Norman told us. "I was out of payoff money. He's going to talk with one of the teachers at the law school about ways we might be able to protect ourselves. I'm hoping the guy has police connections and can find out why they have it in for us. Maybe somebody who really hates us got promoted and now has the authority to come after us?"

The paperboy hurled the newspaper at the glass bricks of the window again that afternoon. Ever since the raid, he'd obviously been trying to show his hostility this way. He was only about twelve and his scrawny arms couldn't have broken a pane of regular glass. I wanted to wring his parents' necks. That kind of reflex rage is practically hereditary. They teach them well from the day they first dress them in pink or blue and give them guns or dolls for their birthdays. Sometimes I wonder what makes the human race think it's so damn superior to other creatures. We may be capable of great achievements, but we're also capable of great destruction.

Norman gave the paper to Lisa as he did every day so she could check for jobs.

"Hey, Norman?" she called over to the bar.

Norman popped his head up from where he'd begun to wash glasses. "You called, darlin'?"

"Did you see the front page?"

"I was too upset to look."

Murph peered over her shoulder and pointed to a photograph. "That's our college!"

Lisa told them, "The college has raised enough funds to buy land for another parking lot. Where do you think they could get land close by?"

Norman went still. "Nowhere," he said with the slowness of dread.

No one spoke, or moved, for a full minute.

Then Murph said, "Unless they plan to tear something down."

CHAPTER THIRTEEN

We all lived close to the bar. I'd stayed across the street in The Avenue Arms for eighteen years, long before Hugh and Norman bought the bar. When I moved into a one-bedroom there, I tipped off JoJo and Carla Jean and they took the two-bedroom I'd shared with Geri until 1958. The bar has been a godsend since then. Hanging out there anchored me in a suddenly lonely world. Geri told me forever, then transferred her affections forever. At The Old Town I could love again, touch again, try to take care of my friends instead of a woman whose loyalty had been a figment of my imagination. I still had nightmares in which I slapped her, once, hard—something I would never even consider in real life—to wake her up to what she was leaving behind. Her new "true love" was an odious, self-serving rodent.

It was strange, seeing bar friends in their homes, seeing their personalities on their walls, in their furniture, and in their choices of where to live. If Murph and Rose teamed up they could together surely afford something better than a rooming house. Norman's apartment would be just the thing. Hugh told us the government started a housing program for renters last year. He went on about it and how the local housing authority would pay a big part of the rent while he and Norman would still own the place. Murph would qualify, he said, and Rose could pay her part to Murph so she wouldn't have to report Vi's insurance money, which might disqualify them.

Right after the start of the new year, 1962, Murph asked me to visit Rose. She was doing better, Murph said, although Rose couldn't stand to leave her room since the raid.

January northwest of Boston can be a bleak affair. The thrill of the first snow is long gone. A longing for spring and for an end to early darkness percolates. I worried about the birds, the feral cats, the lost dogs, the old people who fall helpless in the snow. Dr. Everett had said concussion breeds depression.

The part of town where we live is by the railroad station, a passage to and from other destinations. It's become home to a new kind of retail business. Beatniks, in their dark clothes, have poetry readings at the bookstore. The breakfast and lunch café put an espresso machine in, changed its name to The Den, and now stays open until one a.m., flooding the sidewalk with dark coffee smells, which I missed. The concussion, Dr. Everett told me, sometimes knocked out the sense of smell temporarily. I was ready for temporary to be over. The bookshop now stays open as long as The Den does and specializes in poetry, Edgar Cayce-type books, tarot cards, and posters. Salvador Dali was up there, along with Munch, Van Gogh, museum shows, and Stonehenge.

The railroad station sets the tone. Both melancholy and evocative, the brownstone station was constructed on two levels so the trains wouldn't interfere with horse carriages way back when. At night when I passed it, the lights seemed to beckon and the whistles sang of romance. Many an adventure I had at the end of long rattling trips to Boston and New York.

Rooming houses made sense in this district. When the likes of J.P. Morgan built rail monopolies, many homeowners were hungry to rent out rooms near the station. Of the few sizable homes left these days, some were called guesthouses, as if only wayfarers occupied their beds. A rooming house could be a rambling Victorian with tiny bedrooms, a Federal style with combination bed and living rooms, or even a weather-beaten wood building that looked like apartments or professional offices from the outside.

The place Murph and now Rose called home displayed white scrolled window pediments, an original mahogany door, and bay windows overlooking Pullman Street. The house was gray and would need new paint someday soon. Its windows sparkled clean in the sun.

In warmer weather, high-back wicker chairs painted royal blue and a two-seat swing occupied the deep porch behind the white wooden rail. The landlady really tried to make the house appealing to long-term renters like Murph and Rose—or, as it turned out, renters as much unlike them as possible. On the second floor, where Murph and Rose had rooms, was a bay-windowed space that was used as a common area, with magazines, the daily paper, and a bowl of fruit. Furnished with more porch wicker, this in white, it was an inviting room.

Stairs continued to disorient me as I recovered from the concussion, and I tended to sway every few steps. I rapped on Rose's second-story door. Her little home couldn't have been more different from Murph's. Whereas Murph drew her drapes, Rose kept drapes and windows wide open and winter light soared in like it was looking for a place to shelter for the season. Instead of the clutter in Murph's room, on her wall Rose had two magazine watercolors of Settlers River flowing through town and on into Chestnut Forest Park, winking reflections at people strolling on both banks. I drew a long breath for what seemed to be the first time since the raid; it was peaceful in Rose's room and I could imagine her pretty, a bit overpowering, perfume floating around me.

For all the room's cheeriness, Rose's hostess smile looked as if it cost a major effort. I spotted an angel-shaped perfume bottle on her dresser. She was dressed in a black skirt, a lilac blouse with a pattern of tiny yellow cherubs, and, tied around her neck like a cowboy's bandana, a short yellow chiffon scarf. She'd made herself up. Had she spruced up for company or to bring her spirits up?

I hugged her slight frame. Rose motioned me to a slipper chair while she perched on the edge of her bed. We talked about the weather, the house, everything except the bar. She brought over a photo album, then stood behind me as I turned the pages, showing me what she and Murph had looked like as newborn neighbors, toddlers and playmates, schoolgirls, at their first jobs in a bakery. Rose wore a hairnet over her flaming red hair; Murph was dusted entirely in flour. Rose's hair had lost some of that blaze, as if flour from her early years had settled on it permanently.

Soon after that shot, the geography of the photos changed. I assumed that was when she'd moved to be with Vi. I touched her arm.

"That was at the stone bridge over the brook at Lourdes in Litchfield. We made our little pilgrimage there every year." She pointed to her bedside table. "Those are some of the angels Vi gave me. One for every year. You know Vi was an attorney. She was in the city's legal department. I went to secretarial school in town, you see, and found work with a lawyer who happened to deal with Vi's department."

She fumbled into her bra for a hanky and quietly blew her nose, then wiped her eyes. "I still can't believe she's gone. Older than me, I know, but only sixty-three?" With a burst of anger she railed. "I know she would have lived longer had our lives been easier."

Tears came to my eyes too. Although, like Murph, I'd never met Vi, the depth of Rose's grief spread to me. We held each other and cried. Maybe I was crying about losing The Old Town, about the raid, about The Old Town's troubles, and about the ruthless conspiracy Carla Jean described that wanted to exterminate homosexuals the way the Nazis had killed Jews and homos and Gypsies and anyone else Nazi men despised or feared. I think people who hate us are afraid of us, though I don't know why.

In a voice reedy from recent crying, Rose turned to the next page in the album. She showed me black-and-white photographs of places they'd been. "We lived in a very old little house on a hillside. Vi inherited the house from her mother and father. I thought I'd be living in that house till the day I died. We put so much into the place. It was our hobby and our investment in the future, and now it's gone. Her family—the remaining Derizzi cousins—were ashamed of Vi. Except for one, her second cousin Phil. I came home from the office a few weeks after Vi died and they'd changed the locks on me. Everything the cousins didn't want was in the storage shed we built in the backyard. On the door was an envelope for me from a lawyer I never heard of, and I thought I knew them all, saying I had to give up the house. As if I was dirt under the mat! I planned to stay with Vi until the end of time, no matter what. I did stay until the end of her time, while her family ignored her. I don't know how I could have coped without Phil. He let me stay with him and tried to intervene. He was only a second cousin, though, so he had no say. We keep in touch.

"Vi knew better, yet kept putting off making a will. She was extremely private and hated to put anything about us in writing. She worried that naming me sole heir would reveal us to the world."

Extremely private, I thought, was the polite term for hiding so far back in the closet there was no light at all.

Rose leaned over the thin back of my chair and went on. "Neither of us guessed she'd die so young or so fast. We believed until her last day that she would pull through. I couldn't afford a lawyer once she was gone, and I knew Vi wouldn't want a fight or want me to impose on her lawyer friends. She'd move out before she'd chance being found out and embarrassing the Derizzis. Of course, they already had a nicer, bigger house, across town. I think, aside from the money, they wanted me out of sight. They'd never cared for Vi because she was—peculiar."

We went through the rest of the album. Her voice was angry again and her cheeks redder than her rouge. When I asked if she'd talked to her cousins, Rose said, "Talked? I begged. I said I'd pay rent. All my memories are in that house. This attack on The Old Town brings back everything I went through then. My life was stolen three times. Once when Vi died, once when I lost our home, and now my dignity's been stolen. I'd be ashamed to see Cousin Phil." She shook her head. I'd never noticed her angry before today, even during the raid. Of course, she could have been frothing at the mouth in fury for all the blanks in my memory of that night.

She startled me by saying, "Damn them to hell. Vi and I never missed church. The cousins never even had their little brats confirmed. We planned our vacations around visiting shrines. The last one we went to was Shrine of the Divine Mercy up in the Berkshires. This picture was taken there."

I patted the hand that held the album.

"Vi would have been destroyed if she'd been there for the raid. It's the kind of thing that could have gotten her disbarred. She'd be enraged and terrified at the same time. The two reactions would probably have frozen her. Run? Fight? Keep her head down and hope they'd give her a break? She might have been right behind Deej, taking off, and I'd be at her side, holding her hand as we ran. Or she could have been so fighting mad she'd announce that she was an attorney meeting with clients and try to talk her way out of it, bringing as many of us with her as she could. Whatever she did, she'd make it work. She could make anything work, from a bathroom sink to a municipal law."

She held her hand over her mouth. Talking must have brought back the horror of what she'd gone through.

"I didn't think I could get any lower than when she died. And again when the cousins stripped me bare of our possessions. To go through this, of all things, without her and at the same time be grateful she was spared it and then remember that we'd never have been in that bar, any bar, if she was alive. My heart, my soul, my insides are raked, scraped raw, and exposed. I see myself as a picture of a martyred saint." She bent her neck and looked downward. "I shouldn't because I'm no saint. I'm a sinner, a doomed sinner. I keep praying that neither Vi nor I go to hell for loving each other."

I was sensing that Rose liked the martyr role and wondered what it had been like for Vi, living with Rose. She seemed to be playing at being a lady in reduced circumstances, but you couldn't miss her rough edges. Her grammar, for one thing. She wore a little too much rouge, the wrong shade of eyebrow pencil, and her lipstick was on the gaudy side. I couldn't see Lisa making the same mistakes. No, Vi hadn't quite escorted Rose across the great divide between The Old Town and uptown.

I also saw no pictures of Vi displayed, only the albums. Was Rose afraid someone would jump to the conclusion that they'd been lovers? Vi wore her long hair up, rolled back from her forehead in her younger pictures, and she was in a skirt or dress in every photograph I'd seen.

After an hour or so we met Murph in the bay-windowed room and had tea. The landlady allowed a hot plate in there and gave Murph permission to use the room one last time. I scraped Cheese Whiz onto Ritz crackers. There was a console television in a mahogany cabinet and a matching, well-used coffee table. The floor was green linoleum that, with the play of the sun through white-on-white tatted curtains, looked underwater.

No different at home than in the bar, Murph sat in a wide-backed white wicker chair, legs apart like a fellow would. She looked like a shadow of herself. "How's my Gloomy Gus today?" she asked. She'd warned me that Rose now was completely different from Rose before the raid. I was glad because I didn't understand Murph's passion for her childhood friend. Sure, it was hard to forget a first love and it was natural to want to protect her now. Was her attachment to Rose a shield against getting involved with another woman?

Rose seemed more angry than gloomy, other than that little episode of tears. And here was Murph, a walking reminder of the distance from their childhood friendship to their middle age in a rooming house, a bar, a jail cell. They both had call to be gloomy, if you asked me.

Rose might have taken offense at Murph's greeting, or maybe she was determined to keep up a brave front. "I've been plotting my revenge," she said. "I can't do anything about Vi dying, or about her heartless relatives, or even about your injuries, but I'm not happy with myself. Crying in front of a guest. That was unkind and I'm sorry."

"I'm sure you're not the first woman to cry on Rockie's shoulder, Rosie. I might have done it a time or two myself."

Murph poured tea and handed it around. I commented that she was getting by nicely without the use of her right arm.

"I have to be good for something," she told me.

"Oh, Murph. You're very good," Rose said. "The best."

Looking at the linoleum, Murph missed the exasperated loving in Rose's eyes. I could hear her thinking: *Not good enough for you, Rosie.* Was Rose's look, I wondered, affection for a childhood friend, or growing into something more? I dismissed the idea of anything more without another thought. My crazy heart picks up tremors in the air around other people, and it sensed none around these two.

Rose went on. "I want to enlist you both in a little scheme I'm cooking up," she said. "Vi was, after all, an attorney in this state. She left some close friends grieving. Lawyer friends. Lawyers can't work magic all the time, or change the way the police operate. Some do know a great deal about defending underdogs. Two old friends have business here tomorrow and I'm going to have lunch with them." She whispered, "They're like us."

"Aw, Rosie," Murph said, "you know the deck is stacked against us. We're fortunate to have a gay bar and we'll be lucky if Norman and Hugh can keep it open. Maybe it's time to ask your old pal Frank Goodlette for help? I hear he's a shoo-in for mayor."

"I don't know, Murph. Asking for his help for a bunch of homosexuals? He's the kind who would look to see that I'm registered with the Democratic Party."

"I take it back. That was a dumb idea," Murph said. "He'd probably remember your family was union."

"In which case we'd better start praying the landlady doesn't kick us out before we find places to move."

I was about to tell them they could bunk in with me.

"Prayer." Murph scoffed. "I have trouble believing a smart woman like yourself believes in that guff."

Rose went stiff. She looked like she was rolling bullets on her tongue. "Guff?" she said, then repeated, her tone outraged, "Guff?"

Bite your tongue, Murph, I thought.

Murph responded with an emphatic, "Guff." She turned to me. "Faith is not something I was born with and Rosie, try as she might, never could teach it to me."

"That doesn't give you the right to mock mine," Rose retorted.

"I wasn't trying to mock you, Rosie. I am honestly perplexed. This church of yours condemns you for loving Vi. It thinks you should spend eternity in a hell it made up to keep the living in line. It takes your money so the Vatican boy-os can live in splendor while a sinfully huge number of the faithful starve in rented rooms, tin shanties, or worse. The church thinks women aren't worthy of the priesthood and insists our only use is childbearing and playing second fiddle to men."

"You never hated Catholics like this before. You were born to the church. What have we done to you?"

"Not you, Rose. You haven't done a thing except help shore them up while the rest of us pay the piper. And now you're a martyr yourself."

Rose compressed her lips. "Vi," she said, "thought the church would come around some day. It was a matter of education."

"And in the meantime?" Murph displayed her injured hand.

Rose's eyes teared up. "Poor Murph," she said. "Maybe I'd turn against the church if I'd been through what you have. My life was pretty easy."

"Until it was all stolen away." Murph mumbled so only I could hear.

Shaking her head from side to side, Rose went right to the heart of her problem with Murph and asked, "How can you expect me to be with anyone else when I want to be with Vi in the hereafter?"

"Even in hell?" Murph asked with a bitterness I'd never heard in her voice before.

The tea was gone and only one cookie was left on the plate. When I refused it, Rose pressed it on Murph, saying Murph's boyish figure was skeletal since the raid.

"I'm going back to work Monday," Murph announced as she brushed crumbs off her dark-blue shirtfront. She was in gray, tapered ladies' slacks and white bucks that looked like they'd been whitened too many times. Still, she looked a bit jaunty.

Rose looked and sounded appalled. "Murph! You can't! Your hand will never heal right if you use it too soon. I'm going to go look for jobs next week. I can help pay your rent."

I offered to help too. I was glad my niece could raise a family on what the bindery brought in. I took only out what I needed, except to pilfer the till for things like this.

Murph couldn't help trying to make a joke. "Shall we tell the boy-os we're ready to be their tenants?"

Rose laughed. "Kicked out of a rooming house. And here I thought I was too good for this place! Where can we go if a rooming house by the tracks won't have us?"

This was good, Rose laughing at herself. She might have thought she was hiding from grief, straights, and her meager beginnings. She'd really been hiding from Rose Callaghan.

"Frank Goodlette can't be known to be sheltering desperados like us."

"So he owns this house?"

Murph nodded. "Looks like Frank never sells anything, only buys. What do you say?

For a moment Rose looked closely at Murph. "Let me talk to our landlady first."

"Do you think I'm making this up, Rosie? Do you think I'm plotting to get you into my bed?"

Rose squinted at her over her glasses. "I wouldn't put it past you, Murph, but no, I want some say in all this. I'm not letting the Goodlettes roll right over me."

"They own the town. They can roll over anyone they want."

"Maybe I should move back up North."

"Where you have no one close and a whole house was taken away from you? Where you've already been dispossessed?"

"Vi's law associates—"

"You'd still be there if you'd wanted to depend on them."

Rose closed her eyes.

A roomer paused in the hall, looked in, and waved to Murph.

"Hello, Mrs. Beckner," Murph called.

The woman groped her way down the hall.

"Visiting Millicent, I'll bet," Murph said. She lowered her voice. "Blind," she told me. "Couldn't get along on her own. This is the right place for her."

I asked Murph how she'd explained her injury at work. Probably because she'd looked so banged up, hers was not one of the photos in the paper. Only her name appeared. The newspaper editor was Dr. Everett's patient so neither his name nor his photo was published. Nevertheless, word got around.

"I said I broke my hand when a rock fell on it while I was fishing in the river near the cliffs. Everybody knows how loose the cliffs got when the highway went in. I can do a lot of the job with my other arm, and what I can't, I call physical therapy."

"What about the rest of your life, Murph, you fool?" asked Rose. "Do you think you'll get through what remains of your days pain free?"

"Don't worry," Murph said, with the slightest hint of a grin escaping her gnawed lips, "I've always been pretty good with my left hand too."

Murph winked at me. I was embarrassed beyond words and laughed a bit maniacally. I thought for a minute Rose was going to walk out. Instead, she shook her head at the irascible Murph and smiled. "I'm still going to talk to the landlady."

"Be my guest. I only want what you want for yourself. You know, Rosie, we're like negatives of each other. Both named Rose and from the same street. You left, I stayed. You wanted someone else, I wanted only you. You're one kind of gay girl, I'm another. You bettered yourself and lived comfortably, I bounced around from one lousy job to another and don't have a penny."

"The big difference, dear Murph, is that I can read and you can't."

That knocked the wind out of Murph for a minute. Then she made her point. "We both ended up back in Hansfield, didn't we?"

Murph couldn't read? Rose was probably getting in a little dig. Everyone could read in this day and age.

Before they got any meaner with each other, I took the opportunity to tell them I'd be going. Rose became apologetic again, this time for chasing me away. Murph suggested we walk over to The Old Town together. Rose, as expected, declined to join us.

On our way out, Mrs. Beckner was tapping her way back up the hall. Murph stopped to give her a kiss on the cheek, tell her how stunning she was today, and introduce me. Oh, that Murph, what a charmer.

CHAPTER FOURTEEN

We left Rose after long good-bye hugs. The sun was low, not yet gone. The factories that hadn't shut down for good pumped out enough smoke to stain the sky a strange color. As we walked, the air seemed to be made up of tiny, sharp ice splinters that stung my cheeks, my forehead, and my lungs and froze the little hairs inside my nostrils.

In the past, Murph always had the posture of a soldier on parade. Not today. I imagined, like most of us, she was protecting herself from a lot more pain than she admitted to. I'd lost my nausea and was hoping the constant headache would go away before I depleted the world's supply of aspirin tablets.

Each time I approached The Old Town, I felt a flutter of apprehension at what I would hear. At least once a week the newspaper put something on the front page like, CITY CLEANUP CONTINUES. So far no one had killed her or himself after the raid. Paul, like Rose, went into hiding. Trust me, his seclusion was more extreme than hers.

Norman went to check on him and found poor Paul shrunken inside his bathrobe, his face swollen and infected. His name was on the list in the newspaper so he didn't bother to call the school where he taught and learn that he was fired. He was even afraid to have groceries delivered. He told his sister, who he was normally close to, nothing. Norman reported that Paul's apartment, usually spic and span, was a jumble. The situation was beyond Norman's abilities and Paul wasn't strong enough, either in mind or body, to make things easy. Norman called an ambulance. He visited Paul in the hospital daily. The little guy was on Miltowns, but his fear continued to paralyze him. His parents had long ago chucked him out. He was single. Once his infection was under control he might have to go to a psych hospital. I wanted to take him home with me and knock him out with some pleasant drug for a few months to wipe clean his memory of the raid and get him through some tough plastic surgery.

As Dr. Everett couldn't talk about his patients, a straight regular who was an orderly at the hospital was the one who told us that two of the queens who had been so badly beaten and abused in the kitchen had undergone emergency surgery that night. The third queen showed up for work the next day at the chain auto-parts store she managed, and the chain's owner fired her, hitting her with a rolled-up newspaper in front of the store employees, who then drove her out of the store with kicks and curses. Some queens slowly came back, others abandoned Hansfield for larger cities. One went home to his parents and a friend commented, "We'll see how long that lasts."

All work stopped on the renovations. Murph couldn't use her hand, and Norman and Carla Jean decided against investing more time in the project until the harassment stopped. If it ever did.

The usual Friday after-work crowd was there, minus the defectors, whose absence was costing The Old Town dearly. I was about to call it a night to spend some time grooming Colonel Mustard, laughing with that sweet golden girl, when Deej showed up. As usual, she carried drama with her like a house gift her hosts had learned to dread. She looked boyish, even in a skirt, and this time she was with a tall, broad-shouldered, thick-necked young man. He wore a white sweater with a blue letter on it and pressed trousers. Under the sweater was a button-down shirt with no tie. Mr. Collegiate. I waited for today's *mishegas*.

"He smells like a men's cologne sampler in a department store," Murph whispered, sniffing the air. "Citrus." Sometimes I was glad to have lost my sense of smell.

When Deej came over, Lisa, who was sitting with Dr. Everett, brought her drink to our table. Her figure emphasized by a two-inch red patent leather belt, she walked to the rhythm of "In the Still of the Night," a favorite Old Town slow-dance song. Even her resigned eyes smiled, and Deej was clearly savoring her womanly approach.

"See? I told you I knew queers," she told the boy. I laughed so hard I had to put a napkin to my mouth to catch my drink. Then she turned to us. "This is my fiancé, Russ. I met him through Crista. Remember I told you she went out with the captain of the football team? That's Russ."

I thought it was a pretty lousy thing to do, like bringing a kid to the zoo to stare at exotic animals. Then it hit me. Had she said he was her fiancé? I leaned my head back and groaned. Lisa looked like someone had knocked the wind out of her. She sat. Murph was turning red in the face.

The red wine occasionally brought out Carla Jean's anger, and right then, with cigarette smoke billowing from her mouth and nose, she looked like she was going to explode. "Why in hell did you bring this straight boy here?"

"Straight boy?" Russ said with an unexpected sibilance.

JoJo shed her prized Red Sox jacket as she hustled in for her shift, and Norman delivered the drinks Deej and Russ had ordered on their way in. As Russ paid, Norman looked him up and down, stamped his small foot, and said, "I know you. You go to the swimming hole upriver."

Russ nodded his head, with its neatly crew-cut blond hair, and showed small white teeth in a grin. "You too?"

"We like to watch who goes in to see which battyman."

Russ looked at a loss.

"Battyman is a word we use in Jamaica for homosexual. I used to spend a lot of time upriver, until Hugh," Norman said. "He made an honest woman of me."

"Lucky guy."

Murph found her voice. "What's this about marriage?" she asked Deej.

"I want to be able to get a job when I graduate and so does Russ."

"All the guys in the frat are pinned or engaged. We didn't want to go through that charade with all the double dating and dancing and making out in public," Russ explained. "So we announced that we're getting married."

Deej said, "After that raid, I knew I needed to do something. Why would anyone not want to hide it? Look at the bad stuff that happens."

We all stared at her.

"You obviously didn't come back here to see how your friends are doing." Carla Jean spit her words. "Why are you here? And with him?"

"That's exactly it! I couldn't come back without—"

"A beard," Murph supplied.

"A what?" Deej wrinkled up her young face, her short loose hair like a frame around a portrait of the perfect lesbian.

Lisa stared at Deej, not saying a word. She might have been looking at Frankenstein from the horror apparent in her wide blue eyes.

Murph looked sadder than I'd ever seen her. "To think I've lived all these years and nothing's changed. You shouldn't have to hide like this, either of you. A beautiful young girl, a beautiful boy, forced to lie about yourselves, to draw marriage like a curtain over a window you'll never escape."

Murph's eyes held no laughter. She spoke so elegantly at times, you'd think she was a college graduate. What is it the Irish say? Murph had the gift of the gab.

Deej protested. "We're best friends. We'll be like roomies, only in our own apartment. With two"—she held up two fingers—"two bedrooms."

Russ held his hands, palm up, over the table. "People talk about me."

"We can protect each other. I'll call Russ next time I'm caught in a raid."

"And I'll call the Deej," Russ said. "It's foolproof."

"More's the fool you," Murph muttered, but I was the only one to hear. I always marveled at her language. She'd been born to Irish immigrants. As a result, she could have been transplanted to Ireland and almost fit in. When she mangled a quote it sounded like an Irish expression.

"Can I get another round?" Russ asked.

Murph and I declined. "Plus he'll earn more than me and always has cash on him. Who can afford to live without sharing?"

Lisa's voice was dry and tinny. "How can you have a relationship?"

"Who's ready for a relationship?" Russ asked.

Deej nodded with vigor. She'd bought into Russ's way of life. I wanted to shake her till the common-sense part of her brain kicked in. Marriage was no joke; it was messy with laws, especially if you wanted to end it. I remembered being that age, though, and making a lot of decisions by going eeny meeny miny mo. Why should it be any different for Deej? She was learning who she was.

Murph warned her. "It won't end well, kid. The easy way never does."

"Hey, just 'cause your life didn't work out so great doesn't mean I'm doing it all wrong. Maybe this is exactly what you needed to do."

What a little stinker this one could be, I thought. What drew Lisa to her? I doubted their night together revealed more than physical potential. Deej needed to learn that hers weren't the only sensitive little nerves. Lisa had that frozen look she got when really angry: lips drawn thin, eyes somewhere between staring and murderous.

Murph was all heart toward Deej now that she'd come out. "Live with a man? You're a little scared. I was scared. We're all scared. But I thought there was more derring-do to you than this."

"Well, my mom's unhappy because Russ isn't from an Indian family. My dad is making us wait till we graduate in hopes I'll look further. Right now's when I need that screen you think so little of. It's hard enough for a girl to get work in my field without adding this queer business."

Carla Jean's comment was sharp as a knife. "Oh, for Pete's sake. They'll assume you'll leave to have kids if you're married."

"Another good reason to team up with Russ. I can absolutely guarantee that's not going to happen." She took her second drink from Russ. "Get me another one lined up, okay?" she told him.

"Nothing but the best of both worlds for her nibs," Murph said.

"Why not?"

Murph nodded over her ginger ale. "Sure. Why not? I admit to being a dreamer."

"About what?"

Murph's sad little smile and derisive exhalation told the tale. "I dream of the day we don't have to hide out in The Old Town. I dream of the day we can march in a parade with the Girl Scouts as our own true selves. I dream of the day no one hunts us down or curses us."

Deej and Ross laughed. The rest of us had heard Murph's dream before.

"Rose didn't want me. I was too wild, she said. Of course I was wild. I fit nowhere and looked like no one else. All I wanted was to escape the trap of myself. I wasn't Catholic enough, she said. Of course I stopped believing. I was warned by the church that I would burn in hell for being born who I am. I had no ambition, she said. Of course I have no ambition. Who can look past a horizon of slammed doors? She'd found herself a lawyer! A lawyer! As if a lawyer would cure all ills."

"Oh, Murph, what's wrong with lawyers?" Lisa asked, looking pained now. "Believe me, I'd grab one if I could find one."

"You know why Vi lawyered for the city? Rose told me it was because so few in town would hire a woman lawyer, especially if she had neither husband nor kids, lived with another woman, and could, sometimes did out of necessity, pass for a man. The city kept her in the law library. Sometimes they let her advise people who couldn't afford lawyers, which was what she'd really wanted to do. She stayed on because she wanted some job security, having lived through the Depression years. She was paid little better than a clerk. Most of what she left Rose was in the form of life insurance, and believe me, they didn't live large."

Deej said, "I'm not hearing anything to change my mind."

Lisa's laugh had an edge of bitterness. Deej leaned in to hear Lisa even as she shrugged off what the others said. What was the seven years between them? In time it would be nothing. Lisa told me later that she'd seen, in her mind's eye, Deej in forty years. She was setting dinner on the table in front of Deej, in a small, cozy kitchen smelling of pancake batter and maple syrup. She asked if I thought she'd really seen into the future. Poor Lisa, I wasn't sure if it was Deej she'd seen hungry at her table. If only I was a matchmaker, I'd fix them up for life, if that would make Lisa happy.

We were all looking at Lisa by then, waiting for her to explain her laugh.

"Are you mad at me?" Deej asked.

"I'm angry at you because you're so careless of other people's feelings," Lisa answered. "I'm more angry at my employer because I was let go today."

After the collective intake of breath I could see them all thinking: not another one.

"Why?" Deej asked. "Were you embezzling or something?"

Lisa scowled at the kid. "You can be such a jerk. I was fired because of the raid."

"That was over a month ago," she said.

Murph laughed this time. "Another lesson learned: consequences may not come like a clap of thunder out of the sky. They might not smite you for years. Look at yourself. Did you make this marriage arrangement the night of the raid?"

"Last night. Russ and I went out drinking and came up with the idea."

"The raid was over a month ago," Murph said, parroting the kid.

Deej said, "You should have told your boss you're getting married!"

Lisa asked brusquely, "Where's your pride?"

Deej stepped back. She looked stunned, as if Lisa had hit her.

"Do you think," Lisa asked, "that none of us had the opportunity to hide behind men? I could have stayed married if I'd been willing to live like that."

"Maybe you should have," Deej said.

"Hey," said Murph, "you do what you have to do to get by."

Carla Jean was less forgiving. "I'd be embarrassed. The thought of living with a guy makes me want to upchuck. I guess you're not as black and white as me."

"I don't get it," the kid said, gesturing to Norman and the other men at the bar, Russ among them. He hadn't been able to resist the lure of the admiring guys. "You're friends with them. Why are you knocking them?"

We kind of all looked at one another, without the words to explain.

"It's humiliating, using men for a shield," Lisa said.

"Yeah," Carla Jean chimed in. "We're a bunch of women who depend, more often than not, only on ourselves and we're proud of it."

"Leave her be," Murph said. "She's young and newly out of the closet. We've all made compromises somewhere along the line."

Carla Jean challenged her. "Yeah? What are yours? To lay down and take it when the whole world craps on you?" Even without her wine, Carla Jean was a lit fuse these days. Her family had told her to find another job. They didn't want her managing the office anymore because she was giving the family dealership a bad name by getting herself arrested in unsavory bars. That's the word she said they used, unsavory. When he heard that, Norman had doubled up with laughter and wanted right away to change the name of The Old Town to the Unsavory Town Tavern.

Murph bowed her head and placed the knuckles of her uninjured hand against her forehead. "Carla Jean, you know I think marrying a man is an atrocious idea. Who can tell, though, what's best for Deej in this world today?"

I didn't usually talk much about myself, especially about being a Jew. It's safer to be a listener. My parents taught me that when it came to our religion, be full of pride but keep your mouth shut. These women and men at The Old Town, sometimes it sounded like they thought they were playing a game, playing hide-and-seek with the cops, pushing at the boundaries of the laws, written and unwritten, that straight people and people who passionately wanted to be straight set up to protect themselves from us. Hadn't they learned anything from the raid?

I jumped in, fear for once making me jabber instead of clam up. "Maybe the police will come back and wipe every one of us out next visit. It could happen. When I think what might have been if my family had stayed in Europe…I like to imagine I'd have tried to orchestrate a Jewish rebellion. Who knows, maybe the Jewish women who played it safe are the only ones left."

"You're Jewish?" Deej asked, as if I'd announced that I was a baby killer. My face grew hot. I'd heard the tone before and knew I'd never stop hearing it. Worse, I knew no one else heard it.

Lisa surprised me. She'd caught what I'm sure was the darkest look I'd ever shown this crowd and said, "We're the new witches of Salem."

Deej, by this time seated and attending every word, let herself be steered away from me. "Nobody told me this would get complicated. I didn't know I had to learn rules."

JoJo, half-smiling, said, "Hasn't anyone given her the secret rule book?"

The others grinned at her, and Deej looked up. "Is there one?"

Murph shook her head. "College doesn't fix gullible."

"I'm serious," Deej said. "First there's this raid, and then I try to protect myself and learn I've tarnished the knighthood or something and shouldn't show my face in here ever again."

They all chorused "No, no, no!" except for Lisa, whose face now wore a look somewhere between yearning and protective. She gave a quiet little smile. We all wanted to take Deej home and raise her right.

"That's not what we meant, Deej." JoJo was always the peacemaker, the little diplomat turning her bar apron into a cape and flying to the rescue in the nick of time. "Who can explain anything about women who like women? There is an unwritten code of honor. Do we learn it? Is it something we're born with? And forget umpires. No one's watching what you do or waiting to call you out."

I'd never heard this stuff put into words, and here was our bartender, standing in one place for once and doing just that.

JoJo went on. "We know there've always been marriages like this, like we all know some gay women marry straight guys and never come out at all, or dart in and out of the closet behind their husbands' backs. What you do is your business. What we do is ours. You're a college kid with big ideas, we're bar people. Oranges and apples."

Deej pulled her mouth sideways. "None of you think marrying a gay guy makes sense?" She looked from face to face.

Murph grumbled. "No self-respect."

"Marrying Russ makes more sense than anything to me. A year ago I didn't know about myself and now I might as well be a leper. I don't get why I shouldn't play it safe."

No one responded.

"It's not because I go to college. Look at Hugh, for one," Deej said, but it was clear she was talking to herself. "I admit I'm ambitious. Maybe being Indian-American is making me more careful." She put her hands in her hair, and sat down. Her second Dewar's was empty and she downed half of her next, wincing. "Am I ever going to fit in anywhere?" she asked the glass before finishing the drink.

CHAPTER FIFTEEN

The first time I saw the apartment over the bar, Norman and Hugh had finished painting it and hanging shades. The paint odor was strong. The walls were umber and the wall-to-wall carpeting was cocoa-brown. The second time I visited, at the housewarming party that February, it had a few sticks of furniture from ads in the paper. In the kitchen the guys had planted a mammoth timeworn Norge refrigerator with a clock set in the door. It wheezed and coughed like an old cigarette smoker. They'd hung turquoise drapes. At the start of the party, while tiny snowflakes drifted down outside, the place didn't look very different. Murph and Rose between them had very little.

While Murph brewed tea and Rose piled flowered Melmac plates with drop cookies Murph had actually baked herself, I stood at a window, holding back a drape. I was early and surprised that I wasn't the first guest. Deej sat on the couch with Murph. It was obvious I'd interrupted some deep mentoring talk. Deej had good instincts; she went to Murph. The kid might make us proud of her yet.

Rose was in the kitchen. "Rockie!" she cried, and hugged me hard. I love hugs. I can tell people how much I love them with a big old affectionate embrace. Works better than words, which sometimes scare friends. Rose looked excited. I passed the time with her in the kitchen and she told me all about her plans for the apartment.

Paul came in. "The paint smell is gone!" he said.

"The baking is covering it," Rose explained

Paul was newly released from the state hospital. He was so thin he looked like his flesh had dissolved. His arms barely encompassed the box he held. I hadn't seen him since the raid. He looked like he'd had a stroke, but the drooping eye wasn't as pronounced as I'd expected. It was enough, along with the mismatch of the two sides of his face, to make his beauty a thing of the past.

"I'm only here until my sister picks me up," he warned us. Once released he'd moved in with his sister before I could offer my couch. The poor guy had lost his beloved loft home. "She let me out for good behavior."

"What have you done?" Rose asked, approaching the box. Paul let her open it and she drew out his old bedroom curtains, good thick ones that would keep the heating bill down. They were white and floor-length, with a red-rose pattern.

"Roses for two Roses!" Murph said. "Thank you, Paul. Did you get reinstated at school yet?"

"I wish. My attorney said he wouldn't take my money because I'd never win. I'm going back to waitressing." Paul spread open an imaginary apron while he curtsied. "High-end waitressing, where I can make good money. I've done it before."

It seemed that everyone in earshot turned as one to look at him. His hand went to his scarred, lopsided face as if he was covering his private parts. I heard a collective sigh and Paul looked away.

I wanted to grab Paul and hold him to me. No high-end restaurant would hire someone who looked the way he did and he knew it. I wasn't even sure he could get on at a diner. Accepting that fact could bring him crashing down again. Paul's health insurance ended when his name appeared in the newspaper, so plastic surgery was beyond his reach now. Our poor fallen beauty. Love used to come so easily to him. Now it wouldn't come at all. No one said that. No one warned him. I think we all wanted to maintain the shell of his denial until it broke around him. Norman never stopped watching over him, with a couple of the other men. If he didn't show up at The Old Town someone called him or went to his sister's door.

Outside the windows, snow fell faster. The room got hotter with every new visitor. Deej had gone outside to meet Dr. Everett at his car, a 1951 Cadillac, in, he'd tell everyone, the shade of Corinth blue. That car was the doctor's hobby and great passion. They unloaded a heavy oval wood table that would fit fine in the roomy kitchen. I could see the snowflakes landing on Deej's black hair and blending with the doctor's white mane. Murph and Rose might not share a bed, but a table was a fine thing to share too. Visitors called instructions as they maneuvered it up the stairs.

Paul went to help someone with four unmatched kitchen chairs, each with a blue-checked pad already tied to it. I took each item as it arrived at the door and handed it to the next person. Kitchen curtains scented with laundry detergent, a heavy full-length mirror, a little pinewood secretary, coffee table, television—The Old Town came through for Murph and Rose. Of course, Carla and some of the guys went into interior-decorator mode and spiffed up the apartment with plumped pillows and accent rugs, doodads and gewgaws belonging to Rose and Murph. One of the men used lavender furniture polish on the wooden donations. The fellow who owned the frame shop downtown had matted some of Murph's pictures, and Seneca donated a photo album. Murph's American flag was displayed high up over the bedroom doors.

I sat with Rose on the new kitchen chairs, trying one after the other, laughing as we pretended to test them. She tried to lift my mood after I complained, as usual, that I would never find another girlfriend in this town. I've gotten too flabby, I told her, I laugh too loud, I'm Jewish, I'm old as the hills.

"Of course you will," she told me. 'No one cares about your religion.' She lied and I let her. 'You're not all that old, you're attractive in a cuddly way, and anyone would love your sense of humor. Colonel Mustard, indeed. Maybe, now that Murph and I have an apartment— with her promise that we'll only be roommates—maybe I could get a little dog. I've got my job, but the nights are terrors." She'd hired on as a gal Friday with an attorney in town. "He got me cheap," she told me, "because I haven't worked professionally. Meaning, I never got a paycheck for my work with Vi. How could I explain that Vi supported us both without giving away what we were to each other?"

I commiserated and joked that I'd trade being single for a romance with risk. I have my own business, who could fire me?

Rose looked over her glasses at me. "Do you know what you're saying?" she asked. "Nothing is worth that risk. Vi and I were so careful. And we were because we learned early on what would happen if we didn't take care. Especially in the Depression when no one had money for lawyers. All we needed was for her to lose her job over her home life."

This poor woman was damaged. Lesbian witch hunts, the Second World War, Communist witch hunts, the Depression; I supposed fear must fill half of her brain—and heart. I waited to see if she would tell me what happened.

"My family wasn't the kind to say anything out loud. It wasn't hard to tell from the suspicious questions they asked me that they hated her, sight unseen. For one thing, they'd never forgive Vi for being Italian. Vi's parents, the Derizzis, while they were alive, weren't happy about Vi being how she was, but she was family, and if she chose me they'd treat me well even if her siblings and cousins didn't.

"My family tried to get Vi arrested. The cops went to her office at city hall and questioned her about her 'moral activities.' At the same time the police came to me, at home, and demanded proof of my age. They said they'd make the city safe for decent people and their children by taking Vi off the streets if they ever caught her near a kid. They told me to go home or they'd make Vi's life hell and ruin her business. We were very scared and talked about moving to New York or California. My family, the Callaghans, would lie about going away for the holidays or invent excuses why they couldn't spend time with me. I stopped trying to see them."

I told Rose she'd been through the wringer.

Rose nodded and, while the apartment came together around us, said, "It was almost as bad when another woman like us turned on Vi. It was in 1953. They sat on a committee together and the attorney, not that I blame her for this, fell in love with Vi. At first, Vi would come home and tell me stories. We'd lie in bed and laugh at the woman's antics. And she wasn't a young slip of a thing either," Rose told me. "Her children had grown and left home. Her husband was the nicest man, the principal of an elementary school. The silly woman found excuse after transparent excuse to have business at city hall, sometimes in the legal department itself, and other times she'd say she was there for records, as if a real-estate attorney in a firm big enough to have clerks needed to do her own research. All she wanted was what I wanted, to be close to Vi."

Rose pulled a faded photograph from behind another one in her scrapbook and handed it to me. "That's the itch-bay there. May the good Lord forgive me." She crossed herself. Old-fashioned Rose had to say the word *bitch* in pig latin.

The woman had very dark painted eyebrows, dark hair pulled back from her forehead in two waves, one to each side of her face, a short, wide nose and eyes spaced far apart. Her white blouse over a black turtleneck, with a long black skirt and black shoes and socks made her look like an aged college girl from early in the century.

"She flirted with Vi like a puppy. Vi, of course, couldn't say she was married to me, or to any woman. She was considered single at work. You know how women find one another. This lady had obviously unearthed her different side late in life, as so many do, and meant to test it out on Vi. After a few months of this Vi likened the woman to a pesky fly. She brushed her away again and again; the woman didn't give up. She would appear outside our church and completely ignore me as we exited after mass. I told Vi to be very careful, as the woman obviously had a screw loose."

By this time Rose was as relaxed as I'd ever seen her. She was fine-looking in an old-fashioned way. I guessed she had her blond hair "done" at a beauty parlor, as the upswept style involved a lot of big curls on top. Everyone else was so busy we might have been alone in an otherwise empty room. I considered that telling stories must be in the Irish character.

"The penny dropped in May of that year—spring fever was doing its best. She'd followed poor Vi to the bus stop after work and slipped her a note with the name of a downtown hotel and a room number. Of course Vi ignored it. After a week of simmering the woman showed up in Vi's office. 'Same time, same place,' she told her, 'or I'm going to your boss about you and your little roommate.' Needless to say we thought we were ruined. Vi was a terrible crybaby at home, and she sobbed for days about the meanness of humanity. I was scared too. I held Vi, and comforted her, and told her it would all work out for the best. Really, I think it broke her heart that someone who worked hard to be a good citizen could never be one in the eyes of the world. She went to church, contributed to charity, worked hard, kept up her home, and this madwoman could ruin it all. And almost did.

"Vi didn't know which way to turn, but I knew what I had to do. That Sunday, when the woman approached outside church, I stepped in front of Vi and slapped the woman so hard my hand stung. All around me I heard that sharp intake of breath people make when they're shocked. The woman stepped back, her hand to her cheek. I screamed like a banshee for her to leave Vi alone and stop trying to turn her into a Communist. The parishioners whispered the word *Communist* to one another. I'd decided to fight fire with a hotter fire. In those days, it was as bad to be a Communist as it was to be like us. Maybe worse, because they weren't as skilled as we are at hiding.

"We never heard from that woman again," Rose said, laughing.

I praised her for protecting her mate.

"Not every story has a satisfactory ending," Rose warned me. "You know as well as I that graveyards are littered with homos like us who've been driven to end their lives by circumstances like Vi's. And like the woman's. People are so frightened of us, and so frightened to be like us—that's why this nonsense happens." Her face changed immediately, mirroring her frightened soul. "You see what I mean, don't you? You have to watch every step."

I'm not a particularly fearful person, despite my heritage. Still, fear is the most contagious of emotions and I shivered.

CHAPTER SIXTEEN

The whistling kettle went off yet again. Murph steeped tea bags in a big brown pot. A latecomer brought antique floor lamps with shelves halfway up the stems and shades that showgirls could have worn, tassels and all. The two night-table lights had bases formed like naked Olympians. Rose quickly tied lacy handkerchiefs around their waists. With an amused and accommodating Lisa, Rose spent the rest of the party organizing spices, jars of grains, canned goods, a case of the soft ginger cookies Murph loved, and the rest of the food staples JoJo and Carla Jean lugged up the stairs from the bar's kitchen where customers had donated and stored them. The linen closet was stocked with sheets, towels, and blankets. Dr. Everett and Deej brought in boxes of magazines from his waiting room.

"This is a happy day," Murph announced, as if to turn around my mood. "A day I won't forget." She held up a celebrity-photo spread from one of the doctor's magazines. "I'll be papering the place with these."

How could she, with her hand the way it was?

"You'll be keeping those things in your room, woman." Rose protested with a laugh. She'd agreed to rent the apartment over the bar, next door to Hugh and Norman's own apartment, and with Murph, on the condition that they consider her retired from the gay life. She wouldn't be pushed back into it, she claimed, and would never fall in love again. I looked at Murph. Rose couldn't be serious about leaving the life if she planned to live with Murph. But she'd already hung crucifixes over both of their beds and framed prints of the Virgin Mary in each room.

Most of the guests came and went quickly, partly because of the snow and partly because Rose wouldn't hear of anyone smoking in the apartment. I tapped pictures into the wall with a nifty little hammer, then bumped a carpet sweeper along old braided rugs. Slowly, the activity came to an end and Paul poured champagne. We toasted Rose and Murph, the apartment, the building, Norman and Hugh until the champagne was gone.

"Good heavens, this is a lot of stuff to move again, if the cops get their way," Norman said, hands on hips, inventorying the apartment with a glance.

"I'm praying night and day that you get to keep your investment in this building," Rose responded.

"Is it worth it?" Hugh wiped cookie crumbs from his beard into his cupped hand and mostly missed. "Look at all the people who got hurt in the raid." They'd closed the bar downstairs for these few hours. Hugh and Norman brought up a case of ginger ale for Murph, and they presented Rose with a bag of kitchen utensils, from a church key to a wavy vegetable slicer.

Out the window snowflakes fell, so big they looked like thousands of miniature parachutes rushing to the ground. There were few cars. A bus squealed to a slow stop at the corner.

"I say yes, it's worth it," Paul said. "It's bad enough that they can do this to me." His speech was imprecise, a little slurred. He sounded like it was an effort to shape words. He held up two bottles of pills— drugs to keep him from going off the deep end? Painkillers? "Where would I be if I'd gone through this and was released to find you all scattered to the winds?"

Rose hugged herself. "The police don't even have to come back," she said. "I'm terrified to set foot in the bar."

"That," Hugh said, "is what terrorism is all about. Frightening people so badly and so often that we take over the job and scare ourselves into doing the will of the terrorists."

"What about the bar? Will they close it?" Lisa asked.

Before Paul could answer, Carla Jean stubbed out her cigarette and asked, "What are they going to do? Launch a wrecking ball at the building?"

"Maybe," Hugh said.

"What can we do?" JoJo asked. Her moments of brightness since Thanksgiving night continued to be fleeting. She moved more slowly, no longer a non-stop whirlwind of activity. "Nothing. That's what we can do."

There was a soft knock at the door. A number of people yelled, "Come in!"

In the doorway stood a female replica of Paul.

"You didn't tell us you have a twin," Hugh said.

"Hi, Cissy," said Paul. I laughed, thinking their family had two sissies.

Paul heard me and explained, "We're practically identical. We even both like boys."

They urged the woman to join the party.

I'd always admired Paul's looks and was transfixed to see them in a woman. Small, dark, and handsome; the phrase made me smile. Dressed to the nines for business, she wore her hair short enough that, in men's clothing, it would be difficult to tell the two apart, except for Paul's trace of beard. Cissy was a snow fairy, blown in by the cold wind. I wanted to burst out singing that old traditional song about the prettiest girl I ever saw sipping cider through a straw.

I never even said hello to Cissy. Straight women usually had so few doubts about who they would love—it wasn't up to me to open their eyes any more. I watched her, though, and listened to tidbits about her. In her thirties, she hadn't given up trying to protect her twin, had an on-again, off-again boyfriend she didn't want to marry, lived near the Green downtown, and loved dogs. She'd worked for the college for fifteen years as a secretary in the registrar's office.

While she and Lisa got to talking, Murph and Rose admired a late donation from a couple redoing their apartment in Danish Modern. They'd brought a shiny veneer credenza. Rose immediately stacked old cotton tablecloths inside, most of them white with festive printed designs. The hutch came as she finished and she gave a delighted caw.

Seneca was dealing cards at the coffee table, fanning them like a pro. Spence and two of the gay boys checked their cards.

I caught Lisa gesturing toward Deej and saying something about her to Cissy. Cissy raised her eyebrows, then patted the back of Lisa's hand. Lisa gave her a cigarette. I'd never seen a cuter conspirator than Cissy. I turned my back on them. A few minutes later, when most of the guests were gone, Lisa brought Cissy over.

"You've met Cecelia?" Lisa asked.

"I like Cissy better," Murph said. I silently agreed.

"It's what Paul calls me. You're welcome to call me that too. I've heard how you all tried to help him. Mom and Dad—well, Dad really, never wanted anything to do with Paul." Cissy had the grace to look embarrassed. "What can I say? Paul's always been girlish. To tell you the truth, I don't think our mom likes men much. She's never seemed to mind that Dad's on the road all the time selling belts for machinery. Paul and I used to make up stories about what his other family must be like."

She was so frank and open. Was it because she was straight and didn't have anything to hide? I knew practically nothing about the other world except from my family. I was so in awe of her, I couldn't manage to say hello.

"Did he play sports?" Rose asked.

"Ping pong. Which embarrassed Dad even though Paul has an amazing fast offense and won tournaments. If he'd been a bit taller, with longer arms, he could have been a champion."

Lisa re-tucked her silk scarf, yellow flowers on white with a pink border, into her V-neck sweater and asked, "How is Paul, really? He and Murph got the worst of it."

Cissy paused. "He's always saying how grateful he is that he got hurt. Otherwise, he'd be in jail."

I shuddered as she spoke and thought it was a good thing he'd never been drafted.

"Not in the way you think," Cissy said. "He's afraid he would hurt another prisoner and be locked away for a long time. He's a vicious fighter and a dirty fighter. He had to be to stay alive through childhood. Guys are so cruel."

"Why in hell do you like them?" It was that ever-sensitive Deej, liquored up from a visit downstairs now that the bar was reopened. Her eyes were unfocused, her words crawled into one another, her breath was all whiskey fumes. I hoped she'd quit drinking before she couldn't quit at all.

Cissy didn't answer.

"Coffee time!" Rose and Murph steered Deej into the kitchen.

Lisa said, "I'm so sorry. Deej is pretty newly out of the closet and it's not hard to activate her scrappy side."

"Well," Cissy said, slowly, "it's a good question." She turned to me for the first time, introduced herself, and held out a small hand to be shaken. I said it was no one's business who she liked, just as it shouldn't concern anybody but me that I was a homosexual.

She cringed at the word *homosexual*. I was glad. It showed the wall between us that she might not understand was there. God, she was a tasty-looking morsel. Could the stirrings inside me be a sign that I was recovering from the concussion? A natural response to the horror of the raid and its consequences: a greater will to live and a vital need to love?

"What are you driving?" Lisa said.

The skeptical look on Cissy's face made me suspect the answer was not good news. "I have an old Triumph."

"How old?"

Now, as Cissy pointed out the window to her tiny convertible sports car, she looked plain embarrassed. "1954."

I put my hands on the chilly windowsill and peered down to the street. "How is it in snow?

"I didn't drive here, I slid."

I tried hard not to laugh, but between the car, Cissy's pointy-toed high heels, and the fancy light work clothes she'd worn directly from her office, I couldn't imagine her getting close to her car, never mind excavating it from the snow. I gave in to the laughter. At least she'd worn a tweed wool coat with a lofty fake-fur collar and cuffs. Lisa was dressed more sensibly. We hadn't seen or heard a bus for quite a while.

Rose came out of the kitchen and told us what we'd do. Deej wandered into Murph's room and passed out on Murph's bed so Murph would bunk with her. Rose would get one of the boys to haul Deej's bike upstairs. Lisa would take her, Rose's, bed. Lisa refused and they compromised by assigning the sofa to Lisa. In this game of musical beds, Paul stayed next door with Norman and Hugh, and Cissy would get my bed. I'd enjoy dreaming of her there while I spent the night in a sleeping bag on my couch. I was almost finished reading *Atlas Shrugged*, a big chunk of a novel. Cockamamie ideas in a mesmerizing story. Rose shooed Cissy and me out before the snow got any deeper and put a bag with hot chocolate and marshmallows in my coat pocket to thaw us after we crossed the street. Cissy mooched one last cigarette from Lisa.

I have to admit I never had more fun crossing a street in my life. Cissy had seemed annoyed at me for laughing upstairs. Now, as she sunk her heels into a pile of snow that drifted up against the doorway to the street, she fell against me and I lost my balance and we both went immediately down. Since I was on my back already, I laughed again as I made a snow angel.

"I haven't done one of those since Paul and I were kids!"

I managed to get to my wet knees before she pushed me backward into the same low drift. With hands red from cold, the poor woman pelted me with snowball after snowball before I could rise and pull her up. My cheeks were about to turn into ice balls. By then Cissy was laughing too. I tucked her hand against me and navigated us to paths between drifts. The fur collar was full of static and gave me little tingles of electricity when it touched my neck. There wasn't a plow in sight yet. My building was a distant mountain, I told Cissy, and we became climbers without equipment. The air was thin up here, I said. It was making us foolish with laughter.

Somehow, in my thick-soled, soaked suede loafers, I managed to plant myself, step by step, firmly enough to get us into the lobby and upstairs. I gave Cissy my bathrobe and clean towels and pushed her into a hot shower. At that point the building hadn't lost power and I had hot water. I finished my turn in the shower and emerged to the sight of hot chocolate. Cissy handed me a mug and plopped a marshmallow in.

"When I first saw Paul in the hospital, I thought he was going to die. We're so pale to begin with and he looked—bloodless."

I commiserated with her, not mentioning my own injury.

"It's what I never understood. Why would anyone want to be gay? Paul's a nice-looking guy, has a steady job. My friends hint around that they'd date him in a minute."

Apparently Paul hadn't told her he no longer had a job. He must be pretending to be on sick leave.

"And you," she went on, looking me over. She looked adorable in my pajamas with the legs and sleeves rolled up. "You're boyish. I could make you up and you could get a nice hairdo. Wouldn't you rather be normal?"

Here I'd thought Deej was as insensitive as you could get. I had to excuse Cissy, though. What straight didn't think this way? How else did you talk to a circus freak? I was so tired of justifying myself to the people who believed all the malarkey they grew up hearing. I told her no.

"No? You like being queer?"

She had no idea how rude she was. I have a way of acting confident and superior, especially when I'm mad. This time I told her yes.

"What's so great about it?" she wanted to know.

"For one thing, I don't have to deal with men," I told her. "They're too big, they're hairy, they boss women around, they seem to thrive on wars. Mostly, they hog everything. Who has most of the money in the world? Who makes the laws? Who, if forced to grocery shop, blocks the aisles like everything is there only for him?"

She looked thoughtful. "And who beat up Paul," she said, as if tasting each word. "A lot of the professors at the college are fairies," she added.

Cissy was on my chair, her legs curled underneath her. I was on the couch, first sitting and then, as the hours drained away, I sprawled and, finally, reclined altogether.

"I'd never call you a dyke, though," she said. "You're prettier than that."

I laughed once more in my too-loud way. She was doing most of the talking. I was watching her and nodding, smiling, encouraging her, teasing a bit, relaxing with my arms crossed and one eyebrow up when she got outrageous. Both of us sort of showed off in our own ways. It got pretty late before she started yawning.

Then the lights went out.

I went to the window. Snow, in its whiteness, seemed to create its own low light. Moonlight strained through clouds toward downtown. The wind continued whipping around outside, the blackened traffic light swinging with it, tree branches waving for help in the deluge of snow. No lights. No lights anywhere in sight. Which meant no heat. I'd thought to have a flashlight near and with it lit my kerosene lantern. I handed my one extra blanket to Cissy. Geri had taken the rest. The sleeping bag was mine.

"Do we have to go to bed now?" she asked, like a little kid afraid of the dark. I suggested she'd be warmer under the covers. She started another story, this one about how Paul would protect her when she'd get scared at night. As she recounted incident after incident from their childhoods I realized she was still afraid of the dark. I was tired, though, and got into my sleeping bag. Cissy wrapped the spare blanket around herself. I fell asleep to the sound of her voice. And awoke to the sound of her tears.

Really, all I wanted was to climb deeper into my sleeping bag and keep what warmth I had. Instead I got up, and with my bag and pillow under one arm, I pulled her off the chair and led her into the bedroom. I tucked her in, then lay the sleeping bag beside her and got back in. She used the extra blanket to cover both of us and snuggled close to me, a layer of sheet, blanket, and sleeping bag between us. It had been a while since I'd shared a bed with a warm woman.

Before climbing in, I'd taken a last look out the window through the heavy snowfall toward Murph and Rose's apartment. Would morning find everyone asleep in the same bed where they started?

"I like to imagine I'm safe with you, Rockie," Cissy whispered.

The fact that I dreamed so elaborately and at such length was amazing enough. That I remembered the dream in such detail was unsettling. As soon as I'd fallen asleep, the lovemaking, and the love, began.

Murph and I sat in her living room. Rose was in one of the new chairs, under a donated lamp, with a book.

"Rose is a big reader," Murph said. "She'll read her eyes out one day."

I sort of floated over to Rose and, with great, slow tenderness, took the book from her. She smiled and raised her face toward mine. In that moment, I saw the beauty of her and understood why Murph pined for her. "Murph's wanted you forever," I said, drawing back. Rose took hold of my lapels. I was wearing a men's suit coat and it fit perfectly. Wasn't I the swell in that suit!

Then I was lying beside Lisa wearing only the suit coat, and her large, sensitive hands were on me. Lisa! As if she'd ever be interested in me. In the dream I was thinking what a good friend she'd always been and how I didn't want to lose her friendship, yet what she was doing was sublime. I thought, well, if she touches me while I leave her alone...I knew as I thought it that, in the wash of warmth I felt for her, even though it sprang from friendship, I'd never be able to keep my hands to myself.

Which may be why, in the next and longest sequence, it was not my hands I was using and the woman wasn't Lisa or Rose or even Geri. God forbid it should be Geri. It was my gorgeous new straight friend Cissy.

We lay full-length against each other, her back to my front. The warmth this time was from a soft comforter. It was luscious: smooth, thick, the color of hot chocolate. We lay there for the longest while, breathing in unison, both of us in clean flannel. There was no other sound, only what you hear swimming underwater. We huddled so intimately I imagined us one being, floating yet anchored by the warm chocolate blanket.

With care, I turned Cissy toward me. She nudged me onto my back and pulled off my pajama bottoms, then her own. Our different heights made this nearly impossible, but, while pressing her lips to mine, she rode my pelvic bone. At the same time, her thigh, muscles tense, pulled my pleasure spot to her rhythm. She was making all these happy little sounds and I was trying not to come because she was straight. Cissy grew big with sound. She was flat and wide and warm over me. She was chortling with pleasure. I was holding onto her so she wouldn't float away in her ecstasy. I couldn't hold her close and at the same time refuse my body what it sought. I was sliding under her thigh, embarrassed that I'd covered it with wetness. I'd thought the end of my monthly curse would also be the end of all that. Apparently it was an old wives' tale.

Cissy was so small, so holdable, so intensely lovely. I was her protector. I was strong and in charge even though she took the initiative. I could not have. I was pleased with being gay myself, though this cloud of dishonor always threatened storms of guilt when a straight woman was involved. It made me think, way in the back of my soul, that I was ashamed of who I was. I wish I could find the words to make it real for others: the mixture of fear and defiance, pride and shame to be gay. It brought me to tears, the excitement of being who I am and the anguish of not understanding why it was so wrong.

I found nothing shameful or even carnal about this dream. It was an awakening for Cissy. It was the moment when a monotone life went Technicolor, when the silence after a storm dissipated with a resumption of joyous activity; it was a relief to be alive and a celebration of coming alive.

I woke up to find Cissy, sleepy breath against my back, one hand cradling my breast as if to claim it. Except for that gesture, I might have panicked and tried to move away before she discovered what we'd done. Instead, I returned to sleep, planning to dig out her car or act her hero in some other way. In my sleepy reverie I was certain we were each other's destinies. Paul would be a perfect brother-in-law.

Cissy was gone when I awoke hours later, bright sunlight leaking into the cold apartment. I raised the blind on the bedroom window and saw Paul, Hugh, and Norman on the street, Cissy in her car. They'd dug her out and pushed her little Triumph, her little boat, onto plowed Girolami Avenue, whose gutters ran with melting slush.

CHAPTER SEVENTEEN

"Y ou are such an innocent," Lisa told Deej, without an ounce of her customary charm. No princess now, Lisa's eyes were unsympathetic.

"I didn't mean to make it worse!" A gust of sodden wind had pushed Deej through the door, her hair flat and wet, her clothes soaked through, her shoes squelching, leaving a trail where she walked. She'd come on her bike and wheeled it into the kitchen, out of the way, leaving a muddy track.

Norman was not as forgiving as Lisa. "All my life I've dreamed of having something of my own and making a success of it. Every day I spent in that hospital across the street taking blood again and again all day, all night, weekends, holidays, grabbing every bit of overtime they'd give a pantywaist orderly—it took every cent that I saved and all of Hugh's savings to buy this building and make a success of this bar. Whatever made you think going to city hall would get you—or us—anywhere, Deej?"

The kid turned petulant. "I was trying to help."

Her view of what she'd done was so comical I laughed. Geri once said I could collapse a skyscraper with my laugh. She'd disapproved of a lot of things about me.

It was about a month later, on a Saturday afternoon, raining steadily and heavily, as only a cold March rain could. Umbrellas lined the wall inside the door and water puddled a foot around them. I'd crossed The Avenue in my yellow slicker, hood up, and was perfectly dry. Spring was near and my blood seemed to pulse though me in waves of excitement at the promise of the robins' return, the colors upon colors that would soon break through the ground, the long nights ahead with Cissy.

Murph came over to the bar. She was such a sad sack. She'd probably dropped twenty pounds since the raid. "I've lost the knack for sleep," she'd explained.

Now she asked Deej, "What's this I'm hearing? JoJo claims you refused to leave the mayor's office until you could complain to him about the raid? I'd be surprised if he wasn't the one who ordered it. He's desperate to win reelection over Frank Goodlette and it's always good politics to raid a sinful gay bar. What in heaven's name got into you, child?"

"We should have banned you from the bar, Miss Trouble," Norman said. "Did we? No, we recognized you as one of our own and encouraged you to make this your stomping ground."

"Hey, guys, I'm the one who's risking losing my scholarship. You're sore I stood up for us? What are you, sheep?"

Lisa told her, "I'm afraid you're someone who learns the hard way."

"I told them I'm engaged, for Pete's sake. It's not like I went in there and admitted to being gay."

"No," Norman said, "you stirred up the whole can of worms again by bringing attention to us."

"When I read in the paper that someone was pushing the people next door to sell, I decided it was time to do something."

Murph said, "Listen, what I'm wondering is how the reporters knew to be on the spot when you stormed city hall."

There was a silence. Of course Deej must have alerted them. Who else could have known she'd be there?

Deej stood up. "This is stupid. Do you all hate yourselves so much? It's good that the papers picked up on the story. You'll see. People will help."

"Or they'll burn us down," Norman said.

"Why? Why would they do that? You're not hurting anyone. It's not going to be as bad as you think."

There was a thunk against the window.

"What was that?" asked Seneca, eyes wide.

"The paperboy," Norman said.

"When is he going to learn he's hurting nothing?" Murph commented.

"Shattering my nerves is all." Norman went out in the rain to get the paper and returned assembling the soaked sections and pages. I imagined the smell of the wet newsprint. "The little creep made sure the paper fell apart."

"Even the paperboy is giving you a hard time?" Deej asked.

What a lousy introduction to the gay life, I thought, stretching my legs out on the wooden banquette. Why any of us embraced being homosexual was sometimes a mystery. Estranged from our families, we risked physical harm, endured constant fear, had trouble keeping relationships, gathered only in secret noisy, smelly, smoky, often dangerous places—and still we chose this life, these people, our kind of love. In any crowd, there were only a handful of us, our bonds hidden, yet our spirits so connected we covertly acknowledged strangers on the street when we recognized one another.

No, Deej, I thought, there are no rules, only this strange fumbling in the dark of an underground so vast it can't be measured or defined. Each of us finds her way differently with no guide, no kerosene lantern, and only disguised mentors who might or might not reveal themselves, who half the time did not dare teach their lessons aloud, who often turned their backs on the lost ones and refused entry to their own. It wasn't the first time I thought that it was no wonder so many gay people are too damaged to sustain a union or make a success of their lives.

Norman asked, "How could someone smart enough to be some kind of engineer be dumb enough not to expect flak?"

Murph put her arm around the kid. "You know how you want to protect yourself by marrying that gay footballer?"

"Oh, that's off. It was a goofy idea. I'm not going to arrange my life around being scared. I only said I was engaged at the mayor's office so they'd think I was straight."

There was a kind of bar-wide sigh of relief as Murph squeezed Deej's arm and pulled her closer. "You're not connecting the dots, Deej. You think you can change the world, right? You think that standing up and speaking out will convince people we're more like them than not? It's not going to happen, kid. You know why? Because they *are* us. Inside every straight is someone who could be gay. Nothing's set in stone. No one knows if the devil's in us or our mothers fed us wrong or our fathers should have been tougher or more loving or if we just fall in love. None of the married guys who sneak out to park restrooms or dark movie theaters are going to own up to what they do. They have unhappy wives and make gay jokes at work. And the wives? You're going to hold a few of them in your arms before you're done, if I know my lesbians."

"That makes no sense," Deej said. "If they all said they're gay, there'd be no one to raid."

Norman asked, "How do you explain the way dark-skinned people are treated? Or Indian people born to the wrong caste? Your own family must have stories of prejudice."

"Where do you think I learned to speak my mind? My parents were some of the first Indians in the US motel business. They came over in the 1940s with a little money. The banks wouldn't loan my father more because of his skin color and accent. They saved, borrowed some from another Indian family and bought a falling-down place, put my brothers to work fixing it up. By the time I was born—I'm the youngest—Daddy had three fixed-up motels and my oldest brothers each managed one. We three youngest, we aren't fond of this keep-it-in-the-family-behind-closed-doors deal. We're Indian *and* American. In elementary school, when they did heritage days? They used to leave out Indians. My sister Kala got mad. She wore a sari and brought a curry dish and shamed them into including us every year after that. When the school principal introduced me as salutatorian in high school? He hadn't bothered to figure out how to pronounce my last name so I started the speech with a lesson."

I laughed to myself. I would no more have worn a modest head covering like a Jewish wife and bought challah to school than I would put on a drag show.

"So you thought you could straighten out the mayor," Murph said.

"You have to start somewhere."

This time the sighs were weary. I had to admire the kid's spunk. The rest of us knew nothing was about to change our world. I wished we could put on our native gay costumes and feed acquaintances our traditional meals; I wished we had something of our own we'd be proud to share. Once in a great while I'd hear a little good news, like somebody getting found out at work and not getting fired. I reminded myself that those sparks of hope that things could get better were cruel self-deceptions. Look at the Cohen who changed her name to Cone, the helpless lesbian teacher who witnessed a gay pupil grow up in bewilderment. There was no way to fix how the world was or the way people thought. Still, you never knew.

"Come on with me," Lisa said, buttoning her black wool coat. "We'll talk more at my place. Unless you want to deal with your parents tonight."

Norman held up the front section of the paper. Deej's picture, down to the parka she had on, illustrated the story. "This says nothing about you being 'engaged.' You look like a dykling."

"Let me see that," Deej said. "I made that reporter promise to make a point of it."

Norman wouldn't let go. "Betrayal numero uno? Get out of here, you two," he told Deej and Lisa. "We need to turn this juke joint into a fortress. Take good care of the kid, doll."

Lisa's smile was sad.

Deej tied a woolen scarf around her neck, leaving the leather buttons of her car coat undone. What a little butch, I thought: braving the elements like she's stronger than they are. I followed Lisa and Deej out to be sure they got on a bus safely, then went home for my box camera. I slipped a couple of cards of flashbulbs into my jacket pockets. I'd be lucky if I got away with taking one picture, but I would try for more. If anything happened at The Old Town from now on, I was going to have the guilty parties on film, whether I could do anything with the pictures or not. Deej had me thinking that maybe, someday, someone other than all the gay people in all the gay bars in all the cities and in all the hideouts in rural towns would care that we endured what we did in resigned, immured, besieged silence.

Small chance, I thought, when I returned after walking Colonel Mustard under trees beginning to form what would become buds. I was worrying about my dog and the stories I'd heard of cruelty to the animals of gay owners when I saw Deej step out of a cab. She held the door open for Lisa, who had blood on her face and a smear of it down her coat. Deej looked at me, her eyes begging for help.

CHAPTER EIGHTEEN

I was beside them quick as a wink and we helped Lisa into The Old Town.

"Oh, my God!" Carla Jean cried. "Oh, my God! Why didn't you take her to the hospital?"

Norman dove for ice. "Are they beating us up on the buses now?"

Lisa was groaning, one hand trying to catch blood as it flowed from her small, ladylike nose. Oh, man, I thought. Of all things to be able to smell. I recognized the tinny scent of blood I'd first noticed during the raid. I wasn't sure if my sense of smell was returning or if my memory of the scent was kicking in.

"The hospital?" Deej responded. "A guy in hospital blues with the name of the hospital across the street stitched on them did this."

Carla Jean waved the bar phone in the air while, with the other hand, she clawed at her aluminum case to get a cigarette out. At their shop, JoJo had inscribed the case with Carla Jean's initials because Carla Jean was so hard on cigarette packs and left shreds of tobacco everywhere. "Maybe Dr. Everett can see you. I'm sure your nose is broken."

"He hit her?" Murph demanded.

"No!" Deej snarled. "Don't you know I would've clobbered him?"

"You didn't?" Murph said.

"He tripped her. He did it on purpose. When we crashed down he acted all apologetic."

Carla Jean lost patience with her cigarette case. Instead of putting down the phone, she flung the case to the floor. "I can't stand much more of this!" she cried. JoJo, without a word, picked the case up, opened it, gave Carla Jean a cigarette, and lit it.

Lisa grimaced as she jutted her foot out and quickly back to demonstrate. That led to another gush of blood from her nose. I thought to get a picture of her injuries, but, no, she'd be ashamed of how she looked. The wind was stronger now, and pushed against the front door.

Tipsy chimed in, red in the face. "The lousy bastard." She took the ice-filled bar rag from Norman and pressed it against Lisa's face.

"Ow!"

"Do you want to look worse?" Tipsy asked her.

Deej spewed the story. "Leese walked onto the bus first. I paid, then caught up with her. She was heading for the back. One of the passengers, the guy in blue, a cute guy too, smiling, real friendly looking, was sitting on a sideways bench. He had a newspaper and was looking from the front page up at me, down, then up again. I knew he was matching my face with the picture. I was so worried about being recognized, I didn't see his foot. All I knew was that Lisa was flying forward and I'm reaching to catch her and the driver picked that moment—darn, did he do it on purpose? He slammed on the brakes and threw me off balance, forward into Leese. She hit her nose on the metal hand grip sticking up from a seat."

Murph slammed her good fist on the bar. "Everyone thinks the femmes have it so easy. Not true. They take their lives in their hands every time they step out beside us." She rubbed her hand against her hip. "Yet they stay by our sides. And tell me why, why if it wasn't perfectly natural, would they?"

Carla Jean, who was spending more of her time at the bar than looking for work, said, "The doc's coming over. He answered his phone himself and said he had to let his receptionist go. His patients aren't coming in anymore."

"Poor Doc," said Murph. "That raid won't go away."

"What will he do?" Deej asked. She stood behind Lisa's chair, Lisa's head leaning back against her, a bar towel filled with ice pressed under her nose. I decided I'd be very surprised if they weren't already more than a one-night stand, at least to Lisa, though she hadn't fessed up to it yet.

"What all of us do," Murph said. Her voice always sounded deeper and more hoarse when she was close to tears. "We get by. We get by with ice chips of kindness and hot coals of dead-end passions. We lunge at love and parry our lovers. We set up housekeeping in such secrecy we never have homes. We live in hovels with guilt walls."

She took a seat across from the bleeding Lisa. "You think I've always been a big talker, but there was a time I was so fearful of speaking I hid in silence. Rose can tell you. I'm remembering what shut me up too."

Lisa managed a smile. "Here we go again," she said in a hoarse whisper. "Story time."

As Murph settled in to tell her tale, it was obvious to me she was distracting us from our newest catastrophe. This was another kind of war. I went to the bathroom and wet a handful of paper towels. Deej swabbed Lisa's face and coat with them. It was a war between the homos and the squares. I was too young to remember the First World War. I'd lost an uncle in it. The second, though, was full of memories of fear and deprivation. When the Japanese bombed Pearl Harbor, it had been an awful shock to find America so vulnerable. There was talk of German and Japanese submarines off both coasts, and soldiers came back from the Pacific with tales of heroism, horror, and need. I had one gal working for me who did something in communications. She hadn't been in battles, but she saw what the Germans did over there. A lesbian couple who came to the bar now and then had been fliers. I knew a half-dozen nurses who'd been in field hospitals and told of jumping into foxholes or working with newly released prisoners of war.

I kept busy at the bindery through the war with county and college tracts on subjects like growing victory gardens and living with ration cards. The shortages were hard on business; at times I gave up on getting parts for my machines and went back to hand binding. My crew consisted of myself, one ancient man, and an otherwise all-woman crew. I never let any of them go after the war, though one went back to full-time homemaking. Now and then she'd bring over a cake she'd baked, usually a strawberry one, my favorite. The government wanted me to employ veterans, and I'd have liked to if the plant was bigger. These gals, though, lost their men to the war or didn't have men at all. I wasn't about to take away their livelihoods.

Dr. Everett rushed in. He was a veteran who'd patched up soldiers in North Africa. As he examined Lisa, Murph related an anecdote I'd never heard before.

"I must have been all of eight years old," Murph said. "The Great Depression hadn't hit quite yet. Things were pretty wild and open in those days, even over in Boston. I've heard stories about the old Scollay Square that make these beatniks look like sober Presbyterians at a church picnic. Burlesque was big. The girls didn't wear much onstage, the gags were slapstick silly, and the whole idea was to titillate the guys. 'Decent' people didn't visit Scollay Square, but, as I learned when I grew up, practically everyone had at least taken in a show there."

The doctor announced that Lisa's nose was broken. She'd need a specialist to set it right because he feared cartilage as well as bone was out of place. They squabbled about going to the hospital for an x-ray,

Lisa refusing for fear of running into the tripper, Dr. Everett insisting for fear he'd do her more damage. Deej pushed for the hospital, threatening that, if they saw him, she'd make the tripper regret what he'd done.

"All right," Dr. Everett finally said. "You haven't gone into shock, your breathing isn't bad, and your nose isn't flattened . It could heal fine on its own. You call me if you notice anything that seems wrong. I'm worried about your sinuses. You can take your own chances on your looks. I don't have privileges at the hospital downtown, but you could go there." He gave Lisa more instructions. Deej went to the bar to get him a drink. The doctor wouldn't take money and said he'd drive Lisa home. "You'll have a couple of black eyes in any case."

Lisa's hand flew to her face.

"Now you're sending her into shock," Carla Jean joked.

When Lisa left with Dr. Everett, Murph started again. "Remember, my family was as Catholic as Rose Callaghan. Good Catholics, I thought. See, everything was in black and white for me in those days. You didn't sin or you'd have to go to confession. And they had us memorizing the Ten Commandments. I barely knew what coveting was, and I certainly didn't know the meaning of the word *adultery*. When one day I came home early from school with a cold and walked in on Da in my bed with Mrs. Santangelo from next door and they had no clothes on, I didn't turn away. 'Da,' I said, 'you have to go to confession Friday!'

"He must have thought pretty quick while he covered them up with the sheet. He didn't lie or try to tell me it wasn't wrong. He said he'd go see the priest right away and so would his friend Mrs. S. He made me promise never to tell anyone what I'd seen because another commandment was to honor thy father and thy mother.

"I slept in that bed later that night, with my sister. It was all clammy and, I imagined, dirty. I wanted to ask her, if you had to honor your mother and your father, which one should you honor if you had to choose. I'd been committed to silence and silent I would be. Night after night I wrestled with the question and then day after day. I couldn't ask the nuns at school any more than I could ask my sister. I couldn't ask the priest. I was bound to keep the huge secret about my father, about our neighbor, and about the enterprise I had no name for then: sex. Pretty soon I was consumed by conflict. I was scared silly I'd let slip word of what I'd seen. I spoke less and less at home, then at school, until I clammed up altogether for three years. Doctors couldn't find anything wrong. My teachers gave up on me. Then one day, playing dodge ball in the street, I shouted in protest about some foul or other. The next thing I knew, I was talking a blue streak and never stopped again."

"You didn't talk to anyone for three years?" Deej asked. "How did you stay in school?"

"The church showed no hesitation taking my parents' money and sitting me in a corner to learn nothing atall, atall." The more she talked about her early years as the daughter of Irish immigrants, the more Irish Murph sounded.

"You've certainly made up for lost time," Carla Jean commented.

Everyone at the table laughed.

"You see?" Murph said. "We're laughing. Look at us: we have food, shelter, and friends. They can raid us, jail us, and lose our jobs for us, but we're gay and we'll stay. I had some close calls though. It doesn't take much to upset the apple cart. After Rose left to be with Vi, I didn't care what happened to me.

"I went over to see my folks. We kids were all grown up, my brothers in the service and my sisters married. The folks lived in a third-floor, under-the-gables apartment, and they liked to sit out on the tiny open porch and catch the breezes from the river when it was hot. They'd both worked in the Goodlette hot-dog plant most of their lives. They let Ma go during the Great Depression and she went back to sewing clothes. Ma, she had second sight when it came to her kids. She asked me what was wrong. I told them about Rosie leaving with Vi. I told them flat out that Rose was the love of my life and I didn't see how I could go on without her. Da rocked on his kitchen chair and Ma got up and went in the house for a pitcher of iced tea and glasses. She set the tray on a wobbly little table they kept out there, gray from the outdoors, legs like twists of rope. I was in so much pain with losing Rose I'd forgotten that I was scared to tell them about me.

"Da and Ma always called me darlin' Murph. That started when Rose and I were tiny so we'd know which set of parents was calling who. Rose was always Rose and I'd be Rose Murphy. After a while I became Murphy and that got shortened even more to Murph. 'Darlin' Murph,' Da said, clapping me on the shoulder, 'you're going to live and you're going to love again. You're a Murphy. We're not some kind of sissies who fold when the going gets rough, are we?' I told him I must be the weak link in the family. It wasn't till afterward, when I met other women like us, that I realized how fortunate I was that he and Ma hadn't batted an eyelash about me loving a woman."

As Murph spoke, I remembered that I'd never told anyone in my family except my *Zeyde* Isaak, the man who, thank God, came over here long before it got bad in Europe. He was a farmer and had a sort of natural wisdom. My father was on the road a lot, earning a living, so his father, my zeyde, filled in for him. He took my mother and me to temple, gave me piggyback rides, and taught me skeet shooting. I remember the men who would come begging to our back door. Zeyde Isaak didn't always have work. He'd sit on the steps with them and share a bowl of borscht. There was no sour cream and rarely a meat broth, but beets we had plenty of. Any of the men stuck in the North come winter, my father would let sleep on the porch under blankets he took from his own bed. "I have the *baleboste* to keep me warm," he'd tell them, meaning his wife. Zeyde was a pal and a playmate and the one I told about wishing I was a man so I could marry a little girl in my class. He patted my head.

I was surprised and impressed that Murph hadn't hidden who she was.

"The Murphys don't wear their hearts on their sleeves, but, when I broke down crying, Ma pulled me to her and cradled my head against her chest. 'It'll be all right, darlin' Murph,' she told me. 'There's plenty other fish in the sea. I'll say a little prayer for you.'

"I thanked her and we sat there till dark, them asking questions and me bellyaching about Rose. That was the night they told me about Da's Aunt Una. 'She was small and pretty and loved the girls,' Ma said. 'When her da insisted that she marry, she cut off her long curly locks and took to wearing men's clothing. She talked her way into a job helping a roving veterinary surgeon and often returned to her small town wearing the bloody smock she worked in. Nights, she could be found in a tavern, enjoying the company of women as much as the men did. She lived only till the liquor got her liver, and although she never settled down, your father was told a host of women brought her meals and, sometimes, stayed the night.'

"If I'd been in less pain," Murph concluded, "I'd have got down on my knees and thanked them, these parents who had no problem with me being me. My oldest brother went to prison camp and never got out. Maybe they didn't want to lose another child. They got me through that storm and a few others before I lost them, Da to heart problems and Ma to pneumonia. It makes it hard to understand all the fuss about the queer people when a simple couple who immigrated from the old country, Catholics at that, took the news about me in stride."

Deej didn't take her eyes off Murph. "When was that, fifty years ago? And it was better then? Can you imagine dating women in plain view of straight guys now?"

Murph shrugged. "Half of them their wives. I'm not at all sure how Great Aunt Una got away with it. I've seen pictures of her. She could have walked into The Old Town and fit right in. In the end, it was the drinking got her, though that territory isn't only for us homos. The Murphys have lost their share of straight-and-narrow girls and boys to the barroom Pied Piper. And by the way, it was only about thirty years ago."

Deej lifted her glass, then set it down with a thunk and without drinking. "Is that why you don't drink, Murph?"

"I don't drink because I pledged to Rosie long ago that I'd never touch the stuff. The Callaghans weren't immune."

"I wonder if I have any lesbian aunts back in Jalna."

Lisa tapped a long ash into the aluminum ashtray, one of dozens Carla Jean and JoJo's award shop donated to the bar. She asked Deej, "Is that where your family is from, Jalna? I thought Jalna was in Canada."

"My parents' family came over from the Jalna district. That's in the Indian state of Maharastra. They're Hindu."

"Hindu?" Carla Jean said. "Hindu, like Ghandi?"

Nodding, Deej replied. "I'm impressed you knew that."

JoJo said, "Her hobby is current events. She could go on a game show and make a bundle."

"How are they on the topic of us sinners?" Carla Jean asked.

"Hindus? They're like most people. It depends who you talk to. I was brought up to believe, but I'm not religious. I'm an engineer, a scientist. One neat thing, Hindus believe in reincarnation, and sometimes they come back as guys, sometimes as women. That makes perfect sense of homosexuality: it would be hard to switch who you love from one life to the next. But my parents were taught being gay is wrong. I don't know whether that's from their Hindu backgrounds or something imported by the colonizers." She downed the last of her drink. "My family drinks. Some people of Hindu background think it's wrong."

"You're pretty good to be able to navigate three different cultures," Hugh commented. He'd joined us silently a while back and was stroking his beard. I'd been thinking the same thing.

Deej asked, "Three?"

Hugh smiled with affection and told her, "Indian, North American, and homosexual. How many Indian gays do you know?"

"Only me," Deej replied.

"The conflicts would be enough to drive a sane person over the edge."

Sometimes I thought Deej was pretty close to the edge.

She wrinkled her brow. "I never thought of this," she turned both hands palms up to indicate the bar and everyone in it, "as a culture. I guess it kind of is. Even Murph's aunt had a style like ours. You're right, Hugh, I do have my insane times when I'm a pinball in an out-of-control machine, ricocheting off targets and bumpers and bells until I'm wacky."

"The things parents keep from kids." Carla Jean made a tsking sound. "Think how much easier it would be to come out if our gay ancestors weren't kept in closets. Or locked in attics."

"Why won't they tell us?" Deej asked. "What do they care? What's it to them?"

"Preservation of the species," Hugh said. "In particular the fathers. They worry that no one will carry on the line." That, I thought, is pithy. Hugh and I had long, intense discussions now and then. I enjoyed his earnest opinions.

"We have too many of their species already," Deej said, her voice thin and whiny. "The het species."

"They steal our ancestors," Hugh said.

"What do you mean?" Murph asked.

"When they lie—and omitting the truth is lying—then they're keeping us from knowing our heroes, the people we're like and the people we want to be like. We're stuck seeing only what heterosexuals want us to see."

Dr. Everett returned and told us he'd left Lisa with everything she'd need. Deej used the pay phone to let her parents know she was on her way home from the library. I imagined Lisa worrying the break would mar her fine looks. If it did, maybe I'd stop being so intimidated by her.

The bar got quiet. No one fed the jukebox and the guys at the bar muttered about this latest shock. I knocked back the dregs of my drink and crunched on the last of the ice.

Deej wheeled her bicycle out of the kitchen and took off. Like Murph, Deej brought such spirited color with her, when she left there was a vacuum. She was one of us and so young. She had a lot to learn but seemed to be teaching us all.

CHAPTER NINETEEN

I was at the bar less for the next month. Cissy lived downtown, in one of a line of eight-story buildings along the west side of Garden Square.

She was seeing her boyfriend, but swore she'd never slept with him. The most they'd done, she said, was what we'd done our first night, only fully clothed. Oh, yes, I'd learned the next morning that what seemed to be a dream hadn't been all dream. The boyfriend wanted to get married. Now, she said, she knew why she'd held out.

I was on cloud nine, not one of those fluffy white clouds you see on sunny days. It was a swiftly moving cloud whose shadow briefly darkens everything it passes over. I was dizzy with both the demands of my infatuation and the thud of my common sense putting its foot down, insisting that Cissy was trouble. The boyfriend business gave me the creeps.

"Not that I'm complaining, but shouldn't you be having a period about now?" I asked her, my fingers playing with her down-there hair, as soft as the hair on her head.

She giggled and nuzzled under my chin. "Maybe your menopause is catching."

"You couldn't be—"

"I told you I never slept with him," she snapped.

"Okay," I said, startled. The poor woman, I thought, he must be pushing her hard for this to be such a sore spot.

"Don't you trust me?" She sounded genuinely aggrieved.

Did I? The right answer was yes. I was too uneasy to say it and excused myself by reminding her that I was a little jumpy after Geri's betrayal. To myself I said that the raid made me determined to live life more fully. If I was going to bear the brunt of being gay, I might as well indulge in the good stuff.

Cissy stroked my head. "Poor Rockie. I'd never do that to you."

Despite Cissy's assurances, after a few days apart I'd begun to dread the first kiss, knowing his lips had touched hers. I didn't say anything until one summer-like Wednesday afternoon in April when we'd both agreed to take off from work. Her place was a studio apartment with a view of students from the college lolling on the grassy areas of Garden Square. She'd chosen modern furniture, all angular cushions and chrome legs, slender shiny poles for lamps, and geometric designs on the black-and-white couch. Fake animal skins covered the hard wooden floors. Cissy liked to make love on the furry fabrics. A bed would have been kinder to my tender, aging knees. I laughed, remembering how I experimented in my thirties.

That afternoon the boyfriend showed up at her door while we were buck naked on fur. As usual, the TV was pretty loud, so Cissy couldn't pretend she wasn't there. We stared at the door, holding tight to each other, then dressed. I told her it was a mistake to open the door. He was pounding on it. We probably looked like we'd been making love. I stuffed our underwear under a couch cushion, then sat on it with a bottle of beer, pretending to watch TV like an innocent pal, while Cissy stepped into the hallway to talk.

A moment later, the door opened with such violence it hit the wall. Cissy yanked on the boyfriend's jacket, trying to keep him from looking into her apartment.

"Where is he!" he shouted at me. He was good-looking in a Tony Curtis way, all dark wavy hair and commanding, cocksure blue eyes.

"Who?" I asked. I raised my eyebrows, opened my arms, and laughed to show him there was no man in the apartment.

Fortunately, I was in the clothes I'd worn to meet with a customer. I'd reapplied my lipstick too. I knew it wouldn't even occur to him that someone in a dress could have been making love with his girlfriend a few minutes before.

Cissy was able to get him out and close the door. She must have begged a cigarette from him as she came back in exhaling smoke.

Shaken, I left soon afterward and crossed to the green to await my bus. I was scolding myself for getting involved with a woman on the fence when the boyfriend came up to me at the bus stop. In the background I saw two other guys and a girl monitoring. This was where the dress got in my way; I wanted to run like heck across the square and disappear into one of the big stores or the nearby hotel. I knew my way around this town.

"What's going on with Cecelia?" he asked, pretending nonchalance, as if I hadn't witnessed his anger. I told him to ask her and craned my neck to catch sight of my green bus.

What it is about me that gave his friends the idea I don't know. The girl was yelling across the street to him, "Maybe Cecelia's gone queer on you!"

I could strap myself to the bus-stop sign to keep from bolting. On second thought, the sign wouldn't be buried deep enough in concrete to stay put. I'd have to rely on my own will. Running, in this case, would be as much a confession as a flashing neon sign around my neck.

He turned to me, his eyes ferocious. I threatened to call the bus supervisor at the end of the block. I hated the monster he was seeing: the older lesbian corrupting the younger woman.

"If I find out something's going on between Cecelia and—" He seemed to study my face as if wondering whether what his friend asked was possible. Men should never check out the competition, I thought. It's too obvious who would win.

With a whoosh of brakes the Number 46 slid to the curb. I didn't spare the boyfriend a glance as I grabbed the metal rail and mounted the worn ribs of the black rubber-matted steps. From my seat I saw him, hands stuffed in his pockets, tromping across the street in front of the bus like he wanted to leave footprints in the asphalt.

On the old bus, huffing and puffing as if it was mad too, I dumped myself into a worn seat, its stuffing exposed under the torn woven cover. I took deep breaths to control my shaking. Once again I'd wet my pants a little. The things they don't warn us about when we're handed the manual on aging gracefully.

It wasn't until I was two stops from my apartment that it occurred to me the boyfriend might have gone back to Cissy's place. The minute I got home I called her. She didn't answer. My truck was at the bindery. I had no idea what to do next except change into slacks, which always gave me a sense of invincibility, and walk Colonel Mustard, which normally calmed me. I tried reading the new James Michener book, *Hawaii*. I couldn't concentrate. If I had the truck I'd drive right over there. It seemed wrong to go to the bar when Cissy might be in trouble, but where else could I turn?

The afternoon was waning. A few first-shift workers sat in a line on the stools.

"Spence and Seneca," JoJo said, and jabbed her finger toward the couple. I'd immediately poured out my worries to her. "They have a car."

I was glad to have a man with me when Spence blocked Cissy's car in and the three of us went upstairs.

Cissy didn't answer. I leaned on the bell a few more times and yelled out my concern. Spence tried the door. Locked. A voice called from down the hall.

"What's with the all the banging today?" asked a middle-aged man in T-shirt and pajama bottoms, an open book in his hands. "This is the third time. Enough is enough. She's out. With her boyfriend."

Stan took out his jail badge and displayed it briefly enough to look convincing. "Did she go of her own free will?"

The man stepped back. "Sorry, Officer. I didn't know this was official. I heard yelling from the apartment. The wife looked out the window and saw them leave in a car. Let me get her."

If I chewed my fingernails, that's what I would've been doing at that point. Cissy wouldn't have gotten involved with someone who'd hurt her, I was pretty sure of that. If she had, Paul would put an end to it, based on what Cissy had told me about him. Who knew what a man would do if his girlfriend admitted she was seeing a woman? Could Cissy be that naïve?

"Is Cecelia in some kind of trouble?" the wife asked. "Surely not. We told her about this apartment being vacant, you know. Such a nice young woman. We worked together when she was still in high school. It was her summer job. I work there to this day, you know."

Seneca shushed her with a question.

"No. Everything looked fine to me. He's such a nice young man, you know. I've been hoping to hear they're engaged. I suppose they're taking their time, like the kids do these days."

Kids? I thought. I had to admit they acted like kids.

While we waited for the elevator, the wife stepped back into the hall.

"Hello?" she called. "I don't know if this matters. I saw three other young people in his car. I was a little surprised when the boyfriend put her in the back between the other boys."

I looked at Seneca and Spence. What could we do?

Back at The Old Town, Murph's laugh sounded sarcastic when we told her the wife promised to keep Cissy in her prayers.

"Prayers are not what she needs in a car with an angry boyfriend and his pals."

I went home for Colonel Mustard. We roamed the neighborhood for an hour. Some of the trees quivered with open blooms already. I couldn't enjoy them. Was I actually looking for Cissy? I don't know. Maybe I was kind of keeping my eyes open for her. Before I went back to the bar I called her again and once more got no answer. While I was gone, Paul came in. He looked at me like I was compromising his sister's safety. I looked away; I was guilty. I was older and had been around long enough to know better. I swore to myself—again—that I'd never futz around with another straight woman.

"But Mary," Norman said to Paul, "you celebrated her coming out a couple of months ago."

Carla Jean said, "After what Paul went through, is it any wonder he's worried about his sister?"

Murph waved Carla Jean's cigarette smoke away. "I'm getting tired, tired, tired of all this folderol," Murph said. "I've belonged to the league at Hansfield Bowl for years. My hand's finally gotten well enough to roll a ball. My job helped build it up. I was surprised how easy they went on me at work, letting me take it slow at first. I've always gotten on good with my supervisor."

I was glad for the distraction of one of Murph's stories. I'd drunk my first drink too fast; the room was a little bit swimmy.

She shook her head and took a long swig of her drink. "It was my only splurge other than this silly ginger ale. You work hard all week, it's something to look forward to besides the bar. They aren't close friends, the other women, but I liked palling around with them. I guess they read the papers."

"What happened?" Paul was cracking his knuckles and drinking too fast.

"You'd think, wouldn't you, that after a long absence, I'd get a warm welcome back. It should have occurred to me, when no one called to ask where I was, that they didn't plan champagne to celebrate my return. These bowling buddies of mine, these so-called ladies, turned their backs at the sight of me."

"Oh," JoJo said, like the pain was hers, too heavy for her small frame. I'd always understood why we killed ourselves: this relentless battering could sink the staunchest ship.

"At first I thought to make them talk to me, like if they had their say, maybe they'd remember the Murph they knew and loved, the Murph who'd won so many games for them, because, I don't mind telling you, I was a darned good bowler." She held out her arm. "I suppose those days are over forever."

"You didn't give up and leave, did you?" Norman asked.

"Indeed I did," Murph answered. "I'm wrung out, folks. I am so drained by the consequences of this raid. Thirty years I've been feinting and ducking and hiding under the covers. If my world gets smaller because I choose to cut the straights out if it—present company excepted," she said to Tipsy, Seneca, and Spence—"then so be it. If I'm forced out of my closet, I'll come out with a roar."

"So?" Norman urged her to keep on.

"So," Murph said, getting to her feet. "Before I left, at the top of my loud Irish lungs, I yelled, 'What have I done, you turncoat biddies? Have I murdered your grandmothers? Have I stolen your husbands' jobs? Have I burnt down your homes, sent your sons to war, taken advantage of your little girls?'

"Not a peep out of them. Not a one turned to face me, though one of them, the one I was paired with most often in our tournaments, hung her head and clenched her fists, which I took as a signal that she'd stood up to them before joining their little death squad. I stood there, waiting for a response until they unlaced their bowling shoes, slipped into street shoes, slid their balls into their bags, and left through a side door to avoid looking at me. They gave up their reservation rather than face me or let me back on the team. I've a mind to go back every week and force them to forfeit their fees for as long as it takes."

"Except," JoJo said in her quiet voice, "you're not as mean as they are."

"Amen," Paul said. Then he looked at me. I went back to the pay phone in the restroom hall and tried Cissy again.

She didn't pick up. To be sure I had the number right, I rotated the dial again, then again and again until my fingers cramped around the handset. Paul's eyes looked wide with hope. Murph watched me as if her very soul depended on Cissy's safety. Norman and JoJo, Spence and Seneca, seemed connected to me with the force of their faith that all would turn out well. I would make sure Cissy was all right, then send the others to take care of her.

Cissy's voice, when she finally picked up, sounded as if she'd been screaming for hours.

I told her it was me.

"Oh, God," was all she said with an injured tone.

I couldn't keep away. I'd done this to her. I told her I was coming over and bringing Paul.

"Please, just you. No one except you."

CHAPTER TWENTY

The bus ride back to Cissy's was all red lights. I strained toward the front window, my silent impatience urging the driver, the engine, the wheels, to go faster. Once at the green, I ran the blocks to Cissy's place and didn't bother with the elevator. I rang the bell, trying to catch my breath as I waited. Running had burned my lungs raw.

She answered in her bathrobe, her hair wet from the shower.

"What did they do to you?" I asked.

"It was just him," Cissy said, leading me to the couch. The TV was on low, tuned to an old Ronald Coleman movie, *A Tale of Two Cities*, I guessed. This was beginning to seem like the worst of times.

"It was just him," Cissy repeated. "He dropped off our friends— his friends, I should say. Then he took me to his place and, he said, made me his wife."

She'd begun to shake and I knew where this was leading. She nodded when I asked if she'd been forced.

"When I begged him to wait for our wedding night, like he'd promised, he claimed we'd have our wedding night first and said we'd get the license and the ceremony next week. I've been so confused. After today, I want to marry him, or any man, about as much as I want to live in hell."

Cissy took my hand. Her bathrobe smelled of cigarettes.

"I told him I was afraid I'd get pregnant. All this time I was fighting him off." She showed me the fingerprint bruises on her upper arms and cried. "I thought he loved me. He said he hoped he did make me pregnant, that I'd never get away from him then. He'd make me quit my job and stay home and keep house for him, cook for him. All this time he became more and more domineering, like turning me into his slave was exciting. I got more and more scared, and my strength was draining out of me."

I offered to hold her. She apologized, saying she was one big bruise. I asked if it was too late to stop her from being pregnant. She didn't know; she said she never had to worry about it before. I called the bar and asked for Seneca. She and Spence would be right over.

Cissy told me, "The worst part was that I was starting to believe him. Maybe I was doing something wrong, seeing you. Maybe I was meant to take care of him and have his babies. Maybe my career was less important than all that."

I was so angry I wanted to maim the man.

She bowed her head. "He hurt me over and over. Afterward, all I could think was that I think I know what Paul goes through. I can't imagine living with this fear all the time. You guys always have to be scared of violence, don't you? You have the whole world trying to bend you to its way every minute of the day and night. No wonder you gather together in the bars. You need acceptance and you have no place else to go for it."

It wasn't something I liked to look at. Somehow I managed to see myself as whole and living what I thought of as a full life. Cissy was right, though. It was a half-life.

Cissy cried a while and I watched Ronald Coleman and a lot of stupid ads. When Seneca and Spence came to the door, Seneca took Cissy into the bathroom. They'd stopped at a drug store for something.

"It's not guaranteed to work," Spence told me.

We watched the TV. At the next ad, he said, "You let us know if Cissy finds out she's in trouble down the line."

When Seneca came out of the bathroom, she said Cissy wanted to be alone. They gave me a ride back to my apartment. I told Colonel Mustard all about it as I put her collar and leash on. She looked at me, mouth open in her great panting doggy laugh, as if I was predicting that Cissy and her boyfriend were creating an outrageous mongrel. I told her I didn't think that was funny at all. She kept on laughing. I knelt to her and gave her back, under its soft, clean fur, a good scratching. Her eyes closed in pleasure, she leaned against me. By the time I left her to go to the bar, that doggy had me percolating with higher spirits. One step inside The Old Town, though, and I froze, the terror of the raid assaulting me like the cop who'd rammed my head.

A tall man stood there, a tall man in a blue uniform. I got so nauseous I turned to leave. Carla Jean caught my elbow.

"He's okay," she said.

I stared at her, ready to run.

"It's the good cop."

At that moment he turned his face to me. It was Officer Van Eps, drinking a steaming mug of coffee. I laughed with relief because this Superman had swooped in and caught me mid-fall from a great height.

"We're trying to get him to leave so he's not found out and fired."

He crossed the floor in three long strides, his hand out. "Harry," he said. His grip was both firm and careful. "I was hoping you'd come in. I'm glad to see you're all right."

I thanked him for getting me out of the police station with Paul. I didn't mention the bottle of Empirin I carried at all times for this miserable headache, or the way I'd forget how to do something at the bindery and have to reteach myself. I didn't mention that I'd broken every rule in my book chasing a straight young woman into danger because injuring my head made a hodgepodge of my thinking.

"I told the others. I'm not here to apologize. I don't represent the force. I'm here because this is where I belong off duty."

I remembered what Paul said about what could happen to this guy if the other cops found out about him, and I wanted to tell him to run.

"When the captain gave us the order to raid a gay bar I thought, you know, check the license, card some people, shut the place down for the night. I didn't know an army of us was coming in, or that the captain, the guy who's in love with his baton, called the paper. I didn't know my so-called brothers in blue planned to go on a rampage and inflict so much damage or that your names would be published. My first thought was to quit. Then I told myself to get smart. I'm taking every exam that comes up. The higher I rise in the department, the more influence I plan to have. I'm going to be untouchable. In the meantime, let's see them try to fire me for hanging out at gay bars. Let's show some spunk, people, before we have no place to go."

"How?" asked JoJo, who'd come in and wrapped a bar apron around her waist, pulled two drafts, and was fishing in the draft-beer box for one of Murph's ginger ales. "They don't fight fair," JoJo said.

"Neither do I," said Harry. "I know their secrets."

"That's a dangerous game," Murph told him. "What's to stop them from shooting you and blaming it on some gangster?" The remark was typical of those Murph had been making lately. She'd gotten all negative and woeful, like the effects of the raid kept piling up on her.

"It's all on paper. In a safe-deposit box. In another state. If anything happens to me, my legal representative will deliver that little bomb to the newspapers. And he knows exactly who to take it to locally to make sure it runs—a little gay elf at the tippy top of the publisher's totem pole."

No one spoke. This was inconceivable, that one of us could be so powerful.

"And don't worry your pretty little head," Harry said, his reassuring brown eyes on Norman. "Those who want to do in The Old Town Tavern are going to have to work a little harder at it. Now, who's got some quarters for the jukebox? I want to dance!"

Ben E. King was singing "Stand By Me." It was pretty thrilling to see confident Harry take Paul's hand and lead him to the glowing jukebox. Paul had seen a plastic surgeon about fixing his face, because he couldn't even get a busboy job. Without his long-lashed beauty, he'd decided no man would ever ask him to dance again. Well, the lashes and the small, fluid body hadn't gone away, so I hoped Harry didn't ask out of pity.

I strolled to the bar with Carla Jean. Even inside The Old Town, she exuded an odor of cigarettes strong enough that I smelled it faintly. She finally was receiving unemployment and trying to talk her family into letting her return to work. Her mother was finding it hard to run the office at the dealership with kidney disease. Even if they stayed mad forever, Carla Jean counted on them to need her there. If that didn't work, she and JoJo proposed to move to San Francisco.

After Paul and Harry's dance, a fast one to "This Magic Moment," Norman topped off Harry's coffee.

"I want women on the force," Harry declared. "I want to end this ridiculous persecution. They shouldn't be bothering homosexual bars or bars where the people aren't white or speak Spanish. It's a stupid waste of police time unless something illegal is going on."

Paul looked at Harry with a kind of stunned wonder. "I don't know if you're a visionary or a lunatic."

At her table, Murph applauded. "This boy will go far," she said, walking over to Harry and pounding him on the back. "There's always a silver lining," she announced. Then, returning to her heavy mood, "If you can find it."

"Didn't you get your ribs kicked?" Harry asked her.

"Yeah, and my hand busted," Murph answered. "I've been back at work a couple of months. They gave me my pink slip today."

Oh, no. That raid ruined enough lives. Murph was beaten up enough. Could there be a bottom to her fall? It seemed there was a trap door in the floor under every trap door.

"Murph, why?" Carla Jean asked as she rushed to Murph. She laid her hands to either side of Murph's face and kissed her forehead. "Aw, Murph, honey. I thought you'd gotten back into the swing of things at the laundry."

"I was. No questions about how my hand was broken. No problem that I needed time off. It was as if management didn't read the paper. Or didn't care, which was what I hoped. I was their best worker. And the girls, well, I was a celebrity to them. They wanted to know all about my life now that they didn't have to pretend they didn't know I was gay. Everyone wanted to have lunch with big bad Murph. Some of the most married of them started cozying up to me. I'm beginning to think a lot of them don't much like sleeping with their husbands. "

Norman broke in to tell Harry, "Murph can make an epic out of a nursery rhyme."

Harry held up one hand like a traffic cop and leaned toward Murph, nodding his interest.

"I'd never been so popular in my life. Then, about two weeks ago, it started changing. No more giggling plans to come to the bar with me, no more Miss Popularity in the cafeteria, no more homemade-cookie gifts."

"Why did it stop?" Paul asked.

Murph shook her head, then ran her coarse hand through her mop of hair. Her hair was beautiful, thick and dark, with a natural sheen. "I doubt I'll ever know, although the hospital is owned by the Catholic church," she answered him. "They made sure I can't get unemployment too. They used my absence while I was recovering and how slow I was when I started back, like it was all my fault, and I suppose it was in a way. If I wasn't a queer, I wouldn't have been hurt and would be a better employee."

Carla Jean exploded. "That's ridiculous! Anyone can get hurt, or sick. Do they go around firing people for it?"

Murph looked into the glass she held and smiled like an old crooner singing of regrets. "They can fire anyone they want any time they want for any reason they want. They don't even need a reason. It wasn't exactly a union job."

"At least I have that," Harry said. "The police association. They might not want to defend a faggot, but they would pretty much have to because I'm a good cop."

"One thing I want to know, Harry," said Murph. "How did you ever get the goods on this publisher? How can you make him print a story? How did you learn what you know? Is he family? I wish I knew someone who runs the college."

"Sometimes I think all guys are gay once they stop believing religious rules."

"That's the truth, all right," JoJo said. "Girls too."

Harry explained. "The publisher's son is a raging queen. I mean, he was nelly at five. I remember him in kindergarten, so beautiful and fragile. Even a little girl beat up on him. We came out together in seventh grade, before his daddy started bringing in the big bucks and sent sonny boy off to private school. We saw each other holidays and summers. He's still fragile and even more beautiful. I was his blue-collar boyfriend until last year, when we turned twenty-eight. Maybe always would have been. He decided to play it straight and go into the family business, which required marriage. So much for soul mates forever. And that was the end to getting the dirt on hush-hush deals and which politician is in bed with which businesses. Damn turncoat. Not that I'll expose him. I'll always love him. I'll threaten Daddy, who doesn't want the town to know about his little boy. "

"I wonder," Murph said, slowly, sadly, "if this is how we always survive. With the help of people in high places we don't know are on our side, who use power we don't know they have."

Harry set his empty mug on the counter and slid off his stool. "That's part of it. That, and they don't expect us to stand up for ourselves. I stood my ground after the raid on The Old Town and hurt a couple of them. We survive because we're tough and brave."

"You're talking like we're some sort of team or tribe or—" Paul waved his fingers as if to make the word come to him, "family."

JoJo didn't talk much, but when she did, we paid heed. "I think he's right," she said. "There are so many of us. We're all over the US and North America and the world. If we ever stood together, think what we could accomplish."

The very idea gave me a stomach cramp. We needed to keep out of sight, not expose ourselves. These youngsters imagined they were immune to the forces of hatred.

"Forget it," Paul said. "First, we'd never stand together. Second, if we did, they'd mow us down."

Harry said, "Maybe you're right. I'm personally not willing to sit back and take it without a darned good fight. Let's get together and talk about this some time, Paul."

Paul wasn't about to turn down an offer like that. He wrote his number on a bar napkin. Harry folded the napkin into a precise square, then put it in his shirt pocket and left for his tour of duty.

More cockamamie ideas, I thought, tracing a name carved into the table.

"Ah, the young: afraid of nothing and with dreams grand enough for kings," Murph said.

"But what a beautiful dreamer," Paul said, exaggerating a sigh. "And what a beautiful dream."

JoJo, her nose reddening and her eyes shiny with rare tears, asked, "Where would we be without dreams?"

CHAPTER TWENTY-ONE

The next Tuesday I huddled with an attorney to get my name away from the public eye while maintaining control of the bindery. I was bushed and left early. I spent some time tossing the dolly I'd made out of old socks for Colonel Mustard, then crossed The Avenue through the rainy April night and slipped onto my usual barstool at The Old Town.

It had been six months since the raid, and I was worried sick about my continuing memory lapses. My attention span was shorter than Colonel Mustard's. How could I run a business like this? I couldn't even remember that I couldn't remember, so I had to figure things out over and over.

I'd asked the attorney about protecting the company from my addled brain and he counseled me to be patient. I'd be right as rain before I knew it. My niece was worried and encouraged me to talk to Dr. Everett about seeing a specialist. I walked around in a blue fog, stumbling over familiar furniture or machines that hadn't been moved for years. An odd smell inhabited my nose, a phantom smell, like burning paper dust. We created a lot of paper dust at the bindery and I didn't allow smoking in the building for fear of combustion. It was exactly what smelled, to me, like trouble.

I was afraid Dr. Everett would say this was as good as I'd get. My mood worsened daily. I'd never been a grouch before. Losing Cissy was a blow that proved I was an old fool, more off the market than Paul. When I got testy, Colonel Mustard looked at me with hurt eyes. What good would it do to talk to any doctor? Half the problem was being gay. The raid had ruined me along with everyone else.

Norman set my drink in front of me as I sneezed into a handkerchief. Getting a miserable cold didn't help my day. As we talked, the usual after-work gang meandered in.

"I'll have what she's having," said a guy who took a stool a bit away from me toward the door. I blew my nose, apologizing for my state.

"Darling!" Norman exclaimed to the guy. "You've come back to visit!"

It was Russ, Deej's friend and ex-fiancé. As cool as he seemed to want to be, Russ looked at the door so often it was like he was waiting for the fuzz to arrive any minute.

Norman drew drafts for Spence and Seneca, who sat playing cards at their usual table toward the back of the bar. He returned to Russ. "So tell Uncle Marilyn," Norman said. "What brought you to The Old Town? Aren't you afraid your teammates will find out about you?"

"Hell, no. They wouldn't be caught dead in this part of town, much less in this bar."

"And why is that?" Paul asked, challenge in his tone.

"Ugh!" Russ said to Paul. "What happened to you?"

Paul turned away and joined Seneca and Spence.

Russ answered Paul's questions anyway. "Everyone knows this section of Hansfield has gone to the dogs." Russ was really a handsome boy, if you liked them dense of both body and brain. "There's no one around here except longhairs and gays."

JoJo straightened from dousing glasses in soapy water just long enough to exchange a look with Norman.

"Why," she asked, "would you even lower yourself to stop by?"

This was JoJo's turf and she was proud of it.

Russ swallowed about half of his vodka tonic. "Hey," he said. "I'm not saying I think that. You know how it is. I need to stay in the closet. Anyway, I'm here about the Deej."

Norman asked how "the Deej" was doing.

"That's just it. I don't know. I can't find her."

"Come on," Norman said. "Did you two have a tiff? Are you mad because she's not going through with the marriage?"

"She's not?" Russ asked, his cool-guy attitude disappearing like a shadow in the noontime sun, leaving him one-dimensional.

"Oops, spilled the beans."

"I was afraid that's why she wasn't taking my calls. Maybe she's hiding from me."

"Or she's been making things up to suit the occasion," Paul said, fluttering his eyebrows. He'd recovered from the insult and sat with his good side to Russ.

Russ looked at Paul again and frowned. "What happened to you, buddy?"

Paul now had a black scar running down the left side of his face. His eye was only open enough to reveal the blood in it. The bottom of his eye socket was flat and the flesh sagged.

"Oh, a little run-in with a cop's weighted fist."

"That's why I'm so nervous about coming in here," Russ said.

"Can't afford to look like this?"

Russ shrugged. "Well, I hate to tell you guys: Deej really is missing. Her dad called me and accused me of luring her away. I wanted to tell him she's queer."

"You didn't, did you?" Carla Jean demanded.

Russ was in charge of himself again, obviously assuming Deej had lied to us, not him. I held in a laugh; Russ would be a lot easier to lie to than we would be.

"Of course not," Russ said.

I thought about how that might be hurting us. Gay people adopted lying as second nature. Lying, hiding, pretending to be people our families could love—it was all part of the gay life and Deej was already good at it. There must be consequences. Were we rotting away at our cores from dishonesty? Could I ever love someone so much I'd never stretch the truth, never automatically tell her little white lies?

"Okay." Murph came out of her funk long enough to instruct him. "Why don't you start from the beginning. Have you looked in every nook and cranny she might be?" My mind added the words I could see her biting back: "You big lummox?" She used it a lot when the Patriots flubbed a play on the bar's small TV.

Closeted Russ might be, yet a he had that slight sibilance in his speech. It made me smile, Mr. Big Bad Football Player.

"The first thing I heard about was that Deej didn't show up for her volleyball club. She loves that stuff. I went to one of her games and she was quick and strong. She could spike into next year if they'd let her. A little prima-donna-ish, though. She likes to win the games without a lot of help from the team. It was a kick seeing this little shorty pop up to get a ball over the net when a taller girl was primed for it."

"She's probably shacked up with Lisa," said Carla Jean, who, sloshing her wine a bit, took the seat between Russ and me before lighting a cigarette.

The rolled newspaper thudded against the front door. As usual, the delivery boy hurled it with all the power of his hostility.

Murph looked up. I could see how much she wanted to fling herself out the door to go after that paperboy.

"Lisa? Which girlfriend is that?" Russ asked.

Carla Jean made a face. "How many are there?"

"Oh," Russ replied, "I lost count almost right away. Deej is worse than most college guys. She's brought out so many girls at school the Kinsey Report is going to have to be changed."

"Goll-ee." These days Paul sounded as if he was speaking through a mouthful of cotton batting. "That girl is making up for lost time."

Norman unleashed a girlish giggle. "With Russ setting an example, why am I not surprised?"

Russ gave a little shake of his shoulders like a preening bird might to better display its brilliant feathers. I laughed at him outright, but not to be mean. He was ridiculous and so involved with himself he never looked my way. "So who's this Lisa person?"

"You probably saw her here." Murph poked her finger toward the boy. "Tall for a woman, with the face of a masterpiece, hair pretty much the color of peanut brittle. She's got a sad, striking beauty. You had to notice her." Her pokes got away from her and she propelled a full ashtray onto the floor.

"Notice a woman?" Russ said, with a haughtiness no straight man could manage.

They all laughed. I was taken by surprise when I felt a little jolt in the region of my heart at Murph's description of Lisa. I put it down to vibrations of a train coming in to Hansfield Station. My watch confirmed the train was running right on time. Where was Lisa? Hiding her bruised face from the world?

JoJo appeared with whisk broom and pan for the fallen cigarettes. Norman went to the door and retrieved the paper.

Russ asked, "Do you really think Deej is with that Lisa person? Do you have her phone number?"

No one did, of course. We guarded our safety in rituals so secret that we never even admitted the rituals to one another. I'd never discussed the fact that I feared giving out my phone number; I was a little ashamed of myself for my pervasive distrust. Yet I knew the others did the same. Some of the gals I see at The Old Town are so cautious they won't acknowledge me on the street. When I see a lesbian couple I don't know, or an obvious butch type, our eyes transmit a quick signal of recognition, then slide away with no other acknowledgement. What would happen if I smiled and stopped to talk? Would the sky fall?

Nobody's watching. Nobody. Or maybe one person. That's all it would take to start the talk that would spread the rumors that would reach bosses or customers or our families. Then what would happen?

Most people don't know we're among them. They think homosexuality is a revolting aberration. They think there are fewer than a dozen of us and we only come out at night, like vampires looking for fresh blood. We're as fascinating as horror stories to them. If my family knew, shame would torture them. They'd hide me by telling no one, and I wouldn't tell them details of my life or bring home anyone I loved. They would do nothing to educate themselves. After all, I'd be their only source of information unless they wanted to watch a movie or read a book in which a life like mine ended in tragedy.

"I don't have her number," I said. "I'll go over there right now and see what's what, if someone can tell me where Lisa lives."

Russ clapped me on the shoulder. "You're topnotch. If I'm not here, leave a message with Norman and I'll stop by."

I looked at Norman. He raised his eyebrows and said, "Why not?" Later we'd agree Russ is a rude young queen and that Norman wouldn't mind spending a night with him anyway.

Murph mumbled the address with some reluctance. Addresses are another secret we keep, but this was an emergency. Without enthusiasm, she offered to come with me. I gave her the fisheye and she backed down. Bad enough one of us would see her—Lisa was hiding her broken nose.

In a way I wished someone could have come with me. My awe of Lisa's easy grace, womanliness, and romantic yearnings made it awkward to arrive unannounced at her front door; she'd be embarrassed to be seen bruised and bandaged. What if Deej was there? Lisa was no chicken hawk; I didn't want her to think I was protecting the kid from her.

So why was I going over there? It wasn't to get a chance to ride the Number 46 bus, which, at this time of day when people got out of work, let riders off at every stop. I left the bus at the corner of Highland and Milk Streets, not far from the center of town, about five thirty. It was still light out, sprinkling rain, and I turned up my collar to keep my neck dry. Even here I smelled the burning paper dust; a bonfire of it followed me everywhere. A psychiatrist would say it represented a fear of losing my company.

Lisa's place was the left half of the second floor of a conventional, multi-family home that looked like it was built around 1900, when

Hansfield was thriving. The front door was, for some strange reason, painted purple. I rang the bell for her apartment. A door opened upstairs and I stepped back to see if it was Lisa.

"Rockie?" she asked, leaning over the porch rail. I heard astonishment in her voice.

"Hi!" I immediately regretted not having said something more intelligent.

"Don't look!" she said.

I lowered my head so fast the concussion headache immediately worsened. "I have a question," I told the walkway.

"What?" she said.

I yelled to the ground, "I have a question!"

"Fine," I thought she said, in a normal speaking tone.

"Russ came to the—" I hadn't anticipated having to shout anything. "Came to—to the parade."

"The parade?"

"You know, the grandstand. Where we watch the parades."

"Ah. Okay, I understand." I could tell she was beginning to think I was a meshuggener.

"He said Deej is missing. We thought you might know where she is?"

"What did you say?"

"Deej!" I raised my voice again. "Is missing!"

"Oh, my God," she said. "You'd better come up."

CHAPTER TWENTY-TWO

I have to say it was a shock to see her bandaged face when I got upstairs to her apartment. I was so weary of bandages, bloodied body parts and souls. Right then, I wanted to be taller than Lisa so I could wrap my arms around her to comfort her.

Whenever I was around her, I realized I wasn't the polished, savvy businesswoman I thought I was. I got clumsy and tongue-tied in her presence. She'd grown up in Manhattan, dropped out of college, married and moved to Hansfield, then divorced—I didn't know much more about her. Still, anyone could tell that Lisa Jelane was one classy lady.

"The hell with it," I thought, and took the plunge. It's funny how small a taller woman can seem in your arms. Lisa turned into a soft, needy friend who let herself lean on me. I made sympathetic sounds and stroked her hair. We went to the couch.

"I didn't want anyone to see me in this state," Lisa said.

I averted my eyes.

"That's all right, Rockie. It's just you. You're exactly who I need."

I wish, was my thought. "Yeah," I told her. "I'm not going to like you any less, Lisa. I know exactly how spectacular you usually look."

She laughed and called me a sweet talker. As if to emphasize her point, a small, multicolored cat jumped onto my lap and stroked my neck with its tail. "Who's this?" I asked.

"That's Lana Turner."

"I have Lana Turner on my lap? Va va va voom!"

I was embarrassed by what I'd said about Lisa looking spectacular and didn't want her to think I meant anything by the remark so, while I patted Lana Turner, I filled her in on the news about Deej.

Lisa said, "She called a few days ago and pleaded to take care of me. I told her no. Later, she came knocking on the door. I was sleeping—it's about all I do these days. I pulled a pillow over my head and went back to sleep."

I must have looked grim because Lisa said, "Maybe she needed help more than me. Maybe—are you very worried about her?"

"I wasn't. Now I'm wondering if I should be. Why do you think she might have needed help?"

"Not help so much as..." Lisa sighed. "I told her I wouldn't see her anymore."

"Too young?"

"No. I don't think age should make a difference between two people who belong together."

I tucked that philosophy into my bra for later appraisal. "No, of course not. Geri was nine years older than me."

"That was her name, Geri?"

"That's all water under the bridge now." I brushed my past away with a sweep of my hand. "How do we find out what happened to Deej?"

"It's not at all like her to lose touch with her family. They're very close-knit."

"Okay," I said. "What do we do now? Do you have a phone number for her?"

"At her family's house? You're kidding, right?"

"At a friend's?"

"Not even at work. She said interns don't have phones."

"We could try to reach her with the general number."

Lisa went to get the yellow pages. That gave me a moment to glance around her place and learn something of the inner Miss Jelane.

I touched nothing. At the far end of her narrow kitchen was a tall, light-filled window. The bedroom door was partly open to a midnight-blue wall, the edge of a dark oak dresser, and the foot of an unmade bed with a cobalt-blue bedspread. I imagined dark curtains in there. Did Lisa have trouble sleeping?

Her living room was the opposite. She'd painted the walls such a bright white I bet she squinted when the sun shone in. The window curtains were sheer white and the couch I sat on was yellow. The furniture looked well lived-in, slightly short of shabby. She probably shopped at the Morgan Memorial. Her TV was housed in a square, light-birch cabinet missing one of its doors. On top of the cabinet lay a book I'd been looking forward to reading. Two chairs were upholstered in a fabric so fanciful I laughed: giant discs of moon-white and daffodil-yellow almost orbited across a butter background. Did this make Lisa happy? I stood and went to look at a large framed print over the couch. It was all black lines with a tiny block of yellow and larger blocks of blue and red. It was nice enough, but I go for good strong portraits, preferably of the ladies.

Lisa came back shaking her head. "I called over there. They said Deej wasn't on the company roster and there was no way to find an intern among twelve hundred employees. I guess it's my turn to ask, 'What now?'"

For all her characteristic reserve, Lisa seemed a little lost as she stood with Lana Turner in her arms, nuzzling her neck. It was the kind of lost I'd seen in women whose anticipated life plan fizzled. They had nothing with which to replace it. Would the love of a strong woman be enough to repair the damage?

"Let me think," I said, reaching to let Lana Turner sniff my finger with her cold, wet nose. "You probably know Deej better than any of us. Where else would she go?"

"Another girlfriend?"

"You didn't mind that there are others?"

She looked wary. "That's not something I stay around for once I find out."

I nodded. "Glad to hear it. It's no way to live."

"I don't know why I even care about Deej. Here she is running around with all these girls, including straights who could bring home who knows what kind of infections from men—"

Now I laughed, trying to do it quietly. "You talk about men like they're a diseased species."

Lisa looked me in the eye. "Falling in love with my office mate wasn't the only reason I divorced Dan."

"Oh," I said. She didn't elaborate; I hurried away from the topic. "How did Deej react when you broke up with her?"

"There wasn't anything really to break up. She wasn't dejected, if that's what you're asking."

"You never know. Trust me, I thought of it myself when Geri left, but Colonel Mustard needed me."

"I'm the one who should end my misery. I keep trying and trying and—"

"You know that's no solution," I said.

"Do I? I need a strong, handsome woman waiting at home to share everything with, and I don't see anyone lining up for the job." She rubbed her nose on the cat's head again. "Besides Lana Turner, of course."

I was too concerned to shout *Pick me! Pick me!* Instead, I said, "I'm telling you it's not a solution, and if you ever think about it again you are to call me. Immediately. Here or at the bindery." I dug into my wallet and found her my card. "No excuses. Even if you only want me to come clean up afterward, you call."

Lisa's lips opened slightly and she looked at me as if she'd awoken from a deep sleep.

"You got that?"

"You're always so quiet at the bar. I guess you're not as retiring as I thought."

"Don't change the subject, Lisa."

"I'm to call you if I ever want to end my miserable life."

"Good girl. Now, here's what we'll do about the kid." Lisa was right. I didn't show this side of myself to friends. This was my work personality, very managerial and butchy. I questioned why I was letting it out now. To save her life? More like to save mine.

"What we're going to do is nothing. There's not a thing any of us can do. If the Deej has gotten herself into some mess, she's going to have to sink or swim exactly like the rest of us. Her parents are concerned and they'll take care of this. We have no legal right to do anything. When she comes home to roost we'll do our best to put her back together again."

"'And all the king's soldiers and all the king's men, couldn't put Humpty Dumpty together again?'"

"Do you honestly think Deej might crack up?"

She thought about it. "No one can predict anyone's breaking point." She drew her fingers along Lana Turner's back and up her tail. The cat stretched to keep the touch. When Lisa took her hand away, Lana Turner reached for it with her paw; that was one smart cat. "Part of any woman can be broken. Deej can be such an infant. And so exciting. I hope she's all right."

I nodded, all tender around the heart. "Of course she is. It's been a year of changes for her. She needed to step back and get some perspective. Deej is a smart kid. We have no idea whether her parents did or said something to drive her out of the house. I'd be staying with some friend they don't know about. She'll show up at The Old Town one of these days."

Lana Turner leapt to the rug.

I took that break in our conversation to ask, "Speaking of the bar, when are you coming back?"

Lisa's hand went directly to the splint on her nose. Dr. Everett had gotten her in to see a surgeon colleague. We all suspected that Dr. Everett had subsidized the procedure. No one would ask Lisa, of course, because of her pride. In any case, her nose was properly cared for.

"You look fine," I said. "A little bandaging and bruising can't ruin looks like yours."

"I've been so grateful to be out of work right now so no one has to see me."

"We'd all love to see you. Come on. We're already down one. Don't you abandon us too."

She shook her head. "I'd be so uncomfortable. It wouldn't be fun for any of us."

In the end, Lisa let me do some grocery shopping for her. She hadn't been able to tackle that herself either. She would, in return, cook dinner for me once a week, when I brought the groceries, so I could check up on her.

"Or," she said with a cautious smile, "clean up the mess."

I wagged a finger at her and left, thinking that, strangely enough, I liked her combination of darkness and light. It was the yellow side of Lisa that welcomed my comfort. The dark-bedroom side was the aloof Lisa I'd known till now. It was all up there in her modern-art print somehow, the rigid black lines, the bright patches of levity and warmth. And her cat. Lana Turner was the friendliest, most affectionate cat I'd ever seen.

I was out on the sidewalk when I heard her call from the porch.

"Bring Colonel Mustard!" Her voice sounded a lot happier than when I'd arrived. "Lana would like to meet her."

CHAPTER TWENTY-THREE

The next day, as I hid in my office where no customer could see the company outcast, I thought about Cissy and I thought about Lisa. Cissy was beautiful like Paul, tiny and fine, pixyish and androgynous. I couldn't look at her enough. Lisa's beauty was like a work at the Museum of Fine Arts in Boston, something a sculptor would, with his chisels, hammers, and picks, find in impassive stone to portray a woman's life and trials and pleasures.

That was all behind me, though. I'd settle for my books. I kept the best ones in my bedroom closet, in a shoebox. I'd found a new Valerie Taylor novel, *Stranger on Lesbos*, at the train station in Pittsfield. I was constantly tempted to get rid of the books. What if I died and my family found *Another Kind of Love* in my closet? Regardless, I needed the books. I was getting too old to think about new women. I'd probably call a girlfriend the wrong name, the way I was confusing everything else. Remember anniversaries? A birthday? Forget it. I was too far gone to give any woman the attentiveness she deserved.

At work, I used a desk-blotter calendar; since the raid, I carried one of those pocket Hallmark calendars. Grocery shopping for Lisa was in red. I didn't want to let her down, although every week I half expected her to tell me not to come over. I wrote a reminder to see how Cissy was. Did I want to find out? People are strange about associating bad times and the people they experience them with. I called more than once and got no answer. I laughed. She'd probably run off with Deej. Why not? Everyone else seemed to.

Seriously, I was concerned and decided to check in at the bar. I needed to report on Lisa anyway. I was lucky enough to catch an air-conditioned bus across town; though it was only April, it could have been a summer day.

Murph was standing with her back to the bar, starting a tale. I flopped onto a stool next to Paul and Harry to hear her out. JoJo sped over with my usual, and I set a ten on the bar and left the change there. My eyes met Paul's in the mirror, and I raised my eyebrows. He shook his head. He hadn't been able to contact Cissy either.

"Listen, I lost my new job at the dry-cleaning plant today. Not because they don't like lesbians," Murph was saying. "The place is riddled with us. Or because, after the raid, I now have a big fat arrest record for all the world to see. They let me go because I can't keep up." She showed us her hand. "This isn't getting better." She swallowed a mouthful of ginger ale.

"It hurts you?" JoJo asked.

"Like a son of a gun. I gulp aspirin every four hours. The pharmacist said to ice it and heat it and do this and that. I follow his instructions to a T. No change."

"Oh, baby girl, you don't mean you keep talking when you leave here?" Norman joked.

"I got free advice, didn't I? So before they let me go at the dry cleaners, I talked with the personnel lady and she said how they really like me except production isn't my forte. Would I be interested in doing something in the office?"

Murph looked at us like she was about to confess to killing her family. Twice she started, saying, "I told her…" and twice she looked away. "I told her I can't really read."

Murph appeared as close to tears as she was at the raid.

"Or write," she added.

The shock hit us all. You hear of illiterate people from other countries or up in the hills of Appalachia. I remembered Rose's remark about Murph being unable to read and how I'd dismissed it. I give us all credit. No one looked shocked or asked, "At all?" Instead, Carla Jean, Paul and Norman all volunteered to teach Murph, talking over one another in their eagerness.

"You guys," Murph muttered. She was acting sheepish for the first time in my memory. "You're good souls. I told the personnel lady, who may be family," she said with a wink, "I tried and tried in school. Rosie will tell you. I'd get my letters backward so I couldn't even sound out words. The teachers thought I was the backward one. I couldn't sit still more than a few minutes. In my desk I kept a pink rubber ball. I was always getting in trouble for bouncing it under my desk to keep awake. The kiddos called me thick and showed me no mercy. I excelled only in playground and quit after seventh grade because they threatened to leave me back. You can't imagine my shame."

"Stupid teachers," Paul said. "I'd have given you the help you needed."

Murph sounded like a baffled kid. "They did give me help. The teachers stayed after with me. They signed me up with volunteer tutors, Rosie tried to help me out. They tested my eyes and nothing was wrong. Show me how to do something and I'm fine. Tell me to read the instructions and I'm a washout. Am I stupid?"

Paul went over and hugged Murph to him with one arm. "No, hot stuff, you're certainly not. I've had two or three pupils with conditions something like yours. Maybe exactly like yours. Science hasn't caught up with all these things that go haywire in our brains. We're learning more every day." He tapped his bottom lip with an index finger. His hope, he'd announced recently, was to get a state job and use the health insurance to repair his face. He'd already completed several applications and gone on one interview.

"I have a friend," Paul said. "She does testing for the public schools. Let me ask her for some suggestions."

"You're a pal to offer, Paul. It's a little late now. You can't teach an old dog new tricks."

So this was the crux of Murph's depression.

Harry the cop went to Murph and looked down into her eyes. "You are not old, not a dog, and it's not too late—ever. Are you going to let that raid ruin your life?"

"It already has. Gay girls need our hands."

Carla Jean gave a lusty laugh. "If you don't know a way around that problem, Murph, we need to have a little talk!"

"Paul is an educator," Harry said. "He knows his business. Let him help, okay? There's no shame in it."

"Why did you take so long to tell us, Murph? It's like being born with an allergy. You find ways to fix it," said JoJo, who we all knew endured bad hay fever.

"There's no pill that will help me read." Murph lowered her head and put a hand over her face. "Things are piling up around me. I've always been able to get by. Now I don't see how I can. If I can't earn a living, how am I going to pay Norman and Hugh the rent?"

"Murph," I said, "you tackle this and I'll find you a job at the bindery. We don't fire people for being injured or gay." I didn't know by what means I'd do it, but I knew Murph to be a hard worker and reliable.

"Is that the God's truth? You'd want me despite it all?" Murph asked.

Carla Jean went over and put her arms around Murph, then gave her a smooch. "Aw, Murph, honey. Did you think we wouldn't love you anymore?"

Harry hung his head. "All this because of the raid. I am so sorry."

"It's not your fault, Harry," Norman said, touching him lightly on the forearm. Norman would make a good mother, with his reassuring voice and the tenderness he showed for his boys. "It's always been this way and it always will be this way. I don't know why people hate us. We can't do a thing about it."

As if timed to make things worse, the newspaper came sailing through the door, which was open to the warm day. The paper slid to the end of the bar.

"That little shit could have hit someone," Norman said.

"Stop the subscription!" JoJo reminded him.

"No! No! No! I will never give in to their bullying. Never, never, never."

The mood at The Old Town was not good during the slow spell between the after-work crowd and the night crowd.

I asked if anyone had heard from Cissy or Deej. They all looked so low they didn't seem to care. Norman was stocking the bar, which looked kind of sparse; Hugh was upstairs working on an article for a journal about the use of Latin phrases in contemporary slang. Carla Jean ran over to The Avenue Arms to bring back dinner for herself and JoJo, and a few of us ordered out for pizza. A while later a delivery boy came in. Norman always ordered from the parlor up the street. The boy was one of the owner's teenage sons and actually got flirty with the guys. Norman tipped well. Hugh came down for dinner and I heard the first quiet laugh. I pulled a triangle of pie from the morass of melted mozzarella. Norman spread his newspaper at the bar to read and eat while JoJo worked. I had no doubt the smell of a pepperoni pizza would improve the mood of the gay girls. In a few city blocks we had a perfect tiny city: Chinese, Italian, dry cleaners, library branch, gay bar. What else did a person need?

Norman screamed again.

The regulars turned to him. Carla Jean ran to his side. I wanted to do the same. I kept my seat and hoped the bathroom would be empty when I—momentarily—might need it.

He crumpled the paper in his small hands. "They want our building."

"What building? This building?" Carla Jean, face red with rage, shook a cigarette from her case.

"The college wants to put in a parking garage. They want half the block. This half."

"Hell, no, man," said the used-record-shop owner. "The damn college has shit for brains if they think they can encroach on our street."

His friend the cobbler, beer foam on his beard, said, "Tell them to go to hell. We'll sit here till they drag us out. Or kill us. They'd probably rather do that." I laughed to myself, imagining a parade of these unconventional graduates from the college chugging along Girolami Avenue in their VW buses, tiny red brake lights flickering as they blocked the street to protest the demolition.

Carla Jean leaned over him to read. "Sounds like what the damned college wants, the damned college gets. They've got an in with the city."

"We finished all this work on the place." He looked at Murph. "You may not need to worry about paying us rent."

"Let the city try and take me away from my home. They'll have to evict me by the ankles." She looked plenty scared though.

Norman frowned. "This is probably why no one's bothered us for their annual greased-hand donation. If they think we're going to sell this building…"

"It's worth money now," Carla Jean said. "Danny Bernato sold it to you for chump change."

Norman gave a sputtered laugh. "That pathetic little tub of a queen? He sold it to Hugh and me on the condition that he gets to produce, star in, and take seventy-five percent of the profits from any drag shows here."

"You have drag shows?" Spence asked. "I thought that was a special Thanksgiving event."

"More like no-shows, honey."

"I always assumed," Murph said, "you pitied him."

"That too," Hugh said.

In her quiet voice, JoJo concluded, "At least now we know why they've launched their full-out assault."

Murph stopped cursing everyone she could think of and said, "Rose is getting together with those lawyer friends about the harassment Monday. Maybe they'll have some suggestions concerning this little development."

"Would you ask her to get a recommendation for an attorney here in Hansfield?" Hugh asked.

"We can't afford a legal fight." Norman bit his lower lip. "The publicity would only bring on more harassment."

I nodded. "Why take chances?"

Hugh cupped the back of Norman's neck with a big hand and rubbed his bearded chin on the top of Norman's head. "I think it's time for us to start defending ourselves the best we can, sugar-britches."

I couldn't sleep that night, twisting in my sheets until they tangled around me as I listened for the 3:14 freight train to roll through town. If the 3:14 was on time, everything would be all right. I was desperate for everything to be all right.

CHAPTER TWENTY-FOUR

It was daylight and a hot June weekday, so maybe that's why Rose ventured downstairs to the bar bearing her news. Murph was there on her way to the night shift. She'd signed on with Kelly Girls and worked a part-time temporary job doing quality control at a uniform company until I could find a place for her. I'd taken the day off because the winter cold I couldn't shake had gone into bronchitis. Norman was feeding me hot toddies, putting his fingers to my forehead periodically, and generally fussing over me.

Rose settled her bottom on a stool and motioned Norman over. She opened a small spiral notebook. "I met with my friends yesterday," she said.

"How could I forget after reading that newspaper story!" Norman said. "The lawyers, right?"

Rose nodded. "They suggested I move to Boston."

"How helpful of them," Norman said. I gave a hearty whoop of a laugh.

"I know. When I told them it wasn't an option, one of them promised to look into it. He called me just now to tell me that while the bar itself isn't illegal, we are."

"How the hell can people be illegal?" Murph wasn't even putting on a game face.

"That's my understanding of the law too," said Harry, who was between a college class and work. Three hoods who came in erratically the past week had arrived earlier, according to Norman. I looked around; I saw no enemies now.

"Here's the interesting part," Rose said. "Apparently, the cops go after gay bars either when someone is looking to get votes or parties unknown are agitating to clean up a neighborhood. My friend said it always comes down to power or money, and power equals money. They suggested checking into who would profit by shutting you down. Then we'd know if it's something we can stop."

"The current mayor is running against Goodlette's morality platform," Hugh said, looking thoughtful. "He's using his office to fight back. Closing a gay bar looks good in the headlines. Helping the college to expand looks even better."

Carla Jean filled the silence with her sarcasm. "Well, that's a relief. They don't hate us after all. They're using us to get what they want."

"It's like math, doll," Murph said, as earnest as she was morose. "X plus Y equals Z. We're Y. Z is all the trouble we've been getting recently. X is the unknown. Fill in the formula and the problem is solved. On paper."

It sounded like Murph already knew the basic math she'd need to get by in the bindery.

"And Rose," Norman said, " before you got here, we read that the college wants to put a parking lot you-know-where."

"Ah-ha!" Rose said. "A quick solution to the puzzle."

"Not to the problem," Norman said with a sigh.

"How in hell could the college do this? Don't those jerks know how many gays work for them?" Carla Jean said.

"Probably not. What would the parents say if they knew a gay person cooked their kids' meals or taught them history?" JoJo said with her low ironic laugh as she ran dirty glasses to the kitchen. She started banging around out there, probably working off some anger.

The woman who ran the sterling-silver-jewelry shop came in with her grown daughter. Her long earrings flashed light. A small group of women seemed to have settled on The Old Town for their weekly gabfest. As always, the leather crafter's long-haired wife rushed in to join them, her multicolor floor-length skirt, complete with ruffle trim, clinging to her legs. All three wore long necklaces of varying styles, and the jeweler's daughter had a noisy host of bracelets on one wrist. The spritely little woman in a poodle cut who owned Janet's Hair Studio was sure to be along soon. Would customers like these women care if the bar closed? They'd ordered martinis. JoJo delivered them on a tray with a gentlemanly bow. The women stared and turned away as soon as I caught their eyes. We intrigued them and possibly made them question their own options. The mother grabbed JoJo's wrist and whispered something to her. JoJo looked serious as she asked questions and nodded at the answers.

On her way back to the bar JoJo was looking at me. She made a slight motion with her head for me to follow. We talked by the phone in the hallway.

"I don't know how to tell you this," JoJo said.

All I could think of was Colonel Mustard, but how would that woman know anything about my dog?

"Earrings over there," again she nodded, this time toward the table of straight women. "She went past the church on the corner on her way from her car. There's a wedding going on. She recognized the bride from seeing her here."

"Deej?"

"Said she thought it was odd because the bride was your girlfriend. And she saw the guy who used to be so pretty. That sounds like Paul."

"Cissy?"

Another nod from JoJo, who was working her jaw in a thoughtful way.

"That's not what Cissy wanted," I told her.

"You said she had a boyfriend."

"It's what he wanted."

"Okay, then," JoJo said. "I guess we know where Cissy's been. And what she was doing even before she was with you."

"What do you mean?"

"They don't make wedding gowns with padded tummies, do they?"

"She's—"

JoJo said, "Looked like it to Earrings."

"Why that miserable ratfink," I said. "He must have gotten her pregnant when he raped her."

JoJo gave a grim laugh. "Or it could be the second immaculate conception."

"Will I never learn?"

"To stay away from straight girls?" JoJo asked. "I doubt it."

Cissy might have given in to society. I didn't think so. "We haven't seen the last of her, JoJo," I said. "Not by a long shot. It may be years, she may even raise a family with him. After that, she'll be back in the life."

Carla Jean was listening. "At least I won't have to supply her with cigarettes for a while. Doesn't that woman ever buy her own?"

JoJo gave me a commiserating pat on the arm. "Back to the drawing board for you," she said with a smile.

"Thanks for giving me the heads-up."

The straight women watched as we rejoined the gang. Thank God I had my friends. Not that I ever thought Cissy and I would get together after what she'd been through. I'd enjoyed having a girl again, though. JoJo let the others know. They all looked glum.

"Trouble," I told them. "Girlfriends are nothing but trouble."

"Nothing?" Norman asked, eyebrows raised.

"I'm swearing off women," I said.

"I'm with you." Murph clinked my glass with hers. "With the exception, of—" she added, with a regretful look toward Rose.

Harry and Rose huddled at a table by the window. They jumped when the newspaper hit the glass brick right next to them.

"It would be a pretty sad day," Murph said, "if it took the cop and the lady who won't set foot in a bar ever again to save The Old Town."

"That," Norman said, "would be downright fab-ulous. You could tell that story through the ages."

When Rose went back upstairs, Murph left the bar for Lisa's table. Lisa got a grand welcome when she returned for the first time a few nights earlier. She looked dressy in a sleek, red sleeveless top. To my surprise, Murph's head was on Lisa's shoulder. I caught Lisa's eye as she patted Murph's back. I went over to them. Murph, collar and cuffs frayed, in need of a haircut, looked miserable. She gulped back tears. Even Murph was falling apart.

"When I wake up in the dreary twilight to go to my job, I fear I can't lift the mantle of life." Her stricken eyes were on Lisa's. "There are times I can't face coming here ever again. What will they do to me next? I'd finally gotten on the day shift at the hospital and now I can only get nights."

Lisa's splint was off. The skin around her nose and eyes had a yellowish tinge, but otherwise she seemed to have recovered. "I can't make it better, Murph. All I can do is remind you of the friends you have here."

"My poor friends. You have to put up with my blather when you probably come here to find some peace and quiet."

"Oh, Murph," Lisa said. I heard an echo of Rose's affectionate exasperation in her tone. "Don't you know you're one of the reasons we all come here? You're the ringmaster in this three-ring circus, and we love you for it."

Murph slowly sat upright. "You're telling me that because I'm down right now."

"What Lisa said happens to be true," I told her.

Lisa gave Murph a little shake. "You're always here for us, Murph. Always cheerful or coming to somebody's defense. Long-winded? Yes, but you make us laugh and sometimes cry with your stories, and you never seem to run out. I learn a lot from you, Murph. You've been through it all, yet nothing stops you. You're my life and Rockie's life, and, oh, Murph, you're the gay life, in Technicolor."

Oh, I echoed, for a strong woman like Lisa in my life. Well, she is in my life, I thought. Maybe I'd pay her a bit more attention from now on, besides grocery shopping, though she was far too young and attractive for me, about twenty-five years my junior. I gave Murph a couple of light slaps on the back and went to the phone. Avenue Cantonese would bring me a quart of hot egg-drop soup.

I shuffled back to the bar, stopping to sneeze.

Officer Harry was there.

"We have a sort of plan," he said. "Now that we know who the enemy really is, we may have a chance."

"The college is a vicious fighter," Carla Jean warned us with heated words. "Remember how their architecture department designed that housing project and five years later kicked everyone out so they could expand their gym?"

"Sure, I remember," called Murph. "I had good friends, co-workers who lived there. The college didn't help them move, didn't help them find new places. These people had no money. Mostly not white, they had nowhere to go but back to the same lousy housing they'd left. Usually that consisted of untended turn-of-the-century wood-frame places way the heck out in the sticks, with maybe a tethered goat and some chickens, or of apartments in town you wouldn't walk past at night.

"No one wins against the college in this fricking town," Carla Jean said.

CHAPTER TWENTY-FIVE

I went with Rose, about a week later, on the first prong of the plan. Our mission was to see Frank Goodlette. As I was a respectable businesswoman who'd succeeded with partial funding from the Goodlettes, we thought I might have some impact.

Rose made the appointment, calling herself an old friend. The secretary balked, but Rose had learned, helping Vi, how to deal with protective office staff.

At Hansfield Green we set off in a rumbling old bus, breathing diesel exhaust through an open window. Rose wore her Sunday best, including a small moss-green wool hat with a tiny blue feather. She approved of the long gray flannel skirt, navy blazer, and white blouse I wore to funerals. I hoped this jaunt wouldn't prove to be a funeral for The Old Town Tavern.

Goodlette Franks had grown over the decades to cover acres of former farmland and forest. The city expanded its boundaries to include the plant and laid sewers all the way out there. The city of Hansfield did all it could to be financially attractive to the company. Now small-business owners like me pay higher taxes than Goodlette's does. If Frank got into office that would never change. The firm was too popular, since it provided a living for hundreds of people and put on the annual Frank Fair, which was a bigger deal in Hansfield than the county fair.

We descended the metal steps of the bus. Goodlette's was a world unto itself. I half expected a wooden carousel and roller coaster like the ones I rode as a child down at Riverside Park in Agawam. The headquarters building had remained in the original farmhouse, and the first floor was a museum with the old stand that had served hot dogs on the green. The ancient cookware and the machines used on their first production line were displayed. Rose said the lobby smelled of grilling hot dogs and strong mustard.

A gorgeous dark-skinned woman greeted us. She wore a cheerleader outfit matching the canopy of the old stand and smiled gamely despite her hot-dog-bun hat. The frankfurter-stand logo was everywhere: aprons, barbeque implements, tablecloths, T-shirts, post cards, miniature dogs on buns.

"We bound these," I told Rose, and held up a slim history of the company.

Rose told the greeter we had an appointment, and the woman led us to an elevator that took us up in what appeared, from outside, to be a red silo. Through a long, thick glass window in the reception area we looked three stories down at a factory floor where huge lines of trays, five franks each, rolled past, attended by men in white uniforms and yellow hard hats. At the end of the lines women in hairnets caught the wrapped and labeled packages.

Rose and I looked at each other, eyebrows raised. Frank's family was doing very well for themselves. Very well. That scared me even more. I wanted to keep my hands in my blazer pockets to hide their tremor, but was afraid I'd look too masculine. My head pounded as it might if it went through one of those machines on the production floor below.

"Murph tells me she's tried more than once to get on at Goodlette's," Rose said. "The pay is pretty good for factory work and they have benefits. The problem is, nobody leaves this company once they're in. Now I suppose she couldn't do it at all."

A receptionist beckoned from the end of the corridor. "Ladies, please have a seat," she said.

"Is it okay if I keep watching?" I asked. "This is fascinating. I do some bindery work for you."

"The company prefers that you don't linger at the windows," she said, in an entirely open and friendly way. "Secret ingredients, you know."

Her smile was good business. "You catch more flies with honey than with vinegar," I murmured to Rose. Then I thought, why can't I be attracted to someone like Rose instead of all these straight women I fall for? That was beside the point. "They'll ruin some of our lives to get their way. We've seen that they won't hesitate."

"Shh." Rose looked at the receptionist.

I lowered my voice. "You know somebody's going to make money off this parking lot," I said. "The college, for starters, because it'll bring in more local students."

"I've been thinking," Rose said quietly, "that someone else may stand to benefit. Who owns the college? It's private and a business, like any other. Someone, somewhere along the line, is in cahoots with the college, would be my guess."

We whispered like a couple of conspirators. Rose continued, "We have to find out who that might be and, I don't know, maybe we could put some kind of pressure to bear. Do you think it's—"

The door opened and we were shown into Frank Goodlette's office. The contrast to the calm outer room was extreme. It was a corral of a space. File cabinets lined every wall. Some drawers hung open, fewer did not. Clerks knelt or stretched to overhead shelves. At large tables, more people pored over documents and ledgers, some operating adding machines one-handed, without looking at the keys.

Frank was medium height, thin, and balding, with gold wire-rimmed glasses that disappeared against his tanned skin. He must have gone somewhere on vacation recently, someplace neither Rose nor I could afford. He jumped up at sight of Rose and rushed to her.

"I'd know you anywhere, Rose Callaghan," he said, a smile stretching his thin lips. "You're the prettiest rose in any man's bouquet." He pumped her hand until she pried it from his. Frank Goodlette's memories might bode well for us.

Rose gave him a hug, barely touching him. The poor guy blushed as his staff cheered.

"Get back to work, you laggards!" Frank said with joy in his voice.

Goodlette's was a working atmosphere I'd never anticipated.

Frank noticed me and shook my hand, more briskly than he had Rose's.

"Rochele Solomon," he said. "I see you're wondering about my free-for-all office. The line workers downstairs have fun on the job, so why shouldn't the office workers?" He had one of those tinny voices that grated on the ears. "I take it the bindery brings you a good living?" When I nodded he gave himself a congratulatory pat on the shoulder. "I have an eye for success, don't I?"

He rubbed his small hands and went back behind his desk. "Tell me what I can do for you, girls."

Rose didn't mince her words. "Frank, you're looking at a criminal."

"You?"

"Come on. You read the papers. You know what The Old Town Tavern is and who was arrested there."

Frank reached for a half-smoked cigar in the ashtray on his desk.

"I'm not much for bars, Frank, but they're the only place I can get together with my friends."

The room had gone quiet.

"You're saying you're one of them?" Frank asked.

One of the male clerks stood up from a bottom file-cabinet drawer. I recognized him from the bar at once. He moved farther back in the room, behind another cabinet.

A familiar-looking woman pointedly kept her eyes on her work while the rest of the crew stared. I remembered then that her claim to fame was marriage to a fellow who preferred men as much as she preferred women.

From a side door came a heavy gray-haired man, red veins prominent on a bulging nose. He walked with a purposeful confidence and held up his arms as if to sing an aria. Instead, he strode behind Frank and put his hands on his shoulders.

By the file cabinets, a barrel-chested man with a crew cut pranced, licked his pinky, and swiped it along an eyebrow in one of those universal gestures that mocked homosexual men. The other employees made a show of silent laughter.

"Well," Frank said, shuffling papers on his desk while looking mischievously up at Rose, "now I know why you wouldn't marry me. To think, all this could have been yours!" His look was sly. "And me too!"

"I want your help, Frank."

He laughed. "Or you might have gotten it all in the divorce." He took up his unlit cigar and pointed it at her. "Really, Rose, I'd have thought better of you."

The fat old guy kept squeezing Frank's shoulders. Frank said, "This is Lawrence, my second in command and my sister's husband. I lured him to Goodlette's with Bessie's pretty face."

Lawrence held his chin high.

"Ms. Solomon," he explained, pointing his cigar now toward me, "was one of the first people we loaned to from our small-business fund—and the first-ever Jew. I know how to pick them."

Lawrence patted Frank's shoulders with the palms of his meaty hands. "Then I see you have everything under control." The audience of employees got busy before he turned.

I heard Rose take a deep breath. "Rockie deserved your trust, Frank," she said. "And we're trusting you again today. You have some influence in Hansfield. The Old Town Tavern's been trying to cope with insufferable harassment. Innocent customers have gone through beatings and arrests. Names, like mine, have been published. People have lost their jobs, their families, and, most of all, their dignity."

The man looked kind of like the wizard in the Judy Garland movie. He answered with a cheery chirp. "How do you see me helping with this, Rose?" Then his tone chilled. "As I tell all the people I hire here, they represent the company wherever they go. If they don't have enough self-respect to make good choices, I don't see why I should give them enough respect to keep them on." He waggled a finger at her. "Aside from choosing to be a pervert and breaking state laws, gathering in homosexual bars is neither discreet nor safe."

"You say that like we bring this on ourselves."

"I'm inclined to agree with that statement."

"I didn't ask to be thrown in jail like a criminal, Frank!"

He made a disgusted face. "What you two do together—"

"Rockie and I are friends, nothing more. The love of my life died a while ago, a respected and admired attorney."

"And you're back in the filthy dives already?" He shook his head. "You need a priest, not a city councillor. I don't know what I could do even if I wanted to help you."

"You're going to be mayor, Mr. Goodlette!" I said, more from a sense of chivalry for Rose than out of hope that we'd get anywhere with this. His face lost its glowering look at the assumption he would win the election. "You have some impact. The police come at us like we're hurting somebody. Rose was never even in a gay bar until her lover died. Where else could she go? We're herded into what you call dives by people who don't understand us. At least let us have peace in the few places we've got."

"Thank you for your confidence in my election. If I intervened on your behalf, I'd lose."

"If you cared about the citizens of Hansfield, you'd protect us. Why," I asked with some desperation, "can't you all understand that we're part of the same human race, like a huge family that should be out to help, not hurt, other people? Wouldn't it be better if we embraced our commonality instead of tearing one another to shreds?"

Frank, his voice cold, a smile stiff on his face, said, "I don't see that I have anything in common with your kind."

The big guy was back. The way he was so familiar with Frank, touching him frequently with quick, faux-hearty gestures, was unsettling. If he meant to look fatherly, he didn't succeed. They *were* straight guys, weren't they?

"Frank," Rose said, her voice pleading.

"Don't try that old wheedling trick, Rose Callaghan." He turned to Lawrence. "So much for the innocent young lady I once knew."

Lawrence whispered in Frank's ear.

"All right, all right. I have a meeting in a few minutes, girls. Tell me, if you can, why I should put in a good word for you. And where."

Rose told him what we'd learned about the college. "I'd love for you to find out what's going on, Frank," she said, "out of common decency and fairness."

"You think what you do is decent?" Lawrence proclaimed.

Frank said, "I would have been glad to make a decent woman of you. Any man would have."

I'd heard about Rose's famous temper from Murph and remembered the story of her mad tantrum at the jail.

She put her fists on Frank's desk and leaned across at him. "Oh, I remember how you tried to make a decent woman of me, Frank." She started in almost a whisper. Her voice rose with every word. "Half undressing. Ordering me—"

"Enough, Rose!" He gave Lawrence a quick glance. "I was a normal, red-blooded young man."

"I was an innocent young Catholic lady. We went to the same church, Frank, and that's how you treated me. When I refused, you pushed me out of the car and told me to walk home. Do you remember? Then you came trailing me, begging me to let you drive me home. You feared I'd blab on you, right? I refused, so you followed me in your car—the little rich boy with his car—to keep me safe, you said. You think I haven't noticed that the last thing you men want is decency? You think I don't know that you 'allow' gay bars for your convenience? So you can find another man when you want one? You think you're invisible when you go to the swimming hole upriver?" With a shriek like a banshee's, as Murph described it, Rose said, "People have seen you there, Frank. Is Lawrence your lover too?"

Lawrence grabbed Rose's left arm. She was so worked up she, without looking, lifted her right arm and slammed him in the eye with the bottom edge of her purse. I ducked into a crouch.

Frank jumped and ran around the desk and Rose swung the purse at him too, all the while shouting that he'd never be mayor of Hansfield as long as she had a voice and a memory. I wanted to jump up and down and clap my hands like a kid. Rose was my fury, the fury of all us timid, go-along-to-get-along queers.

She pivoted, purse carving an escape and, as we made for the door, yelled back, "You'd damn well better do something, Frank Goodlette!"

I was pulling the door closed behind us when Rose grabbed the knob and slammed it as hard as she could. I blocked her in the nick of time to stop her from using her purse to smash in the glass on the door. What a spitfire.

Rose wouldn't calm down even when we reached the bus stop. She kept muttering about the lying bastards inside and how they'd talk their way out of this. I told her that their employees would talk, they'd play town criers. As we got on the bus, a police car, no, two, swung up to the old Goodlette homestead, and four officers leapt out, guns drawn. What did Goodlette tell the police?

"We're getting off the bus," I told Rose.

She was deflated by then. She cried. She'd apologized to me several times. "Why?" she asked.

"We'll duck into Woolworth's and use their pay phone to call a cab and get you off the street and home. They won't know where to find you. They certainly won't look over the bar."

"If they do, I'll go to the newspaper. That slick-looking article with the eyes of a sneak-thief won't be able to protect Frank then."

"This is dangerous, what you're doing. A lot of money and power is at stake for Frank Goodlette."

She followed me in silence. I made the call. We went through the store and, when the cab arrived, out the back door. At The Old Town, I dismissed the driver. I led Rose by her elbow up the stairs.

"I'm sorry you saw me like that."

"You did a good thing, Rose. I'm proud to be your friend, but if I was frightened before, I'm panicked now—for you. Stay indoors for a couple of days, will you? Give me a ring if you need anything. I'll be keeping my head down too, except for taking Colonel Mustard out. We'll see what comes of one person in this whole world being willing to stick her neck out."

CHAPTER TWENTY-SIX

W hen Cissy rang my doorbell in July, I wasn't prepared for the limp-haired, colorless sweatiness of her. Her flat little belly was all distended. She rocked when she walked through the doorway. On the couch where we'd spent so many pleasant hours, she untied her tennis shoes, complaining, "I don't have a pair of shoes that doesn't strangle my swollen feet."

Pregnancy is pretty revolting. The way they make it happen and then to have something growing inside you, feeding on you. I don't get why anyone would go through that on purpose.

Despite Colonel Mustard's happy welcome, Cissy pushed her away.

She'd come to apologize, she said.

"I heard you'd married. Him?"

"He was sorry for what he'd done. Said he'd make it up to me by marrying me. I wanted to laugh in his face. I was stuck. My pregnancy survived that drugstore concoction Seneca tried on me."

"A baby?"

"Twins, I think. His twins," she said, as if spitting. "Paul said they'll be born with horns."

"Why do you think they're twins?"

She shrugged and lit a cigarette, as if I'd asked a stupid question. "I just know."

I brought her a bottle of 7UP left over from her visits and thought of Carla Jean's question. Cissy certainly had someone to buy her cigarettes now. "Why did you marry the devil?"

"I told Mom. She told my dad. He went berserk. I mean, really berserk. We barely stopped him from calling the police on the devil.

He made me choose: go ahead and marry the man or take him to court for rape."

I must have caught a touch of that indignation of Rose's. "Who was he to limit your choices?"

"I was so confused, Rockie. I knew he'd be like that. I told Mom not to say anything. Dad was really concerned. He didn't see how a single woman could raise a child by herself. He thinks it's better to have a father in the house, even a man who forced himself on me, than to have none. The more he talked, the more he convinced himself that Rick wasn't a devil. He was a man tempted beyond reason. My mother had the nerve to ask what I'd been wearing that day, like I'd raped myself."

We looked at each other for a long moment. I couldn't believe this was the woman I'd worshipped with my eyes and hands and mouth. She was so grossly animal right now; such a short time ago I thought her ethereal. The idea of touching her *treyfe*, swollen body, with something growing inside her, disgusted me, as if she really was unclean, forbidden. It wasn't only her looks, though. It was the marriage. The thought would not leave my mind that she was not made to be a het. I knew how uncomfortable I would be if I shared a bed with a man. To know he owned me.

"Will you stay with him?" I asked.

She turned her hands palm up, and I saw that he'd given her a shoddy little wedding ring and no engagement ring. "What else can I do? My dad was right. I can't raise two little ones on what I make."

"Couldn't you get help from the state?"

She looked abashed. "Rockie! What do you take me for? I would never stoop that low. Besides, Paul will help. He said he'll take care of them while I go back to work."

I shook my head to get the confusion out. She would marry a man even though she'd learned she preferred women, a man who was violent. She would have children she thought of as a devil's spawn. She did what her father and husband told her to do. With all that, she was too proud to ask for help from the government that took her taxes?

At least I knew with certainty where she'd gone. Women tended to try out the gay life then skulk back to safety.

"I didn't like not being in touch with you, Rockie," she said.

I took her hand. "There wasn't a future for us, Cissy. Enjoying you while I could was all I wanted."

"You're not mad?"

"At you? No. At your husband and father—you bet."

"It's not so bad." She sounded timid. "He has an outside girlfriend so he doesn't bother me much."

"Already? He just married you, for land sakes."

"It's not his fault," she was quick to say. "I've learned how to stop him. As long as he pays for what I need—"

"Oh, don't defend that piece of dreck!" I was disgusted. At the same time I understood. Not everybody can hack the gay life. Cissy had a choice. She'd seen what happened to her brother. I didn't blame her for wanting to protect herself. My mood, though, was setting like the sun on the first day of winter when there was nothing to look forward to except the doom of even less daylight. Colonel Mustard lay at my feet, licking a spot on her leg. She was wearing away the fur. I told her to stop and she did.

What was it about being gay that could upset my applecart so easily? It wasn't pride, like I'd set out to turn Cissy and failed, but when a gal went back to men it did stick in my craw. It was so easy for some of them to go straight and turn on us, the women they'd loved, the people who accepted them and always would. It was a loss; there would be one fewer of us at the ramparts when they came for us, or was that my overactive Jewish imagination? I knew I wasn't so much personally rejected as collectively rejected. They didn't like what I loved, or, more often, they wouldn't let themselves like it.

What, exactly, was there to love? The secret connections, the undefined signals, the ecstatic wanton camaraderie of a dance floor? The softness of another woman, the thrill of introducing her to her own sexuality, falling in love with the forbidden?

I wanted to have a parade whenever someone threw her or his lot in with us. Every person who realized she or he was gay cheered for every other one of us. The knowledge that we are a giant hidden people everywhere on earth, including all sorts of famous people, is thrilling and comforting. I puff up with pride every time I hear that some talented and successful person is one of our own. As unfair as it was, even being illegal, even having our secret touches condemned was exciting beyond reason. Like an explorer who finds a new place, or a mountain climber at the top, being gay was an accomplishment. I could not understand why anyone would give up such a tremendous kick.

Now that she wasn't one of us, Cissy lost all attraction for me. I couldn't wait until she left. Was that wrong? I'd been down this road so many times before, they ought to write a song for me: "Straight

Gal Blues." Maybe someone had. How would I know? Some singer in Nashville might be composing it on his guitar right now, but it would be about straight boys and never be recorded.

What did Cissy want from me? Forgiveness? An affair? Her look was pleading, though her chatter was about how awful it was to be pregnant. Oh, and how good her brother was being to her. Paul was thrilled about the babies and excited about being an uncle. I realized she wasn't even as smart and witty as her twin. Once again, I'd fallen for a pretty face.

"I would have married you," Cissy was saying. "You'll never ask now, because of the babies."

"You mean you want me to rescue you from him? Now?"

"Well…" Trust me, the woman's eyes had dulled since our days together. The spark she'd shared with Paul was gone. She batted her eyelids the same way Paul did.

Was I wrong? Should I accept Cissy and her distorted body and the problems her husband, and maybe family, would cause? Should I agree to support these near-strangers? The child might be a boy. I'd never choose to live with a boy. But did I have some responsibility for this? The husband might not have raped her if Cissy hadn't been with me. Did I have a responsibility as a homosexual to another homosexual? Was Cissy even gay? Did I want to spend the rest of my life with this woman? Was being with her better than being alone?

Oh, my God, no. No, no, a thousand times no. Even so, would I talk myself into taking this one on?

That's when the thunderous knocking at the door began and Colonel Mustard broke into mad barking.

CHAPTER TWENTY-SEVEN

W e both stood. I raised my eyebrows at Cissy.
"He couldn't follow me here," she said. "He's at work. I called him to make sure."

I was on my way to look through the peephole. "Good way to tip him off that you're up to something," I muttered, only half wanting her to hear.

The knocking began again. "Open up, police!"

He sent the police after her? This was too much. They could haul her home for all I cared. What a schlemiel to come here. I was really sore at her. The businesswoman in me opened the door to a couple of officers in plainclothes and welcomed them. I'd never seen them before.

"Sorry to disturb you, ma'am. May we come in?" asked the thinner of the two over the Colonel's barking.

Instead, I stepped into the hallway and pulled the door shut behind me. My gut growled. I left one hand curled around the knob.

"How can I help you, officers? I'm sorry your knock upset my dog. She's usually the soul of calm. I don't want to chance a biting incident by asking you in."

"We'd like to ask your help in locating a certain Rose Callaghan. We have been made to understand that you would know where she resides."

So formal, I thought. Where did they learn their lines, *Dragnet*?

"What's wrong?" I asked. "Is she all right?"

The two, both white, clean-shaven, and wearing fedoras, looked at each other. Once again, the smaller one spoke. "The individual was reported to be involved in an altercation at a local business. Witnesses place you there at the same time and, as a matter of fact, allege that you accompanied her."

"Yes?" I asked.

He yelled over Colonel Mustard's concern for my safety. "If we went inside, ma'am, you could probably quiet your dog."

"I doubt it."

The heavy cop sighed.

The other one said, "Then perhaps you would accompany us to the station."

"Where it's quieter?" I asked, putting on a look of disbelief. "Why don't you tell me what you want and I'll answer the best I can."

Big guy couldn't keep his mouth closed any longer. "Look, we need to find her. Tell us where she lives."

I pretended to mull that one over. "You know, I don't think Rose ever told me. She's new in town. One doesn't exchange such information right off the bat. Not if you live alone. I think that's something the Hansfield Police Department advises, doesn't it?"

"We believe she might reside with you, Miss."

I shook my head as much to cool the sweat as to correct him. "No. I used to have a roommate, but," I lowered my voice as if I was taking them into my confidence, "I learned my lesson. If you know what I mean." I winked at the little guy.

He looked confused. "And you don't have any idea where she might be?"

"No."

"We'd like to take a look around your apartment."

"Oh, that wouldn't be possible right now, officers."

The big guy protested. "Of course it's possible."

"Why don't we set a time then. Say, tomorrow evening? I'll have my neighbors take care of my dog while you're here."

Big Guy looked like he wanted to push past me and grab the doorknob; Little Guy knew better. Small business or not, maybe I counted. Nevertheless, Big Guy said, "We can be back here with a warrant in an hour."

"I hate you to go to all that trouble, Officers. For me, it's a matter of principle." Meanwhile, I envisioned what it must have been like for my ancestors. The same knock on the door. Big Guy in boots. Never seeing their homes again. Keeping vigil over their starving families. This was America, wasn't it? My concussion headache was back in full swing and I was growing nauseous. I leaned back against the door.

Little Guy motioned for Big Guy to move away. "You're within your rights, Miss Solomon, but you're making me wonder what you're hiding. Or who."

I managed to say, "I'm hiding nothing. I'm protecting my life."
Then the nausea hit in a flood from my gut.

"You okay, lady?" asked Little Guy.

"Sick," I croaked out as I covered my mouth and fled inside. I
managed to lock the door behind me. Colonel Mustard crowded up
against me as if to make sure no one had hurt me. The bathroom was
too far. I grabbed the kitchen trash can and was sick, then sick again
until my throat was sore and my mouth and nose sour. I'd probably
gone back to work too soon. Or was this a reaction to the threat outside
my door? I'd respected the police before the raid.

They would expect me to sneak Rose out the back of the building.
Fortunately, it was Cissy I'd been protecting from their view, not Rose.

"Why didn't you say you're sick, Rockie?" Cissy asked when I'd
freshened up.

"Trust me, I wasn't. Until they showed up."

Cissy picked up her pocketbook and held it to her chest. "I can't
take a chance," she said as she lit another cigarette, probably to cover
up my smell. "The babies could catch something."

I laughed despite my embarrassment at having been sick. "And I
could be dying. You've answered my question."

"What question?"

I didn't respond but told her to stay put. I checked the hallway, the
stairs, and the elevator, then hustled her out the door. If the cops lurked
outside somewhere they wouldn't know this mother-to-be was visiting
the queer on the second floor.

Was this any way to live?

The nausea passed, but my eyes stung, my stomach burned, and
my sense of balance disappeared. I wanted to sleep for a week. Or
maybe until life got back to normal. If there ever would be a normal
again. Instead, I called the bar and told Norman to warn Rose. She and
Murph didn't have a phone yet. Anyone who needed to get in touch left
messages downstairs. Norman said he'd run right up there and tell her
to catch the next train to somewhere, anywhere.

I brushed my teeth and ran a wet cloth over my face, then grabbed
Colonel Mustard's well-worn leather leash to walk her while I was
able. Outside I looked around. No sign of Big and Little Guys. Maybe
finding Rose wasn't as big a deal as they said. Nudniks! How they
made my head hurt.

Upstairs again, I lay on the couch. It was no good going to bed
yet. I'd have to take the Colonel out once more before I could sleep for

the night. Could I sleep? Nothing doing. I was as nervous as a lightning bug in a jar. I was no longer sick to my stomach, though, so I got up, laced my shoes, and went across the street.

Murph sat at a table, some kind of workbook in front of her.

"What are you up to?" I asked.

She shook her handsome head. I was shocked to see her in glasses and said so.

"Turns out I can't see much better than a bat," she said, with her lusty laugh. "Paul has me doing this assignment. I hope your job offer stands, because I'm working my tail off for it."

"Don't worry about that," I told her. "I've got plenty for you to do. As a matter of fact, the binder who doubles as delivery person is getting married and moving to Kansas. We can spread his binding duties among the others. That will leave me short someone for part-time pickup and delivery. Do you have a driver's license?'

Ah, Murph, Murph, I thought as she scrambled to pull her wallet out of a pocket and show me the license. She was so eager to work and more hopeful than she'd seemed in a very long time.

"And I'm strong," she said. "I don't need my right hand for lifting. See?" She raised the table in front of her with her left hand and her right forearm. "I can earn my keep, given the chance."

Norman brought my drink over. "Oh, goodness gracious," he said when he couldn't set the glass on the table. "You are such an adolescent boy sometimes, Miss Murph."

"Okay, okay. You've convinced me," I told her. "How about giving me somewhere to put my glass?"

"I had the muscles of a boy all my life," she said. "Why, there was a time—"

Norman pretended to jog backward. "Run for the fallout shelter, Rockie! Murph's about to tell a story. It's in the air!"

Murph set the table down. "Get your tail behind the spigot, barkeep! I don't recall inviting you to stick around."

"You'll have me in stitches, you two. You're like an old vaudeville act. This was what I needed," I told Murph as we laughed at Norman's antics. "If I could only bring Colonel Mustard here with me, my life would be complete. I know full well they'd take her in a raid, though. Plus, I wouldn't add to the risks Hugh and Norman already put up with for us."

"Nor would I," Murph said, in a quiet voice. "Hey, did Paul tell you what he's up to?"

"He's going to be a full-time babysitter for Cissy," I said.

"That too, but he's going to start a publishing company while he's taking care of the kids."

"He's going to publish books? What kind?"

"Kids' books! He wants to do books that make kids like to read. And books for kids like I was so the teachers and parents know something's wrong. I was able to fake so much and to sweet-talk my way into passing grades. You know, the adorable tomboy type. They figured I'd stop swinging from trees and get down to work when I got older. I fooled them!"

"What made Paul decide this?"

"You know how discouraged he was. He can't teach because he's gay, he can't be a waiter because his face is so messed up, and his left eye is worse."

"I didn't know."

"He may lose the vision in that eye. When he heard he was going to be an uncle, he had a new purpose in life. He's starting small, maybe with a kids' magazine. He'll probably talk to you about using the bindery."

"I can see him making a success of something like that. I can recommend a printer for him too."

"Harry the cop has gotten the newspaper publisher to give Paul a start. Paul may move in with Harry, you know," Murph said, and winked.

"The babies will have two uncles then."

"And an Aunt Murph," she said. She was so proud of those unborn children, you'd think she was the dad.

We sat quietly for a few minutes. I kept shaking my head and smiling. The ways we overcome adversity. The ways we pick ourselves up and go on. I hoped like heck Paul could make a go of his new business and being boyfriends with Harry. I'd heard of gay couples lasting all their lives—thirty, forty years. Maybe Harry and Paul had a shot at it.

"So, *bubbaleha*," I said, "tell me your he-man story."

"I was mortified, to tell the truth. I was new at the hospital laundry and thought I had it made. Getting on there isn't easy. The wages don't break any records. It's the health care and job security people are after."

Every time someone came through the front door, I checked to make sure it wasn't a cop. "Where's Rose, by the way?" I whispered.

"On her way down Maine," she whispered back. "She got on the first train to Boston. She'll switch in Boston and go up to Old Orchard Beach where her sister lives."

Murph cleared her throat, as she often did before starting a story. "It was a couple of months after I'd started my job at the laundry, and one of the women, she was trying to reach a gown she'd dropped behind one of the machines."

Rockie took a sip of her Buffalo Rock and pushed back her hair. "Well, wouldn't you know it. The woman, who was on the substantial side, got herself stuck half behind and half between machines. She's long retired now and should have been then, but, like I said, they stay and stay. It was management's fault, really. They needed to put in the bigger machine we have—they have—now and get some space for people to access more than the front. Anyway, there she was, old Murtha, wedged in there like a rusty bent nail in a plank, so red in the face she looked like she might have a heart attack. She screamed for someone to get her out. The supervisor went to get the floor manager, who went to get another man to help him move that mammoth machine. I knew I couldn't do it. The thing was big enough to swallow Murtha whole."

She ran a comb through her hair and perfected the dip onto her forehead. "I have to admit we called her Moby Murtha out of her sight. She was a royal pain in the behind."

"The point, Murph!" one of the boys at the bar called. "Get to the point!"

"Aw, Denny, the fun is in the telling! I got her out of there is the point."

"How!"

"Thighs of steel, that's how. I shimmied up to the top of that washer, put my back to the wall, my heels against the machine, which, thank the Lord, was flat at the back and angled up toward the front. I pushed the damn thing forward and away from poor old Murtha exactly enough that she could wiggle out. The whole place broke into applause, and when the floor manager came back with two maintenance guys and an orderly in tow, we laughed them out of the laundry. I was afraid I'd be fired."

Every ear was attuned to the story. For all their teasing, the other customers enjoyed Murph's tales. I enjoyed listening to her modest bragging. I told her then, what happened at home with Cissy and the police.

"They came to your home? Might as well be a Catholic in Northern Ireland as a homo in America. And to come hunting sweet Rose Callaghan. That takes the cake. Was she really so bad at Frank's? She left me her purse to have the cobbler repair its strap. I hope she didn't draw blood."

"Let's just say she's better off in Maine until Frank cools down."

"She's going to write to her lawyer friends and ask if they can get the charges dropped."

"They must think she's lost her marbles. Maybe I have too. Since the raid I've done too many things I was afraid to do before. It's all got to catch up with me." My spirits sagged and I must have looked it.

"Hey, buddy," Murph said, her tone as soft as it was gruff. "Don't let this ruin your day. We can't help who we are and we don't want to be any other way, so we roll with the punches."

"It's not like we're out in the parks trolling for sex. It's not like we're selling sex or buying it. Maybe that's wrong, maybe it's right. They look at us and all they see is sex, sex, sex. We're so much more than that!"

Murph winked at me, her nice duds gone now. She wore loose dungaree pants, pressed, and a neat long-sleeved shirt. I assumed she couldn't afford to replace her good clothes or didn't want to risk losing whatever was left. Her new style was more rascally. "You can believe it. Remember, too, we're so much more than them."

I was proud to be her friend. "After the broken hand, after the broken ribs, after jail, after losing your jobs and your home, you're holding your head up and know you're whole?" I was ready to cry.

"What about you?" she asked. "You're in trouble for Rosie's actions, your home isn't safe, you've been dumped by a girl without the courage to leave the man who's practically destroyed her to get his way."

"Colonel Mustard!"

"What?" Murph asked.

"They could have gotten a search warrant by now. Colonel Mustard went nuts earlier. What would they do to her?"

I was up and hurrying out the door, Murph behind me every step of the way as we ducked between cars stopped at the traffic light to get to my place.

CHAPTER TWENTY-EIGHT

W hen I unlocked the door the Colonel was wagging her tail and smiling.

"I have never been so relieved in my life," I said, going to my knees and hugging her. She was panting. The July heat didn't let up in the evenings. I turned on the floor fan.

"Does it look like they've been here?"

"I don't think so, but I shouldn't have left her alone. I may curtail my social life, such as it is, for a while."

"Ah, Rockie," Murph said, and crushed me in a hug that couldn't have been more welcome. We stood there, my arms around her ribs, her arms around my shoulders. We might not say how important we were to each other in words, but this hug couldn't make that plainer.

"As you'd say, it's cockamamie!" Murph said. "Did I pronounce it right?"

We stepped away from each other, laughing, not meeting eyes, a bit self-conscious after hugging like a couple of ladies.

"I guess I'll head on home," she said.

"Why? Let me make you some coffee. Stay and look around. You've never been here before."

"That I haven't. After all these years you'd think, well, that we'd get to know one another better. More than our drinking choices at least."

"Your stories tell us a lot about you," I told her as I moved into the kitchen.

"Don't trust those. They're a little truth, a little exaggeration, and a little tall tale."

"That says it all right there."

"That I'm a liar?" Murph asked.

I laughed. "That you have a great imagination."

"It's the Irish in me, that's all." She was patting my dog. "Why did you name this poor girl Colonel Mustard?"

"For her color. She's much too dignified a dog to be called Mustard though. So I gave her the title."

Murph whispered, "Does she know it's from the game?"

I whispered back, "No. We only play chess together."

Murph thought that was a knee-slapper.

When we sat—she on the couch, me in my club chair, big, soft molasses ginger cookies on a plate between us—I asked, "So, what do you think about the bar's chances?"

"Oh, come on, Rockie. That's like asking me what I think about our chances to marry our girls in this lifetime."

"Doomed, right?"

"Maybe, maybe not." Murph tilted her good hand one way and the other. "At least the bar is a business. Businesses always count more than people in this world. What about you?"

"I think we have shot at it. Because of where the business is." I'd thought about this a lot. "This neighborhood is sort of a new other side of the tracks. Not only poor people or people with darker skins. The students help keep the area alive, and all these bearded types, hair too long, some of them wearing ratty dungarees and sandals all year round, the women cut from one pattern, hair down to their waists, tall boots, an astonishing amount of makeup, are here to stay. This third side of the tracks is the different side, the weirdo side. We may be able to blend in."

"I never thought of this neighborhood as a melting pot for our kind of people, like all of America is supposed to be," Murph said.

I'd turned on the radio when I walked in. Sinatra was singing.

"How I hate that man," Murph said.

I went to turn the radio to another station, but Murph held up a hand.

"It's not the singing I hate," she said. "It's the man."

I sat again.

"Why is this rat-mafia guy so popular and successful? There are lots of great voices out there—and better-looking singers. It's because he's in a gang of some powerful guys who use him for their gain and protect him all the way."

She leaned forward and squinted at me. "What if Hansfield College is the crooner in this town? It's the equation again. The college is A and the sum total is protection, or *C*. I'm looking at it like A plus X equals C. Who's the gang? Who are the protectors? How does the college rate the protection? How did they get in with this gang?" She tapped the coffee table with a fingertip, wincing because it was her injured hand. "We figure out X and we know how come the college is throwing its weight around."

Whatever method Paul was using to teach Murph, his results knocked my socks off. Murph was not only picking up fractions, but applying mathematical reasoning to yet another problem.

I said, "Maybe the question we should have asked Frank Goodlette was not how he could help us. Maybe we should have asked who could help us."

"That's the ticket."

We both leaned back. "Will you talk to Rose about this?" I asked.

"Sure, sure. I was planning to. She's going to call me at the bar tomorrow night."

"Mazel tov. Meanwhile let me freshen your tea."

When I returned, Murph held up a cookie. "Where do you buy these?" she asked.

I hesitated.

A big smile took over Murph's face. "You made them, didn't you?"

It sounded like a teasing accusation. I thought of the moment when we'd hugged, revealing a whole other part of ourselves that we never showed at The Old Town.

"Would you," Murph whispered, as if anyone else could hear in my apartment. "Would you teach me how? I want to be able to cook for the babies."

CHAPTER TWENTY-NINE

After that, I stayed in at night for three weeks, four? I don't remember, but it was until late August or early September. I was feeling more heartsick every day, thinking too often that I was one tiny speck of life in a city of tens of thousands of similar specks making dinner, talking to our dogs, watching *The Avengers*. I stood by my living-room window, short of the drapes, singing along with a Sinatra LP of ballads I never heard on the radio. I caught sight of the buses hurtling souls to and from their random destinations. Like the birds and squirrels on overhanging branches: we foraged, always foraged, for our next meals, for nesting materials; delighted in puddle baths. Our days ranged on and on, from one sunrise to another until we ran out of sunrises. Some stranger came along then, some young bus rider grown older, and took over the nests we'd made in aging brick buildings.

I'd think about how this was only one city in a whole world of speck-filled cities. How we all were trying to get by with as much joy and as little pain as possible. I chided myself. I was normally the happy-go-lucky one at the bar. In those months after the raid, my head throbbing, my neck stiff, I was glad to spare my friends the company of someone sunk so low in the doldrums.

One night I heard a gentle knock on the door and almost didn't open it, fearing the police. I stayed stock-still in my easy chair, light from the floor lamp both exposing and curtaining me.

Before I could decide what to do, Lisa, in that sexy, unexpectedly deep voice of hers, announced herself. Then, I thought as I got out of my chair, there are the specks of beauty, the sheer enrichment of life you get from hearing a "Moonlight Sonata," reading a novel by Herman Wouk, resting your eyes on a piece of art or a person who turns on the lights in your mind and resuscitates your heart. I understood right then and there that Lisa Jelane did that for me. Of course, even with the tiny new misalignment of her nose, hers was a beauty beyond the reach of this humble businesswoman.

I fumbled with the door chain but managed to let her inside. I told her, "You arrived in the nick of time. I was about to get maudlin."

"No wonder. Do you leave this place? No one's seen you in weeks."

I backed up through the foyer with my thumbs hooked into the loops of my slacks. "Like the cowboys say, I've been laying low."

"You need a cat to keep you and your colonel company. Lana Turner wouldn't approve of a cat-less household. Show me around?" Lisa glanced over my living-room walls.

She looked so splendid in my place, it became shabby. I kept the hardwood floor highly polished and the walls decorated with pictures of Hansfield. Through the years I'd collected paintings and photographs, often buying them at county fairs, the local library, or restaurants that showed the work of local artists. While it wasn't always first-class art, I had the works professionally framed. Lisa spent some moments at each piece, nodding, not commenting.

I'd done some tile work myself in the kitchen, and she studied that for a long time, looking at and touching a counter of fruit and vegetable tiles, which I'd found in an antique store. Another set was from a home-decorating place downtown, whose manager learned to call me when something new was offered. Those lined the walls at about eye level, all of them herbs and spice plants.

"It's a harmless hobby," I said.

"And a beautiful one. I'd love to cook in this kitchen."

"Be my guest any time! I'd bet you're good at it."

Lisa smiled with great warmth. "It would be my pleasure."

She said she loved the little tchotchkes I'd appropriated when my grandmother died. She picked each one up, including the nesting peasant dolls and the miniature kaleidoscope. She was silent and barely moved; only smiles betrayed her delight. She especially liked a porcelain turquoise elephant on a pedestal because it was crouched and its skin was in folds. I was particularly fond of that elephant too.

"It's good luck when the trunk is up," she said. At my tiny copper tea kettles, three of them in different styles, Lisa asked, "How do you keep these so polished?"

I told her it was a monthly chore I'd pledged myself to.

She looked at me with raised eyebrows, as if reassessing me. "Such discipline."

"I haven't done well in business by fooling around."

"The mortgage office I worked in served all kinds of clients. I saw the nitty-gritty of success and failure every day."

My bedroom was the last on the tour. I stood in the doorway as Lisa looked around.

"This room is so different from the others," she exclaimed.

I'd painted the walls a white-yellow to warm them up. "My inner sanctum."

"Is that a water bed?"

I'd built a mahogany platform for my bed about three feet off the ground. I stored all my linens and clothes in drawers that rolled out from the platform and wedged a set of steps between two of them. The rest of the room was bare except for heavy white drapes that insulated me from the sounds of the street.

Lisa looked at me, one eyebrow cocked.

I explained. "I need a place that's quiet and calm. The bindery is full of machinery and people constantly on the move. It smells of glue and industrial oils and paper dust. You know how loud the bar can be. After I'm assaulted by the world, I come in here, lie on the bed, and see nothing, hear almost nothing. This room is for sleep and rest and peace. Right now I'm trying to quit being so low in my spirit."

"I would never have guessed you'd have a sanctuary, Rockie."

"Now you know. I must have been a monk in another life."

Lisa laughed. "Somehow that image doesn't fit you. You're such a charmer."

"You must be thinking of some other Rockie Solomon."

"I might agree if your bed wasn't so big."

"That's so Colonel Mustard can share it with me," I said, one quick word tripping over the next.

"Uh-huh," Lisa said as she pivoted out of the room.

I offered her coffee—or tea.

"Thank you. I'm here to take you across the street."

I looked at my feet.

She chided me. "Never mind shaking that silky white head at me. There's strength in numbers."

"I suspect I'd be a weak link now."

Lisa came right up to me and put her hands on my shoulders. Her touch was light at first, then her fingers dug deep as she made her points. "The Old Town lost its liquor supplier, Rockie. Somehow, since Prohibition, this part of the state has slowly allowed one supplier to take over the distribution of liquor and mixers to the bars and restaurants."

"I don't see how I—"

"Glue. What if your bindery couldn't get glue anymore? The men are taking turns driving over the state line to buy from the New Hampshire state liquor store. It's obvious that can't go on forever. Someone has squeezed the supply line shut, Rockie. We need your brains, we need you back on our side."

"I'm on your side."

"All right, by our sides. If you're over here with your shades drawn and door locked, it looks like you've turned your back on us."

"I have to choose the bindery, Lisa. It burns me up inside that life is this way, but I'm supporting so many people. I can't indulge in my own pleasures at their expense. That's so irresponsible."

Lisa sat, crossed her legs, and pulled out her cigarettes. She lit one and waved smoke away from her face. "I'm no big thinker, Rockie, so I can't explain my reasoning. Aren't you saying you're not as important as your employees? And you're not as important why? Because you're gay? Would you say business comes before a straight marriage and kids? Are our gay lives a sinful indulgence while people who put their straight families first are doing the right thing?"

I covered my face with my hand. Was she right? I said, "Bar friends change, fall in love and move on. I like to think of The Old Town as my family, but we all know it's more like a foster family with no long-term promises."

"It's as close as we can get when we're queer," she said, a blade of rancor piercing her usual calm. "They don't let us have that marriage or those kids. Aren't families the people who stick by us, who we play with, who we go to when we're down and out? Isn't that what a family is, Rockie?"

She stubbed out her cigarette in my grandmother's standing ashtray, the kind where you pushed a button and it opened up, then swallowed the butt so no smoke escaped. The sight of Bubbe's ashtray, of all her beloved possessions, brought a hot flash of fear to me. They'd come for my relatives in Europe twenty-odd years earlier.

"With every fiber of my being," I told Lisa, "I want to stay here and hide."

She first looked chagrined, then I stood and got my jacket out of the hall closet and she smiled. I thought the Colonel would be safe with the deadbolt I put in.

At The Old Town, I opened the door for Lisa. She made an entrance Princess Grace couldn't beat. Despite the lack of a police presence on

Girolami Avenue this evening, I hurried inside like a scared rabbit and jumped at the gang's welcoming shouts. They hugged me and clapped me on the back till I threatened to go home. You'd think I was the Messiah.

Once everyone settled down and got back to socializing or drinking, playing cards or seducing or dancing or all at once, I wondered why I'd stayed away. This was the most innocent of spots. Who did we hurt? Why did anyone even care that we were here?

I asked Lisa to dance, which I'd never done before. Our recent contacts had opened my eyes to the pleasure of her company. I'd never danced with a woman taller than me, but she was a good dancer and I barely noticed her height. Too bad, I thought, again, that she wasn't twenty-five years older, but then, look at Rose and Vi.

Lisa, laughing, said, "I've always dreamed of a partner I wouldn't tower over."

She'd only be sixty when I was eighty-five, I thought. She'd end up taking care of an old wreck instead of dancing with someone who suited her. The song ended, and, like Lisa did with Deej, I let the fantasy go.

Poor Murph. I ordered her a refill. She groaned. "Norman can't get Buffalo Rock anymore," she told me. "Canada Dry from the First National is the best we can do right now."

"I offered to fly down to Alabama to pick some up if she'd pay for my ticket. Love those Southern men," Norman joked, hands fluttering as if in flight. "Believe it or not, Murph's stories are few and far between these days. Maybe a good ginger ale would loosen your tongue again."

"If only ginger ale was the worst of our troubles," Murph said.

Norman turned to me and sighed. "Did my New York glamor girl, Lisa, tell you about our own personal liquor embargo?"

"Do you think that was imposed because of the visit Rose and I made to Frank Goodlette? Or Deej's trip to the mayor's office?"

Norman sighed. "I don't know. I really don't know."

"When you're dealing with gay people," Murph said, "you're damned if you do and damned if you don't. And some say just plain damned."

"I wish I knew what started it all." JoJo darted behind the bar with a huge glass jar of pickled eggs. "And why we're damned." She grunted as she tried to twist the cap off the jar, refusing Norman's help.

"Stubborn little butch," he quipped as JoJo, red-faced and out of breath, triumphed over the vacuum seal.

I said, with a shock, "You know, it never occurred to me that there was a time we might not have been damned."

"Was there?" JoJo asked. "Really? If there was, I'm heading for the nearest time machine."

Hugh placed his briefcase on the bar. "The very concept of homosexuality is nineteenth century."

JoJo squinted at him. I wished she'd wear her glasses more often. "You mean you guys never did it in the Dark Ages?"

"Tell me another one," Murph said.

"It wasn't called homosexuality until about a hundred years ago. We had our ups and downs through the centuries, but you're right, Murph, we've been doing it since the beginning of time. Some societies have been more accepting than others. It's run the gamut from being considered perfectly natural to executing us for loving one another."

"I don't get why they're so shook up about us," JoJo said. "I never have understood and never will."

"They're afraid someone else is having more fun than they are." Murph swung her barstool in a half-circle and added, "They're right."

"I beg your pardon," Tipsy said with a mock-indignant tone.

Murph patted her on the arm. No one knew Tipsy's real name; her nickname fit so well, no one cared. It started because Tipsy was in the habit of declaring, "Why, I think I might be a little bit tipsy." There always seemed to be one flirty old gal who adopted a gay—or neighborhood—bar and acted as an elder mascot. I worried about bag-of-bones Tipsy, who seemed to imbibe little other than alcohol. She acted happy, though, and was old enough to decide how she wanted to leave this world. She could count on the men if she needed help while she was still around.

"You old reprobate. You like the boys as much as I do the girls," Murph told her.

Tipsy asked, "How is your friend, that other Irishwoman?"

"Rose? Scared to come home." Murph's smile disappeared. "I wouldn't have believed it of her, that she could attack Frank."

"I'm not sure she believed it of herself," I said. "She was ashamed afterward."

Norman said, "She should be proud. She'd probably held that rage inside all her life."

"Not that gentle soul," Murph insisted. "She's talking about staying down Maine permanently. Says she loves being near the water.

I even tried to lure her home by telling her she could be an aunt too. It didn't work, I've lost her again."

"So Rose is abandoning us," Lisa said.

"Can you blame her after all that's happened?" Murph asked.

"No," Lisa answered. "It makes me sad to see her driven away."

"Rose is the one with the lawyer connections," I said. "Safe, out-of-town lawyers."

Murph pulled a folded piece of stationery from the pocket of the tan-suede blazer I'd given her and told her to keep after the raid. The blazer was worn in all the right places, suited her, and at my time of life I doubted it would ever fit me the way it once had. The style didn't flatter me anymore.

"Rose mailed me this information—I think it's about the lawyers," Murph said. "I don't know how to talk to lawyers. What if they gave me something to sign and I couldn't read it?"

There was a look of pure terror on Murph's face. She was thrusting the paper at anyone who might relieve her of it. What an awful secret to have to keep for forty years, that she was illiterate. Thank goodness she'd told us. The squares might think gay bars are for the dregs of the earth, and I'm not saying you can't find any dregs in them, but you can also find stars. Paul volunteered his time. Hugh visited the college's education department and set up testing for Murph. Both of them found resources for adult tutoring in addition to Paul. In turn, Murph gave us Rose and, through her, maybe some help. I was thinking of help for the bar and for those of us who had criminal records from the raid. I'd heard of expunging records; could these attorneys find a way to do that?

"What about the apartment upstairs?" I asked Norman.

"Rose kept up her share of the rent," Murph said. "She's staying at her sister's rent free. Of course, that can't last forever."

Norman was avoiding my eyes. I imagined he and Hugh needed that rent money as much as the next person.

Someone pushed the bar door open. Two large wheels appeared. A wheelchair? This was a first. I could have kicked myself for my shock; of course gay people sometimes needed wheelchairs. I imagined what it would be like to be unable to cross the street to get to The Old Town. What a nightmare.

When I saw who it was—

Norman was the first to recover. "Honey Delight!" he cried, and scuttled around the bar to greet her and her companion, who called herself Scarletta when in drag. Tonight he wore black chinos with a shirt and an argyle vest. He looked feminine whatever he wore. He gave the chair a last shove over the lintel. Honey Delight held tight to a crocheted blanket that spread across her lap and over the sides of the chair. She was all made up and wore a platinum-blond wig.

"How are you, darling?" Norman was asking. I couldn't understand what Honey Delight said in reply. Although I'd heard she'd got the worst of the beatings in the kitchen the night of the raid, I hadn't come near to imagining the scope of her injuries. I realized, seeing her, how lucky I'd been to suffer no more than the effects of a concussion.

Of course Norman and Hugh had visited her in the hospital, then at the nursing home where she'd gone to relearn how to walk. It appeared that she wasn't ready to dance yet. The blanket hid her legs. They might be strapped to the chair. With her left hand, she took turns waving a brilliant-patterned scarf at everyone and patting her forehead. Was the perspiration from nervousness or pain? Her smile was wide and warm, like that of an actress who must go on with the show. All the regulars hugged her or kissed her on the cheek.

"When will this fallout from the raid ever end?" Lisa grabbed her pocketbook and headed, with some urgency, toward the bathroom.

After greeting Honey Delight, I followed her. I might as well have been socked hard in the gut. Lisa was at the sink, salvaging her makeup through tears. I held out my arms.

"I am so sorry," Lisa said. "This was the wrong day to lure you back."

"Not at all." I patted her on the back. Cissy was so petite compared to this rangy woman. Lisa wasn't as thin as Tipsy, but she needed more flesh on those bones to protect her if we got caught in another raid. Oh, Lisa, I thought, it could have been you in that wheelchair. "It was exactly the right day," I told her. "Seeing Honey made me even more determined that we can't let it happen again. Whatever they destroyed in Honey Delight's body or mind, they're not storming in here a second time if I can help it. I've been considering getting in touch with that new Civil Rights Commission."

She was crying, enough that her tears dampened the fabric on my shoulder. "What the hell good would that do?" Her tone was demanding. "They don't care about our kind."

Lisa pulled away from me and leaned on a sink. I went into a stall and wound toilet paper over my hand. She took it, dabbed at her eyes, squinted into the mirror, and reached into her purse for makeup.

"What happened to your resolve?" I asked.

She glowered at me, a lovely-looking woman. "I would rather die than end up like him."

"Honey Delight is back, Lisa. Despite everything, here she is again."

"Maybe I should have stayed married. They tell you not to turn queer, that you'll go to hell. What they don't tell you hell is right here, in a bar in Hansfield."

"Aw, Lisa," I said, and made to comfort her in my arms again.

She backed away. "I can't live like this. I thought, with you here, I'd get my nerve back. It's not working."

"Why me?"

"You're always so strong and upbeat about things. You're always here, reliable, ready with a joke and a laugh. Now—now I don't even want you here, in danger. I don't want to wheel you in some day. If you waited for me at home, I'd never come to a gay bar again."

I laughed at that, at all my wanting, and hearing her say I was what she wanted. The irony, I thought, yet couldn't bring myself to tell her. Sometimes I believed laughing was my secret weapon, the way I got through all this dreck life threw at me. Tell her. Tell her. Instead I was all caring reason, perhaps a bit motherly, though it was killing me. "You'd still need friends. You and your lover would still need a social life. You could even have kids somehow. Maybe adopt."

"Kids! Let Murph and Cissy bring up the kids. That didn't work out so well for me. And what if Cissy has boys? Can you imagine bringing up boys?"

I agreed. "That would be pushing it, but I doubt Murph would mind. She could teach them to climb trees and toss a football." I thought about Murph's hand. "Maybe not a football."

She straightened up. I could sense every muscle undulating to life as she did. She shook her hair from her eyes, a deep pool of hopelessness in them.

We both started when the bathroom door opened.

"Hey, you two," JoJo said. "Deej has joined the party."

CHAPTER THIRTY

Lisa plunged a hand into her purse and shooed me out of the bathroom while she reapplied her usual light, very effective makeup. Deej was back all right. Her hair was longer. In women's slacks and wearing makeup, she looked like she'd stepped out of a magazine ad for college coeds, except I'd never seen an Indian woman in such an ad. I shook her hand. She was antsy.

Norman, with a salaam, presented her with a drink. It looked like tonic water topped by a cherry and a parasol.

"You're a teetotaler like me now?" Murph asked.

Lisa came down the hall like a fashion model on a runway. Deej saw her and turned away. I held a chair out for Lisa and she sat, puzzled eyes on Deej.

"I can't stay." For all Deej's straight trappings, she came across like a cocky little gay girl. "I'll get kicked out of school if I get caught in a gay bar."

"Why, girlfriend?" Norman asked. "Nobody knows you were here for the raid."

"Somebody did. And that somebody went right to the dean of women with the information. I guess they couldn't prove it or something because the school left me alone until I shot off my big mouth at the mayor's office."

"What happened?" Lisa asked.

Deej looked at her from under her thick, dark brows, as if she'd be vaporized by directly meeting Lisa's gaze. "Looks like the mayor's tight with the college president. The dean called me and my parents in. First she told them about my visit to the mayor's office. They kind of defended my good intentions until the dean said I'd barely escaped arrest during the raid. The dean threatened to expel me. My father went into his humble act, begging the white lady to excuse my behavior, explaining that it wasn't the Indian way and promising that I would rather die than bring shame on the college and my family. The dean said the college president was willing to give me one more chance based on my good grades and, get this one, the difficulty of being the only woman in an all-male department. She thought I was confused. Ha! I was confused until I found The Old Town."

"Didn't you want to strangle her right there and then?" Murph asked.

"I wanted to graduate more. Once school is behind me I can do what I want. Meanwhile, I'm on what they call social probation."

Murph said, "It took nerve to come here today."

"I wanted to tell you that I didn't walk out on you. I'll be back as soon as I'm free."

Murph gave a quiet snort. "And if your employer disapproves of the company you keep?"

The old Deej shone through when, with a grin, she said, "I'll be up shit's creek without a paddle."

We all laughed to hear such an expression from Deej. She seemed too well brought up for casual cursing.

"Your fiasco with the mayor," Norman said, elbow on the bar, chin on his fist, "made the paper. Who would squeal to the college about the raid, though?"

Behind her hand, Honey Delight whispered something in Scarletta's ear. Her blanket shifted. She'd been covering a bag partly filled with a yellow fluid. I averted my eyes. Honey Delight fixed the blanket. I didn't want to think how badly those men damaged her.

Scarletta looked wary. "John reminded me: that straight-looking girl was here at Thanksgiving. Funny how she left right before the raid."

"Wasn't she sleeping with Deej?" Norman asked.

"Maybe she got caught. Maybe the college wanted to throw her out and she blew the whistle on our private party to save herself," JoJo suggested. "Sorry, Deej." She filled two glasses, one in each hand, from the ice well.

"That's okay," Deej said. "I was starting to wonder about her too. After the raid, it was like she didn't want to know me. I assumed she'd been scared away."

The door opened and Deej looked panicked. I held my breath until I saw it was Spence and Seneca. I could hear a train braking at the station and imagined men headed home to their wives and kids, so normal, so boring. I could use some of that boring normality.

"If you see me run out the back," Deej said, "you'll know why."

"What do you know about—was it Chris?" Murph asked.

"Crista, that's her name. Cheerleader. Her dad's head of emergency management with the city. Crista's an honor student, an education major." Deej grinned again. "Great dancer, great in—"

"Never mind that," Murph said, with a swipe at Deej, who ducked like a boxer and swiped back, hitting Murph's hand.

Murph's eyebrows rose and she clamped her mouth shut. She cradled her hand without touching it and rocked. A hiss escaped her lips.

"Oh my God," Deej cried. "That's the hand they hurt! I'm sorry. I'm sorry."

"It's okay," Murph said, coughing. "I started it. Shouldn't start something I can't finish."

"No," Deej said. "You guys are right. I'm nothing but trouble. I hurt you, Murph. The raid was my fault. I don't even have the guts to hang out with you anymore."

"If only we had someplace to go other than the bars." It was Lisa. "Why are we always in the bars, like animals in a cage?"

Deej looked at Lisa now. "I'd better get out of here before it's too late."

"It's too late now," Lisa said.

Murph said, "It was too late the day your mother gave birth. You're like us and always will be, come what may."

"That doesn't mean I can't have a career," Deej said with a tone of desperation. "There must be gay engineers out there."

Murph used a napkin to wipe sweat from her forehead. "Of course there are, kid. And you're going to be one of them. Last question. Crista plans to be a teacher?"

Deej nodded.

"She has even more at stake than you. The schools for sure won't hire a homosexual."

"So you think she reported me?"

JoJo made staccato guesses. "Maybe someone found out about her. Maybe she got called into the dean's office too. Maybe she traded information for graduation."

Murph enumerated her points with the fingers of her left hand, one by one. "Let's see now. Crista is the one who didn't secure the front door when she took off. And I've been told that she's the one who took the trash out back while she was helping in the kitchen before the raid."

"She was always doing that," Deej said. "Leaving her car unlocked. She was careless and too trusting."

Murph touched another finger. "Sure, and Miss Innocent knew only gays, other than Seneca and Spence, were here for the day after Thanksgiving. I saw her, with my own eyes, watch you flirt with Lisa, Miss Always-on-the-Make. Could she have been hurt that you carried on with Lisa? Could Crista be our boogeyman?"

"Like I said, I started wondering about Crista too. So I asked some questions. My favorite instructor at the college is also Hansfield's city engineer. He told me Crista's dad used to be a cop. He got hurt during an arrest and they created the emergency-manager job for him. His brother's a cop too." She narrowed her eyes. "He's captain of the vice squad."

"Oh, boy," Scarletta said.

"*The* vice squad guy? The wild-man cop?" Norman's chest heaved the way it did the night of the raid.

"So it's personal," Lisa said.

"Maybe," Murph said. "Remember, the college wants this land."

Deej looked absolutely diabolical as she reached into an olive-green canvas bag slung from her shoulder. With a smile both wicked and triumphant, she displayed a gun straight out of the Wild West. I was *plotzing*, it looked so deadly.

"Oh, sweet Jesus," Murph said, backing her chair toward the wall.

"Jeezum!" Norman cried. "You're mad!"

I remembered what Hugh had said about Deej's three cultures and how the conflicts they would cause could make someone unhinged. There was no denying that our Deej could at times be genuinely mental. Carla Jean too. She was born to an old-fashioned Italian family and juggled their ways with gay ways.

"Deej." JoJo's voice was so quiet and firm it could have calmed a panicked animal. "Put that away and leave. Now."

Deej put it away, but stood her ground.

"Where the hell did you get that?" Murph asked.

"At home." Her grin narrowed one eye and pulled her mouth sideways. "Of course my father has a weapon. He owns a downscale motel. This is his .38."

"And what, my dear," Dr. Everett asked, "do you plan to do with that thing?"

"Use it on someone like Captain Vice if he ever tries to touch one of us again."

"No. Deej." Murph pleaded. "Put it back. Leave all of this alone. Go to school. It won't be much longer. What good would another gay girl in prison be to the world? You have dreams. Don't ditch them."

Lisa got up then. "Murph's right," she said. "I'm sorry if I was hard on you." She opened her arms. Deej hesitated. Lisa went to her and rocked her in her arms, then stepped back. "Go. Change the world with your talent, Deej, not with fireworks."

The kid grabbed a napkin from the bar and blew her nose. It sounded like she was choking down a sob. "It's just—so—unfair! How else can we fight back?"

"When you get older, Deej," Murph said, "it won't matter so much. We have food on the table and roofs over our heads. You'll be okay."

I wondered if Murph was worrying about being a homosexual and bringing up babies. Could they be taken away?

Deej looked at Murph as if she was the one who was acting crazy. She shook her head and made for the door. "See you later, you guys."

"Come back when you can," Murph said. "If we're here."

The kid paused. "They'd better not take this place away. Where would I be without all of you?"

"You'll be okay," Murph repeated.

Honey Delight squeezed Deej's hand. "Don't take it all on yourself," she said in a hoarse whisper. "Bless you." Then she waved Deej out the door with her brilliant scarf. They'd ruined her voice as well as her body.

I think we all got wet-eyed. Leave it to a queen to know exactly the right thing to say and do.

"Why did you tell Deej she'd be okay?" Lisa asked.

Murph said, "Because the kid's going to meet some girl, or get a job far away. Listen, we want her to have a place to come to, but she's young. She needs to be free to go."

"You sentimental slob," Lisa said with an affectionate smile. A bolt of jealousy singed me.

The mood, once Deej left, was pretty depressed. Where we used to have so much fun at The Old Town, now there was only an occasional bark of laughter from the men at the bar. Carla Jean came in and stopped in her tracks. "Who died?" she asked.

I knew what was going through my brain was going though everyone else's. First, what if Honey Delight took what Carla Jean said wrong? Second, some of us had come very close to death and, for all we knew, we might yet hear of a raid-related suicide. Carla Jean could be a little insensitive at times, like a cloud of her own cigarette smoke insulated her.

"No one!" Murph shouted. "We're all alive and getting along fine!"

All at once the bar was lit up with smiles.

"Yeah!" one of the men at the bar yelled.

"Ain't that the truth!" Seneca called out. Spence hammered his fist on their table to emphasize her sentiment.

A lightness filled the room. Murph was right, we carried on despite everything. Lisa was a gutsy lady; she'd land a job. Honey Delight would improve with therapy. Eventually I could emerge from my closet at the bindery. Murph was better off for confessing that she needed help, and with Rose gone she could let go of that hopeless dream. All the loose ends needed tidying up yet: Paul, Lisa, the bar itself, the list of repercussions from the raid were endless. Who knew, for example, what would happen in the future for those with the raid police records?

There was more laughter at the bar and from tables of beatniks who'd come in for pitchers of beer. They'd brought pizza with them, and the room smelled like someone had sprayed Italian-food room deodorizer. My stomach growled.

"Let me take you out for dinner," I said to Lisa.

She looked at me like she was trying to determine if this would be a date. Her cigarettes lay on the table. She edged one out of its pack with two fingers. Darn, if that wasn't one of the sexiest things I'd ever seen. I assured her I wasn't asking her on a date; I was hungry and would enjoy her company. She nodded yes, her eyes locked with mine as she touched a match to the cigarette. I thought, Lisa's let Deej go. I wished I could fill in her emptiness, because it was plain to me now that this was a woman who would never believe she was complete without a mate. I sighed, again wishing myself at least ten years younger.

Murph came over. "I'm pondering the city connection," she said, massaging her injured hand with her good one. The pain of her two useless fingers, she'd once whispered, never let up. "Her dad has a political appointment so we know he's tight with the city movers and shakers."

"Keep going," Carla Jean said.

Lisa said, "Deej remarked that Crista is petrified of her dad's temper."

"If he's anything like his vice-squad brother, the beast who led the raid, I don't blame her." Murph shook her head. "The captain that raided us has some temper."

I imagined what she was thinking. "Did you just find an answer to your equation, Murph?" I asked.

"Shhh. I'm concentrating. How about this? The college wants this land. The college prez is pals with the mayor. You with me so far?"

Lisa and I nodded.

"The mayor tells the cops to make trouble so we'll want to leave. They started watching the bar and taking pictures before the raid. The captain sees Crista's photo and rats her out to his brother, Crista's Papa. Papa's mad as a hornet and assumes we're the ones corrupting his innocent daughter. The election's coming up. He's going to kill two birds with one stone. First, bring down the bar as a lesson to his kid. Second, make the mayor look good doing it. He happens to have this weapon, the captain, who's glad to wreck some queer lives for whatever reason."

She raised her eyes.

"I'm with you so far," I told her.

She pressed her lips together and grimaced. "I'm at a dead end. The whole cockeyed shebang is tied up together, I know it is. I'm damned if I can figure out how to stop it."

CHAPTER THIRTY-ONE

We could have gone down the street to Avenue Cantonese or to Brigham's, but I wanted to inject a taste of romance even though I knew it would go nowhere. At the same time, I wanted someplace up to what I thought were Lisa's top-shelf standards. I decided to take her to Hank's House, a semi-swanky eatery famous for its prime rib and stuffed flounder. I was a regular and they gave us a comfortable booth. There was an unobtrusive piano player on the other side of the room I'd gone to college with. I'd seen him at the bar downtown. We'd never done more than nod when I ate at the restaurant. He seemed to be one of those homosexual men with no taste for the company of women.

Lisa was in a navy-blue dress with a cinched waist, a wide red belt, and a silk scarf in red, patterned with blue flowers. She looked better than any woman in the place. At least, I think she did—

I couldn't take my eyes from her.

The waiter wore a bow tie and a black-bibbed apron with HANK'S HOUSE stitched in red. Lisa ordered the Cobb salad. I asked for a plain strip steak. As she talked, she unfolded her cloth napkin and placed it on her lap with care. She used all the right silverware. She blotted her lips between bites and drank in dainty sips. The day hadn't been one to work up appetites, but a bottle of good wine helped. Before I knew it we lost ourselves to giggling, heads tipped toward each other like two goofs in a funny factory. No matter how weighty the subject, we got silly about it. I'd never seen this part of Lisa; I liked it—liked it a lot.

She motioned for me to look over my shoulder. Frank Goodlette was hanging over the piano player.

"Look, the high-muck-a-muck and his grand pooh-bah brother-in-law, Lawrence!" I told her. We watched them make their way back to a table with two middle-aged women.

"Do you think the wives know they're boyfriends?" Lisa asked me.

This set us off in unrelenting giggles.

We calmed down over coffee. I was drained; I hadn't laughed so much since long before Geri left. Or had I? That night, in the snow, with Cissy—but that was the only time with her. Everything got too serious, too fast, like a kiddie-park ride I fell off.

"Do you really think something is going on with the cops and the college and city hall?" asked Lisa.

My mouth was full, which gave me time to think. "It sounds like business as usual to me."

"Political corruption never dies, does it?" Lisa let a stream of smoke waft from her lips.

"I don't think they even see it as corruption. A gay bar isn't worth a second thought to them. Maybe no business would be, and certainly not one that caters to perverts. "

"Oh," Lisa said. "I dislike that word. It's so ugly. When someone talks about us that way, I know my daughter is much better off living with normal parents like her father and his wife."

"That's so sad," I said. "You'd be a wonderful mother."

"What kind of a mother brings home girlfriends for the night? And some of my girlfriends came across as—I'm looking for the right word—coarse. That's why I like the women at The Old Town. None of the girls, and not many guys, are showing off or trying to impress themselves. I don't go there for excitement, I go for companionship. I think most of us do. Maybe I'd meet more women downtown," Lisa said, eyes downcast. She met my eyes then. "I guess I'm trying to say I'm looking for quality in a girlfriend, not thrills, though I forgot that for a bit. For," she explained, now watching her finger make circles on the gold tablecloth, "my few hours with Deej."

That darned hot jealous burning made me move us on. "So your daughter doesn't know you?"

"They don't want her to."

"Her father and his wife?"

She nodded.

"You agreed to this?"

"What choice did I have? Go to court where he would expose me to the world and the judge would most certainly give her to him legally and forever?"

"You stepped aside."

"Let her grow up without all the disturbance I'd bring into her life, like chronically bad weather."

"I understand," I said, mulling over her options. There must be a way, I thought, looking at this perfectly fine woman who was so obviously in distress over her decision. It would be best if I stopped probing.

"It sticks in my craw," I said then, "that the college, which is supposed to be a place of enlightenment—or at least that's what they told us when I went there—isn't more sensitive to us or to the neighborhood. Maybe they don't approve of their bearded students or the coeds with big earrings who gravitate to Old Town Hansfield."

Lisa laughed again, lifting her chin to show her long white neck. Why was this woman single? I considered matchmaking for her, but found jealousy again burning my gullet. Romantic dinner or not, I'd be damned if I'd let myself fall for her.

She said, "The parents don't want to scrimp and save to send the kids to a good college and have their little perfect little boys and girls turn into poets or have sex before they marry. I can't imagine which they'd think is worse. Don't they remember how they carried on at that age?"

"I certainly do," I said, laughing with her. It was a weeknight. The restaurant was far from packed. I was full of a sense of well-being. Then I thought of The Old Town. "Look at us here, blabbing happily away when Honey Delight, Murph, Paul—hell, all of us have been through the wringer."

Lisa slapped my hand, which was lying on the table. "I forbid you to say another sad word tonight. We need a goddamn break."

I smiled and told her, "I love a strong woman."

"Well, you've got yourself one tonight."

I tried to turn my mind away from the swamp of misery the raid caused.

"Tell me," Lisa said, leaning my way. "Did you turn gay very young?"

"Turn? I always wonder why we use the word *turn*. There was nothing to turn for me. I've been a stubborn tomboy since I took my first steps." Great change of subject, I thought.

"You're lucky. It was confusing for me, to be girlish yet have no interest in guys. I loved dressing up and cooking and playing dolls. And I didn't understand why I couldn't keep playing house with my girlfriends. We could be mommies together! I knew it wouldn't be any fun to do what I loved doing by myself while my husband was at work. And it wasn't at all."

"I'll bet it wasn't any fun when he came home at night, either."

"He was a good man. And funny. I even wanted a child with him. He couldn't help it that he was male."

"How can you say that? He took your daughter."

"He remarried. Quickly. He makes good money. His wife is a homemaker, with the kids when they're not in school. My little girl has a brother and a sister now."

"She must want to see you, though. You could go to her school."

"Her stepmother decided to tell her about me. She isn't old enough to understand anything except that her mom is different. I could kill that woman for not waiting. My child refuses to see her 'bad mommy.'"

"That's a heartbreaker," I said.

"And you snuck in a change of subject, didn't you?"

"You don't want to know my ancient history, Lisa."

"Of course I do. What was her name?"

She looked sincerely eager, so I told her my first was a girl named Polly. "She's a nurse at the hospital now," I whispered.

"No," Lisa said. "Polly Cerreto?"

"You're joshing me."

"Black hair? Kind of chunky?"

"Sounds like her."

"I went out with her a few times after my divorce." Lisa put out her cigarette. "I have never been so bored before or since."

My laugh seemed to fill the room. Other diners looked our way. "Sorry," I said when Lisa noticed. "Let me tell you, she wasn't boring the night she brought me out!"

"You could have been celebrating your twentieth? Thirtieth anniversary?"

"Uh-uh. Her girlfriend got wind of it."

"How, Rockie?" she asked with a laugh. "Did you have witnesses?"

"Right. And a notary public. Someone at a party saw us dancing together."

"I guess you learned your lesson early."

"Which lesson?"

With a delighted laugh, Lisa said, "You're quick tonight!"

I'd half-noticed that the restaurant was emptying out. When the waiter stacked chairs on the table next to us I looked at my watch. "You're more fun than a barrel of monkeys," I said.

"What time is it?" Lisa swiftly looked concerned. "The last bus is gone! How did it get this late?"

"My fault. I was enjoying myself too much. I'll pay for your cab home." I asked the waiter for the check and a cab call, then helped Lisa with her light sweater.

"We'll have to do this again sometime," she told me as we waited outside.

"It would be my pleasure," I said. I wanted to kiss her; our quarter-century difference held me back. I leaned toward the street and watched for the taxi. "I love downtown Hansfield at night," I told her.

"So do I," she said. "It's a miniature big city: old brick buildings, neon lights, enough traffic to know you're not alone in the world."

The light at the corner went red, then green, then red again. A yellow car slowed across the street and popped its roof light off. I heard a song in my head, "Secret Love." That was silly, I told myself.

"The cab came too soon," Lisa said.

I dared take her arm as we crossed the street. The driver would think I was her mother. Lisa squeezed my arm and I let go.

"I never knew how much fun you are, Rockie," she said. She gave me a peck on the cheek. "How will you get home?"

I snapped out of my dreamy daze, embarrassed, and fumbled a ten from my wallet to pay the driver. That kiss set me off. I hadn't thought about it. "Why don't you ask this guy to call in that I need a ride?"

"Why don't you get in, silly? Drop me off and have him take you home next."

"You wouldn't mind?" I thought of *To Kill a Mockingbird*, the newest library book waiting on my nightstand. It wasn't as appealing as it had been earlier.

"Of course not."

In the cab, we stopped chatting. I was desperate to come up with a joke or even a comment on the weather. Was I getting shy in my old age or was I out of practice? Cissy took the lead, and I was so much younger when Geri and I got together. Why was I even having these thoughts? My birthday had come and gone. You're fifty-four, you're fifty-four, you're fifty-four! I kept telling myself. Then I remembered Lisa's recent birthday. Big deal, I thought.

God, it was hot in that cab. I unzipped my hooded sweatshirt.

Out of nowhere, Lisa's fingers touched the back of my hand. I froze. I didn't dare look at her. What was I thinking? I'd be dead when she hit my age. I closed my eyes, melting down from the heat and her so-tentative touch. If she's asking, the answer's yes, but is that the right answer? Looking straight ahead, I turned my hand over, opened it, and enclosed hers. As we slowed for a light, she squirmed a little closer.

The driver swiveled enough to look at us and our entwined hands. I tried to pull mine away, while Lisa held on tight.

"That your mother?" he asked Lisa.

Before I could say I was and save us some grief, Lisa piped up. "No. She's my friend."

"Friend," he said, scoffing. He shook his head and scowled. "None of that in my cab," he said, eyes on me, then on our hands again. When we didn't jump away from each other he said, "Or you'll walk."

"Let us out here," Lisa told him. She pushed the ten back at me and took a dollar from her purse. The meter read $1.25. "Give me a quarter," she told me. I did. She dropped the money on the front seat as I held the door for her. I'd barely closed it when the driver went into a screeching U-turn.

"Let's look for a phone booth," I said. "I'll call—" There was only one cab company.

She reached for my hands and whirled me around with her. I peered into the dark store windows. The apartments above had closed venetian blinds. I whirled with her.

"Race you to the corner!" she said.

She was only a few inches taller, but she was light on her feet while I was burdened with middle-aged blubber. She turned and held her arms open. Her head tipped back so I could see the waves of laughter coursing up that proud neck. I walked to her. We held each other, perfectly motionless, hearts thudding together, until we heard a car heading our way.

"Let's walk," she said. "It's not more than a mile. Can you do that?"

I gave her an insulted look. "I walk more than that around the plant every day."

Out of the confined backseat of that taxi, we chattered again. That mile went too fast too. I really needed to get back to Colonel Mustard somehow. Upstairs, as I turned from locking the door behind us, Lisa whirled once again and, in a very unfemme-like maneuver, pinned my arms to the door while pressing her lips to mine. She tasted as sweet as a bruised peach.

We both breathed heavily when she released me.

"I thought I'd cut through the awkward part," she said.

"I—"

"And I don't have the patience to let you pretend to be all picky and choosy. I've seen how you look at me. I don't know why it took me so long to catch on that you're the one I've been looking for."

"I'm too ol—"

She shut me up with a bevy of kisses. "I may be too young for you, but you're not too old for me."

I couldn't help thinking of her past tries: Murph hadn't held much promise for her and I suspected Lisa knew that; she'd brought Deej out and Deej was too young to stick around. Was I her last resort? Lisa was a prize catch, a plum, the brass ring on the merry-go-round. What would she want with me?

I remembered where her phone was, entwined my fingers with hers, and walked to it.

"Rockie," she said, "what if you get the same driver?"

I smiled at her and squatted to pat Lana Turner, who was winding around my ankles. My neighbor answered the phone and I apologized for calling so late. Fortunately, I'd fed their birds last month, when they went to Europe, and was assured that I'd never call too late. They'd been about to run downtown for the Sunday paper and would love to take Colonel Mustard with them. Could they keep her overnight? Of course they would. To tell the truth, the Colonel loved to go over there. They kept a shoebox full of toys for her and always had treats. Like grandparents, they could enjoy the dog and she'd go home the next day.

I pulled Lisa toward me by her silk scarf, then slid it off her neck.

CHAPTER THIRTY-TWO

Lisa was looking sexy and hungry. I was nothing *but* sexy and hungry. We took turns in the bathroom. She laid out towels, a packaged toothbrush, and unopened toothpaste. I appreciated a woman who respected the etiquette of cleaning up. I was drawn to the same quality in Geri too. That and how cerebral she was. I'd ask what she was thinking and she'd talk about applying some mathematical premise to a theoretical problem about the hypothetical something of something. I'd tried to read an article she'd written for some math journal and hadn't tried again. Her brainpower amazed me and, who knows why, ignited my passion. Me, I was happier with my kind of books. Bernard Malamud, who I tried to get Geri to read, was brainy enough for my tastes.

In the case of Lisa, it was her grand womanliness that got to me. It occurred to me that a wedding night should be like this. She was slightly propped on pillows, the white sheet covering her to the tops of her breasts. I stopped at the side of the bed to admire her unthinkably strong, lovely face, that straight cider-colored hair, those teasing brown eyes, her freckled shoulders, the secrets under the sheet.

She unveiled a long arm and pulled me to her by my belt. With both hands, she unbuckled it and then slid it fully loose from the loops that held it. She studied my eyes and, with a fast and sure movement, pulled my blouse free of my slacks.

"I like a woman who knows her mind," I told her.

"You fill the bill, Rockie, you really do fill my bill."

She unbuttoned my blouse from the bottom up. This wasn't something Geri ever did. She'd wait for me to disrobe her. I liked that. It defined us. Cissy was the same, maybe because she was new to lovemaking. This, what Lisa was doing, was even better. Lisa, on her back, was playing aggressor. She was bold enough to electrify me, while leaving the next, more definitive step, and relinquishing the control she'd established, to me.

By my age, I was no novice at lovemaking. Lisa's bed was against the wall, so I stripped, slowly pulled the sheet off her, and nudged her away from the edge. I loved her long legs. And I have to say, I suddenly didn't mind this younger-woman business. While, except for the flab, I was in fairly good shape because of my job, Lisa didn't have to work at it yet. What a portrait some painter could make of her.

We kissed, touched tongues, I licked her nipples. The way Lisa twisted under me, I knew I could get right down to business. Enough time for the art of her and for enjoying her slowly later. We wanted fireworks.

Every woman is different. One likes a really light touch, another something a little harder, and some can only come with the touch of a tongue. Lisa, to my surprise, didn't leave me guessing. With her wet mouth at my ear she told me and went off like a rocket. When I touched her again, well, I'll just say she was more exciting than anyone before her. She used her long limbs to good advantage, and those long, well-formed hands.

As soon as we'd stopped, Lana Turner was up on the bed, pushing between us. We both scratched her neck, one from each side.

"Oh, you're perfect," she said. "I knew you would be."

"Are you kidding? I'm old enough to be your mother."

"And experienced enough to be a really fine lover."

"You're not so bad yourself." I sat up and gave her a grin. "For a youngster."

"You make me wish I was a young girl. I wish I'd never been with anyone besides you, Rockie. Do you believe in soul mates?"

I thought about that one. "I'm willing to," I finally said.

"You old bear." Lisa hugged me and ran her tongue along the edge of my ear. "You are love. You're walking, talking, loving love."

She lay back and lit a cigarette. I watched her smoke, then took it from her hand and stubbed it out. She didn't stop me. I took my time urging her legs apart. I bent her knees toward her and laid my head between her thighs. I stayed there a long time, resting on my elbows, holding her lips apart with my index fingers, letting my widened tongue run up and down the length of her and periodically touch the button that made her whip her hips around and gulp air.

It was like a button. She was so small down there, compared to her overall build, so delicate, all lace-like and foamy. What made people soul mates? If clicking physically was a sign, then that's exactly what we were.

We napped, made love, napped, made love, all night. We drank pitcher after pitcher of ice water I brought to the bed. I got up at daybreak, as soon as the buses started running, took some coffee to her—and a saucer with a splash of milk for Lana Turner—in bed, and didn't say what I was wondering, which was which of us would give up her place, Lisa or me, so we could live together. Was that a homosexual thing, or a thought any woman would have after a first night with a lover? Sex and moving in together. Where did love fit in? I'd been attracted to Lisa for a long time and could enumerate things I loved about her. Would that list grow?

It hit me then: I hadn't been having sex with a tall woman or a short woman, or any woman who was nothing more than a body or someone who was going to leave me. I'd been lovingly touching Lisa Jelane, touching all the bits that made her Lisa, all the warmth and sadness and playfulness that made Lisa lovable. I'd been slowly, deliciously, making love, real love, to Lisa.

What the hell? When did this happen? What if Lisa didn't want my love? It didn't matter if she could love me; only that she let me love her.

I left her in bed with her cat, sitting up with a china saucer on her lap, sheet gathered to her waist, steam rising from her cup. Maybe I shouldn't have given up my two-bedroom apartment after all.

I rode the bus across town with the morning commuters, on top of the world. I smiled at every one of them that met my eyes. The neighbors came out of the building with Colonel Mustard as my bus pulled up. I took over, walked her, then quickly showered, changed my clothes, and met the cab downstairs, same time as usual. It was a hectic day; I could barely take time to walk the Colonel at lunch. I finally broke away and who did we find sitting at the picnic table I'd set under a tree outside the back door? Lisa Jelane. She opened a big tote bag and took out sandwiches, sodas, napkins, and straws.

It was all I could do not to throw my arms around her and give her a kiss. I was flabbergasted. "You made lunch? And brought it all the way out here on the bus? For me?"

She patted the bench next to her for me to sit down. "I wasn't about to take a cab after that driver last night," she told me.

I wasn't intentionally staring at Lisa with my mouth open, and stopped as soon as I realized I was doing it.

Tears came to my eyes. "You're really nice!"

She laughed. "Don't look so shocked."

I immediately became flustered and got up to walk the Colonel.

"I'll come with you," she said.

It occurred to me that my employees might notice, but it was about halfway between their lunch hour and their breaks, and what were they going to do? Quit their good jobs?

The Colonel led us toward the little wooded area behind the plant that she liked to explore. In New England rocks stick up all over. The trees closed behind us as we followed my dog and our path took us around a seven-foot boulder and we ended up behind that rock kissing my lunch break away, my hand up Lisa's skirt, Lisa pressing down against my fingers until the Colonel nudged me and I got busy wiping Lisa's lipstick off my mouth. Lisa pressed me to take a sandwich back to my desk.

"I love that you want to feed me," I told her with a laugh.

That night, without discussing it, we both went to The Old Town. We hugged hello, long and gently. We touched hands across the table. The regulars observed and smiled as Lisa and I, without a word, announced a new "we."

And that's the thing about gay people. Squares think all we do is have sex when all we want is love. Even the boys, for all their monkey business, usually really want a good man to go home to at night. We'd been at war far too long with stupid laws and hypocritical religions that left us weak, dispirited, despondent. Despite the boulders blocking our way, we managed to keep on, or hide behind them. Somebody ought to write a song for us and call it "We Will Survive." It would be playing in every gay bar in the world. For now, we played a lot of Andy Williams singing "Lonely Street." Some theme song that is.

Lisa was giving me more details of her coming-out story when Murph asked if she could join us. That made us officially an item. At The Old Town you never asked; you sat where you wanted unless you smelled romance in the air.

"Speaking of coming-out stories," Lisa said, "I've never heard yours, Murph." So Lisa had questions about Murph's love life too.

Ignoring Lisa's prompt, she squinted at me, then at Lisa. "It's about time somebody snapped you up," she said to either or both of us.

I couldn't have been happier at that moment if a rabbi had officially blessed us.

Lisa imitated Humphrey Bogart. "Of all the gin joints in all the towns in all the world, she walks into mine."

That cracked Murph up: the most feminine woman at The Old Town growling out those words. I was falling more in love by the second. We chatted, mostly about the space race between us and Russia. Murph boasted that of course America would win while Lisa and I held hands under the table, not exactly in the mood to argue.

Without warning, Deej burst into the bar, so loony-tunes angry that she slammed the door into the wall. It sounded like a shot. Already jumpy, about half the customers stood.

"She's dead! Crista's dead! They killed her!" Deej yowled, like a hurt animal.

For a moment, it was as if some little green guy from Mars had doused us with a paralyzing ray gun. Trust me on this—for once the bar went completely still.

"Oh, my God!" Carla Jean screamed. "She was a little girl! She didn't even get to live past the toughest years."

Then the questions started. What was Deej doing back at the bar when she'd get thrown out of school? Was Crista really dead? Did she kill herself? How could we help Deej?

I remembered my own flirtations with suicide. It's nothing I'd consider now, but when I was younger I was more vulnerable, and stupider. Life is the most valuable thing we have, I'm not about to squander it. As a homosexual kid, though? You don't have the tools to fight back. You don't have anyone to talk to or books to consult. You become cut off from everyone. You don't have a solution and can't imagine that there are any. I didn't even know what the problem was; what made people so upset? You only want to stop the pain. Everybody says you're bad so you start to believe them and to believe the world would be better off without you. I was forced to make a conscious decision to live, to keep going. I believed the rabbis were mistaken in their opinions about homosexuals, but if I'd had easy access to a gun back then and my father found me out—well, I'm grateful I've always been a deliberate person and not unfocused and impulsive like Deej's Crista.

Finally Hugh, probably the biggest person in the bar, guided Deej, probably the smallest, to a table next to ours and sat at the banquette. He held her and she let herself go, crying silently into his beard while her shoulders rose and fell and his big hands stroked and patted her back. Soon she was telling the story.

"Russ. They called Russ to tell him."

"Who?" asked Carla Jean, standing behind Murph at their table, her hands on Murph's shoulders.

"Her family. I don't exist. They know about Russ, so they told him and he called me."

"What exactly happened?" Carla Jean asked.

"That little girl wanted for nothing," Murph said. "What did she go and do that for?"

The questions set off a new torrent of tears; Deej couldn't answer. Lisa was squeezing my hand like she was holding on for dear life. It was a while before the kid said, "She used my dad's gun."

I looked at Murph, concerned that she'd lose the gains she'd made in her mood. "That damn gun," she said. "I knew something like this would happen."

Deej turned on her. "You're blaming me?"

Where was the appealing little butch now? Deej wore a plain dark skirt again, with a print blouse, a cardigan, lipstick, and dirty saddle shoes, one of them untied.

"Now, did I say that, kid?"

"Might as well have," Deej answered in a sulky voice. "She asked to borrow it. How did I know she was going to kill herself? She said it was to protect her while her parents went out of town. Some guy was bothering her."

Carla Jean asked, "The parents came home and found her? Those poor people. Why? Why did Crista do it?"

Deej accepted some bar napkins from the ever-ready JoJo and cleaned up her face. "She was pretty confused last time I talked to her."

"You were seeing her?" Carla Jean pronounced rather than asked. She took a cigarette from a flattened pack. JoJo, who didn't smoke, fished in a pocket and lit the cigarette with her lighter. Carla Jean had inscribed a lighter at their shop so she could rely on JoJo for a light.

"Not after the raid. When her dad found out, she was lucky he didn't kill her."

"No wonder she ended her life," Hugh said. "One day she was the perfect daughter, the next she was an outcast. Some folks can't take that kind of condemnation."

"I told her not to take it personally. They don't know any better. I mean, she wanted to see me anyway, as friends. Well, we still fooled around some, when it was really safe. And she went out with boys from school to keep her family off her back. She told them she was at The Old Town with a boy when it got raided."

"So many, many lies," Murph said, hands in fists. "Pretty soon you don't know what's the truth and you're away with the fairies. Or you choose the damned final way."

Norman brought Deej a refill and she drank it down without stopping.

Lisa frowned at Norman. "Relax," he said, drawing out the word. "It's soda water."

"Thanks," Deej said, wiping her mouth with the side of her hand.

Norman grabbed his broom and went back to sweeping the floor, stabbing and scraping like it was the enemy.

"So," Carla Jean said, sounding scornful and sarcastic, "Crista had sex with you, but dated guys. Did she like them?"

"She was pretty and fun and they showed her a good time. I couldn't do that for her, not after her uncle blabbed."

"How did it happen?" Carla Jean asked.

"I was over there all that afternoon, with her parents gone. It was one of the best times we ever had." She shook her head quickly, as if to get rid of her sadness. She said as soon as we graduated, she'd give up guys and wanted me to promise not to see any girls besides her." She hung her head. "I should have promised, but, you know, she was dating and I didn't see why I couldn't too."

"You had a fight?"

"No, nothing that bad. It was sad. If I could have been with her I would have said yes, but she didn't, maybe we didn't, dare."

I took Lisa's hand again, thinking this must be a little painful for her to hear, with her history.

"She didn't give me any guarantees, you know? She could decide it was safer to marry some jerk and then where would I be?"

"So…" Carla Jean urged her to keep talking.

Deej shrugged. "So I left. I wasn't going to watch her get all decked out for a guy."

"And then she shot herself?"

Deej winced. "No. She went with the guy to a drive-in theater. She said she was going to the ladies' room and called me from the pay phone. He was trying to maul her, she told me. I told her where to kick him. She was afraid if she did that it would get around campus that she didn't like men. 'You don't!' I reminded her. She was quiet till the operator asked for more money. She said good-bye. I was yelling into the phone for her to call me later."

"Did she?"

"No. I thought maybe she got in late and was afraid to wake my parents. They have to answer the phone at any hour because of the motel. I should have stayed awake and kept trying. I don't know what time she did it."

"Funny," Murph said, "that the girl who ratted us out should be the one to die."

"I refuse to believe Crista ratted anyone out," Deej said.

"She's the only one who left early." Carla Jean had her arms folded, looking like a one-woman judge and jury.

"That doesn't prove a thing. Crista would never do that."

"Not to save her own neck?"

"What about all the people who didn't come at all? Why couldn't it have been one of them?"

"Or," Norman paused as he swept behind the bar, "the police could have noticed all the activity on a day we normally closed."

"Not likely," Hugh said. "Those operations take a while to plan and coordinate. They don't drop everything and say, 'Let's go raid a gay bar, gentlemen.' Not on a holiday weekend when they want to be home with their families."

"We all ought to go to the funeral," Lisa said. "Show them we're decent, respectful people. It's her family that killed her, not us. We welcomed Crista as she was."

"Maybe we ought to go," Carla Jean sneered, "and maybe her uncle the captain would recognize us and toss us out of the church or temple or funeral parlor. A lot of good that would do us."

"And Crista," someone said.

"And your father," Carla Jean told Deej. She drained her glass. "When they find out he owns the gun."

"That won't happen. It wasn't registered. Someone left it at the motel." Deej put her head in her hands. "Not that it matters. Not that anything matters now."

CHAPTER THIRTY-THREE

I hated to see Deej leave on that note. She'd noticed the time and needed to get home so her parents wouldn't suspect she hadn't been at the library. Hugh, such a worrier, went to the bus stop with her.

For the next weeks, through September, The Old Town was like a funeral parlor during the wake given for the mother of one of my crew: politely downhearted, yet a little riotous, with mourners reuniting after years, somber when examining the deceased in her coffin, all smiles as soon as that was done.

"It's a sad day to be new," Murph said, looking at us. She smiled and told Lisa, "You could have done worse than this one, doll."

We no longer hid our hands; we held them tight together on the tabletop. Lisa squeezed mine. Her late grandmother's modest, well-cut diamond ring pressed into my palm. Lisa was otherwise reserved about public affection.

Neither of us could give Murph an answer. When it was time to walk Colonel Mustard, Lisa stayed behind. It was a good pause. I strolled in the light rain with only a hooded jacket to keep me dry. I'd checked the thermometer outside my kitchen window: it read close to seventy and this rain wouldn't be enough to break the heat.

As I walked I thought: how many times could we grieve for this same reason? No one cared enough to count suicides, I supposed. I was sure more homosexuals took their own lives than normal people. Why this poor girl? Nice-looking, well-brought up, decent family, except perhaps for her father and uncle's tempers, and smart enough to get through college. She was lucky to be gay. I kicked at a falling yellow leaf.

What was wrong with parents anyway? They have a juvenile-delinquent child or a child who stammers or marries someone of another race or religion—do they stop loving her when they find out? Sometimes, I admitted, but not nearly as universally as they do their gay kids. I didn't get it, why there's so much shame attached to us. We don't care that they're straight.

I said all this to Lisa later. She had no more answers than I did. We spent the night in each other's arms, our energetic passion like a stage curtain we closed to shut out life's film, always a tragedy, except for the pleasure of each other. Lisa's astonishing pageant of femme hands at play made me fall deeper and deeper into love with her. I scared myself with the accelerated opening of my heart. Sunday morning we walked the Colonel together, picked up the newspaper and some pastries. She laughed when I chose prune Danish, and I indulged her with a couple of Napoleons. I can't help it, I have a terrible sweet tooth and prunes are among the sweetest fruits on earth. The trouble with sweets, I'd noticed, is the same trouble with drinking a lot—you sometimes come crashing down.

"We need to talk," I told Lisa after another intense bout of lovemaking. I never had trouble coming, and now with Lisa, I didn't have a stop button. Not that she did have one, but I'm in my fifties now, past menopause; I should start paying attention so I wouldn't overdo.

"If you want to end this before we start, I don't want to know about it, Rockie. We're not some freak accident. We fit. Don't you recognize it?"

"What I know is that I'm very, very lucky to have this time with you, Lisa."

She was still naked. We both were. Lisa wriggled around so she was looking up at me. She gave me an impish look and opened her mouth to take in my breast. I let her stay like that, her tongue flicking my nipple, each touch sending a tentacle of excitement through me. What a pushover I was for this woman.

"Lisa," I managed to say, "when you're my age I'll be almost eighty years old. I don't think it's fair to you to start something I can't finish."

She didn't stop.

"What am I going to do with you?" I asked, laughing.

She sat upright, then, her lovely little breasts decorating her chest like—well, like a woman's breasts should.

"Rockie, Russia could drop the bomb on us tomorrow. It'd land on the coast and the radiation would kill us over here. I think we both take enough baloney from this world every day without manufacturing our own."

"I probably thought very much like that at twenty-eight. Look at it from my perspective, though. It's not going to take long for you to get bored with me."

"So that's what's bothering you."

"Is it fair to either of us? You're so gorgeous, Lisa, and I wasn't anything to write home about even in my twenties. "

Lisa laughed. She stopped. "You're serious, aren't you? Rockie, I don't know what you looked like back then, but today you're so distinguished looking, I can't keep my hands off you."

"Distinguished? Me?"

She smoothed back my hair. She ran her fingers up and down my biceps, which embarrass me in summer clothes. They're unavoidable when you spend your days moving boxes. You can't do it all with a forklift. Then she made a fist and punched my thigh.

"Ow!" I cried, rubbing the spot. "What was that for?"

"Your thighs are rock hard."

"It's my job. Like Murph's. You can't stay soft."

"Who wants soft?" Lisa asked. "You don't get it, do you, Rockie? I find you wildly attractive. Just looking at you in the bar turned me on."

"Hey, I was there for the asking."

"Not that I could tell. You're older, have your own business and money enough to give people jobs. I know you helped Murph out when she needed it and probably others too. Your heart's so big. There was Geri and then your breakup. You wouldn't dance or go anywhere with anyone. It was your job, your dog, and a couple of drinks at the bar. I knew you never noticed me. I was a kid to you."

Lisa's revelations astonished me. "Of course I noticed you. Even when I was with Geri I noticed you. I wasn't free and I was no cradle robber."

"Oh, you're a big kid yourself," she said, collapsing on top of my prone body. I let my fingers spread across her bottom. It was such a satisfying bottom to hold.

"It doesn't matter to you that I'm Jewish?"

"Rockie!" Lisa looked like I'd slapped her. "Remember, I'm from New York. At least half my neighborhood growing up was Jewish. My husband was Jewish. My daughter is Jewish."

"My Empire State woman." Even while my brain fought, my heart told me then and there, like in some sappy song, we were meant to be. At the same time, I needed to protect her.

"Look," I told her, "what if I die first and you're, say, seventy?"

"You think I'll be all washed up by then? That no one will want me?"

"I don't like the thought of you being alone."

Her finger was on my face now, following my jawline, my cheekbone, as gentle as a summer raindrop. "If I don't want to be alone, and I think I'd rather be alone if there's no you, Rockie, then I won't be alone. If I'm alive then, there'll be a few gay women still standing."

"Young ones, too, I'll bet." I kissed her finger. "Those young Deejs will flock to you and beg to take care of you."

"I'm thinking you're going to leave me so well taken care of— in every way—that I'll take up knitting and bingo and pass my days recovering from your energy and enjoying my memories."

"It bothers me."

"What about you? Aren't you taking a chance too? If I'm so young and attractive, women will be trying to steal me every time you let me out of the house."

My silence lasted too long.

"You won't," Lisa said, "listen to reason." She flung her arms wide. "You won't even tell me your coming-out story."

"Me?" I said. "What do I know about you? Your family?" I wasn't trying to fight with Lisa. I knew every story would be told in its own good time. Darn it all, she wasn't playing fair.

She was up, dressed, and out the door before I could think of what to do or say. I considered going after her. I didn't want to saddle anyone with my old age, but I knew what I was feeling, and what Lisa was saying, took us way out of range of an affair, and I was scared.

The coming-out story wasn't a big deal. It did hurt to talk about it. First I lost Bette, then Geri. Lisa would be my third strike, my third out, fourth, if you counted Cissy. I was afraid Lisa would think I was some kind of schnook and wouldn't want me anymore.

I peered from the window, shivering in the shirt I'd pulled over my head. She crossed to the bus stop. She stood there, hands hugging her shoulders as if to keep herself from shattering into pieces where she stood. Was I being unreasonable to be cautious? I'd hurt her. Did I trigger her fears? Crows lined the electrical wire above her like a row of judges discussing our chance at happiness.

Was loving someone who loved you back always right? If it wasn't, I was glad Lisa was suffering the hurt of months rather than two or twenty years. Or did she have a point? Was I protecting her—or myself—too hard? I was on the verge of flinging open the window and bellowing out her name when the bus, with a fanfare of noisy brakes and streaming exhaust, blocked my view and carried her away.

CHAPTER THIRTY-FOUR

I lay on the bed as it was, unmade, and breathed in our scents. My sense of smell was getting stronger, and I was more grateful than I could have imagined, but what would help my dilemma? My college ethics course hadn't taught me how to deal with this, or much else I'd encountered in my life. The Colonel rested her chin on the edge of the bed, watching me with what looked like pitying eyes. All the light was gone from my day. I even worried that I'd lost The Old Town a customer, Lisa, when Norman and Hugh least needed to add to the exodus in the wake of the raid.

Lisa was too far a stretch for me. I was a pretender companion to her throne.

"Come on, girl," I said to Colonel Mustard. I'd given her a soup bone while Lisa was there, and the Colonel always drank herself to bursting once she'd finished a bone. I clipped her leash to her harness and we went walking. And thinking. And noticing more and more FRANK GOODLETTE FOR MAYOR signs anyplace they could be displayed.

By the time I got to The Old Town, I was ready for distraction. Murph came right over and pounded me on the back.

"Good to see you, old buddy," she said. "I thought we'd lost you to Lisa for good."

She spoke with such a tone of relief I looked harder at her. She wasn't jealous, was she?

Murph wandered off, thumped someone else. Came back and started talking. "There was a time, fellow and gals, when not having Murph on the job was a calamity. Who repaired the machines? Who pulled her load and that of some poor individual whose back went out? Did I tell you about the time I rescued someone stuck between—"

"Yes!" cried Norman, who, with JoJo, was stocking the bar for the night. JoJo was moving at double time, while Norman dawdled to flirt and talk. Apropos of nothing, it occurred to me that the least conventionally attractive guys might be the biggest flirters.

Murph looked at her feet. "You're right, of course. I did." She meandered back to the bathroom.

"What's the matter with Murph?" I asked. "Why's she putting on her hale-and-hearty front?"

With a loud sigh Norman said, "She lost another job today."

"Because of her reading?"

"No, Paul's doing a great job on that. It's her hand. She can't handle the work."

"Can't she get unemployment?"

"Murph?" JoJo, on a step stool, stretched to polish the mirror behind the bar. "She's too proud to take help from the government. Pretty insane, right?"

I said, "I'm afraid all this—the raid, the jobs, the injury—have driven Murph to the brink of sanity."

"She's been mumbling to herself and spouting off since she came in."

I got a table and motioned Murph over when she came out of the john. I'd give her a taste of my reality, maybe jolt her out of hers.

"I'm afraid I ruined things with Lisa," I said.

Murph lifted her ginger ale. "Join the club," she said. "Listen, I was actually hoping you two might work out. Lisa's kind of touchy, isn't she?"

I thought of Lisa's touches and the breath left my body for a second or two. "It's me who's being touchy, Murph." I explained my concern.

"What does Lisa say?' she asked. It was working; she sounded like her old self.

"Before she walked out I might as well have been as green as a traffic light."

"That's Lisa all over. If it was the end, she would stake her claim to The Old Town. She would be here."

"Unless she's given up on all of us."

"You're going to have to go get her back, Rockie Solomon. For all of us."

"I don't know. She's not even thirty."

"She will be. And forty and fifty. Are you going to let her spend those years in misery? Or being happy together?"

I laughed without restraint. "Maybe I'll buy a house." Talking to Murph was doing me some good too.

"You wouldn't be avoiding the subject, would you now?"

"It would give her some security. So even if I went first…I'd put it in her name and there'd be no question of inheritance."

Murph folded her arms and now nodded at me, looking like a sage. "Make sure it's in the neighborhood, will you?" She reached into her pants' pocket and brought out one of those soft rubber change holders that open when you squeeze them. She gave me a dime and pointed to the pay phone.

I patted my watch. "She won't be home yet."

"I'm keeping an eye on you, so don't think you're leaving without using that dime. And no blathering to her about *ifs*, *ands*, and *maybes*. Thank your lucky stars a fine woman like that wants you, be it for a week or forever. I would have taken either with Rose."

"If I may be frank," I said.

"Be my guest."

"Sometimes I think you like being stuck, Murph."

"Stuck? Me? Of course I'm stuck. I'm downright impaled. They've got me pinned to a wall. I'm fighting one-handed now that my right wing is broken." She held up her ruined hand.

"I'm not talking about physically or about the awful things the world has done to you. I know you're giving your all to overcome that. It's Rose. You're telling me to take a chance with Lisa, while you won't take a chance with anyone. You won't let any woman measure up to your idea of Rose. I mean, she's a nice-enough lady, but I think you're stuck somewhere in your teens. You're in love with the excitement and sensations you had back then for Rose."

Murph was glaring at me.

"It's never going to be like that again, Murph. Stop chasing that phantom thrill. You're telling me to quit refusing this gift Lisa's offering me. There are gifts out there for you too. This raid thing has knocked us all for a loop, and I think it's making it harder for us to take risks because we're on such unstable ground right now. No one has ever seen you with a lover of your own, for heaven's sake. Rose isn't real, Murph. You need a new dream."

I didn't know if Murph was going to stomp off or cry. Or both.

Someone put quarters in the jukebox. Elvis singing, of course, "Are You Lonesome Tonight?" Did God think he was a comedian or what?

"Well, look who's back," Murph said so quietly I could barely hear.

My innards did a little flutter of hope that it was Lisa. No such luck. It was Cissy.

"Cissy?"

"In the flesh," Murph said. "Lots of flesh from the looks of her."

Cissy got fat? I turned to see her. She immediately started toward our table. "It's the pregnancy," I said to Murph out of the side of my mouth.

"I'll bet that's a first for The Old Town," Murph muttered back, but she was grinning at Cissy.

Cissy carried a suitcase in one hand and a very large straw pocketbook in the other. They looked heavy. Murph quickly stood and took the suitcase with her left hand.

Between Paul's injuries and Cissy's state, life had stolen away with the family good looks. Maybe the baby would revive them. I mulled this development over. Cissy was having a kid: a narrow escape for me. I said hello, excused myself, and took Murph's dime to the wall phone.

As I dialed and waited for Lisa to pick up, I watched Murph be all courtly with Cissy. Lisa wasn't answering. I slid the dime out of the silver return chute and headed back to the table. Carla Jean, Seneca, and one of the beatnik girlfriends surrounded Cissy, oohing, touching Cissy's distended belly, and offering cigarettes before Cissy could even ask for one. I motioned for Murph to escape to the bar with me. She ignored me, smiling and laughing with the baby admirers.

Now, I have nothing against propagating the species in moderation. Acting like Cissy personally cured cancer, climbed Mt. Everest, or won the cold war against Russia, though, was a little overboard. Look, almost any woman can get pregnant, and most of them deliver and raise the little darlings. I've never seen anything to get excited about. Murph looked entranced. She'd never shown an interest in Cissy until motherhood redefined her. Maybe our little talk was helping already.

Cissy's hair was long now and drawn back into a lank ponytail. The confidence that once made her seem to sizzle was replaced by an empty-eyed forlornness. I could see it in her stooped shoulders, in the wrinkled dress that looked a couple of sizes too small.

"I didn't know where else to go," she was telling her avid audience. "He has such an appetite for sex, he wouldn't even let up once I started to show. I think he's between girlfriends. It's like he's mad at me all the time and that's how he shows it. I begged him to be careful for the baby's sake. Every night—" She sobbed once, then stopped herself.

There was a babble of sympathy.

"I hoped I'd find Paul here.

"You left your husband today?"

"I packed my suitcase as soon as he went to work this morning. I hid it under my desk at the college."

She looked at me. "I should have stayed with you, Rockie. I was afraid he'd hurt you if he found out," she said. "I'm sorry I disappeared on you."

I assured her I understood and she was right. He would hurt me and her and anyone else who interfered with his will.

Murph asked, "Won't he find you at work? Follow you home?"

"They have good security. I could ride to work with a friend's husband who works there—he's my supervisor. He knows what's going on. As of today, I don't have a home." A sob escaped her again. "I'm sorry. I can't even go to Mom and Pop's. He'll go straight there."

"Oh, sweetheart," Seneca said. "You can come stay with me and Spence for a while. Our place is tiny, but we have a couch."

"Really?" Cissy said. "It would only be for a couple of days."

"I have another idea," Murph said. "Would your supervisor drop you off here at the bar?"

"He did. My husband knows where my supervisor's family lives, though, so I can't go there. The bar was close."

"You know I live upstairs."

"With Rose."

Murph looked at me. "Rose moved down Maine. It's a stretch for me to pay rent out of my savings. I'd welcome a paying roommate if Norman and Hugh wouldn't mind."

Norman had joined the women to give advice about diaper services. His family was filled with nieces and nephews so he thought himself an authority. "That wouldn't be a problem for us as long as your husband doesn't come and tear the place down."

"That's the genius behind my plan, Norman," Murph said. "Cissy gets dropped off here, where there are plenty of pedestrians and cars around—including the police. She comes in the bar and disappears from sight, up the stairs through the kitchen."

"What about the baby? You'd want to live with the baby?" Cissy asked.

Murph chuckled. "If I could help with it." She actually blushed. "I love kids. That's why I was a Girl Scout leader."

Cissy looked at me. Did she want my approval? That reminded me to try Lisa again. As far as Murph's offer to let Cissy move in, I couldn't think of a better way to get her mind off Rose. I nodded at Cissy.

"Don't forget the city wants to rip this place down," Norman said.

Murph said, "It wouldn't look so good for them to evict a pregnant lady."

"Why didn't my devious mind think of that angle?" Norman asked.

Murph stood and picked up the suitcase. "A Girl Scout is always prepared," she answered, winking.

This time, Lisa was home when I called. I asked if I could come over and tell her my life story. If I was setting myself up again, at least I could say I tried.

CHAPTER THIRTY-FIVE

Life became pretty tense. Thanksgiving was coming up next month. Would The Old Town repeat the day-after-Thanksgiving dinner? Should it be held somewhere else? That seemed like a dumb idea when we had a perfect spot for it. The newspaper hadn't mentioned putting in a parking lot lately. We sensed a tension under the calm, though. Like soldiers isolated on an atoll, we knew the enemy could come by sea, by air, any old way they liked, and any time they wanted.

It didn't help that Frank Goodlette's face loomed over us from yet another election billboard on top of a building down the street.

Cissy expected her kid or kids sometime this month. The more miserably uncomfortable she looked, the more enthralled Murph seemed with the arrival of new life. Murph wouldn't let anyone give cigarettes to Cissy in case they might be bad for the baby. She replaced Cissy's martinis with ginger ale. She hovered over Cissy as they, and some of the rest of us, spent more time upstairs than in the bar. The view of the darned billboard was even closer upstairs.

Lisa and I stumbled back toward each other and away again. Well, I was stumbling and she danced toward me and away in an enticing, glittering cloud. I liked telling her about Bette and Geri—certainly better than refusing and losing her.

Bette, pronounced with the "y," came into my life in 1942. She was a WAAC when it started as the Women's Army Auxiliary Corps. I bid for some war business and got it from her unit, which worked stateside. The government printing presses couldn't keep up with the amount of material they needed. Bette Himes, a gal from Maine, was all dark curls, cheekbones, and smiles under the Hobby Hat named for the WAAC's director. The hat matched her olive-drab woolen winter uniform. Bette drove a funny little motorbike with a closed sidecar for deliveries.

I'd heard that many women who joined the corps turned funny. Twenty-four-year-old Bette was very feminine and seemed square. I'd done no more than fool around with other straight women. I looked forward to her visits more and more. She was so high-spirited and full of laughter! We entered the war after I took over the bindery business, so I was exuberant with my accomplishment at age thirty-three and ready for more excitement in my life. In my office one day Bette came around my desk, sat on my lap, and put her arms around my neck. I liked her weight on me.

"What's this?" I asked. She answered by kissing me. As soon as our lips touched I knew I was wildly in love with this firefly of a woman and she was with me. We spent every weekend together after that. Her uniform was anywhere except on her body once she stepped into my apartment. It was a hot winter and the most colorful spring I ever saw. We walked to remote areas of Chestnut Forest Park where we could hold hands out of doors and sneak kisses behind trees. I stocked up on cereal, cheese, bread, and butter when I could get them and would cook a chicken from one of the local farms or prepare a canned-salmon salad before she arrived. We didn't waste time heating up anything besides our randy selves.

In 1943 the WAACs became the WACs and thousands of them shipped to Europe. Maybe Bette didn't want to tell me she was planning to throw away what we had, or maybe she was simply twenty-four and ready for someone new. Once, after the war, I borrowed my father's car and drove to the town where she'd grown up. She'd never given me her address so I puttered up and down every street and out every country road. I never saw her or a mailbox with the name Himes on it. The postal clerk claimed not to know of the family. Did she even tell me the truth about where she came from? Did she die overseas or was she living a wild life in Paris? To this day I wonder where Bette Himes went.

After I told Lisa my little story and gave her more painful details about Geri and me, she regularly joined me to go through the houses for sale in the paper. I wanted something in the neighborhood and found some decent buys. Not that we said aloud that we'd live together, but I wanted her to like the place, and she said she wanted to make sure I made a good investment. She'd worked in a mortgage office for a number of years.

I worried, though. As predicted, the symptoms of my head injury slowly disappeared. I realized one day that my headaches were gone. My mood shot up with Lisa on the scene. Also, I made it a practice to visit the river every few weeks before work. I tore up some bread and with each piece cast my sins, and also my troubles, on the water. It was a little ritual I'd adapted from Rosh Hashanah. I tossed each of my symptoms into the current and took time to thank whoever was in charge of such things for taking them away from me. The ducks and hybrid geese acted pretty grateful for the treat. Loaves of bread or not, my balance and my concentration stopped short of fully normal, and I feared I was selling Lisa damaged goods. I submerged my hands in a little river riffle to cleanse them.

One early fall day JoJo was manning the bar by herself when Norman and Hugh appeared in the doorway and paused. Everyone turned to look at them.

Norman dragged his tie off like it disgusted him. He pushed his way through a group of customers to go behind the bar. Hugh took his regular seat around the corner of the bar by the window. Though his beard hid his jowly face, I could see that his jaw was slack from what looked like sadness, shock, or both.

"You two look like you were at a funeral," Murph said.

Hugh nodded his big head.

"Rat bastards." Norman's voice was unusually deep. Uh-oh, I thought, no more Mr. Nice Guy. I hoped Norman's queenly antics weren't gone for good.

"Who?" Seneca called from the table where she and Spence sat with Cissy.

"The city," he spat. "The college. The mayor and his whole city-hall crew. The cops. The double-dealing neighbors. The useless lawyers. Anyone who takes advantage of homos to enrich themselves." He set a drink in front of Hugh. "There you go, baby. You tried so hard. You're so good at working with those impossible people. Tell our friends the sad story."

"Rose called us with the name of an attorney here. Her friends consulted him and he agreed to meet with us. I'd already talked to someone at our law school. I was only able to bring up the property issues with him, not the gay harassment." He took a long draft from his drink. "He told me that the city has the law on its side as far as taking our building."

"Eminent domain?" asked Dr. Everett, who appeared to be making the bad news a good excuse to drink more.

"One form of it. It's a little tricky for the city because they'd be taking the land and then selling it, for one dollar, to a private owner, the college, instead of for public use, such as a highway. That's technically legal. We could challenge it if we could afford to and wanted the publicity, which we don't. The other reason not to challenge it is because the city will claim that it's taking into account the property's highest and best use—read its most profitable and morally acceptable use. Who would win against an institution of higher learning?"

"Where you're trying to get tenure," Norman added.

"The city can also say it's been planning to change the zoning to avoid blight. As if The Avenue is a rundown slum."

One of the bearded regulars laughed and held up his beer. "To the homos and the demon beats ruining the neighborhood!"

"The drunken students too!" yelled a drunken student who wore small round glasses like my father had when I was a kid.

Hugh went on. "Today we met with the gentleman Rose's friends referred us to. We talked to him about the raid, the toughs hanging around, and the beating outside. We told him how one cop lured a guy into our men's room so he could arrest him and get us in trouble."

"And?" Murph added.

Hugh chewed on his lower lip. "What we do together is illegal. Period. A police raid is not. That's it in a nutshell."

Shouts, curses, high-pitched whining, and complaints immediately filled the bar. Lisa grabbed my hand—as if I could protect her or anyone. Someone dropped a drink. JoJo rushed over with bar cloth, broom, and dust pan. The Old Town's communal rage simmered to grumbles.

"So no one can help us. As usual," Carla Jean declared.

Norman was quickly filling glasses after the great uproar. Anger, I thought with surprise, is good for business. He said, "Not as long as this administration is in charge. The lawyer told me the only way out of this mess is to take the money they offer for the building and move on. He'd done his homework. Some of the homeowners around us have signed their intention to sell."

"Like hell we'll sell!" Carla Jean cried. Hmm, I thought, so she did have a stake in the bar.

"That's pretty much what I told this lawyer today," Hugh said. "He suggested it might be worth our while to offer a trade. We sell to them if they sign a promise never to raid any bar we open again."

"A free pass would be a winner for your customers if the city would agree," Dr. Everett said, then coughed, long and moistly, after drawing on a cigarette.

"They'll never agree to that. Why would they?" Carla Jean asked. "All they have to do is condemn the building and take it."

Murph slammed a fist on her table. "Look, there's nothing wrong with this place. An inspector would have to ruin a few dozen things to condemn it."

"That's a legal term. It doesn't mean the property is rundown," Hugh explained.

Norman said with a tone of truculence, "I don't like losing, and I don't want to give them their way after what they've been doing to us."

"It sounds like we don't have a leg to stand on," Carla Jean said. She didn't wait for a light from JoJo, but viciously scratched a match across a matchbook. She and JoJo kept the bar supplied with The Old Town Tavern On The Avenue matchbooks. "What if we found a better place? Maybe with more rentals upstairs. The city has to pay us enough to buy and renovate, don't they?"

Norman folded his short arms. "Oh, sure, running would spare all of us scads of grief. On the other hand, what customers? If we move too far, we'll lose everyone."

Would they lose me? I'd never spent this much time in a bar before Geri. I might walk a couple of blocks more, though not as often. I held up the paper. "I happened to notice the building around the corner from the bookstore is for sale." I read out the number. "The ad says it's zoned for commercial use."

"That's an old rattletrap," Carla Jean said.

Hugh moved behind me and rested his big soft hands on my shoulders, reading the ad.

"No, Hugh!" Norman said. I thought he would cry, this increasingly tubby, increasingly bald little guy with a heart the size of New England who took such care of us. He'd filled himself up with more and more alcohol since the raid and was as weepy under the influence as Carla Jean.

"Options," Hugh said. "Let's consider all our options."

"After the work we put into this place?"

"And," Murph added, in her disgust practically spitting the words, "after the work we'd probably need to put into another when I can't help because of the hand they ruined."

"It'll only encourage them to use this tactic elsewhere," Spence said.

"Where I come from?" Seneca added. "Way over on the other side of the tracks? The police don't bother to put names in the paper. My brother said they call the captain who attacked you 'massa' because he thinks it's his job to keep us in our place."

"Gestapo," a man in a beret said. "He'd nuke your neighborhood and this whole street if he could."

"The man's got a problem, all right," Seneca said.

"Let's sit down on them," one of the long-haired women, dressed all in denim, suggested. "If they come to take your future away from you, we'll make a human chain. They'll have to drag us out. We're not going to sit in the back of the bus anymore either!"

"Now there's a good way to get a job: have myself arrested again," Murph said.

I was going to have to find Murph something to do at the plant and some way to afford her wages soon. With the approach of our slow season, I worried about taking on a new employee, but I wanted to help. She was losing her self-respect. I'd noticed the last time she wore her fancy three-piece suit that it was getting frayed around the ends of her sleeves. At least Cissy, who was installed upstairs, had her job as secretary to the college registrar. The college would hold her job for her when Murph's baby arrived. We'd taken to calling it Murph's baby because she fussed so much about it. She went with Cissy to each doctor appointment, made her lunch for work. I wondered how Murph would be at sales work. I suspected if I put her on base plus commission she'd earn Cissy's kid a college education.

"Are you sometimes convinced we're all on a cliff and about to fall off?" Lisa whispered to me.

We'd been talking about the Russian missile bases being built in Cuba and the crisis that seemed about to explode over them.

"If the Russians start peppering us with nuclear missiles, it won't matter if there's a bar, who's mayor, who wants a parking garage, who's gay," Lisa said.

I nodded into my drink.

"There's nothing we can do about that." Carla Jean held out her wineglass for Norman to fill.

"Aren't you the one complaining about your hangovers getting worse?" Norman asked, his own eyes glassy.

Carla Jean insisted by shoving the glass closer to him. It went too far, toppled, and broke.

"For crissake," Carla Jean said as she went around the bar and grabbed the broom.

The white-haired upholsterer from the next block spoke up. His hands looked as bunged up as Murph's. His lower face was covered with white stubble. "Sure we can do something about Cuba and the Russkies," he said, the cigarette hanging from the side of his mouth wagging up and down. "You younger people ought to be going into the service, protecting our country instead of all this fussing about gay bars and who has rights and whatnot." He squinted at a couple of the younger men.

"They don't want sissies, Arnie."

Arnie harrumphed. "You can carry a rifle as good as anybody."

"Tell that to the secretary of defense."

"McNamara? Now there's a sissy. Embargo won't do no good. Go in there and blast them out of the water."

The gay people closed ranks rather than talk politics with Arnie, who was always hepped up on the subject.

"What about the day after Thanksgiving?" asked a quiet gay man in a motorcycle jacket, helmet under his arm. "Are you going to do it again?"

"The Soviets may atomize us by then," said Lisa. I patted her hand and assured her we'd be all right because Colonel Mustard would take care of us. Laughing, Lisa intimated that my dog wasn't exactly behind the eight ball protection-wise.

Norman and Hugh looked at each other, but Carla Jean spoke. She amazed me: one minute she was a short, fat drunk and the next she was as shrewd a businesswoman as they come. "Not without some assurance from the city. I don't want to see another person hurt in this bar," she said.

"We'll have to make a decision pretty quickly then," Norman said.

"Why don't we check into that building," Hugh suggested. "It might help us to look at a real alternative."

"Unless," JoJo said, not moving for once, "the college isn't after property at all."

Carla Jean finished for her. "They might only be interested in driving us from the vicinity of their campus. Which wouldn't interfere with the mayor's plans in the least."

CHAPTER THIRTY-SIX

O f course we had a quick celebration in the bar to greet the arrival of—Cissy was right—the twins. October babies, I was relieved for them that President Kennedy had gone for the embargo rather than start a nuclear war. She and the babies came downstairs, Paulette in Paul's arms and Murphy in Murph's. Once everyone oohed and aahed over the little ones, Murph handed out cigars as she did the day of their birth, some with pink bands and some with blue. The fear level stayed pretty high, though, so Cissy opened the few gifts, and the three proud parents—Cissy, Paul, and Murph—went back upstairs with the kids.

Lisa had been seated when I arrived at the bar and only now did I see how incredible she looked. She wore her tweedy pencil-skirt suit and a cream blouse wide open at the neck. Va-va-va-voom!

"I can't stand all this cigar smoke," she whispered to me. Even Carla Jean was puffing away.

We went across the street to get Colonel Mustard, who'd been alone long enough. After our walk, we each carried a shopping bag of gifts up to Murph's apartment.

As we climbed the stairs, Murphy was wailing. Paul let us in. Colonel Mustard had no experience with newborns and barked at the infant shrieks. "Colonel, I know he's crying. Thank you, but *ixnay* on the howling-wolf business." The Colonel calmed down as we handed over the shopping bag.

"Oh, look!" Cissy sounded both doubtful and delighted.

The Colonel went directly to Paulette and was licking a tiny ear. "Paulette's in!" I told Cissy. "She's been chosen to be a member of the pack."

Paul scooted Murphy into Cissy's room for a diaper change. Lisa now held Paulette. She offered her to me and I backed off. Babies, to be truthful, give me the heebie-jeebies. They're too fragile for this rough old lezzie.

Cissy was looking more like her old self. All of Murph's hovering must be having a positive effect on her, I decided. She'd cut her hair and it looked bouncy and bright. She fit into her old clothes. The apartment smelled entirely like babies: their powder, faintly of diaper pail, and the stuffiness of too much heat.

I asked her if the father bothered her at all.

"No! The opposite!" she answered. "He served me with divorce papers. He wants to marry the woman he was seeing on the side. I'm upset for Paulette and Murphy. The man isn't even asking to see them." She resettled Paulette in her arms and told her, "We'll have to make it up to you by loving you twice as much, won't we?" The baby slept on.

Lisa asked, "Will they have his name?"

"No. Absolutely not. Their birth certificate has Paul's and my last name. I like the sound: Paulette Lillegård. Murphy Lillegård.

Murph made tea and set out cookies. I tried one and smiled approval at its chewiness. Murph winked, a good sign. "No laughing. I made these—with the help of a Betty Crocker mix, of course."

I made a face and exaggerated a tiny bite. "They're pretty good anyway!" I joked, and laughed. I asked Paul, who brought a happier baby Murphy back, to tell us about turning into a publisher.

"Pouf! I'm a publisher," he responded, throwing invisible fairy dust on himself. "But, seriously, I am so lucky. No one can stop a homosexual from being a teacher if he really wants to be one."

"This isn't going to get you health insurance that would pay for reconstructive surgery."

"The good news is that, because it happened while I was employed, I'm covered by the school policy. They didn't officially terminate me for six weeks and told me I wouldn't be covered. I got hold of the state-government insurance office and the ombudsman set them straight, so to speak. I don't know if it's a quirk in that particular group policy, but I'm seeing a surgeon next week."

"That's wonderful!" Lisa grabbed Paul's hand.

"I won't be as pretty as Cissy—or Lisa. At least people on the street may not stare at me anymore."

Officer Harry showed up then. He hugged us all and I recognized the autumn scent of gun-cleaning solvent from my childhood when my father hunted.

"I'm moving into his loft with him," Harry declared. "The minute he told me he'd lost it and had gone to live with his sister, I went to the rental office and snapped it back up. He's made it beautiful. Plus it's bigger than my place."

"You're such a martyr," Paul said. "Don't saddle yourself with this old wreck."

"And," Harry continued, "we're going to enclose a separate space for his company. You wait and see, he's going to have a very sufficient income from this business. When I retire," he looked at his watch, "in about twelve years, I'll work with you. The business will be big enough by then that you'll need me, right?"

Paul gave a dramatic sigh and said, "I'll always need you, Harry."

Harry grinned. "I'm going to run home and get out of this uniform. What a day. I've been guarding the mayor all over the city on campaign visits. He's disgusting—acting like emperor-for-life. I'll be back in a jiff, okay?" He grabbed a fistful of cookies and made his getaway, waving them in the air and laughing.

"What a man," Paul said.

Lisa asked, "Is he always this cheerful?"

Paul groaned, grinning. "Sometimes he's more cheerful. I swear, I might not have pulled through all this if not for him—and Cissy and the infant noise machines."

"Oy, *gevalt*!" I said, when Paulette screeched on cue. Cissy had pried away her teddy bear and carried her to her crib.

Lisa glanced at me with a knowing look and said, "Yeah, we're never having kids."

"Darn," I joked, snapping my fingers. "Paul, what's with the magazine?"

"All the kids have now is *Scholastic Magazine*, and when I was young, it bored me silly. The drawings scared me. *My Weekly Reader* is a little better. What about a home magazine? A colorful, playful monthly that makes kids want to read at home. Forget current events. That's all about adults and through adult eyes. I want to teach them to have a bigger vision. I want it to be written by kids themselves. What do you think about that?"

Lisa and I threw Paul a dozen questions. He fielded them well. He'd obviously been thinking and planning this for a long time. It was heartening to see his excitement.

"Here's the big question, Paul. How are you financing this?"

"Naturally I'll sell my body."

He got a hearty laugh out of that.

"No. I have my pension money. Harry is good at saving money and is pitching in. Dr. Everett wants to help and thinks he can get some others to pony up for a good cause. And, of course, Harry's 'persuaded' his newspaper contact that he needs to add a magazine to his little publishing empire."

Murph was the one who finally quieted Paulette. She was so like a proud dad. You never saw stains on her clothes at the bar, but tonight she was in pushed-up sleeves, with who knew what all across the *schmatte*, a clean diaper she'd tossed over her shoulder to protect her sweatshirt.

Cissy brought a load of clean diapers into the living room. Paul took them from her and, keeping up his end of the conversation, folded them as if he'd been doing it all his life.

"Where did you learn to fold like that?" asked Lisa.

"Murph, of course. The laundry maven. She's hell on wheels," Paul said. "She gave us actual training sessions before the babies arrived. These kids will not get within a mile of a germ or a wrinkle, if Murph has her say."

"And have my say I will," Murph announced, rejoining us. "Did I ever tell you about the time my sister's kid—"

We all laughed.

"So she's like this even outside the bar," Lisa said. "Full of stories."

Murph looked down with a happy smile as Cissy laid a hand on her sleeve. "What would I have done without Murph?" she asked.

Lisa and I exchanged glances. We had learned nothing about Murph and Cissy's romantic status. I doubted they were together, myself. Lisa didn't see how they could seem so close otherwise. We'd talked with JoJo, the great listener, and even she didn't know. Carla Jean, arms around Murph's neck, cooing her question, asked Murph outright. She said Murph launched into a long story about a couple she knew who never did more than sleep in the same bed and hold each other because they knew anything else would be wrong. And they'd been together since Sunday school. Lisa was right. To this day no one knows if Murph ever actually had sex with a woman. Or if she did, whether it was reciprocal sex.

Cissy went on. "My parents love Murph for taking such good care of me. Dad hates the idea of his unmarried daughter having kids. Me living with Murph and Paul living with Harry, though, that's not a big deal for him."

"He thinks I'm like an older sister to Cissy," Murph said. "Her dad's a big bowler. Once things settle down here, we've got a date to play at his favorite alley. And am I going to whip him!"

Cissy laughed. "Of course you won't. He's won trophies!"

"So have teams I've been on!"

"Not the same!"

They certainly seemed to enjoy each other, I thought. It was sad that Murph thought she'd be able to bowl. What did I know? Maybe she would. Maybe her poor hand was salvageable for that at least.

I asked if they had any news about their apartment. Hugh and Norman hadn't said much since their visit to the lawyers.

"As Harry says, The Old Town is an institution," Paul told us. He held the neat pile of folded diapers on his lap, patting it to line up any stray edges. "They looked at the other building and said it would do, but they want to stay on the main drag right where we are."

"They're going to fight?" I said, amazed.

Murph raised her fingers in a gesture of victory that went back to the world war. "What we think happened," she said, "is that Rose's lawyer gave up before he could start. Hugh's college pals didn't want to get involved. All the advice sounded lousy to Norman, so he asked around and found this guy who fought the highway."

"I remember that," Lisa said. "That highway forced good friends at work to move into the projects. It went right through their bedroom."

"The lawyer lost that time. He's won other fights against that kind of thing," Paul said. "He's going to bring suit against the city, the college, whoever he has to, based on the premise that the parking garage would ruin a historic neighborhood."

"He's right," Lisa said. She reached for my hand and held it. I got a thrill every time she did that.

"Then Murph may be able to stay!" Cissy said. "She's asked me to move in permanently." She gave Murph a loving look. "The school is so close and so is my job. Paul and Harry are only ten minutes away even at rush hour."

"Listen, my heart is in The Old Town neighborhood," Murph said. "It even smells like home: braking trains, restaurant-foods smells fighting to be dominant, the mix of cigarette smoke, spilled beer, and air conditioning coming out of a bar. The brick buildings are stained, they have faded ghost signs, the house paint is sometimes peeling, the billboards block the sunlight. On the other hand, the storefronts are these bright blues or reds or haven't been painted in thirty years.

You get ambulance sirens at night and squealing tires by day. Half the time the street is hot and sticky with something, and the other half it's covered by rain or snow or ice. It's a jumble of activity from mothers pushing baby carriages to men wheeling handcarts and whistling. I'd love to stay here."

"It all depends on whether they let the building stand and," Cissy looked down, "Murph wanting the three of us."

"It sounds so impossible," I said. "We managed to make the Soviets back down on Cuba today, so who knows what miracles lie ahead."

"We won?" Paul said. "Maybe President Kennedy would like to help prevent our disaster too."

"Weren't you glued to your radio?" I couldn't believe he hadn't noticed that the world almost ended today or, at the very least, that a war was averted. I was terrified. "We made a bit of history."

"Gays don't make history," Paul said, with a dismissive movement of his head. "Or if they do, nobody knows they're gay."

"Don't be such a spoilsport," Murph countered. "The Old Town is a neighborhood bar as much as a gay bar. It took a while for us to sort this out: what they raided was a private all-gay party. They wouldn't dare raid the place when the squares are here. Seneca and Spence don't count as squares, of course, because of the color thing."

"How did the police know it wasn't going to be a mixed crowd?" Lisa asked. I watched her review the Thanksgiving diners.

"That's the mystery," Paul said.

"And when we find out I'm going to give them a knock on the noggin like they never got knocked before," Murph added.

"I'm a walking question mark," Lisa said. "Where will we live, where will you live, will we have a bar, will Goodlette be mayor, and will the Russians drop a bomb on us? Will your kids grow up gay?"

"Not if I have anything to do with it," Cissy said. "No mother would want her children to go through this." She nodded at Paul's face and Murph's hand.

I wanted to defend being gay. At the moment, I couldn't think how. I continued to be in the closet at work and forgot things all the time. My niece made a habit of double-checking me. My recovery was taking too darned long. I was trying, as a matter of fact, to remember something Lisa said. I knew I should pay attention to it.

Wait, did she say we? She was asking where we were going to live? Did that mean she planned to live with me? I looked at her over with Cissy, talking babies. I stuffed my hands in my trouser pockets and determined to assume she'd keep house hunting with me and moving in would be the next natural step.

When Harry returned, one of the babies woke and bawled. Tall Harry and tiny Paul crooned at it like a couple of mismatched birds feeding their brood while they changed its diaper. Paul, I'd heard, hadn't been at the bar in a long time. When I asked, he told me he was too happy at home. So Harry hadn't been futzing around; he really cared for Paul.

Lisa tugged at my hand and whispered. "I'm so glad you only have a dog to take care of."

"And I'm so glad you only have a cat."

As we left, I told the gang we would be at the Paradise.

I'd expected the bawdy laughter that came, but we weren't off to bed. We went to dinner at the Goodlette hot-dog stand, the long, bun-shaped landmark downtown that replaced the old cart. Then we headed to the Paradise Cinema to see *Dr. No*.

CHAPTER THIRTY-SEVEN

On Halloween night the little trick-or-treaters wove in and out of the small shops, which stayed open to give out candy. From other streets we could hear Frank Goodlette's station-wagon loudspeaker alternately blaring patriotic music and his cajoling voice. His campaigners covered every incumbent flyer with Goodlette handbills promising reform and improvements. I was surprised to see a row of Goodlette placards across the bar's window.

Deej came in, as she infrequently and boldly did, with yet another young woman on her arm.

"I stopped by because I heard your good news!" she told Lisa, flapping her arms under a Superman cape. She wore a full-face mask.

Cissy had friends in the bursar's office at the college. Their assistant bursar was leaving, so, despite Lisa's qualms about working for the employer that was trying to tear down the bar, she'd gone to see the bursar.

"Hell," I told Lisa. "A third of my business comes from the college. If I gave that up, I'd have to take jobs away from my crew."

The woman who was hiring was delighted not to have to search for a candidate and offered her the job as soon as Lisa's references checked out, one of whom was me. Tonight we celebrated. Lisa was dressed as a flamenco dancer in a scant black top and ruffled red skirt. I wore a black-brimmed hat, black vest, black slacks, and white shirt. Every once in a while I'd stamp across the floor while Lisa twirled.

Deej propelled Lisa's hand up and down as she scanned her costume, until Lisa tugged away. "Let me buy you a drink," Deej said.

Deej looked at the girl—dressed as a ballerina—she'd arrived with and nodded to send her to get the drinks.

"I figure this is the best night of the year to visit my Old Town pals," she announced. "Even if we're raided, Crista's uncle won't recognize me. And I'll run."

"Who's the lucky girl?" Murph, gestured toward the bar.

"Oh, that's Anita. She's a freshman and the second girl to get into the engineering department."

"You turned her already?"

Deej shrugged and grinned. "Someone's got to. Might as well be me."

Lisa said, "After what happened to Crista? You're not worried that you're putting this girl in danger?"

"I'm not exactly twisting her arm, am I? She thinks a raid would be exciting. Anyway, she's in costume too."

"Someone like that isn't planning to put both feet in the fire, kid. Watch your heart." Deej laughed off the warning.

I was sitting close to Lisa, with an arm around her shoulder. Deej came out of her Romeo shell long enough to notice.

"Hey, what's this?" she asked. "Are you two going out together or something?"

"Or something," Lisa answered. Though she changed the subject quickly, I thought I heard a warm pride. "How did you escape from your parents tonight?"

"I said I was going to a Halloween party at school. And we will, right after we leave here."

"So you're sticking it out."

"Yeah, I'll finish school—I have to make a living. I have the rest of my life to be gay in Boston, New York, Chicago, wherever I won't have to waste my time hiding from the cops. Maybe I can help make life better for homosexuals."

"A waste of time," Murph said. "It's the way of the world for people like us."

Lisa told her, "Stop up your ears, Deej. Murph's discouraged. I wish you could stay in Hansfield. You liven up The Old Town."

"I'd like to. I also hate to leave my family. Even though they hate it that I turned out this way, they say they love me. I'll miss Jarjar most. He's my next-oldest brother. Jarjar's my nickname for him—it means kind of kooky in Hindi. He might as well be gay too. He should have been the girl, not me. I'm the one following in my parents' footsteps—they were engineers before they emigrated. He wants to move to India, which he's never even seen, and be the next great Indian poet.

My parents want to know if they give us our crazy ideas in American schools."

There was some commotion at the bar. We followed with our eyes as JoJo and Carla Jean removed a very drunk woman in a scarecrow costume, escorted her to a cab, and leaned in to pay the driver. They used this guy regularly, tipping him well to get rowdy customers home.

Lisa whispered to me, "We should have gotten that driver and paid him double for minding his business."

"Not tipping ours was too satisfying," I said. Lisa laughed. At this stage of the game we agreed about almost everything.

"So what about you two?" Deej asked, turning back to us. "When are you moving in together?"

"Any time Lisa wants to," I said.

Lisa gently slapped my hand. "It's a little soon for that."

"Oh, come on. I've never seen you look so happy," Murph told Lisa.

Lisa ducked her head onto my shoulder. Her lips spread into a grin against me. Her hair must have been newly washed, because I could smell the shampoo she used, clean and not overly perfumed. I couldn't help myself and gave a big laugh at the thought that she could be one of those Breck girls.

"Okay, Leese, tell me why you'd go to work for the college," Deej said.

"Why not? No employer in Hansfield is going to love gays."

"They don't have to love us. Simply leave us in peace on our time off."

Lisa lit a cigarette. "Get me another offer and I'll consider it."

I realized that Deej's new girlfriend had never returned from the bar. She was tête-à-tête with a good-looking little show-off in a sailor costume. Deej seemed unaware of the competition. For her, girls grew on trees. I hoped she had what it would take to really love someone. Unthinking, I squeezed Lisa's hand. She looked at me, one eyebrow raised. I said, "Let's go house hunting together tomorrow. There are three open houses in this neighborhood."

From her frown I knew she was uncomfortable.

"That doesn't mean you'd move in with me," I whispered. "I'd appreciate your good sense, though."

She said, "All right, but only because I adore your company."

Deej was answering a question from Murph. "Of course I have a gun. We have more than one motel that needs protection. My father will think Jarjar threw both guns out. Jarjar's an anti-weapons man—nuclear, handguns, you name it. He despises violence."

"Would you consider tossing the gun in the river?"

Deej shook her head so vigorously her mask slipped down her nose. "I would consider never being in a position where this lady, or any lady," she said, indicating Lisa, "will ever be in danger again if she's in my company."

"Let me tell you a little story," Murph said. I nodded with enthusiasm. Murph's stories were far and few between since the raid. She was starting work at the bindery on November 1st; maybe that would help her spirit.

Deej said, "My night wouldn't be complete without one."

Lisa laughed. "You're quite the smart aleck, Deej."

"So, let me guess. Some guy found you with his wife, right?"

"Look, kid, not everything has to do with sex," Murph said. "It was when I lived in town, in the north end of Boston where the ladies are Italian nine times out of ten. And married to Italian guys. There was no love for the Irish, especially me: a woman superintendent? It wasn't right to take a man's job, they said behind my back. The tenants, like as not, had guns.

"There was one couple who fought tooth and nail. Every night I'd get complaints from the neighbors about the screaming and yelling. So one night, I went over there—it was a three-building U-shaped complex. I lived in the basement by the street, they lived in the back.

"Well, I arrived at their door and there was dead silence. It was like being down in a tomb—you can imagine. To tell the truth, I wasn't sure what to do.

"The apartment doors on either side of the fighting people each opened a crack.

"'They went at it up till five minutes ago,' an old guy in a plaid bathrobe said.

"Out of the other door two little kids peered at me.

"'Shoo,' I told them.

"I started knocking on the middle door again. Next thing I know there was a loud bang. I looked at the old guy. 'Was that a gunshot?' I asked him.

"'That's what they sounded like in the war,' he said. This guy was two sheets to the wind, and I decided, from the looks of him, it was the Civil War he'd been in.

"Now, I didn't do the renting, so I knew nothing about who was inside the middle door. It was like that TV show, the one where you guess which door has the big prize. I told the veteran to call the cops. Meanwhile, I'm not banging on the middle door or yelling for them to open up any more. I don't want anybody blowing a hole in the apartment—or me.

"I backed slowly along the wall and sped down those stairs. I didn't stop till I'd arrived at the street ready to flag down the first police car I could see. From the back building I heard a shot again. Later, I found out the old guy went back inside, called the police, then got his old service pistol out. Was he showing off for his wife? Trying to be a hero? I don't know. His wife said he went and pressed his ear to the door, then tried the knob, hollered that he was coming in, and pushed the door open. That's what brought on the second shot. It went past him and hit his wife. She'd been at the door yelling for him to get back into their apartment.

"So there you have it: three guns, three tragedies. The old guy's wife wasn't dead, but she'll never be the same. She's in a nursing home. The woman who'd been yelling and screaming originally was dead, shot by her murdering ape of a boyfriend. Once the old guy saw his wife hit, he went in there and shot the heck out of the boyfriend and wound up in jail at the tender age of eighty-two." She took a long swig of ginger ale.

"Do you think I'm some kind of jerk like those people?" Deej asked.

"If you have that gun in your book bag you are."

"I plan to shut the bullies up, that's all. It's not loaded."

Murph answered, "You'd best treat that weapon like an atom bomb. People and guns are unpredictable."

"Uh-oh," Lisa said, looking over Deej's shoulder.

CHAPTER THIRTY-EIGHT

The sound of a campaign loudspeaker came through the door as it opened. Everyone at the table turned to see who it was.

"Shoot. Am I ever in trouble now," Deej said, backing away. "That's Crista's uncle, the rabid police captain."

Murph took her arm and stopped her. "You're in costume, remember? Stay put."

"He's not in his good-guy costume, the uniform, but I'd know that face anywhere," Lisa said, darting her arms into the sleeves of her long black coat and pulling the coat tightly around her. She'd told me she'd had that coat since her first year of college; it was so well-made I couldn't tell it was old. "Can't we get the hell out of here?" I wasn't sure Lisa was aware that, now and then, she delicately stroked her nose at the exact place it broke.

I shook my head. "Murph's right. We don't want to bring attention to ourselves." I put more space between us. "Am I glad we voted this morning."

When she noticed the captain, Carla Jean flung herself on him, a screeching warrior. She hammered his face with her fists. One of the louts who'd been intimidating everyone by hanging out at the bar came in behind the captain, carrying a shotgun. He wrenched Carla Jean away, swung her around, and threw her at the unlatched front door so hard she was propelled into the street. She kept her balance, ditched her cigarette, and charged back inside.

"He's looking for somebody," Deej said. "Who else could it be unless it's me—because of his niece, Crista?"

The lout locked the front door and leaned on it, gun at the ready. What was this? Did they come to punish someone, anyone, for the suicide of the captain's brother's child?

Deej shook off Murph's hand. She went to the empty middle of the bar floor. The lout held Carla Jean in front of him, huge hands encircling her upper arms. Deej, facing the captain, looked like an avenging gunslinger in a movie Western where the Indian is the good guy and the white man is the bad guy.

With her left hand she ripped off her mask.

"You scum," the captain said to Deej. "I prayed to Jesus you'd be in this hellhole." His eyes were slitted and red-rimmed, like he was drinking a lot. He moved toward her, his buddy coming behind Deej so she couldn't back away. "You killed that beautiful girl. You took her life the same as if you killed her with your bare hands."

This was a personal vendetta, then. The college was an excuse this time. If I hadn't seen the captain before, here and at the station, I'd think he was a criminal, not a cop.

Though the jukebox pulsed with neon, it ran out of music. The Old Town was as silent as the mirror on the wall.

I had a frightening thought. I pulled Deej's book bag to me under the table, lifted it between my knees, and fumbled for the gun. "Hell's bells," I whispered to Lisa. "Deej must have slid that damned gun out of her book bag and tucked it under her cape. Even a kid should know better, especially a college kid."

"She's the jarjar in her family," Murph whispered.

"Like so many of us," Lisa said in a murmur, and I thought back to all the broken gay people I'd known. Did we turn gay because we were crackpots to start with? Or did living in the homosexual world drive us nuts? Raids and breakups, drinking and living from paycheck to paycheck. Some of the nelliest boys unable to get or keep a job, some of the toughest girls breaking their bodies trying to do men's work. Our families might be strangers to us; our hearts broke when friends found out and dropped us.

"Don't you dare touch one person in here ever again," Deej told the captain. At least her voice was quaking. I'd really be worried if she'd shown no fear.

Did they have guns off duty? Would they shoot her, even with the rest of us watching and within range? If I hadn't been so afraid to make a sudden movement, I'd get under the table. Instead, I slowly dragged Lisa and myself lower, so we'd be smaller targets. My innards roiled.

Then Murph was up. She bellowed from the floor, "Leave her alone!"

The captain sneered and moved closer to Deej, who stood her ground until the captain nodded and his sidekick kicked her feet out from under her. She fell to her knees and he shoved her in the back with the flat of his boot. She lay sprawled on the floor, flailing. She tried to get up and he kicked her spine again. I was ice-cold with fear by then, sure Deej would come out of this paralyzed or dead. One of the neighborhood straight guys approached the captain and was shoved back so roughly that he tried to break his fall by reaching for Norman beside him, and knocked him to the floor. Norman scrabbled to all fours and went behind the bar that way.

The captain spit on Deej. "You're not even worth the time and trouble it would take to give you what you deserve, you degenerate import. I don't know why they let garbage like you into our country."

The lout lifted Deej by the collar. Once upright, she lunged toward the captain; his henchman pulled her back.

The captain slapped her. "I know where you go to school. I want to know where you live with your family, you commie pervert."

Deej challenged him with her silence.

"Find her ID," he told his ape.

The man lifted her up and made a big show of checking her pockets, then plunged his hand into her bra. Deej lowered her head and bit his hand. It took two tries before he could pull away. When he did, his hand was missing a chunk. She spit out the bloody flesh. One of the captain's blows had broken half of a front tooth and she'd used its sharp edge as a weapon. The thug raised his other fist and that's when she pulled the gun from her waistband.

"See if you like it, buster!" Deej yelled.

Murph hurled herself at the kid and the gun, and for one endless horrific moment I thought Deej would pull the trigger, but Murph tackled her in time, uttering the deafening yell of a *dybbuk* gone mad as she landed on her injured hand. The men wouldn't be held back then. Murph rolled on her back holding her hand. The thug kicked it. The captain lurched for the gun. Where was Harry the cop when we needed him?

Deej tried to get up and help Murph up at the same time. Several people took advantage of the chaos to leave The Old Town. Others dove behind the bar or into the bathroom and kitchen when the gun came out. Tipsy was the only one anchored to her stool. She'd kept her back to the scene at first, probably watching in the mirror. Now she left her stool, cigarette in one hand, Manhattan in the other, and flung her drink into the captain's face.

"Okay, Robin, that's enough," she announced. *Robin*? I thought. The man must have had to become a monster to survive his name.

Tipsy had a brief fit of coughing, then went face to face with Captain Robin and, while he was still blinded by the alcohol in his eyes, with the heel of her hand she smacked his chest, pushing him back toward the door. "You've scared the bejesus out of us, now you can go protect the people of Hansfield from real criminals. Is this all about Election Day, for heaven's sake? Are you mad your man is about to lose his job?"

She pushed him again, and his henchman made an opening for the captain to back through, still covering him with his shotgun. He couldn't be here officially, I thought, or he'd object to Tipsy's orders. He'd come at the behest of his family, or was using Crista's death as a smokescreen for more abuse from the city and the college.

"You should be ashamed of yourselves. I've a mind to tell your mother about this behavior, Robin. I'll bet you haven't told her about these after-hours antics you've been getting up to. You were a big hulk of a bully as a child and you're a big hulk of a bully today. I told them to take a stick to you, but no, you were the son and heir. She's so proud her Robin is a policeman. Why in the world did the city give you a gun and a badge?"

Another push. The captain seemed to be collapsing at the middle, bending forward like a collapsing inflatable parade float. "Don't you dare arrest anyone for the gun. You drove the child to it and I'll swear it's my gun. You wait till the new mayor is installed. There goes your Hansfield Tammany Hall. Get out of here. Both of you."

I'll never forget the sight of Tipsy stamping her high-heeled shoe, knee peeping out from under her too-short skirt, blue-hued hair glowing under the dim lights, with a Manhattan glass in one hand and the other pointing them toward the door.

"Shame on you," she said, as the captain turned and left with his goon.

"What in heaven's name?" Norman cried when the door closed behind them. He was limping. I wiped sweat from my forehead. Lisa pulled her tight top away from her chest to cool off.

"Oh, that's my nephew by marriage." Tipsy gave a little giggle. "I suppose he'll tell his mother that her rabble-rouser widow-in-law is a homosexual because he found me here. That's all right though. She knows I like good-looking men. Maybe I'll bring her here one of these days."

Tipsy set her glass down on the bar and marched over to Deej.

"Of all the asinine things for a girl to do," she said, "this takes the cake. You don't have to go and get yourself killed because your girlfriend ended her lily-livered little life. And here," Tipsy said, trying to tear the gun from Deej's hands. "Give me that damned pistol. I'll have the cabbie stop on the bridge while I drop this in the drink."

Deej wasn't letting go for anyone. The poor kid must have put all hope of safety into that gun. She opened it like an expert. "It really is unloaded," she said, showing Tipsy.

"Heaven be praised," Tipsy said. She spun back toward the bar and said, "Well, who's going to buy me another drink. Do I have to do everything for you people?"

JoJo was already rattling the shaker. "On the house," she said.

Lisa and one of the gay men inspected Murph's hand for new damage. I could see it was no longer shaped like a regular hand, but remained cupped. Tears and sweat slipped down her face. She hyperventilated. Someone brought more ice. Her start date at the bindery was going to be delayed unless I could think of a one-handed task. I could have murdered Deej myself. Murph needed the job for the health insurance as much as for the wage.

I soaked paper towels in the women's room. This seemed to have become my job during these crises. There was something reassuring about their brown, soggy smell. Every one of the stalls appeared to be locked shut.

"It's okay, girls," I called to the queens, "they're gone."

Scarletta, who was plainly crouching on a toilet seat, straightened and looked over the door. "You're sure?" she asked.

"Yes, all clear."

'Thank God Honey Delight wasn't here. She'd die of fright in her chair."

Little Minnee Mouse emerged from the other cubicle. "My knees can't take much more of this," she said.

"If it's the only bending they do, girlfriend, you need a boyfriend."

"Isn't that the truth."

I left them there, fixing their wigs. Hugh was walking out the front door with Murph, supporting her. I went to Deej. Her school friend was long gone. No one was tending to her. I'd heard the grumbling; the overall opinion was that she'd brought this on herself and, by introducing Crista to the bar, on all of us.

"You can't go home," I told her. "Let's get you to an emergency room and then you can bunk at my place." I saw no response in her eyes.

"Who's got a car?" I yelled. "We need to get the kid to the hospital."

The silence couldn't have been more disapproving.

Carla Jean bustled over. "Come on," she said brusquely. "I'll bring ours to the front door."

CHAPTER THIRTY-NINE

It was after their visit to Frank Goodlette that Hugh and Norman started acting strangely. They'd met with the mayor-elect right after the election, a couple of weeks ago.

"Did you hit Frank with your purse like Rose did?" Lisa asked with a teasing laugh.

Norman kept his eyes on his work as he replied, without a trace of his famously exaggerated effeminacy, "No need. We get along pretty well."

Lisa looked at me, meticulous eyebrows arched in her suspicious expression. I looked at Murph.

Stroking the new bandages on her hand, Murph asked, "How'd you manage that?"

Norman met her eyes. "They were very understanding."

"Maybe a couple of pretty boys can accomplish more than a battalion of women. Do you think—" Murph asked, "I've been wondering since Rosie went up there if Lawrence and Frank are family."

"I don't know." He hurried away to serve a table of longhairs across the room.

I watched Hugh. His eyes evaded mine. "*L'chaim*," he said. "We'll do what it takes." I didn't put it together until that minute that Hugh was also a Jew. It wasn't just the word; other little signs popped into my memory. This must be killing him, I thought, like it was me. Did he have family left? Why hadn't he ever told me?

In time, it became an open secret that the bar was getting weekly visits from a man who collected an envelope from Norman.

Murph griped. "I don't know. Not only do I doubt those boys will stick with our crowd. I think they're in on the whole scheme now."

I told her I understood their yearning for protection.

She looked disgusted. Lisa and I left soon after.

"Protection?" Lisa asked as we lay on my bed at The Avenue Arms, she naked except for the string of pearls I'd retrieved from the jewelry store she'd sold it to. She told me some weeks ago that she sold the necklace to get by until her job came through. It had been her grandmother's, the one precious item that made it through the Depression.

Lisa was smoking, a beanbag ashtray between her breasts, one arm behind her head, her nails long and painted a peachy-pink shade. I was on my stomach, reaching toward the floor to scratch the dog behind her silky ears, trying not to hear the ringing in my own ears that had let up only a little since the raid. My whole left arm tingled when I crooked my elbow, which Dr. Everett said probably meant nerve involvement in the neck. He thought this would eventually improve on its own.

"You mean improve like go away or improve like fulfill themselves as unrelenting, full-blown torture?" I'd asked him.

The doc had laughed, as I meant him to. I remembered he didn't comment. I'd always carry reminders of the raid inside me.

Lisa bought me some candles and the bedroom smelled like roses. I was so glad to be able to, faintly, smell again, that I loved every scent in the world.

She was staring at the ceiling. "Why else would Norman be giving these people envelopes?"

"Then it's an organized-crime payment? How does that work? Criminals can't keep the police—or people like Crista's uncle—away." I didn't expect an answer.

She stubbed out her cigarette. I rolled toward her and put my hand between her warm thighs.

"Oh, Rockie, I don't think I can, again."

"I think you can."

I rubbed my knuckles lightly on her still-wet parts. "I'm so thankful the blow on my head wasn't any worse. What if I hadn't been aware enough to enjoy you?"

Lisa launched herself at me. "Hey!" I cried.

"Hey, yourself."

She wriggled south and licked north. I cried, "Hey!" again, toppled onto my back, and let my legs go where they would. Darn it, this woman was good at getting past my defenses. I opened my eyes and saw her crown of hair. It tickled my thigh. I thought, she can do anything she wants with me. The sensations took me over. I grabbed her hand and held on, aware only of Lisa, the source of this pleasure overflowing from me. She rose to her knees and slid, straddling me, a few inches at a time, toward my mouth, then lowered herself, hands gripping the top of the headboard. I wallowed in the smell of her sexiness. My view, as I tightened my tongue so it would be firm as she touched it, was of belly and breasts, closed eye-shadowed lids, and her loose, swaying hair. She didn't move much, didn't have to, lifting herself away so my tongue would touch her more and more lightly. "Rockie," she breathed. "Rockie, you're the best, the best, the best." And she lay atop me, her lips puckering softly at my neck.

I never imagined being this appreciated as a lover, nor had I ever appreciated a lover as much. She was ideal: feminine enough to entrance me, skilled enough to please me, smart enough to engage me. If only I can keep her, I pleaded with the heavens.

The front door slammed. "Rise and shine!" Deej yelled. "I'm home!"

Lisa fell back on her pillow. I called through the closed door, "Be right out."

"Good, 'cause the bagels are warm!"

"So am I," Lisa whispered, and grinned, eyes closed. She'd spent the night, after we met at The Old Town, as had become our ritual.

Last night Murph confronted Norman and Hugh, and got nothing out of them about their reticence. Dr. Everett, however, told her that the photos suppressed by the newspaper publisher, including the picture of him holding the injured Paul, had somehow got into the hands of Frank Goodlette's election team—and were destroyed. He'd admonished Murph not to be too quick to condemn people with good intentions.

Naked, I stretched under the sheet and realized my body was as relaxed as it had ever been. "Are you getting up?" I asked Lisa.

Lisa shook her head. "I think I'd rather nap than have breakfast with your boarder."

"Boarder! More like freeloader!" I whispered, laughing. "I really don't mind. She can stay until she graduates and moves to a city next spring. Unless we find a house before then."

"We?" Lisa asked, running the backs of her fingers across my nipples. I shivered at the sparks she ignited in me, then finished dressing.

"I won't make a decision without Miss Jelane, my financial advisor."

She pulled the covers to her chin and lay silent, smiling, while I dressed and went out to the kitchen.

Deej was spreading cream cheese on her bagel. The toast smell made my mouth water. No more burned-paper dust in my smeller, I thought. Mouth full, she pointed to the refrigerator and I knew she'd brought me whitefish. I'd left out money for groceries. I used the bathroom and then pulled together my breakfast.

Deej swallowed a last chunk of bagel and said, "They were campaign contributions." Her broken tooth caused her to lisp.

"What about them?"

"That's what's in the envelopes. At the bar."

"Wait. Slow down. You're telling me Hugh and Norman are contributing to someone's campaign? How do you know?"

"I followed the guy after he came by. On my bike. He went to Goodlette's office."

"So? How does that make it political money? Umm. You got him to give you good whitefish."

"I finally figured out to tell him it's not for me, it's for my bubbala. He wasn't about to give an Indian the best fish."

"Now I'm your grandmother. Answer my question. How do you know it's campaign money?"

"Figure it out. Now that Goodlette is mayor, after Norman and Hugh's support, he's not going to drive their business into the ground."

"Good. You're one smart cookie. It makes sense. Campaign money, protection money, bribery, all rolled into one. There remains the problem of the college parking lot. Changing their minds won't happen overnight."

"It might discourage the college enough to look for a less-controversial site. Like taking down one of the old factory buildings that are falling apart along the railroad tracks."

"That wouldn't get rid of the homos." Lisa was standing in the doorway, dressed in the clothes she'd brought in an overnight bag.

"You heard the kid's take on this?"

"Sorry, I didn't know you stayed over, Leese." Deej grimaced as she sat straighter. "I brought enough breakfast stuff for an army. Help yourself."

Lisa took a bagel. "Here we voted for anyone except Frank Goodlette and now he's not only going to be mayor in January, he's our big protector? What is he—part of some mob?"

Deej told us, "Murph says so. She says Norman and Hugh sold their souls to the devil."

"I don't know about that," I said.

"Look at the changes they've made there," Deej said. "The big wood tables with all those carved hearts and initials, they're gone. The new tables look like spindly bar stools. You can hardly fit two glasses on one. And they taped over the window in the kitchen door. What are they up to?"

"I know they don't want this kind of thing happening to their customers any more than Cissy wants it to happen to her kids." I pointed to my head, to Lisa's nose, and to Deej, whose hair was growing back over her stitches. She'd shown me the enormous bruise at the bottom of her spine. They'd x-rayed it at the ER and told her to see an orthopedic surgeon. So far she hadn't. She was afraid to go home. Since it was her parents' health insurance, she'd told them she fell. Deej had always been jittery and restless, but I was pretty sure she didn't change positions as frequently before the kick in the back. It worried me.

"The guys could compromise and move the bar," Deej said. "I don't see why it can't be as much an institution around the corner as where it is."

"Oh," Lisa said. "That's obvious. The police would come around the corner and bother us."

"Even if they got their parking lot?" Deej asked.

I gave them my most cynical smile. "We're always good for some action."

"Oh, hey, I found something else out. Remember Russ? It was him."

We waited for Deej to quit chewing before she could continue.

"He got caught in his dorm room with a sophomore and told the dean about the plans for the day after Thanksgiving at the bar."

"That *dummkopf*!"

"Take it easy, honey," Lisa said, stroking my arm. "Why?" she asked.

Deej shrugged. "In exchange for not kicking him out. Besides, he was mad at me for not going along with his marrying plan. He knew darn well his dean would tell the college president, who told the mayor, who knew he didn't have much chance against a Goodlette running on a morals platform and needed ammunition like shutting down a queer bar."

I raised my voice, indignant. "You shrug? That idiot ruined how many lives and you shrug?"

Lisa looked at me with alarm. It's nice how much she worries about my blood pressure and my health in general. To me, I'm a youngster.

Her? She's a little afraid I'll keel over and she'll lose me. I admit my heart was racing a bit. I drew a deep breath.

Lisa asked Deej, "How did you find out?"

Lisa wouldn't have worried about Deej having blood-pressure problems if they'd worked out, like she did with me. On the other hand, Deej thought she could save the world and survive.

"One of my classmates is marrying him," Deej answered. "I heard her bragging to some other straight girl in class."

"Does she know he's gay?"

"I doubt it. If I told her I'd have to say how I knew. And if I tell on him, he'll tell on me." She refilled our coffee cups. "No. It isn't worth it."

"And it wouldn't be right to start pulling people from the closet." I didn't want to think about the misery that would cause.

"Oh, Deej. That poor woman," Lisa said. "Someone should warn her. He's going to ruin her life too."

"She gets her wish—marrying a pretty football player. She'll be busy bringing up their kids."

"The poor kids!" Lisa cried.

I said, "That guy is the most selfish person in history."

"He'll get his," Deej said. "I don't know how or when, but he'll get his."

Lisa lifted her arms. "I hate all this drama. I hate living under layers and layers of secrets."

"It won't always be this way," Deej said. "I like how Harry Van Epps thinks."

"You two scare me with all your ideas," I said. "This isn't like sitting at forbidden lunch counters in the South."

"It isn't?" Deej asked.

Sometimes the kid had innocent insights about life that I envied. I remembered my own idealism. I was going to make a lot of money and be a philanthropist so there wouldn't be a Great Depression II. I'd learned I couldn't do any more about how the world was run than I could about how straights treated homosexuals. My ambitions stayed strictly small-scale these days, helping one person at a time.

Deej replied, "It *is* scary. The hatred of homosexuals has long, tough roots in civilization. There's an endless struggle for power going on. Guys mostly. They get their power from property and possession and kooky ideas. A man," she explained, "can lose everything if he can't prove a woman is his wife and her kids are his. So he makes up these rituals and rules to prove everything belongs to him and his sons, and he gets all the other guys in his tribe to back him up, and pretty soon it's the law."

I was trying to follow. "What for?" I asked between bites of bagel. "What's the big deal for them?"

"They lived in the desert, or the jungle, or other places where the more they owned, the better their chances of survival. They didn't want some other guys coming by and stealing wives and their stuff. These rules go so far back nobody questions them."

"What does all this have to do with us?" Lisa asked.

"I'm working on that. I think it has to do with, if a man doesn't own a woman, she could ruin his whole deal. And if gay guys don't play along, they could too. The only way men think they're safe is by corralling all the women and making everybody play by the rules he makes up. Plus his sons can't be gay. They have to reproduce. Get it? If the heir doesn't reproduce, the dad no longer lives on. His physical features, his ideas, his stuff, all that he is gets dispersed to nomads or whoever. Without his intact bequest he not only loses his survival kit—the woman, the kids, their possessions—he might as well not have lived. They can't stand that."

"You have quite the head on your shoulders," I said, trying to catch up to Deej's thoughts.

Lisa looked puzzled. "That kind of makes sense."

Deej laughed and said, "Good. Then you can explain it to me. I can't swallow all this heavy thinking at one time." She pointed to the newspaper. "You two going to look at houses?"

We did and left Deej to study. I had an old delivery step van at the bindery that I'd bought from the local dairy when they stopped delivering milk. That's what we used for house hunting. I sat on the only seat to drive while Lisa made do with a stack of two milk crates—no seat belts—and hung on with both hands. We drove along Settlers River, slowing, stopping, lingering, moving on. Anything for sale near The Old Town was either too run-down or too spiffed up for my tastes or my wallet. The search could take years, but I didn't want it to. Now that I was enjoying life so much with this princess at my side, I dreamed of being with her night and day for the rest of my life. I was looking for a place we both could call home.

CHAPTER FORTY

It wasn't one for the records, but we had a quick, show-stopping snowstorm that next February, in 1963. I called my niece and asked her to let everyone know not to try to come in until the roads got better. The radio said the buses stopped running because snow had piled up on yesterday's ice. Colonel Mustard and I walked with leery steps over to the bindery to open up and take calls. I hate cold slacks against my bare legs. I should have worn long underwear.

The house we found had been vacant for a while and was only two-tenths of a mile from work. It was hidden from the road by an old apple orchard. We planned to clear the wild backyard in the spring. Even now we could see the river, with its chunks of ice and dumped snow, from our bedroom upstairs, and we could watch—and hear—the trains roll along the opposite bank. We'd wanted to be moved in by the holidays, so we packed like fiends and a mover brought a big truck to pick up Lisa's belongings, then mine, and hauled both households over at once. I still ached from lifting and my headaches threatened a return. Nevertheless, I was happy: this house was our wedding ring, as close to legal marriage to each other as we'd ever get.

Although The Avenue Arms had another two-bedroom available, we both wanted to start new, away from the lives we'd been mired in for too long. Deej found two roommates and took over my apartment. We never even asked where they all slept. She got a job and will finish school with night courses. Her mother slipped her money now and then.

Lisa fashioned a verging-on-luxurious modern home for us in that old farmhouse complete with deep front and back porches. It turned out—to my surprise, relief, and good fortune—that Lisa's standards weren't as top-shelf as I'd assumed. Love is funny like that: it was a quality that attracted me, but when I learned that Lisa's tastes were pretty similar to my own, I fell even harder for her. The more I got to know her, the deeper I fell.

When the sun hits the dusty hardwood of the floor I smell the history of the house and our future in it. We planned to buff the floor to a shine as bright as us. The living room we wallpapered in broad pistachio and off-white stripes that Lisa picked out. The fireplace was set high and framed with brick painted white. Lana Turner and the Colonel both loved a fire. We used our mismatched couches like sectionals to either side of a three-tiered table. Already the table held novels from the library—we loved to visit the library together. A carpet of beige-and-white swirls would do until we could replace it. Other furniture we needed we'd find at the Morgan Memorial down in Pittsfield. Our two bedrooms were smallish. The kitchen was a ready-made treat for my lady, with new dark-green linoleum, glossy white cabinets, and appliances with silver handles. I had a pile of decorative tiles Lisa had picked out for the counters. "Everything except a live-in cook!" I said.

"For $14,500 you'd think they'd include one," Lisa replied with a laugh. I put the down payment on it, and she paid a little more on the mortgage each month to catch up.

Normally, we walked to the bindery in the mornings together with the Colonel because the river-route bus stop that brought my crew was right out front to take Lisa to work at the college. She stayed under the covers this morning, and I smiled to think of her all warm and toasty in the white silky pajama top that molded itself to her breasts. I expected to be with her forever, but, then, I couldn't remember if I was always like this the first year.

I quickly cooked a bacon-and-egg sandwich and ate as I walked to work, the salty, greasy smell of the bacon strong in the chilled air. I laughed aloud at the Colonel's face, white from burrowing in the snow for the crusts I dropped. With each step I took, snow crunched. The world was quiet otherwise, except for the sound of a heavy pickup that passed me on studded tires and chains. Here and there I sank to my knees. Tiny balls of ice hung from my gloves. I hooked the Colonel's leash to her harness and we walked more easily in the street where the snow was already packed down. As we passed a little patch of woods, I breathed in pine scent, my favorite. A brook emerged from beneath the road at one point about halfway to the bindery. I could hear it chatter past pebbles and roots on its way toward the river.

Someone jogged in place outside the bindery's back door, obviously trying to keep warm. Murph, I thought. She always sacrificed comfort to style: no boots, thin black gloves, and my blazer instead of a real winter coat. I wore a heavy jacket that was too small for me. Maybe I should forget my intention to get back to my age-twenty size and give Murph that jacket too.

Colonel Mustard danced around her, kicking up snow.

"God forbid you should wear a hat and mess up your hair."

"For the love of God, would you unlock this door?"

As I did, I said, "Where's your key?"

"Left the apartment too fast to find it. Johnny Lakey came to get me. Remember? He told me any time I needed a ride in weather he'd come for me in his Scout." Inside, she stamped the snow off her feet. "Boy, did that old Scout plow through the snow. He fish-tailed a couple of times, but brought it right back."

"The four-wheel drive does the trick," I said.

"If I ever have a car, that'll be it."

"Didn't you get the call not to come in?"

"Yes, but I thought you might need someone." She pointed to the mess we'd made with melted snow and went for the mop.

Murph, Murph, Murph. How could I ever forget Murph? Charmer, raconteur, ex-embroiderer, semi-literate loyal friend. Seldom in her good outfits these days, she still was a hoarse, rough-edged forty-something, a handsome, dashing talker. More modest now, less boastful, always loveable. Ever since Murph had started to work at the bindery, she'd been desperate to please me and my niece enough to keep her job.

"You could have come to the house."

"Aw, Rockie, I knew my buddy would be here," she said as she placed an arm around my shoulder.

That day there was no one but the two of us in the drafty wood building. Usually the heat of the machines and a dozen or so bodies brought out the smell of the paper and even ink and almost made me dizzy with the chemicals in the glue. I had a rush job and decided to try Murph out on a machine in the forwarding department. Deej had come up with a simple fix so Murph could operate it one-handed—one-and-a-half-handed, to be precise. I went into the finishing room and used the brass hand tools. Even with her new injuries, her thumb worked, thanks to the exercises Dr. Everett gave her. If the rest of her hand wasn't flexible, it was usable. I was convinced she'd be good in sales, but I wanted her to know the business inside out before she took that on. If the phone didn't ring we'd be done today.

She was rubbing her hurting hand and I was massaging the small of my back by the time we broke for lunch. The college sent someone out to get Lisa, who'd originally planned to hike over with lunch, so Murph and I foraged in the tiny bindery refrigerator, which could use a new box of baking soda, I noticed. We found mustard and Sunbeam bread, orange juice and pickles. And a pint of Brigham's hand-packed butter-crunch ice cream in the freezer.

"How did that manage to last in this place?" Murph asked, and laughed as loudly as I did as we grabbed for it. I spooned it out. "Hey, you got a spoonful more than me!" We played swap-the-bowls for a while and then enjoyed the creamy stuff. Colonel Mustard got the carton.

"Haven't seen you at the bar lately," Murph said.

"We've been busy. The new house."

"To tell you the truth, I've only gone down a few times to wet my whistle." She looked up from her bowl. "The kids keep me busy."

"Not Cissy?" I prodded.

"Oh, Cissy doesn't want to go downstairs. She says that's all she needs, to get in the drinking habit. She thinks gay bars are a plot to kill us all off, calls booze love poison." I remembered Cissy's lectures about the dangers of alcohol. "Paul and Harry visit us a lot and Seneca comes up, but, no, we live in a complete madhouse, what with work and the kiddies."

I shook my head. "I love to be home with Lisa. We have fun like you wouldn't believe." Murph's eyes had a longing brightness. "Now and then, though," I admitted, "I have a real pang for The Old Town. The way we seemed to be a big family. I thought Thanksgiving was the start of a beautiful tradition. Instead, it was the end."

"It was a fine celebration, till it wasn't. Maybe homosexuals really can't be happy. If the heavens catch us enjoying life too much, watch out—here come the thunderbolts. It worries me. I'm afraid to be too happy with Cissy and the babies."

"Does the ex-husband help at all?"

Murph laughed and licked her spoon. "Paul and Harry do, and her parents have come around. They foot the bill for daycare."

"Do Norman and Hugh visit?"

Murph shook her perfectly combed head. "They have me baffled. They're nice enough, but it's not the same. Did you hear they bought out Carla Jean and JoJo?"

"I thought the boys were short on capital."

"That was my impression too. Ever since they got in with the new mayor's backroom crowd, though, all Norman and Hugh's problems have disappeared. The liquor suppliers came back as soon as Goodlette won the election. The hoodlums are gone. Norman wears a skinny black tie and white shirt behind the bar. Oh, and Crista's uncle, the bully, hasn't been seen since."

I was stunned by all this news. "Did Goodlette tell Norman to can the fag act? To cancel his public persona?"

"I don't know. I have no idea what's going on. Cissy says the boys are in cahoots with the authorities to keep us in these dark caves, the bars, all rounded up and drunk, so no one, from popes to rabbis, to Hindu priests and presidents, lets on that we deserve light too."

"What in the world is so valuable to the authorities that they bribe our own people to keep us hidden?"

"Or do the boy-os love us so much that they want to protect us? Are they cooperating with the enemy for the sake of their hearts or for the sake of their own safety and prosperity?"

"In the end, does it matter? Like Carla Jean asked, is it all a ruthless conspiracy?"

"It is, it is," Murph said. "Carla Jean and JoJo will be okay, though. They'll use the money from the bar to expand Girolami Awards enough to keep JoJo busy full-time. Carla Jean's mother wore herself out so the gay daughter is running the office at the car dealership again."

"You know the Doris Day song, 'Que Sera, Sera,'" I said. Then I thought, maybe Carla Jean will cut down on her drinking. And her smoking. It could turn out for the best for all of them.

Murph took the kind of long breath she seems always to take before a story. "I'll tell you, Rockie, it's been my experience that the gentlemen will always be there for one another, whether they're homosexual or not. There's a big men's club out there called You Scratch My Back and I'll Scratch Yours. Maybe Frank and Lawrence enjoy Hugh and Norman's company. Maybe they have heated chess tournaments among themselves. Or play poker. Or—" Murph threw her arms wide and knocked her ice-cream bowl off the table. She bent to retrieve it. Colonel Mustard beat her to it and licked the sticky remains. It tore me up to imagine Norman and Hugh giving the cold shoulder to their regulars.

"Don't say it. I don't want to even think about the four of them—"

"Whatever saved it, The Old Town Tavern is an institution."

"I'd like someplace else we could go. The bar downtown is so loud. You can't hear across a table."

"I'll give you no argument on that."

Murph seemed sad that day. I sensed there was another reason she'd come to work. I asked, "How are your babies?"

"They couldn't be better, Rockie. I swear they get bigger every day." Her face didn't light up the way it usually did when she spoke of them. "Cissy doesn't want me there anymore."

"What?" I said, my breath leaving me, my heart giving a sudden thud. "It's your place."

"She needs it for the babies."

"What's wrong with her? You've been so helpful."

"She doesn't want to sleep in the twins' room any more."

"She doesn't sleep with you, Murph?"

Murph shook her head. She wouldn't meet my eyes. "At first she was pregnant and after the babies came, well, I'm not half the catch you are, Rockie. What chance do I have?"

"Doesn't she know those kids have taken over your heart and soul?"

"I know, I know. I shouldn't have let myself get so attached. I thought maybe now I could take in some foster kiddies and raise them if the state would only entrust them to us homos. This was my one shot at a family of my own."

"Is it a family, Murph, if all the love comes from you?"

"I don't want to be like Tipsy and spend my life in a bar," she said with such passion that her out-flung arms sent the napkin holder to the floor this time. She picked it up and continued in a plaintive tone. "I'll do whatever works. I'll sleep on the divan. Cissy said no. I asked what I did wrong. She said I've done everything right." She shrugged. "It was the family life I was after, Rockie, any touching took second place."

"Murph! Have you let the raid take the starch out of you?"

"Probably," she answered, like she was carrying the weight of the world on her shoulders.

"I miss your stories."

"What do I have to say anymore? Maybe you're right. I'm not what I used to be. I read kid stories to the twins, did I tell you that?"

"You read to them? That's perfect, Murph. The more practice, the better." I realized I heard shame in her voice. "Is there someone else? For Cissy?" I asked.

"Oh, no, no. I'd guess she's making room for someone, sometime."

"Where would you go?"

"Who'll rent me a room here? No one who reads the paper. I thought maybe I'd go down Maine, where Rosie's settled."

"Oh, Murph, even you know that's crazy. Besides, you'd leave me in the lurch."

"If anyone's replaceable here, I am."

"Why don't you let me be the judge of that," I snapped at her. Colonel Mustard looked up. I seldom used that tone. I could see by Murph's face she'd been taken aback too. "I'm sorry, Murph. I didn't teach you to run that machine today because Irv wasn't here. It's because I think you can, injured hand or not. My niece has gotten some new accounts so we'll use it quite a lot. You'd earn a few dollars more that way. I want to move Irv into the finishing room."

She looked at me as if she suspected my motives.

"Honestly," I told her.

"The way my fingers are stuck in a sort of claw almost helps me to use the controls and move things along. I'm fortunate beyond belief that the nerve damage from that second go-round with the killer captain numbed me up—if you could call anything about the whole encounter fortunate. It's the way of the wicked world." She sighed.

"That's settled then. Now, about the other. The years are piling up behind you, Murph, not in front of you. Why don't you stop tippy-toeing around Cissy and let her know you're interested in more than the babies. You don't want to ignore the writing on the wall."

"You mean, seduce her?"

"Did Cissy ask you to move out, Murph?"

"Just about. What else could she mean when she says she doesn't want to sleep with the little tykes?"

I didn't say a word, but I watched her eyes as they came alive with comprehension.

"Rockie, you don't suppose Cissy is asking for an invitation?"

"And getting tired of waiting, I would think."

She was clearly panicked at the thought.

"It's like riding a bicycle, Murph, if that's what you're worried about."

Her face was flushed. "I took one of my brothers' bikes when I was four. It was a two-wheeler. I thought if he could ride it, I could, so I climbed aboard. He'd dropped it at the top of a hill and gone off to hunt bugs. I got my balance—the bike was too large for me so I stood on the pedals—and pushed off. It was the most terrifying moment of my first four years and many thereafter. I hit a curb and flew into the street where a car raised an awful stench as it burned its tires. After that, no one could get me on a tricycle, much less a two-wheeler."

"You'll find your balance, Murph. We all do. Cissy will help you—trust me on that." But she had one last ocean of disquiet to cross.

"What if Rose comes back?"

Had Murph really saved herself for Rose all these years? It would explain a lot if sex was virgin territory for her. I was glad to help kick down, as kindly as I could, that particular wall, if only to see Murph's grin return, broader than ever and heightened by a glint of resolve in her eyes.

CHAPTER FORTY-ONE

We hadn't been back at work after lunch more than thirty minutes when my crew straggled in. The sun had won its skirmish with the snow clouds and made the streets passable. The other arrival danced in with her book bag and waved an envelope at us—it was Deej. She raced through the production floor and found me coaching Murph.

"I got in!" she yelled over the machinery.

We stopped the machine.

"What school?" She'd applied to a few with graduate degrees in her field.

"THE school! RizDee!"

"RizDee?"

"RISD—The Rhode Island School of Design. They are so cool. The school was even founded by women, can you believe it?"

"Where is this place?" Murph asked.

"Providence. Man, oh man, providence is right! I can't wait!"

Murph and I looked at each other. This was one happy young woman. I could see my crew's curious glances so we moved into my office.

"You remind me of Tigger," Murph told Deej. "In this book I read to the twins."

"Tigger? I love Tigger! You read them *Winnie the Pooh*?" She rushed forward and squeezed Murph in a hug that made her squeal. "You're reading, Murph!" Then, as if to cover any embarrassment she might have caused, she said, "I'll bet they have about a dozen gay bars in a town the size of Providence."

Murph shook her head. "What have we done to our children?"

"What's the matter?" Deej asked.

"Rockie and I were talking about how we'd love somewhere to go that's not a bar. Why haven't we given that to these kids?"

"Who ever thought about the next generation?" I asked, and realized, as I did, the truth of those words.

Deej showed us her acceptance letter and told us about the graduate courses RISD offered. I was suddenly a dead weight of sadness, regret, guilt, hopelessness, shock, and self-disgust. Was there anything I could have done so every Deej could have more to look forward to than bars? This young woman was a professional. She'd be highly educated. If no one found out who she really was she might be respected in her field.

I dropped onto my office chair. The Colonel was in her basket next to my desk.

Deej said, "I'll find the bars and see if I can get something started. A club, maybe, for us. Imagine if we could have a parade of our own, a Saint Sappho's Day parade. We'd march down The Avenue! I mean, The Old Town is good, it got me into the life, but hangovers are for the birds, and I can't spend all my time off in bars—"

She clapped a hand over her mouth. "Oh. I didn't mean there's anything wrong with bar life."

I got up and went over to her. "I think that's a fine idea, Deej. If you're patient and persistent, I know you'll do it. And," I held out my hand. "Mazel tov!"

She shook my hand, a grave excitement in her dark eyes. "You'll tell our Princess Lisa? I never see her any more. When I'm ready to settle down I'll find someone exactly like her."

Murph laughed. "I'm not sure Rockie's Lisa can be duplicated," she said. "In the meantime, Rockie, maybe we could organize a group like Deej talked about for us older gals. I've heard of one, daughters of somebody, I think it's called."

The thought brought back my glad spirits. "Okay," I said. "Maybe it isn't too late for us."

"Or maybe it is," Deej said. "At The Old Town."

"What's happened?" Murph asked.

"I don't mean to be catty—the bar has changed. While they don't exactly toss women out, it's really uncomfortable now. It's all well-dressed white guys and the cutest of the college boys."

"Do the neighborhood straights go?"

"Fewer and fewer. Norman gives them watered-down drinks, the cheapest draft, surly service."

"Norman? Surly?" Murph said. She looked doubtful.

"To us, yes. Not to the pretty guys. Oh—and they've turned the kitchen into a big dance space. Who knows what else goes on back there."

Now Murph looked truly shocked. "Our Thanksgiving kitchen is gone?"

Deej shrugged.

"Well," I said, "it's their business, but it sounds like a betrayal." I thought of Lisa, who, like the rest of us, believed The Old Town was like a family. Oh, well, I told myself. I knew all too well that families drift apart.

Murph said, "More like a kick in the butt."

"The lights are different too. They've replaced those neato-keano table lamps with electric beer-ad wall sconces. Plus they've strung green-and-gold grape swag lights over the bar. It doesn't even smell like The Old Town. They use some sort of air freshener in there and I think they've got a contraption that sucks out a lot of the cigarette smoke. Russ loves it there now, without all the riffraff." Deej grinned. "That's what he said. And there's a gold statue they stuck at the end of the hallway. Everybody calls it The David, or The Duh-veed, like they worship it. I mean, who wants to see a naked man while she dances with a girl?"

I gave a rowdy laugh. If I ever had any doubts that Deej was true family, that remark set them to rest.

Murph laughed too, and looked at me. "I guess that's us, the riffraff."

Deej jounced on the balls of her feet. "Hey, this riffraff needs to get going," she said. "Night classes aren't cancelled. I don't want to mess up now, when things look so good." She regarded the bindery. Although she'd been here before, she seemed to study it now with some intensity. "How did my idea for this machine work out?" she asked, and pointed to the controls and feed on Murph's machine, where she'd been able to lighten the pounds of force needed.

Murph kneaded her left hand with her right.

Deej tightened her lips and nodded. "I'll think more about it. Ergonomics—you know, how to make work compatible with the human body—really got off the ground during the war. Maybe there's some literature on units like this one. I mean, why should only people with two good hands be able to open doors? Isn't there a device besides a knob we could put in houses?"

Deej could invent an embroidery machine that would work for Murph, I thought, suddenly connecting Murph's needleworking skills with patches for Carla Jean and JoJo's awards shop and with the bindery, which did custom decorative work.

We walked Deej to the front door, Colonel Mustard at our heels. The sunshine was warm. The Colonel's feathery tail waved like a flag. I laughed. "You smell exactly like a wet dog," I told her. She looked up at me, eyes eager, mouth open in what I thought of as a smile. You'd think I'd given her a compliment.

"You're kidding," Murph said at the sight of Deej's bicycle. The dumb kid had ridden it all the way out here through the barely plowed streets.

"Nothing else was moving," Deej said, and took off, waving.

Murph and I stood in the warm sunshine.

"Look at that kid bound out of our lives and into her future," Murph said. "Our future."

She was more innocent than Deej. I bet Cissy was her first and would need to lead the way. No matter her experience, Murph took whatever the world dished out to gays. Yet, like Deej, she had faith that things would get better for us all.

I, on the other hand, watched Deej bike away through the snow with a wobbly uncertainly that I'd never seen in her before and which could blight her life. I saw our past repeating itself, but hoped my foolish friend Murph was right.

The End

About the Author

Lee Lynch published her first lesbian fiction in "The Ladder" in the 1960s. Naiad Press issued *Toothpick House*, *Old Dyke Tales*, and more. Her novel *The Swashbuckler* was presented in NYC as a play scripted by Sarah Schulman. New Victoria Publishers brought out *Rafferty Street*, the last book of Lynch's Morton River Valley Trilogy. Her backlist is becoming available in electronic format from Bold Strokes Books. Her newest novels are *Beggar of Love* and *The Raid*. Her recent short stories can be found in *Romantic Interludes*, *Women In Uniform*, and at www.readtheselips.com. Her reviews and feature articles have appeared in such publications as *The San Francisco Chronicle*, *The Advocate*, and *The Lambda Book Report*. Lynch's syndicated column, "The Amazon Trail," runs in venues such as boldstrokesbooks.com, *Letters From Camp Rehoboth*, and *On Top Magazine*. Lee Lynch was honored by the Golden Crown Literary Society (GCLS) as the first recipient (for *The Swashbuckler*) and namesake of The Lee Lynch Classics Award, which will honor outstanding works in Lesbian Fiction published before awards and honors were given. She also is a recipient of the Alice B. Reader Award for Lesbian Fiction; the James Duggins Mid-Career Author Award, which honors LGBT mid-career novelists of extraordinary talent and service to the LGBT community; and was inducted into the Saints and Sinners Literary Hall of Fame. In 2010, *Beggar of Love* received the GCLS Ann Bannon Readers' Choice Award and the ForeWord Magazine Book of the Year Bronze Award in Gay/Lesbian Fiction. She has twice been nominated for Lambda Literary Awards and her novel *Sweet Creek* was a GCLS award finalist. She lives in rural Florida with her wife.